CORDELIA

A NOVEL BY

WINSTON GRAHAM

THE BODLEY HEAD

LONDON SYDNEY

TORONTO

All rights reserved
ISBN O 370 00555 4
Printed in Great Britain for
The Bodley Head Ltd
9 Bow Street, London WC2E 7AL
by Unwin Brothers Limited,
Old Woking, Surrey
First published 1949
This edition 1963
Fifth impression 1977

CORDELIA

In October, 1866, Cordelia Blake married Brook Ferguson of Grove Hall. There were three reasons for the marriage, and these were Cordelia's youth, her health, and her good manners—in short Frederick Ferguson's requirements for his son's second wife.

Cordelia learned her duties quickly. She must adapt herself to the rigorous routine of Grove Hall, manage the household, care for and comfort Brook, obey her father-in-law. Already others in that household had yielded to Frederick Ferguson's will: his sister Letitia, who was too simple-minded to do anything else; and his brother Pridey, who had retreated into his two preoccupations—music and his treatise on mice. But even Uncle Pridey's attempts to divert Cordelia did little to alleviate the gloom.

This curious marriage might have continued indefinitely if Stephen Crossley had not come into Cordelia's life. Although she was sheltered and restricted in the severe tradition of her time, Cordelia found the strength to accept Stephen's love and the even greater strength to face the crises which followed her precipitate decision.

Ross Poldark
Demelza
Jeremy Poldark
Warleggan
The Black Moon
The Four Swans

Night Journey
The Forgotten Story
Take My Life
Fortune is a Woman
Night Without Stars
The Little Walls
The Sleeping Partner
Greek Fire
The Tumbled House
Marnie
The Grove of Eagles
After the Act
The Walking Stick
Angell, Pearl and Little God
The Japanese Girl
Woman in the Mirror

The Spanish Armadas

CORDELIA

It is there on the mantelpiece still, about two feet from the base, carved with a small sharp knife or a fretwork tool: COR-DELIA, 1869. The letters are plain and regular and level, except for the A, which slants away from the rest, and the date has a wavy careless look as if the carver tired of the task.

The house is dusty and old now, given over to uses it was not designed for, but the name persists, faded and dirt-smeared, in that upper room. Two notes echoing like notes on a tuning-fork, losing themselves far back in the passages of yesterday. Cordelia, 1869. The lettering is not quite the lettering of a child. Then why was it carved there? As a girlish prank, as an act of defiance, as a gesture before the hands began to tremble into senility?

It has been a pleasant room, square and lofty, facing south, with a dressing-room leading off. A venetian blind in good condition is still fitted to one of the windows, and the brass gas brackets are firm in the peeling walls. The doors and the shutters are of bird's-eye maple, and the ceiling is heavily moulded with a centrepiece from which an un-shaded electric light now hangs.

One can picture it furnished in the fashion of the time, one can try to peer in, as through one of the wide sash windows, at people living and loving and talking inside, moving in the familiar friendly rhythms of custom and habit, like us but not us, links in the eternal chain. One sees them now as through a glass darkly, conscious of deep differences of outlook misting the scene but unsure whether the idiosyncrasies are all theirs or partly our own.

Well, here is the Victorian house already fallen from its distinguished usage, and here is the name, symbol of a time past, of a personality, of a woman, maintaining its own dignity, its own reserve among the shabby humiliations of today. And that woman? Is all the intimate personal detail of her life already blown away, lost for ever in the dust? Not quite, for when the name was carved Cordelia was young. . . .

BOOK ONE

CHAPTER ONE ❧ On the fourteenth of March, 1866,
Brook Ferguson's first wife died. On the fifth of April he started looking
for his second.

If he had been left to himself he might have stayed inert for years,
thinking idly what would happen if he did this or that, biting the skin
round his fingers, and dreaming his own dreams. There were, too, all
the usual obstacles to any early move: the frowning brows and whispering voices of convention, the raw new memories like railway cuttings,
bitterness, and some grief. Yes, grief, for one did not live with a woman
for six years without gathering ties of memory and association.

But he was not left to himself.

"Brook," said his father, after Monday night's supper, when the
maids had cleared away and Aunt Letitia had gone to find her sewing
and Uncle Pridey to feed his shrews. "Brook, I hope you won't allow
yourself to brood over poor Margaret's death."

"No, Father, I'll try not," Brook said, tapping with his long thin
fingers on the arm of his chair.

"When your mother died," said Mr. Ferguson, "only the consolation
of religion saved me from serious illness. Twenty-eight years. The
break-up of a life companionship is the greatest tragedy that can happen
to a man. You were only nineteen at the time, and perhaps you didn't
realise all that it meant. . . ."

"Oh, yes," said Brook, his eyes filling with tears. "I realised exactly
what it meant." There was no one like her. She understood me. She
knew how I felt, what I hoped for.

Frederick Ferguson went on: "I came to realise—in time, thank God—
that it was wrong of me to grieve or to rail against His will. My responsibility remained to the living. I realised that in good time I should rejoin
her. Until that appointed time I must go my lonely way alone."

Brook got up and thrust his hands into his pockets.

"My lonely way alone," said Mr. Ferguson, and lowered his fine
head. It was a good phrase. Then he said: "But your case is different,
Brook."

2

"Oh, yes, in degree," said Brook. "I know. I know that. I was fond of Margaret. She had her faults, but——"

"You are young," said Mr. Ferguson, puffing out his lips and staring at his son's thin, round-shouldered figure. "With all your life still before you. You should grieve. That is natural. But not to the detriment of the life you have yet to live. Margaret would not wish it. Nobody would wish it."

"I don't suppose I shall," said Brook. "I never said I would." On the defensive, he added: "Haven't I been down to the works just the same, carried on much as usual? I don't really see there's anything to complain of. After all . . ."

He was going to say, 'After all, Margaret's only been buried a fortnight, I think I've stood it damned well.' But, as often, the sentence slid away.

Frederick Ferguson got up.

"My dearest boy, I never for a moment suggested there was anything to complain of. Your fortitude has been admirable, and I deeply respect you for it. But your interests, so close to my heart, as you must know they are . . ."

He waited.

"Yes," said Brook.

"With your interests so close to my heart, out of my greater experience, I offer you this advice. You have a sensitive and affectionate nature. I thought it necessary to have this talk with you."

"Oh, that's all right," said Brook, mollified.

Mr. Ferguson went over to the port table and poured out two more glasses.

"I am an old man now, Brook; I expect you realise that."

"Oh, no."

"Well, an old man for the kind of active life I lead. At sixty-four life is very uncertain."

"It's uncertain at any time," said Brook, thinking of Margaret—who had shared his bed, for whose footsteps and voice and nervous throat cough one still listened.

"I know; but more than ever so at my time of life. And when I am gone, responsibility will fall on you, Brook."

He brought the port back and stared into his son's soft inward-looking brown eyes.

Brook turned away, avoiding the direct gaze. "Oh, a certain amount, I suppose."

"A great deal. The direction of the works; its welfare and continuity. All the other interests. The maintenance of this fine house. The well-being of your aunt and uncle, if they outlive me. All this. I'd hoped that Margaret would be at your side to help you."

"Oh, I shall get along somehow."

"I don't want you to 'get along somehow.' I want to feel assured of your future and the future of all the things I care about. You should be firmly established. As you know—there was one circumstance of your marriage to Margaret that I found disappointing. . . ."

The port was warming Brook. It comforted his mind, covering over the qualifications and hesitancies, the defeats and the humiliations.

"I know. You weren't the only one who was disappointed. We were too."

Mr. Ferguson walked with his glass across to the large sash window. The curtains had not been drawn and the gaslight glimmered upon the sallow wintry lawn and on the wet leaves of laurel and rhododendron.

He said: "Much as I liked and admired Margaret," and brushed a crumb or two from his waistcoat. He was a man who conveyed a lot by implication. "Oh, she was a lady and brought a gentility to this house it's not quite had before. Why pretend? We are an educated and intelligent family but we haven't yet the background, the connections. It's only a question of time. Indeed, we're accepted and esteemed everywhere it's worth being accepted." He turned and met his son's sombre eyes. "But when I first saw your interest in her I thought it an admirable match. An old Cheshire family with county connections. *Your* son, I thought . . ."

"Her brother was damned rude the other day," said Brook. "He made all sorts of sneering remarks and pretended to think . . . Oh, well, you know the sort of things he pretends to think."

"You need not worry your head about Dan. He'll drink his way into the poor-house. With an ordinary man one would perhaps expect a little gratitude. . . . Ignore him, Brook, he'll forget his grievance when the flat racing starts."

"Even her mother pretended to think Margaret had been unhappy here. I mean, I know you and Margaret got at loggerheads at times, but she meant permanently unhappy, suggesting——"

"Well, it would be too much to expect them to admit that Margaret had been a sickly woman all her life, should never have married, wouldn't it? I believe Maud will be the same in another ten years."

Brook stared round the large sombre dining-room. From here he could see himself in the mirror above the fireplace, the mirror framed in plush with the heavy carved mahogany overmantel. From here, too, he could see Margaret's chair, and for a moment pictured her there with her tightly drawn hair and black eyes and soft moist hands.

"I shouldn't be surprised if we see nothing at all of the Massingtons

4

from now on. All that unpleasantness." He began to bite the skin round his fingers. "And at heart they're snobs, every one of them."

"Well, let them go. It's better that than the other way. When you marry again you'll not want them calling here at all times."

"*When* I marry again," said Brook, with a half-nervous laugh, a little startled at the thought—or at the blunt expression of it. "*If* I marry again."

Frederick Ferguson turned from the window. "I should like you to marry again, Brook. And soon."

"Why?" The port had given defiance as well as comfort.

"For the reasons I've told you."

"Oh, perhaps I may some time. I don't see the hurry."

"It should be perfectly plain to you. I think you should re-marry."

"I know no girls."

"You can't be expected to. But there will be plenty willing to marry you—given the opportunity."

"You think so?" said Brook, with a little unbidden interest.

"Well, of course. What girl wouldn't accept money and position and an agreeable and indulgent husband? Indeed, an overindulgent husband."

There was the echo of old strife in this, but Brook allowed it to pass. "Perhaps. I don't know."

"There's no perhaps about it, my dear boy. You can pick and choose—and I hope you will."

No more was said that night. The seed was sown. But on Easter Sunday Mr. Ferguson found himself unoccupied—a rare and unpalatable state—and his energy, which had helped him to double his fortune twice in ten years, his desire for progress, which had put him among the leading Liberals of the city, the need that was always in him to fill every passing hour, forced him to come to the subject again.

They were all there. Brook was playing some of Field's Nocturnes, Aunt Letitia was dozing inanely over her crochet work, and Uncle Pridey was turning the pages of some notes he had made that morning. At midday dinner they had all eaten too much, and they were feeling slothful—all except Frederick Ferguson, who had eaten the most of all and whose food, as well as turning ultimately to fat, seemed like a child's to turn at once into consumable energy.

For a few minutes he stood by the piano, watching Brook's fingers move over the keys. He knew nothing about music, but Brook, he felt, played the piano as he did most things, with insufficient zest. It was not a technical failure but an attitude of mind.

When the piece was finished he said: "Have you thought any more about our discussion of the other evening?"

Brook glanced uneasily round the room at his uncle and aunt.

"Not a lot, Father."

"I think you should. It's important to your happiness—and indirectly to mine."

Brook moodily turned over the music. "Surely, it can wait."

"Anything definite can wait. But consideration. It's a step that needs active and early consideration."

"I don't see how one can begin when there's no one to consider."

"You have no friends?"

His father knew very well what friends he had and had not. Was he to make an inventory of the few young people who came to this house, or the sisters of the men he met at the Athenæum, or the clogged and shawled daughters of poverty he saw each morning at the works?

He was saved from answering by Aunt Letitia, who looked up and said: "Eh, Frederick, let the lad play. Don't stop the lad playing. It soothes me."

Frederick, as usual, ignored his sister. He had long since found that there was nothing to be gained from carrying on a conversation with her.

"On Wednesday evening," he said, "St. James's Choir will be giving the 'Messiah.' You'll come, Brook?"

"Oh, yes, I think so." Margaret had been buried at Alderley. No bar to visiting St. James's.

"More than I will," said Uncle Pridey, wagging his beard. "The tenors are always metallic and the contraltos low like cows. I know. The thing should never be attempted except by professionals."

"The choir will be augmented," said Frederick, half to Pridey but half, significantly, to his son.

"I didn't know you were that interested in music, Frederick. Next time we have a Gentlemen's Concert, come along, and Karl Hallé will teach you what music really is."

"Walk with me to the door, Brook."

The young man got up, and they went together out into the over-furnished hall.

"On Wednesday," said his father. "Look along the choir stalls. We shall be able to see them from where we sit. A family. There are two or three daughters. It is just a thought. Naturally no more."

Brook stared. All his instincts were to shy away from such a sugges-tion. This was nothing to do with bereavement, it was something born or grown in him, a backing away from any positive act.

"Do I know them?" he said at last.

"Not socially. You may have seen them in church."

"What are they called?"

6

"Blake, I believe. There's a large family of them."

"No, I don't know the name." He said this with a sense of relief, as if it was an added barrier. "Where are you going?"

"Just a walk. So should you. It would improve your health if you took more exercise instead of crouching over the fire."

"It's not a very nice day."

"Their father keeps a watchmaker's and jeweller's shop on the Oxford Road."

"A shop?" said Brook, surprised out of his sulkiness. "That's rather a change, isn't it; a change from the Massingtons of Alderley Edge. I mean . . ."

"My dear boy, don't take this too seriously. A casual suggestion thrown out to you. And Mrs. Blake is a tolerably well-educated woman. I think she married a little beneath her."

Brook put his hands in his pockets. "Wouldn't I be doing the same thing?"

"Well, as I was saying the other evening—was the other sort of marriage wholly a success? It's for you to say. If we could recall Margaret, of course we would. But since we cannot, do we want another sickly woman about the house? We don't need money, you know that. Your choice should be wide and quite free." Frederick Ferguson patted his son's shoulder. "This—this is the merest suggestion. Don't hesitate to put it aside."

He opened the door and went out, turning down the Grove towards the house of his friend Mr. Slaney-Smith, who, although not a churchman, seemed to know the whole history of the family of Blake.

CHAPTER TWO ❧ The parish church of St. James's was crowded when Brook and his father entered it. They were the only representatives of the family, since Pridey had stuck to his refusal and Aunt Letitia had been discouraged from coming. Frederick Ferguson liked to maintain his sister in comfort, but he did not want to be seen about with her. There were limits to one's philanthropy.

They came up the aisle dressed in black frock-coats and carrying glossy silk hats with broad crêpe mourning bands: Brook five feet eight inches and weighing nine stone ten pounds, Frederick six feet one inch and weighing nearly seventeen stone. People whispered together as they passed up the church, and one wag muttered: "Reckon service can begin now. Fergusons 'ave come."

The church was decorated for Easter, and when the choir filed in it sat amid daffodils and primroses and bits of green moss tucked in by anxious maiden ladies on the Saturday before. Normally the choir was male, but on special occasions two rows of women and young girls were admitted to the stalls. From the Ferguson position—in the family pew Frederick had bought—the women were plain to be seen, shiny and smooth and bonneted and self-conscious, fingering their music and keeping their eyes down.

Brook had not been looking forward to this evening. Beside him his father was breathing and settling into the pew; after seating himself in any public place Mr. Ferguson seemed to simmer, as if it took a time for all his dynamic energy to come to rest. Brook's eyes travelled along the choir. He had been married at twenty-one, and had not known any girl intimately before he met Margaret. Margaret had been a case apart. She became in time not one to be included under the generic title of 'women,' who were still unapproachable and mysterious; she was his wife, a special dispensation of nature, separate and distinct.

If he married again he would be starting afresh. New difficulties and problems would be on every hand. These thoughts would have frightened him off a second marriage, if they had stood alone. But he was not unhappy in the company of women: he enjoyed talking to a woman—some women—much more than to a man; and he sometimes thought romantically of finding in a second wife all the virtues of sympathy, delicacy, and understanding that Margaret had not seemed to have.

The oratorio began. Two new soloists had been engaged, and Brook felt that Uncle Pridey would have been forced to swallow his intellectual pride and admit this was good.

Music did things to Brook. Under its stimulus his mind floated away into glorious daydreams, rich and full and satisfactory.

He thought of his marriage to Margaret in this church. Margaret had looked a little sallow in her orange blossom. The guests crowding with their perfunctory smiles; two waves meeting, the county and the commercial. Dan, tall, thin and cynical, and Margaret's mother with her creaky voice going on and on about the old lace. The honeymoon at Filey, walking along the cliffs, fatigue and anxiety and disillusion. But there had been times, little happinesses, kindnesses to recall; they had got used to each other.

Then his mind swept on and up with the music into the far rosier future, where, with a confidence he never knew in real life, he was wooing a lovely young girl, who was enchanted by his looks, his manners, his talk.

Frederick nudged his arm. "There are the three Blakes. You can see them now in the front row. Next to the tall woman with glasses."

8

Brook flushed crimson, for his father's whisper had a resonant quality.

Pleasant, fresh-looking girls, singing brightly under wide-brimmed straw hats. One was dark; then there was a fair girl, and then a shorter girl, younger than the others. Brook glanced at his father, but Mr. Ferguson was watching the soloist with a determined look, as if all his thoughts were concentrated there. Only Brook knew that this was the habitual expression of the man—his face didn't ever really relax, it only altered its focus of attention.

He looked back again, and at the profile of the second, the fair one, with the corn-coloured hair. She had a lovely pale fresh skin and a pre-occupied other-worldly expression, like a young madonna. (She was in fact at that moment thinking about her new straw hat.) For a time Brook stared at her fascinated, puckering his brows to try to narrow the distance between them. He fancied he could hear her voice above the others.

After the oratorio was over, people stood in groups outside in the quarter darkness of the mild fine night and chatted and gossiped and raised hats and stroked beards, and about them the beech trees rustled and the old grey gravestones slept.

While they were waiting for Tomkins with the brougham there was a brief whispered angry argument in which Brook was overborne, and then Mr. Ferguson steered his son across the grass to a group standing under the shadow of the tower. There were five in the group. Brook still hung back.

Ferguson said: "Ah, good evening, Mrs. Blake. A good performance, I should say. We ought to be proud of our old church and its choir."

Mrs. Blake turned.

"Oh, Mr. Ferguson, now isn't that kind of you to say so! Well, we all did our best; we're just waiting for Teddy to take his surplice off. Yes, I think it went well."

She was like a big bee on an autumn afternoon, humming and great with honey. They were there in the shadow, three girls and another older woman, white figures against the grey wall of the church, with glinting eyes and teeth. Introductions, and his father with a turn of his hand brought him into the circle. The older woman, an aunt, Mrs. Higginbottom. How d'you do to her, and then the girls. Abruptly they seemed to step out of the darkness, out of anonymity for ever.

"This is Esther Jane, my eldest. And this is Cordelia. And this is Emma. Emma has only just joined the choir since she had her seventeenth birthday." Mrs. Blake went on talking, explaining the unexplainable, which was that one woman, plethoric, commonplace, talkative, with wisps of hair falling all over her face, could have produced these

9

three buoyant smooth-skinned creatures, all so different, so young, so unapproachable.

Quick glancing dark eyes and an impudent nose—that was how Brook remembered Esther Jane that night, and his hand, he knew, was beginning to sweat when he touched hers, and he could say nothing but a muttered "How d'you do," and then he saw Cordelia, and this was the one he had watched in the choir; quite different full face, still a little remote, a little preoccupied, but with a grave quicksilver charm to her expression that turned his heart over; and Emma had fair braided hair like great gold chains over her shoulders; and the fat Mrs. Higginbottom was breathing a smell of camphor over him and trying to tell him something about the choir at St. Ann's where she usually went; and then a tall youth with an ungainly, tumbling sort of way with him came out of the vestry door and was introduced as Teddy.

"Are you a singer, Mr. Ferguson?"

Brook said: "No, I'm afraid—er—not. . . . I play the piano, though." What does Father want me to do? he thought. Esther Jane too vivacious, Cordelia too beautiful, Emma too young. If any, it would have to be Emma for her extreme youth. But they're complete to themselves. If they do think of marriage, it's not to someone nervous and a bit delicate like me, it's to someone younger and more lively who can laugh and joke with them and meet them on their own ground.

"Most of my sisters play a bit," said Teddy, "but not me. I sing: it's easier. And the trouble with them is that there's really too many of 'em to learn on one piano. Have you any sisters?"

"No. I had two brothers, but they both died when I was a baby."

"Ah, too bad. It's happened to us. Is that your carriage at the gate?"

"Yes."

"She looks a lively mare. I should think she'd go a spanking pace with something lighter behind."

"Yes. Oh, yes, she does."

Teddy glanced at Brook curiously. "D'you ride much, Mr. Ferguson?"

"I have a horse. I go for a canter sometimes." (But not before Tomkins has taken him for a gallop to work off his first exuberance.)

Teddy was thinking what a queer stick this young man was. He was rich and probably had everything he wanted, but he didn't seem to find much fun in life. How Mother's purring, Teddy thought.

"You must come round and see us one evening during the lighter weather," Mr. Ferguson said, his voice, his eyes steady, ice-blue, confident. "Bring this young man and your daughters, Mrs. Blake."

"Oh, thank you. We'd like to do that, wouldn't we? That's a real pleasure we'll look forward to, Mr. Ferguson. I often pass your gates on the way to my sister's, and in the spring I always stop to admire the lilac and the laburnum, Mr. Ferguson. It will be full out, I suppose, quite soon?"

"Quite soon." He was too well aware of his condescension to need to take the hint. "Well, I think we must be going now. We shall meet your husband some time, Mrs. Blake."

"Oh, yes. Yes, I'm sure he'll be that disappointed when I tell him about us meeting. He often speaks about you."

They parted. Brook shook hands with the boy, whom he had rather taken to, and bowed to the ladies and followed his father over the gravel path among the gravestones, taking with him a last impression of soft voices and smooth cheeks and a disturbing, walled-off femininity. Did he wish to climb that wall? A burglar breaking into a strange garden.

Tomkins was waiting, hand on the open door, touched his cap, shut them in, jumped up to his box. They drove off.

Mr. Ferguson said: "The aunt is a little common. It confirms my earlier view."

The carriage jolted and rolled in the ruts of the country lane.

"I wish they'd do something about the road," said Brook. "Even cinders."

"I must meet the father. I'm told he is worthy—wrapped up in his family. What did you think of the girls?"

"I didn't see much of them."

His father's bulk shifted impatiently. "Naturally you couldn't come to know them in ten minutes. I suppose you got some impression?"

"They seemed—very nice. Er—what makes you specially interested in this family, Father?"

"It is for you to become 'specially interested' where you choose," said Mr. Ferguson, breathing his irritation out. "I think those girls are suitable in *type*: young, healthy, modestly well-mannered. I have good reports of them."

"Who from?"

"They're unlikely to put on their opinions the sort of *misplaced* importance that Margaret would sometimes do. Not well connected or rich, but one of them, I think, could make a suitable wife for you, could become a suitable mother for your children." He lowered the window. "Very close in church tonight. If you get to know them a little better and then don't find them at all to your taste, they can be dropped. Indeed you should look elsewhere while considering them."

The carriage crossed the main road and Tomkins whipped up the mare to a better pace as they moved into the wooded darkness of the residential suburb. The night was thick and warm about them. Brook took a deep breath. Oh, well, this was just an idea of his father's. It was in such an early stage there was no need to fret about it yet. (He knew these ideas of old but tried to forget how often they came to fruition, how often before he'd found himself manœuvred into a position from which there seemed no reasonable retreat.) He tried even to forget his father's voice in the pleasure of the drive, to remember the fine surging music of the 'Messiah.' As so often before, he turned away from life and found security and comfort in a daydream. He thought of himself writing music as fine as Handel's, listening to it being performed by massed choirs in the Gentlemen's Concert Hall. His answers were increasingly absent-minded for the rest of the way home.

CHAPTER THREE The Blakes lived over the shop in Oxford Road. They were a healthy family; and although there was never quite room for them all in the house at once, they bore the inconveniences of overcrowding with good humour.

Ten of the children were living from a total output of fourteen. Esther Jane was twenty-one, Edward was twenty, Cordelia nineteen, Emma seventeen, Anne twelve, Sarah ten, Mary eight, Penelope six, and Winifred two. Virginia was minus a third, though everyone was at present hoping for a John James.

Teddy worked as a junior clerk at a grey cloth merchant's, Esther Jane taught at a kindergarten school, Cordelia was apprenticed to a dressmaker, Emma helped with the shop and the house, and the others were at school or in rompers.

On a warm evening in July the Blakes had important visitors. It was late enough for all the workers in the family to be home, but the shop was not yet closed.

It was a tall, narrow building bounded on one side by a pork butcher's and on the other by Bates's Wine Lodge, which was a public house in disguise. There were three steps into the shop, and down these Brook stumbled, leading the way for his father, who followed close behind. Outside Tomkins leaned against the step of the phaeton and the two horses shook their harness and put their noses together.

The shop was small and crammed with ailing clocks, many of them surgical cases. Grey-faced grandfathers leered with empty bellies at cuckoos frozen in the moment of calling the hour. German chimers rubbed uneasy shoulders with bow-legged walnut Frenchmen. Marble bracket eight-days leaned against decorated ormolus. And dozens of convalescent clocks ticked.

Mr. Blake was working behind a narrow counter—a small man with sloping shoulders and a long neck in a collar much too high and too big.

Without looking up, he said in a slow voice: "Good evening. It's warm. I'll not be a minute."

Brook, sweating, turned to look for an empty chair, but his father did not move, so he gave up the search.

"Good evening, Mr. Blake. Is your wife in? I don't know if you have a side entrance, but we could not see it."

Mr. Blake looked up. His tired, prominent, quizzical eyes took in the callers.

"Ah, Mr. Ferguson. And Mr. Brook." He fitted a magnifying glass into his eye and peered down at the watch.

"We've come," said Mr. Ferguson, "on a somewhat important personal matter, concerning yourself and your wife and one of your daughters."

"There," said Mr. Blake, and ran his hand through his fine grey hair. "It's the compensation balance. They've used some sort of alloy muck instead of brass. See?" He came round from behind the counter, picking his way slowly across. "Cheap watches, sir. Never buy a cheap watch."

"My own watch was given me when I was twenty-one," said Mr. Ferguson, towering, seeming to fill a third of the shop. "By my father. It has served me ever since. I made the same present to my son, didn't I, Brook? The best is always the cheapest. But I am not interested in watches——"

The time was a quarter to nine and Mr. Ferguson found himself interrupted. He had a strong voice, but it could not compete against twenty-seven chiming clocks. With impatience he waited until they had done. Mr. Blake listened to them with an interested but critical expression. At the end he nodded a slow judicial satisfaction.

"As I was saying," Mr. Ferguson resumed, "although it would be——"

He stopped again. Two clocks had been half a minute late off the mark. All the satisfaction instantly vanished from Mr. Blake's face. He clicked his tongue and frowned until the noise had ceased, and then as Mr. Ferguson took a breath he wandered off to put things right.

"It's the Louis Quinze," he said. "And of course this Handsworth thing. Quite erratic." He turned his thin neck within its collar and looked at them. "It's all a question of balances. Did you wish to see my wife?"

"Yes, and you too, Mr. Blake."

Mr. Blake took out a handsome watch and looked at it.

"It's not about clocks?"

"It is not."

"Well, I can't close yet. . . . I'll get Teddy to come and mind shop."

The house had been built with a gloomy basement kitchen; but in his early married days, before his children had begun to come so quickly off the assembly line, John James Blake had had a new kitchen built out on the ground-floor level. This had become a common room whose population was continually in a state of flux and change. The only constant was Mrs. Blake, who cooked there, laid the meals, washed up, dressed and fed her children, propelled them off to school or work, and was still there to welcome them on the rebound.

On the evening that the Fergusons called, only Emma and her three youngest were with her; Ann and Sarah were upstairs playing duets on the upright rosewood piano, and Esther, Teddy, and Cordelia, having just finished their supper, had been sent out by Mrs. Blake to pick peas and dig potatoes before the light failed. Mrs. Blake worked hard herself and she had a talent for organising her children's lives so that nothing was wasted. The spring which set off her inventive brain was to see one of them sitting down.

But in the warm early dusk of the garden not much work was being done. They had stopped to talk, and talk had led to good-humoured argument. The two sisters sided together and Teddy, finding himself getting the worst of it, had maliciously begun to flip peas at them with his finger and thumb. There was no retaliation for a time, until he added weight to his ammunition with a small potato. This bounced off Cordelia's head and left bits of clayey soil in her hair. She squealed and dropped her basket and picked up the two largest potatoes that had so far been unearthed. One of these hit Teddy on the shoulder, but the other was a wild miss and went rolling down the path to fetch up at the feet of Mr. Blake, who at that moment came out.

Mr. Blake had a powerful influence over his children, but it was not the influence of a heavy hand. He stared a moment at the potato touching his toe, then looked up at the three and opened his mouth in one of his queer soundless laughs.

"Teddy."

"Yes, Father?"

"Look after shop a few minutes, will you? Fergusons are here and want a word alone with Mother and me."

"All right, Father."

They went indoors and the sisters were left to gather up the split peas. They bent together, with their wide-spreading skirts flowering like giant mushrooms from small curved waists. After a moment Esther said:

"I wonder what they're here again for?"

"Phew, it's hot! There's thunder about somewhere."

"It must be important if old Mr. Ferguson's come. He's too busy to waste his time on us."

"Perhaps he's taken a fancy to Father."

Esther eyed her sister. She knew that Cordelia was by no means as ingenuous as she pretended.

"Or to you."

"Why to me? I'm sure he's made far more fuss of you."

"And left you to Brook." Esther giggled. "I confess I like Mr. Ferguson better than his son. He's got a comfortable waistline and good gentlemanly manners. Seriously, Delia, has Brook ever said anything to you?"

"What? Oh, of course not. There's nothing like that about it."

"I thought at that last concert he was looking at you in rather a sentimental way."

Cordelia said with a slight heightening of colour: "I feel sorry for the poor man. He's so shy and delicate and—artistic. But it was the music that was making him sentimental, not me."

"What must it be like to live in a big house with servants to do everything for you?" Esther stretched her arms and yawned. "Smith, dig those potatoes for me, Jones, sweep the path. Very pleasant, I should say."

"Mm . . . That should be enough for dinner. . . . They're a bit on the small side this year."

"The rows are too close together. That's Teddy's fault. . . . I wonder how long we're supposed to stay out here. Shall we go in as if we didn't know that they were there?"

"No, no, we can't do that."

"How those two *thump* the piano." Esther frowned at an upper window. "It'll need tuning again in no time."

"Essie . . ."

"Yes?"

"I wonder what they *have* come about?"

"Go in and see."

"No. Wait a minute." Cordelia turned and her eyes moved slowly over the house.

The kitchen had a flat roof and in the roof was a large open fanlight. Against the corner of the kitchen wall was an old and battered tree. It had been much used for climbing until Sarah had fallen out of it one day like an over-ripe pear and cracked her arm. Cordelia had not been up it for three years. Now she was impeded by all the inconvenient spread of her crinoline, but the way was too familiar to put a foot wrong. Presently she was on the roof and waving down in triumph at Esther. She took off her shoes before tiptoeing across the leaded roof.

As she stared down her father was just lighting the gas. It bobbed and flickered for a moment and then as he turned it up the noise developed into a steady hiss and the flame flickered yellow out of the top of the globe.

The Fergusons had not been quite successful in getting Mr. and Mrs. Blake alone. Mrs. Blake, enormous now in semi-disguising draperies, was sitting on a rocking-chair before the fire with Winifred on her knee, drying the child's hair. Beside her was the small soapy bath which had just held Winifred. At the kitchen table Mary and Penelope, with round, thoughtful, distant eyes, were scooping up bowls of bread and milk. Mr. Ferguson's bulk overflowed the edges of a small armchair, Brook sat turning his hat and biting the skin round his fingers.

Cordelia had never been able to take quite such a detached and unhurried view of the Fergusons before. She stared first at the father and saw all his exceptional bulk, the great weight of his shoulders, the thickness of his strong legs, his broad, capable, well-kept hands. It was all bulk rather than fat, power rather than ballast. Strong sonorous voice, phrases and words that came easily, that flowed. Ice-blue eyes which stayed a little cold even when they were smiling. There was something about him which was thrusting yet secure, unsatisfied yet confident. He was a leader, a doer, a mover of men; he would be conspicuous in any company.

She looked at the son and saw his slender build, his soft, easily startled brown eyes, his thin artistic hands, his high smooth forehead with the hair brushed forward and round. She wondered what the mother had been like, for there seemed nothing the same between these two.

She knew her mother was highly flattered by this friendship, and in a way she was pleased with it too. The Fergusons were superior. The Fergusons were known everywhere and knew people the Blakes wouldn't ordinarily have met at all. She had been to a dance at the Athenæum, which was very superior; and she had been to Grove Hall where they lived. Both father and son had put themselves out to be nice, and she liked them in return. It wasn't hard to like people. Old Mr. Ferguson had a finger in every pie, and the son was deferential and refined.

Mr. Blake lit the second gas with a pop, and the burning spill shook in his hand before he threw it into the fire.

"Well, Mr. Ferguson," he said, with his soft, quiet, level voice as if he was adding up. "I can't say I'm not surprised. I've never been more surprised, not since that Brunswick thirty-six-hour I was repairing. . . . You remember that, Mrs. Blake, eh? And promised for the following day——"

"But in this case a pleasant surprise," said Mrs. Blake, towelling away. "We never thought, of course, that dear Cordelia . . ." The child on her lap began to cry. "There, there, my little pet. Yes, *quite* a surprise. I'm sure she'll be quite taken aback when she hears."

At the fanlight Cordelia was as taken aback as her mother could have wished—was held by a sudden frozen fascination.

Mr. Ferguson said: "I take it then you've no objection to an arrangement of some sort being come to?"

"Mummy, can I 'ave some more bread?" asked Penelope.

"Mummy, can I have some too?" said Mary.

"Yes, yes, but what d'you say?"

"Please," they piped together like little birds.

"Excuse me," said Mrs. Blake, getting up and handing Winifred to her husband. She went to the bread-bin in the corner and began to saw off two crusts. From the parlour on the first floor came the turbulent trills of the 'Huntsman's Chorus.'

"It all," said Mr. Blake, shaking his youngest daughter absent-mindedly, "it all really depends on Cordelia, doesn't it? She's a very good girl. Very good indeed, and it's her happiness we want above aught else."

"But naturally," said Mr. Ferguson, "you have some parental influence."

"Of course," said Mrs. Blake. "And I fancy we should know what is best for the dear child's happiness. *Dear* Brook! May I call you Brook? I'm that convinced you and Cordelia are meant for each other. In my heart, here, here, I believe I've felt it from the start!"

Pushing hair up from her face, she moved round the table and seemed about to squeeze him to her; but Mr. Ferguson had other subjects to bring up, and Cordelia, cold a moment ago, cold as she'd never been before in her life, but now hot, listened unbelieving to his strong self-controlled voice.

"I am a widower," he said, "and an old man. I should want Brook. They would live with me at Grove Hall."

"Of course, yes."

"Brook's wife would be expected to live in the style we're accustomed to and she wouldn't be stinted of money in doing this."

"Of course, no," said Mrs. Blake. "Cordelia's a very good girl, as Mr. Blake said. And the clever one of the family. We've always said that, haven't we, Mr. Blake? Three prizes she won at school, and if Mr. Blake or I are ever wrong in our monies she can put us right in no time. And as for fretwork . . . Did you see that decoration over the mirror in the shop? When she was twelve . . ."

Shut up, Mother, thought Cordelia, shut up, Mother, shut up.

". . . Simple people, and I should be there to give her any advice she needed. There are times when I might be away and Brook might also be away, but I do not think your daughter on the whole would find her life too lonely."

"Of course, no, Mr. Ferguson. Why ever should she be?"

Mr. Blake had been trying to get a word in. Now he passed the baby back to his wife and blurted out:

"We're—grateful for this offer, Mr. Ferguson, but——" He hesitated, and they all looked at him, Mrs. Blake in horrid astonishment, while he put a finger inside the rim of his large collar. "But I'm Cordelia's father, and it seems to me—not being ungrateful, mind you—it seems to me that it's up to the girl to choose—and choose quite free—who she'll marry and when."

He was going to go on but he was too slow.

"Nay, of course she will, John James," said his wife indignantly. "Nobody thought anything different. But if I know my dear child, she'll choose the way we want her to."

"Why not call her now?" suggested Mr. Ferguson. "Then we could proceed."

"I think it might be a sudden shock for the dear girl," objected Mrs. Blake, but her husband had already gone to the back door.

"Cordelia!"

There was no answer. It was growing dark in the garden.

"She's out here somewhere," said Mr. Blake stolidly.

"You go and fetch her, Brook," said Mr. Ferguson.

"Oh, no," said Brook. "I hardly like to. Wouldn't it be better——"

At that moment the echoing jangle of twenty-nine clocks came to them from the shop, and almost at once two cuckoo clocks on the mantelpiece opened their doors and began to explode.

"Do you know how a cuckoo works?" asked Mr. Blake, diverted.

"I do not," said Mr. Ferguson.

"It's really quite a nice bit of machinery. Remind me to show you some time. When the hour comes, a wire gives a push to the body of the bird——"

"Mr. Blake," said Mrs. Blake, "go and fetch your daughter. And tell Essie to stay out for the present."

"Was it me you wanted, Father?" said Cordelia.

She came in out of the falling dusk, in her pink striped skirt with its frilled hem and white apron; and there was a piece of old blue ribbon about her throat. No one—except her mother, who had come to distrust extreme innocence in her second daughter—supposed any connection between this lovely girl with her natural reserve and dignity and the scraping sounds they had all heard on the roof.

18

CHAPTER FOUR 🌿 A few hours later she lay in bed watching Esther at the dressing-table brushing her hair. Her own hair lay in a cloud on the pillow, looking darker than it really was against the white linen. Her eyes were at their most thoughtful. Yet behind the thoughtfulness was a hint of humour, as if she wanted to laugh at life even when life held her in its closest and most humourless grip.

"Well, go on," said Esther, "what then?"

They never modified their voices when talking in the bedroom; experience had shown that whispers would wake Sarah and Mary in the other bed, but ordinary speech seldom.

"Well then," said Cordelia slowly, "I said—simply out of panic and to gain time—'What sort of an offer?' Old Mr. Ferguson looked a bit impatient, but he smiled and I think he was going to say something, only Mother spoke first. 'The only sort of offer a gentleman can bring,' she said, and I could see how excited she was. I've never seen her so worked-up before, though I believe she was doing her best to hide it."

"What did Brook say?"

"Nothing—at least, not then. I didn't look at him. Just then Penny upset her bowl of milk and it gave me something to do to wipe up the mess, but Mother stopped me and Mr. Ferguson said something about him being happy at the idea of the match and he was sure his son had made a wise choice. Then Papa took out his watch and began winding it—you know how we always used to mind our step when he did that when we were young. And he said: 'Is this a surprise to you, Cordelia?'"

"And of course you said it was?"

"I said it was! And it had been five minutes before! Oh, Essie, up on that roof I could have died——"

"Go on. You said it was a surprise. What did Father say?"

"He stood there fiddling with his watch and made such a queer little speech, slow and steady and careful and wise, almost as if he was talking to himself, about this was just as much a surprise to him and that he was very mindful of the kindness meant, but that he didn't want anything—*anything* that had been said to something the main point—I've forgotten the word he used--which main point was my happiness, and of course Brook's happiness; and although he thought it right that I should be told at once, he must insist that I didn't answer tonight even if I should have no hesitation in saying yes. Winnie was crying now and making everybody have to say things twice to be heard, and Penny had turned her bowl upside-down and was beating the top of it with her spoon. But Mummie seemed too upset at what Papa was saying to take any notice of any of this; and then Teddy came in from the shop to know if it was time to close."

Cordelia paused and looked at her sister. Esther was plaiting her hair.

"D'you think they were annoyed when they left, Delia? I thought Brook looked a bit down, but perhaps that was the lace curtains."

Cordelia said: "I wish he'd asked you, Essie."

"Oh, pooh!" Esther turned. "I'm glad he didn't. I should have told him . . ." She stopped. From now on the Fergusons were no longer material for joking. All that was changed. "I wouldn't have been any good to him at all."

"Yes, you would." Cordelia paused. "Why not?"

"Oh . . . I think Brook needs someone more like you. You're the practical one. You'd be able to look after a big house and not let it worry you. I'd be off my head. And you're kind and understanding. . . ."

Cordelia sat up and hugged her knees through the bedclothes. "I'm not kind and understanding, Essie! No more than anyone else. It's rubbish to talk like that. I'm selfish—I want to be happy, happier than most people. I want comfort and an easy life. Oh, Lord, I don't want to be a dressmaker always: pins and needles and lengths of serge every day from eight in the morning till eight at night. And being crushed up and short of money . . . I want all the things, the good things, there are in the world. I want to travel and to have time to read and to think—to meet people, intelligent people, and to hear music and to go to dances and to give parties—of my own, in my own home. . . ."

Esther dropped her plaits behind her shoulders and climbed slowly into bed beside the other girl. She understood her sister's feelings.

They did not say anything more for some time, Esther with her hands behind her head on the pillow, Cordelia sitting up, leaning back against the painted iron bedrail. However much one tried to consider it so, this was not just an offer of marriage from a rather kind, delicate man seven or eight years older than oneself.

Not only were the good qualities in her appealed to; but all the instincts she felt in her heart had no right to be considered—and all the dreams. If as a child she'd ever tried to snatch the biggest plum; if she had ever given way to pride; if she had ever felt lazy or envious or wanting to be better than her fellows or to shine in the eyes of the neighbourhood, or to be a benefactor of one's family . . . If she had ever dreamed of becoming beautiful and rich . . .

"D'you love him, Delia?" Esther asked.

"Oh, I like him," said Cordelia quickly. "I like him very much. I think perhaps . . ."

"When have you promised to give an answer?"

"Papa said next Tuesday, but Mother looked as if she was going to be ill, so we agreed on Sunday. They're to drive us home from church and I've to tell him then."

Esther knelt on the pillow and turned out the gas. The steady hissing died away and there was a sharp plop. She settled into the bed again.

The new darkness gave her courage and she said:

"What's it to be?"

Cordelia wriggled down on to the pillow, letting out a slow and not quite steady breath.

"I wish life wasn't so mixed up."

"How d'you mean?"

"I wish one didn't have to have children—and all that sort of thing."

"Don't you want a family?"

"Oh, yes—some day. It's not the family I don't want. . . ."

There was a long silence. Far away in the distance came a rumble of thunder, lazy, reluctant, moving across the roofs of the sleeping town.

Esther said: "I forgot to starch my cuffs. It was all the excitement. Hang."

"I've got a pair you can have."

"Thanks."

There was another silence.

"What are you laughing at?" Cordelia said.

"I'm not laughing. At least, not the way you think. I was only thinking how funny it would be to have a sister who lived at Grove Hall."

So even Esther really, privately, took it for granted. Teddy too. Over cocoa he had had his revenge for their teasing of him. But beneath the chaff Cordelia had been able to see that he was counting on the marriage and was quietly excited about it. Already they were all counting on it, building it into their picture of the future. 'My daughter, Mrs. Ferguson.' 'My brother-in-law who owns the printing and dye works in Ancoats.'

There was really only her father who stood out against all this pressure, who refused to let her hurry herself. Thanks to him, she had at least some time for reflection. But was her choice really free when she knew her mother would practically die of the disappointment, and she expecting to be confined next month? Cordelia didn't want a repetition of last year and the year before, when they had lost Clara and little Elizabeth: her mother sitting in front of the fire crying with her hair down and all the children round her crying too. She didn't want to feel responsible for such a scene.

And Brook? Could she make him happy and in so doing be happy herself? Before they left he had come across and touched her elbow and said:

"I'll wait for Sunday. I'll—I'll hope you'll choose right—the way I want you to choose. It would make me very happy."

It was the nearest he had yet come to speaking of his own feelings. She felt warmer, comforted by remembering it.

"Essie," she said.

"Yes," said Esther indistinctly, being nearly asleep.

"Oh, it doesn't matter."

She lay quiet until she heard her sister's regular breathing, and then slipped quietly out of bed and went to the window. She stood in her long nightdress against the glass with the curtain parted by her outstretched hands.

There was a moon somewhere, but the night was heavily overcast. She stood there and thought: All the selfish little things, pride, position; all the unselfish little things, compassion and liking for Brook, wanting to please and help my family; if they are all piled up one on top of another . . .

She would be able to help her family, that was certain. They were always hard up. Much of Mr. Blake's work was visiting the big houses of the country to attend to their clocks, and for this work he seldom got paid more than once in three years; some had even run on for seven. To found a family of her own, surely found it in comfort and security and position. Wrong to feel pride and excitement in that? Her children would not need to be brought up anyhow—they could go to fine schools, perhaps be trained for things even above dye works and Grove Hall. To throw all that away . . . She thought: The first I shall call John James and the second Edward Blake and the third, if there is a third, Brook. But what of *this* Brook? I felt more for that boy Teddy brought home when I was thirteen. Yet I like Brook. We get on well. He's clever, plays the piano much better than I shall ever be able to, he writes poetry, is a gentleman. Mrs. Brook Ferguson of Grove Hall. Get thee behind me, Satan.

Heavens, I'm excited. I shall never, never sleep!

Talk to Father tomorrow. He's the only one who's keeping a level head. But what can I tell him? I can't shift the decision to him. It must be mine, *mine*.

She turned from the window and came slowly back to the bed. The sound of quiet regular breathing met her in the darkness. Three of them there, peacefully asleep. I wish it were Esther, she thought. (Do I, truly, honestly?) I wish I could put off deciding for three months. I wish . . . I wish . . .

She climbed slowly up into the bed, and Esther turned over restlessly

22

as the bed creaked. Cordelia looked at the figure beside her and thought: Esther . . . Brook, Esther . . . Brook.

A little shiver went through her limbs, and she pulled the bedclothes up to her chin.

CHAPTER FIVE Seven months and three days after the death of Margaret Ferguson, Brook signed the register in St. James's Church a second time.

There had been a good deal of argument over the wedding arrangements and Mr. Ferguson had wondered once or twice whether he had been wise to choose a girl with such an obstructive and independent father. It was not at all what he had expected.

Mr. Blake had insisted on all his rights, and the marriage had almost foundered on Mr. Ferguson's suggestion that the wedding breakfast should be held at Grove Hall. Mrs. Blake, now nursing her fifteenth, had needed all her hysterics to persuade John James that the reception need not be in the tiny parlour over the shop; and eventually they compromised by holding it in the Albion Hotel. There in superb dignity only offset by his slight build and roomy collar, Mr. Blake followed Mr. Ferguson's speech with one of equal length, though far fewer words, in which he likened life to the building of a great clock and the partnership of marriage to the fitting together of two cogwheels which turned ever afterwards in precision and harmony.

She had gone through it calmly, detached, and a little surprised at her own detachment. A few days before she had been terribly excited, wound up, but on the day this strange calm.

Someone was marrying Brook Ferguson. O God, who by Thy mighty power hast made all things of nothing; who also did appoint that out of man woman should take her beginning; and, knitting them together, didst teach that it should never be lawful to put asunder those whom Thou by Matrimony hast made one, O God, who hast consecrated the state of Matrimony to such an excellent mystery . . . She saw it all with extraordinary clearness: the nervous perspiration round the corners of Brook's nose; the thick rimless eyeglasses and swinging black cord of Tom Griffin, the best man; that other tall young man with the friendly smile who seemed so taken with Esther's vivid bridesmaid beauty; the slightly common effect of Aunt Higginbottom's coral beads of which she was so proud; the new clergyman, Mr. Shrike, with his new Dundreary whiskers. And later Mr. Ferguson's dominance of the whole scene, his beautiful white waistcoat and shiny silk hat, her mother's

23

tears—which might have been of regret at losing a daughter or relief that the wedding had come off after all; Mr. Ferguson's friend, Mr. Slaney-Smith, who made a dryly witty speech but really rather took too much on himself by seeming to claim credit for the whole affair; Brook's shabby out-of-date aunt, whom everyone seemed so unkindly to ignore, and Brook's eccentric uncle; the fashionable breakfast Mr. Blake had ordered, beginning with a sardine and ending with some sort of cheese no one had ever tasted before. If there was one thing that disturbed her during the early part of the day, it was not any of the ordinary embarrassments of a bride but the thought of how much her father was spending on her, how little he could afford it, what her family might now have to do without during the coming winter.

Brook, she could see, felt it more than she did, even though this was his second adventure. Curious how little she thought of his first wife; but she'd never known her, not yet even seen a photo of her; she had no twinges of jealousy, no curiosity to know more; Margaret belonged to Brook's past and she did not yet try to visualise it.

After the breakfast Mr. Slaney-Smith sang 'Tell Me Mary How to Woo Thee' in a thin clear tenor, and then a male quartet with quiffs as shiny as their shirt-fronts came in and gave 'Thy Voice O Harmony' and 'Glorious Apollo,' while the bride and bridegroom were upstairs changing.

At the door, after she had taken leave of the whole family, she turned back for a moment and looked at all the people who had been at the breakfast. They were smiling at her and crowding together, and some of the younger ones had got rice ready to throw. She thought: This is really happening to me. And the circumstance which suddenly pulled aside the veil which had been separating her from life all through the day was the expression on her father's face as he shut the door of the carriage—of sudden pain and doubt—and then she had touched his hand for what seemed the last time and someone shouting and laughing had come between.

The carriage began to draw away. I am Mrs. Brook Ferguson. My home is at Grove Hall. The shop, the kitchen, the garden, the little parlour, the upright piano; I shall come to them as a stranger revisiting old places. The familiar routine, the easy jokes, the homely smells. And all the clocks chattering and chiming, something which has been with me ever since my first memories of warmth, of the rocking-chair, of the singing kettle.

"Phew!" Brook said. "I'm glad it's over, dear, aren't you? I got so hot in the church, and then it was cold in the dining-room. I hope I haven't caught a chill. What time did Father say we got to Blackpool?"

"Half-past four," she said. "Will there be a lot of people on the train?"

"Not in the first class."

She stared out at the passing traffic, at the big black bulk of the Infirmary and the stone drinking-fountain with the three beggars sitting beside it, at the bus with its brown horses and the street barrows and the horse-drawn drays, at the old ladies in their black velvet cloaks and black bonnets and the urchins in ragged coats and bare feet. She glanced at her husband, who had drawn the cloak around him, at the fine silk hat slightly overshadowing his sensitive, nervous, petulant face. And she thought: We are strangers. Polite words, touched hands, a nervous kiss. Little spun silk threads of contact; you could crush them and blow them away.

But it's not fair to doubt now, to think sentimentally of the things left behind. Sympathy and affection were his due. Already, merely by his proposal, he had given her so much. Somehow true feeling had not been possible while the two families had been there. All day she had been dried up, unattached. Now that would change.

She said: "What are you thinking?"

"I wish it wasn't October. It goes dark so soon."

"It doesn't matter, does it?"

"No. No, I suppose not."

One hand was on his knee and she put hers over it.

His pale face instantly flushed with pleasure.

"Cordelia," he said. "We're away from all those confounded people at last. I hate staring people wondering what you're thinking and feeling. It's nice to be alone. I'm very fond of you, Cordelia. I hope we'll get on all right. I want to give you things and make you happy."

"You don't need to give me things, Brook. I'm happy now."

They reached Blackpool in sunshine and drove straight to their hotel, with a strong westerly breeze pushing and thrusting at the hansom. The season was over and there were few people in the hotel. At her suggestion they went out again almost immediately to make the most of the daylight, and strolled along the front, stopping now and again to sit on one of the big black stones which stood in ridges overlooking the pebbly bar sloping down to the sea. They came back through the centre of the village, where a few people were finding amusement in the vulgar peep-show machines, and where a few of the shacks were still open and loud-voiced men invited you to buy cheap jewellery or an indigestion cure. They stopped among the shops, and Brook bought her chocolates and a stick of 'rock' and a new handbag. He wanted to buy her more things but she would not let him. Then he got some cheroots for himself and they stared at a little shop which had a notice in the window saying 'Smythe's Improved Photographic Portraits. The brilliance and warmth of tone gained by this amazing new method . . .'

They made an appointment for the following day, strolled back past the little cottages to their hotel.

They watched the afterglow fade and then went in. A few more people were about, two elderly gentlemen and some silked and velveted old ladies. A porter was just lighting the oil lamps. Brook had taken a private sitting-room, and for the first evening they decided to have a meal up there to avoid the interested inspection of the other people.

She had tasted champagne only once before but liked it instantly in spite of the way it made bubbles burst in your nose. It was strange, this liking, she explained to Brook, for she didn't care much for beer or port or brandy. Champagne had a sort of clean taste like cold water gone sour.

They both laughed at this. Brook began to tell her about his poetry. She knew he liked talking of it, and she liked to hear him. The little hesitations slipped out of his speech. During the cotton famine the *Courier* had published two of his poems, and occasionally he got an essay in one of the weekly papers. There was a suggestion that he might some time give a reading of his poems at the Athenæum. If he had had his way, he said, he would have taken up literature as a career.

Time passed quickly while he talked, and she encouraged him to go on.

At length he said: "Well, I'm tired. Are you? I expect you are. I think I'll just go downstairs and smoke a cigar before I turn in. Would you like anything more?"

"No, thank you, Brook. I shall be all right."

"Very well." He got up and rang for the maid and put on his cloak and hat and went down.

In the hall he stopped to light a cheroot, feeling master of the situation. He was not drunk but had taken just enough to feel for once that he had a firm grip on life instead of being at the mercy of every eddy that came. He knew he had talked well and had interested her. None of Margaret's condescension. She was young and untutored and poorly off and fond of him and desirable. He was knowledgeable and rich and mature. He had all the advantages. Life was good.

Only, in a way, he wished she was not so beautiful. In living reality, and at close quarters, her loveliness unnerved him. It was always the way: the life of his imagination was subtler and easier than reality.

There was a balcony leading off the smoking-room which looked across the road to the sands and the sea, and he went there and leaned against the rail looking out. A single lantern hung over the entrance from the french windows. Another man was at the other end of the balcony, and Brook nodded a brief good evening.

He was glad of the prospect that for a fortnight he would be free from his father. On this fortnight they should do everything, go everywhere they possibly could. He looked forward to showing her all the things she had not seen and teaching her all the things she did not know. With Margaret it had never been possible. Apart from the difference in age, she came from a family which had inevitably seen more and knew more than he ever had. He remembered how Margaret had looked that first wedding night. Ever so slightly superior and passionless—and ever so slightly resentful. It had given him a sense of inferiority, of amateurism, though he knew in truth she was as innocent as he.

"Right unseasonable weather we're having, sir," said the man in the other corner.

"Yes," said Brook.

"We've seen naught of the October gales yet. It's been a strange autumn, has this. Why, I was walking along the South Shore this morning and watching the people shuttering up their windows and sealing them with clay, and all the time the sun was shining and it was as warm as August."

"We—only came tonight. I shall be glad if the fine weather holds a day or two more."

"Eh, but the gales are healthy, lad." The stub of a cigar showed up a fierce brick-coloured old face, whiskered and alert. "Always come for 'em. Have been coming for 'em for near on forty years. Blows the cobwebs away for the winter."

"Yes, I suppose so." He had to be grateful to his father; without him it would not have been possible. One resented so often the things that he did, so reasonable, so ruthless. One resented having things decided for one, and yet . . . The girl in the grey churchyard had become his.

"Only missed one year, and that was when the wife died. She'd been a diabetic for some years, but in the end it was a stroke that took her. . . ."

There was a strong salty smell coming in from the sea; it filled one's lungs and enriched one's blood. That champagne . . .

"From Manchester," said Brook, wishing now he had not chosen this place for his cigar.

"I was there three months ago. In hospital for an operation. Stone, it was. You wouldn't think you'd come through it at my time of life, would you? How old d'you think I am? Nearly seventy-eight. The surgeons were right surprised when I told them. They said: 'He's got a strong heart, has Mr. Wainwright.' "

On that other honeymoon his father had come over to Filey at the end of the second week; Margaret had resented it. It had been the first of many clashes. . . . There'd never been any real peace between Margaret and his father all the years, only a sort of armistice between quarrels.

27

"The things they can do nowadays. They wanted me to have an anæsthetic, but I said no." The old man moved nearer and stared into Brook's face, searching it for expression and interest. "Never lost my wits in seventy-eight years and not going to start now. D'ye see? It's not really an operation, lad, not a cutting, that is. . . ."

"Yes," said Brook suddenly, feeling a bit sick as the story came home to him. Up to now he had kept the old man's nonsense at bay. The words had fallen on his ears and meant nothing. "I see. Well, I think——"

"They crush the stone. With an instrument. Like a thin pair of pliers almost."

How would you like this to happen to you? The nightmare of his life was fear of pain.

"Look, I'll tell you. It's really a matter of making up one's mind to it. They say the Greeks . . ." He went into details.

God, shut up! Leave me alone. Go away, old man. I want to think of youth and health and pleasure, not age and disease and pain. I've always got something the matter with me, some trivial thing that might *not* be trivial. Do I want to think of such things tonight?

"What went wrong with me was that they cracked it in two but only one piece was crushed. So they said to me, 'Will you go through with it now, Mr. Wainwright, or have you had enough?'"

Brook sat down and took a deep breath. The sea air was sweet.

"They said many a man half my age . . ." The old fellow put the tip of his cigar back among his whiskers. "They said it surprised them. What's to do, lad? Reckon that cheroot's a bit strong, eh? They're always a tidy mouthful, are those long thin ones." His fierce old face was peering, questing. "Got something with you, eh? I had a nephew once——"

"There's nothing wrong with me," Brook said, standing up. And that queer distaste for offending people made him add: "Thank you. I think it's time I turned in. Good night."

He went in through the darkened smoke-room, knocking into a table in his haste, and hurried through the hall. He went up the stairs and fortunately there was a chair on the landing. There was a plant on a wicker table beside it and he crushed out the cheroot and dropped it in the pot. Angry and humiliated, he sat quiet for a few moments and began to feel better.

He got up and went into the sitting-room. The table had been cleared and Cordelia was not there. He pottered about a few moments. He had brought a few books with him, and she had arranged them on the top of the display cabinet. He took one down and stared at it, then replaced it and went to the bedroom door.

The bedroom was ornate, with a faded red carpet and a crimson and gilt Fleur de Lys patterned paper. The furniture was of heavy polished walnut, with lace antimacassars, and there were two improving texts on the walls: 'The memory of the just is blessed' and 'I sleep but my heart waketh.'

He had never seen her with her hair down before. He went forward and sat on the edge of the bed.

"Cordelia . . . You're lovely."

The colour flushed up to her cheeks.

"Am I, Brook?"

He put his hand over hers.

"You're cold," she said. "And pale. Are you all right?"

He stiffened.

"Of course I'm all right." He got up sharply and went to the decorated mirror over the fireplace. Yes, he looked sallow, ill. She had seen it, she with her abounding health. Perhaps already she despised him. So perhaps it was all to be just the same.

"We'll leave here tomorrow," he said.

". . . *Leave?*"

"And go to Bailey's. It's a better hotel—more modern."

There was silence.

"Just as you say, Brook. I shall be happy anywhere."

"Will you?" He turned. "Will you, Delia; that's what I want to know."

Her eyes widened in astonishment. "Of course I shall. This is all new to me, Brook. And it's our—— I don't mind where we stay. Brook, I was thinking while you were out just now—are there gypsies at the South Shore? A girl I knew came here last year and she said she bought a pretty basket and had her fortune told. I'd like to go there. It would be fun, wouldn't it? Can we go tomorrow?" As he did not respond she said: "What's the matter? Have I said something to offend you?"

"No. Nonsense. Nothing at all." He leaned against the mantelshelf, looking at her, conscious he still felt far from well. "We'll leave first thing tomorrow morning," he said defiantly. "Father should never have booked here; he only did that because he and Mother used to come here in the old days."

"Where's Bailey's?"

"That big place we passed near the centre of the town. There'll be more life there." He said with a sudden rush: "We'll go out to the Star Inn tomorrow for lunch, if you like. They have wonderful oysters. Then we can go and see your gypsies. I'll buy you baskets and you can have your fortune told as often as you like. Afterwards, tomorrow evening, we'll go the other way. . . ."

He stopped, thinking suddenly that to talk so was to show his nervousness, not hide it.

"It's like a new life beginning," she said.

29

"Have some more champagne?"

She shook her head. "No . . ."

"Mind if I have some?"

"No . . ."

He went out and drank a glass and felt the warmth creeping into him again. He drank another glass and went back.

He sat on the bed and took her by the shoulders and kissed her.

"Brook," she said. "I . . ."

"Well?"

She shook her head. "Nothing."

He tried to look into her eyes, but their clear depths looked past him, seeming to seek escape and detachment beyond the confines of the room. He could smell something on her hair and the faint perfume of her body. Then panic took him and he suddenly accepted her instinctive solution. Keep self-consciousness and personality out of it. Forget self, forget sickness, forget Brook Ferguson.

He kissed her on the neck, the cheeks, and the hair, and she half turned away, then checked the movement, checked revulsion and fear and turned towards him, accepting this baptism of experience that he was about to bestow.

CHAPTER SIX ✿❧ The leaves were falling. It took Farrow and Bollard nearly all day brushing them clear of the drive as they drifted down from the sycamores and the beeches. It was a nice house, big and square and grown with ivy, mightily furnished, nothing spared, and six indoor servants to do your bidding. Cordelia settled into it with the determined happiness of her nature but a little overwhelmed. They'd never had even one servant at home; the girls had graduated from one job to another as a younger sister came on.

She had spoken truly when she said to Brook that this was a new life beginning. *Everything* was different. As she grew to know her father-in-law she found that.

At home authority was democratic. You said what you liked and did what you liked within unwritten limits, and if you overstepped them the family quietly sat on you. Mother had a sharp hand with the young ones, but Father was more like an elder brother who had graduated out. Many a stern parent had shaken his head over the follies of the Blake household.

In Grove Hall one sun blazed and the others were satellites who drew their light from the parent beam and moved round it.

Not that Mr. Ferguson was master in a pompous way. It was only in time that you felt his authority, and then you couldn't call it the rod of iron: he seemed to do everything with an admonitory finger. Even during the day, when he was out, no one was quite free from it. The household moved and lived under the influence of one question: What would Mr. Ferguson like?

He was too intelligent, too broad-minded, too considerate to be a bully. Yet it was almost impossible to relax in his presence. You sat down ready to get up; you read with an ear expecting some interrupting comment; if *he* read you were self-conscious about keeping quiet. Sometimes she thought it was his breathing which made you unable to forget him. Its audibleness was like the beat of a dynamo—but, unlike a dynamo, it was not regular, and a quickening usually meant he was going to say something. A quickening, even if he said nothing after, was enough to draw attention to his being there. He wore elastic-sided boots and was very light on his feet, so that often his breathing was the first thing you heard when he moved about the house. Then, too, you came to hesitate about giving your own opinions because his when they came were so much better phrased and better reasoned. You were in the presence, you felt, of an original personality whose views you could *never* predict beforehand.

You moved to a steady routine. Life began at six-thirty when Mr. Ferguson took a cold bath in the cellar. After this he went for his morning walk across the fields to Birch and was back in time to read prayers to the household at seven-thirty prompt. Breakfast was at seven forty-five and was cleared at eight-fifteen. For half an hour he sat in his study dealing with the affairs of the house, and Cordelia and the servants were expected to hold themselves in readiness to go and see him, as and when he summoned them. At eight forty-five his carriage was at the door and he and Brook left for Town.

This was normally the last that was seen of them until six in the evening, but about two days a week, quite unexpectedly, Mr. Ferguson and Brook—or sometimes only Mr. Ferguson—would arrive back with panting horses at twelve-thirty for dinner; and the constant expectation of this always kept the household at a stretch until twelve thirty-one was past. At six-thirty in the evening there were short prayers, followed at once by supper. The evening would generally be spent according to Mr. Ferguson's plans, and if they were at home there would be evening prayers at half-past nine, followed by another meal, though a less substantial one this time. Unless something special was on, the downstairs lights of the house were expected to be out by half-past ten.

The routine did not break when Mr. Ferguson or Brook were away for a day or two. Mr. Ferguson had interests in Oldham, and it was necessary to visit them; but you could never be certain that he might not come back unexpectedly. His talent extended in many directions.

The first time Cordelia felt any of the weight applied to herself was over her father's wedding present to them. This was a Swiss grandfather clock, the pride of his collection, which he had bought when broken and persuaded into working order by endless toil and patience: a superb thing with a great brass face decorated to look like a smiling old man. Its supreme virtuosity lay in the striking of the hour, when a long brown tongue slowly protruded from the old man's face. Mr. Ferguson thought it vulgar.

It had been put in the hall while the happy couple were away, but soon after they came back, Mr. Ferguson suggested they might like it in their bedroom.

Anxious as she was to be agreeable in all things, Cordelia found herself opposing this.

"My dear child," said Mr. Ferguson. "A charming present, I've no doubt. Quite—original. And I know you must attach a certain sentimental value to any wedding gift—as I would. But I'd put it to you. When I bought this house, I furnished it adequately and completely after a particular style. To insert among items of furniture which harmonise together one piece which is out of period . . . Why, I should say the same if it were a Sheraton armchair!"

Cordelia glanced at Brook, who was idly crumbling his bread. He was uncomfortable but was not prepared to weigh in on her side.

She said: "Could it be put in here, do you think?"

"Eh, yes," said Aunt Tish, looking up from her soup. "Why not have it in here, Frederick? I think it's proper quaint."

For once Frederick chose to answer his sister; she was a convenient target for shots aimed elsewhere.

"If I put a clock of that type in here I should be laying myself open to the contempt of those who *understand*. Things should exist in harmony or not at all. I dislike the disharmonious. And in my own house it would be unforgivable. Quaintness, Letitia, does not make up for lack of taste."

The clock went upstairs. There it had to have its strike stopped so that they could sleep in peace through the night.

Aunt Tish, people whispered, had been frightened by a gypsy when she was three. It must have been a bad fright because it had so far lasted fifty-five years. She was untidy and rather dirty, and sometimes had lice in her hair, which she called 'bidies.' She never changed her style of dress; a full flounced skirt and a laced corsage with a soiled white over-jacket of embroidered muslin. It was about a quarter of a century out of date. When the weather was cold a dewdrop formed on the end of her nose. She was simple-minded, generous, on her dignity with the servants, boring in conversation, and in awe of her brother Frederick.

Uncle Pridey was none of these things. He was in the late sixties and very tall, with a rather untidy imperial and grey eyebrows that reminded Cordelia of caterpillars because they were continually on the move. He had an alert, mischievous mind which kept too closely to the limits of his two hobbies, music and mice.

Except for being an indifferent 'cellist, he depended for his music on the performances given in Town; but the mice, the shrews, and the white rats he kept in his bedroom upstairs, where he bred and cross-bred them at his own discretion; and sometimes on Saturday nights he would put on his oldest clothes and take a selection of them down to sell at Shudehill market.

It was flattering to be suddenly wealthy, to be a married woman, no longer an untried girl, to have the attentions of a well-mannered man, to find herself accepted in this strange new world. These were the pleasures. And to those duties which entailed taking up the reins of this house she brought a peculiar interest which surprised even herself. Even the fact that she and not the housekeeper was expected to keep a record of every penny spent and to render her accounts to Mr. Ferguson at eight-fifteen every Saturday morning did not after the first few weeks upset her.

As for the rest, she wondered sometimes if she loved Brook, but more often she blamed her own youth, feeling that she had perhaps married too early and a new happiness would come later on.

While they were away, Mr. Ferguson had redecorated and refurnished their room, and she was grateful for this as it seemed to draw a line after the dead Margaret's occupation and to allow her to start afresh.

Nevertheless the room was not without its souvenirs.

One day she lifted the lid of a narrow-necked jar on the mantelshelf and found it full of wispy black hair. She told Brook about it when he came home.

He flushed. "I thought—it had been taken away. I thought everything had gone."

"I didn't move it," she said slowly. "I felt somehow . . ." She felt that if she were Margaret she wouldn't want another woman to touch it.

Brook said: "She was saving it, you know. Her hair had been coming out during her illness, and she thought it could have been made up into a tail or whatever it's called."

He picked up the jar and shook the hair out upon a paper. He screwed this up and looked at the firegrate, then he glanced at her, coloured again, and left the room.

Only that day, as it happened, she had been looking at the miniature

33

which was the only reproduction of Margaret there seemed to be in the house; she had stared at the dark young woman with the pale cheeks, the pronounced eyebrows, the looped dark hair, and the young woman had stared back at her—it seemed with a hint of hostility, as if to say: 'Know me if you can!'

A patrician, a fastidious face.

"Was she much older than you, Brook?" she said when he came back.

"Oh, Margaret? Well, nearly seven years."

"What was the matter with her? I never liked to ask."

He hesitated. "Pernicious anæmia. She—had an illness and then didn't seem to pick up her strength. She wasted away." He looked at his wife. "You haven't found anything else of hers, have you?"

"No," said Cordelia—and felt she didn't want to.

But she did.

At Christmas Mr. Ferguson arranged several evening parties. The first was given to nine of his business associates, who came, frock-coated and bearded and sober and a little self-conscious, and sat round the groaning supper-table and talked in slow, cautious, level-headed tones of the price of cotton and of the laying of the Atlantic Cable. They were nearly all Liberals and nearly all dissenters, yet they were less progressive in outlook than Mr. Ferguson the churchman.

Cordelia, introduced and then courteously disregarded, listened intently to their views. Some of them shook their heads over the coming enlargement of the franchise; most of them did not believe in education for their sons—it might teach them to be gentlemen but not how to work: *their* children would go into the counting-house at fourteen; and all of them looked on organised labour as a dangerous challenge to the peace of England. The cotton famine was only just clearing up and Mr. Ferguson thought the time ripe for employers to make some gesture which would disarm the men by meeting their just claims in advance. He thought it policy as well as generosity.

Their view was that the Monster's appetite would grow with what it fed on. For them the trumpets of the French Revolution were still echoing on the banks of the Irwell.

After a while, summing up with a sort of Olympian calm, Mr. Ferguson said: "The trouble, gentlemen, is that you see these workers as a single many-headed beast—the sort of mob they band themselves into in time of trouble. But really they're separate individuals. Like ourselves. It's the only Christian basis—a working basis. We need not *fear* them or shun them or try to organise ourselves against them. They're quite reasonable creatures if given their rights. Indeed some of them are nearer to God's truth and see more clearly than we do."

There was a hesitant disapproving silence. A man called Jakin Robinson said:

"Did they see more clearly when they tried to blow up Ashton's house last week? And why did they do it? Because Ashton was a bad employer? Nowt o't sort! They did it because he makes bricks by machinery and they want to go on making 'em by hand. D'you call that seeing clearly?"

"Most unclearly. But perhaps they had not been invited to see it all. Perhaps they think machine-made bricks means starvation. Hallows, the port."

"You think we're behind the times, Ferguson. But you don't defeat laws o' commerce by saying they shouldn't exist. Let's forget bricks an' turn to our own trade. If you reduce hours o' work you cut production; if you increase wages you increase costs. Either way turns profit into loss. Then the mill closes down and where are your grand schemes? It's better a man should live than starve. There's been enough poverty in these last few years."

"And more than a little of it their own fault," said a husky old man at the end. "If they'd not supported Lincoln and his blockade . . . They should have followed Gladstone."

Mr. Ferguson said: "It takes grit and courage to risk starvation for a principle. And that sort of courage doesn't arise among a mob of thoughtless folk. They think for themselves. They deserve fair treatment."

Two or three gave low grunts of grudging acknowledgment. They prided themselves on their enlightenment and had suffered in good causes themselves. But Jakin Robinson said:

"Fair treatment! Well, who's not giving 'em fair treatment? Wages an' conditions in my mill are as fair as any in country. And if there were none of this damnation banding together——" He stopped. "Begging your pardon, Mrs. Brook."

"Cordelia," said her father-in-law. "You may join us later."

"Please let me stay, Mr. Ferguson," she said. "It's all new to me. I'm very interested."

But they were all waiting for her to go. What they were talking of wasn't women's business. It was an oversight, she realised, an error of taste on her part not to have left when Aunt Letitia left.

As Brook held open the door for her and she went out she heard Mr. Ferguson say: "You may smoke now, gentlemen."

It was a cold night and a big fire burned in the hall. She warmed her hands before it, wondering what to do. She felt restless, dissatisfied.

She heard a rustle behind her and saw Uncle Pridey stalking across the hall in his carpet slippers. When he saw her he veered towards her like a ship caught by an unexpected breeze.

"Ah, there, young woman. Going to freeze tonight. You'd best give instructions that these fires are kept in or the house will be as cold as a morgue in the morning."

She smiled. "All right, Uncle Pridey; I'll see you're kept warm." She found she could call this old man uncle much more easily than she could call Mr. Ferguson father.

"Afraid of their backs," said Pridey, energetically cracking his finger-joints in front of the blaze. "All servants these days are just the same. That lazy scoundrel Hallows. Are they still in there?" He nodded his head.

"Yes. Won't you go in?"

"While the birds are sitting? I should flush them. Let em sit on their schemes and see what'll hatch! Have a sweet."

"Thank you."

She peeped into a big paper bag he produced and took one. The old man's head was temporarily on a level with her own. Seen so close, his face seemed lop-sided with eccentricity.

He suddenly looked up from peering in the bag to meet her interested gaze. "At a loose end, young woman, eh? Ever seen my mice? More interesting than old greybeards who've forgotten all their natural instincts twenty years ago."

She was afraid of mice, but she said: "Thank you. Are they nice mice? I'd like to very much."

They climbed the stairs to Pridey's bedroom. A strong 'brown' animal smell met them.

"Now," said Pridey, "over here," and padded across to what must have been intended as a dressing-room but which now was lined all round with shelves and glass cases in all the dark corners of which were to be seen tiny bead-bright eyes and nibbling noses.

"You see," said Pridey. "My little friends. Far more faithful than human beings, eh? Come on, my pretties, come on then!" He pursed his lips and made little popping noises like drops of water splashing. Then he opened a door and six or eight white mice ran upon his hand and up his sleeve and moved sniffing round his collar.

"Showed them to Margaret," said Uncle Pridey, shaking his head. "She pretended to be disgusted, said they made her feel faint. What nonsense! They're clean, healthy little things, healthier than men and women. Look at this one. Look at his soft little belly. Look at his legs going like pistons. *And* he doesn't need a cold bath every morning. What's all this fetish of baths, young woman? My brother's crazy about 'em. A bath's a necessary evil, no more, no less. Once a week or once a fortnight you pop in, scrub down, pop out. Quicker it's over the better. Hot water. Soap. Steam. Towels. But no one's improved for smelling of a

tar barrel. People think it's progress. But it's back to the days of woad."
He paused, having wandered from his point.

"Yes. They're sweet," said Cordelia with great calmness, keeping a watch on each individual mouse so that none of them should get lost. "Esther likes mice. That's my sister. She—really likes them more than I do."

"Well, you've got pluck. Can see that. There, that's enough, my pretties. Lady's edgy. Back you go." Pridey picked them off himself, his great fleshy thumb and forefinger seeming to threaten each mouse with broken ribs as he put it back. Then he shook two out of his sleeves and shut the door. Cordelia let out a breath.

"Why *do* women fear mice? Peculiar. Nothing to show for it. Nothing to see. You'd find no evidence on the dissecting table. One of the imponderables. Yet people these days think they can find evidence for everything. They want evidence of God; evidence against God; proof of the pudding *before* the eating. Its childish. I laugh. Let me show you Mr. Gladstone."

He opened a cage set separate from the others and put in a great hand. While he fumbled about he watched her. Presently he withdrew his hand and had in it, held firmly by the hindquarters, an enormous old brown rat.

Cordelia took a step back and he wrinkled his restless eyebrows in good-humoured interest.

"Something's happening inside you now, young woman. Wonder what it is. Juices stimulated or something. But he's quite harmless. Far more harmless than his namesake, I assure you. *This* Mr. Gladstone's not concerned with spending seventy millions or whether he can take a penny off the income-tax. He's concerned with the important things in life: good food, good friends, a proper use of leisure. Eh, aren't you, now? Aren't you?"

He set the great rat on his shoulder and it squatted there, its long tail hanging down his sleeve, its old, wicked, blood-shot eyes suspiciously on the girl.

She said: "Where is Mr. Disraeli?"

Uncle Pridey showed his yellow teeth in laughter. "Good. Good. Pluck, as I said before. And a sense of humour. *Very* unusual in a woman. Think I'm going to like you. Better than Margaret. Brook's done well for himself this time, though how it came about . . . Should be a law against it; how old are you: sixteen?"

"Twenty," said Cordelia, flushing. "Why didn't you like Margaret, Uncle Pridey?"

"You want to be knowing, don't you? Only natural. Curiosity. But

37

who said I disliked her? Did we say so, Mr. Gladstone? Not at all. Have another sweet?"

"You remind me of my father," said Cordelia. "He has a hobby, but it's clocks. He's coming to supper tomorrow night. You didn't really have a chance of getting to know him at the wedding." (But, she thought, Father's queer little twists are on the surface. Uncle Pridey's are deeper set, sharper, spikier. And there's a sort of malice. But it's not towards me.)

"They gave me the wrong flavours today," said Pridey, chewing. "I hate these purple things. I shall complain. Is he an idealist, a progressive, a radical, a reformer like every third person you meet in this benighted town?"

"He doesn't take much interest in politics. You see, with clocks and children . . ."

"I shall tell him to stick to his clocks. His clocks. Safer and cleaner. Demagogy's in its infancy, young woman. If your father-in-law was younger he'd be in Parliament in no time. Come and see my skeletons."

He took her to a cupboard and showed her five tiny skeletons mounted on wood and beautifully built up with fine copper wire, one of them a mouse, the other four shrews. He also showed her a rat's stomach preserved in spirit and a shrew's brain floating in an Epsom-salt bottle. Afterwards she had to admire the live shrews, which Pridey kept in separate cages because they fought if they had to share. "The family instinct, young woman; we should all live in separate houses, and then there'd be good will among men." He took one of the animals out and pulled back the upper lip to show the tiny crimson-tipped teeth. "Notice the smell? Like Stilton that's been left too long. He doesn't like you. That's his way of showing he's frightened." Uncle Pridey's small, quizzical, twinkling eyes scrutinised her a moment. "More advanced than man, you know. Man's cruel when he's frightened. Better if *he* only made a smell."

Back went the shrew at last, having had all his finer points inspected, and Cordelia, glad to escape, made her excuse and left.

When she reached her own bedroom she was surprised to find Brook there. He had paper and pencil in his hand but had written nothing.

"I came out," he said moodily. "They didn't want me. I'm useless at this politics stuff."

"Why do you always run yourself down? You have just as many thoughts and ideas as they have."

"Have I? I don't know. If it occurs to me to say something, I put it badly, and if I take time to think out how to put it, then the chance is gone and they're talking of something else!"

"That's only because you're not as used to talking as they are. Practice would make all the difference."

"Oh, stop consoling me," he said snappishly. "I know I'm no good."

There was a moment's silence. She looked at the tall old clock in the corner. "I've been seeing Uncle Pridey's mice. They're nice and tame and well behaved, but I wanted to scream. Why are we frightened of mice, Brook? It seemed quite natural to be until Pridey thought it strange."

"He's writing a book on them," said Brook like a sullen boy. "He's been rat-mad as long as I can remember."

"It's half-past nine. Do you want to stay up till they go?"

"I expect Father will expect me to."

"Brook, why were they talking so much about cotton tonight? I thought it was calico printing and dyeing that we—that your father was in."

"Oh, that's our own works, yes. But Father's been—two years ago he put money in some cotton mills in Oldham; and after that he got interested in a cotton merchants. He's been trying to bring them together—into one company. That's why we invited them here to supper tonight."

She shivered. "Well, I'd better go and see Mrs. Meredith about the fires. It's bitterly cold."

He caught her as she reached the door. He was embarrassed.

"I'm sorry I—you know—I didn't mean to be irritable."

She smiled quickly. "It's all right, Brook. Really. I didn't think anything about it."

Which was the truth. Forgiving and even-tempered at the worst of times, she did not pause to think as she flew down the stairs why she was not more often hurt by his occasional peevishness towards her, why he sometimes seemed to want to rebuff her. She didn't reason that she might have felt it much more if her own feelings had been more deeply taken.

CHAPTER SEVEN ❦ Next day the Blake family—the elder and more portable half—came for the afternoon and evening. This was the first formal visit paid by the family since the marriage.

To her it was as if a great gush of fresh air had suddenly blown in among the overbearing mahogany furnishings and the ormolu ware, the heavy patterned velvet curtains, the tasselled overmantels, and the quiet respectful servants. Chatter and normality had arrived. The fact that they were slightly less restrained, slightly more noisy than those of the

Fergusons' friends she had met was something she noticed for the first time, but it did not upset her. She returned to its welcoming arms with joy and a little relief.

For her the day was more of a success because an hour before they were due Brook came home with word that his father was kept at the works and would not be home until very late.

Instantly she said: "Brook, do you mind? I'd like to ask Hallows. He could help me carry Papa's clock down into the hall, just for this evening."

He had brought back flowers for her; but underneath this pleasant gesture, perhaps because of a developing cold in his head, he was irritable again.

"Father won't like it. I know him better than you do, Cordelia. You'll never hear the last of it. And after all—it's his house."

"But it's such a little thing," she wheedled. "It won't corrupt his old furniture for one evening, my love."

"You don't know Father."

"I really *don't* believe he could be annoyed. But I know what we'll do! They're sure to go by eleven and we can whisk it upstairs again as soon as the front door closes. Hallows won't mind a bit if I ask after his rheumatism."

"He's sure to get to know. Aunt Tish or one of the other servants."

"Not if I ask them not to. Please, Brook. It was Papa's most precious possession. I'd hate him to be hurt."

"Well, I'm having nothing to do with it," Brook said. "It's entirely your own responsibility. I specially didn't want *you* to—to get at loggerheads with Father."

He blew his nose and went into the drawing-room to play the piano. She looked after him a moment, ill-at-ease, then shook her head as if to shake away the depression his attitude left, the possible implication of the emphasised word. When the representative seven of the Blake family came the clock was ticking and striking satisfactorily in a corner of the hall. It was a clock that hated to be moved, but Cordelia understood its inside nearly as well as her father.

Brook had conquered his ill-temper and in between blowing his nose and husking his throat played the host to them with good grace. In fact he found himself rather enjoying his new role; they were so different, so much more appreciative than his other in-laws. News of the family was passed about for Brook's benefit. Esther Jane, after a whirlwind courtship, was almost as good as engaged to the tall young Scot called Scott whom she'd met at their wedding.

Hugh Scott had been at school with Brook and was still one of his best friends. He was a journalist on the *Manchester Courier*, and it was agreed how jolly it would be if two sisters came to marry in this way.

At Cordelia's suggestion, Uncle Pridey took Mr. Blake and Esther to see his rodents, and after supper they played a round game of cards. A noisy game, and the merriest hour the drawing-room had seen for several years. Mrs. Blake's hair, tidy at the outset, had barely seen supper and sherry through in good order, and by the time she had built in front of her a pile of counters which meant five hundred per cent return on capital, there were hairpins all over the floor.

On this agreeable scene came Mr. Ferguson, frock-coated and imposing, gracious, dignified, suavely agreeable but somehow casting a blight over the game. They played two more rounds under his benign breathing supervision and then Mrs. Blake clutched at a falling coil and said they really must be going, and Mr. Blake, who had been strangely silent since the other man's arrival, took out his own great silver watch and got up and said slowly: yes, the children would be yawning their heads off tomorrow; and in a moment all was movement and self-conscious stir.

Just for a few seconds, while Cordelia was helping him with his coat, she was alone with her father, and when she'd done it in the old way he turned and looked at her and opened his mouth in a smile.

"Very nice, Delia, my dear. House is more human-like than when I saw it last. Perhaps it's you being in it. You and dear Percy. Does he keep good time?"

"Excellent, Papa."

"I thought the chime was a bit flat. Has he been moved much?"

"Perhaps he's not quite level. I'll look at him tomorrow."

"It was against the grain not to tinker at him myself. Sometimes it's hard to remember to be polite. Who looks to the clocks in this house?"

"I don't know, Papa. I think they just go on and on until all the wheels fall out."

Mr. Blake tutted. "Very bad policy. Are you happy, Delia?"

She wished he was not so close to her, suddenly felt irritated because she did not want to meet his eyes.

"Very, Papa, thank you. Don't I look it? Don't I radiate it? You should hear me singing in the mornings."

"You don't mind me asking?" He touched her arm. "When I sell a clock I don't just lose thought for it. Neither then when I give away a child."

She said: "Of course not," and kissed his cheek. She added lightly: "But you haven't really given me away. I'm much harder to get rid of than a clock. I come back twice a week in a carriage and you'd be sure to notice if you heard me chiming flat. I must have been born to be a lady, I like it all so much. Riding about and having servants and ordering a house . . ."

"All the things I couldn't give you."

"Of course not," she said lightly, but embarrassed. "You gave me all the more important things. Far more important. I—only like these things as well. I'm really a glutton. Gourmand! I was telling you how everything helped."

Outside in the hall Mr. Ferguson's deep voice could be heard explaining one of the dark oil paintings to Mrs. Blake.

Mr. Blake twisted his thin neck. "Did we stop too long? Didn't he mean to stay out till we'd gone?"

"Of course not! There was a breakdown at the works."

Mr. Blake glanced at her. "You'll think me a testy old man. Sometimes I need you to poke fun at me, Delia. The others are not so good at it. I wonder if your mother has finished admiring that foggy old picture?"

The farewells were said. Mr. Ferguson had offered them a carriage home, but when they deprecatingly said it didn't matter, he did not insist. A bitterly cold night again but clear and still. It would be pleasant for walking, Mr. Ferguson said when Hallows closed the door.

Cordelia flitted into the drawing-room to tidy up the card table, but Patty and Doris were already there putting away the cards and rearranging the tables. She picked up some crochet work from the sofa, said good night to Aunt Tish, who had settled down again like a fall of sand, and, if not disturbed more than three times by her brother, would sit there dozing and lacking the initiative to go to bed for at least another hour.

Thinking of her father, she walked humming to the stairs when Mr. Ferguson said:

"Cordelia."

She turned.

"Yes, Mr. Ferguson?"

"Did you have this clock brought down?"

"Oh—yes." She flushed a little and smiled. "I—meant to explain but just for the moment I forgot. My father—you see, it was my father's favourite clock. To give it to me—I mean to us—was a big thing to him. I felt if he didn't see it in one of these rooms . . ."

Why did this imposing stout old man make one hesitate and stumble over words, a failing she'd never suffered from?

"You know I don't like it in here."

"Oh, yes, but I knew you wouldn't mind for one evening. My family wouldn't know whether it suited the room or not, and no one else was coming. It made all the difference to Papa's evening to see the clock. I'll have it carried up again first thing in the morning."

He said with quiet, sombre persistence of manner: "Nevertheless, Cordelia, I think I do mind."

She looked at him in surprise.

"I'm sorry. I'd rather hoped—Brook said you wouldn't be back until midnight, and I'd hoped . . ."

"D'you mean that I shouldn't know?"

"Well, yes."

"Wasn't that rather deceitful, my dear?"

Her flush suddenly deepened. "It wasn't meant to be."

Brook came out into the hall, blowing his nose.

"Did you help Cordelia with this clock, Brook?"

He hesitated.

"Brook knew nothing about it," she said.

Mr. Ferguson's eyes came round and she met his ice-blue Olympian stare. It was the first real clash because it was the first time Cordelia's spirit had been roused to opposition. He instantly recognised it.

The three of them were alone in the hall and he came across to put one hand on the bannister.

When he wanted to speak with emphasis his tongue was slightly too large for his mouth, so that he lisped. "Of course, this is not the clock but the principle. You agree? You feel hardly done to, my dear? Well, so, I confess, do I. You have been here two and a half months—under my care —under my tutelage, one might say. Have you received any unkindness or lack of consideration?"

"No," she said.

"I have watched—with interest and some affection. Growing affection. You are not one of many now, my dear. You must stand alone, all your actions be open to the general gaze. You have a high place to fill in this house. Do you feel that we've lacked any confidence in you, that you haven't been treated fairly or generously or straightforwardly?"

"Of course not! Certainly not. There's no question of it. But I——"

"Yet without first asking me about it, you have the clock brought down—arranging it with my servants in secret. They become a party to the deceit."

"It wasn't intended to be deceit at all," she said in distress. Why couldn't he see that in her sight it looked *quite* different? *Awful,* to be hauled over the coals, with Brook listening, perhaps servants; to feel the conflict of impulses, to want to explain, to ingratiate, yet to feel her own cause just. She had never quarrelled like this—and so petty. Mr. Ferguson, her guide, her benefactor. "I don't want to offend you or anyone, but I've tried to explain why I did it. It never occurred to me to look on it as——"

He said: "I don't think we need go any further with this, Cordelia. It's a small thing, no doubt." He brushed the lapel of his coat, brooding on her behaviour. "Perhaps you think I have made too much of it. But it really depends on one's code in these things, what one is brought up to regard as important——"

She stiffened. "I was brought up to respect my own father and to consider his feelings!"

He had said the wrong thing for once, strengthening her opposition when he had wanted to undermine it.

"Yes," he agreed, nodding slowly. "Perhaps I am expecting too much in too short a time."

"And I shouldn't want to change."

He stared at her. Not the benefactor but the judge. "My dear, when you were married, you took Brook as your husband and me as your father. We have our faults, of course—our faults—but one of them is not lack of confidence between one member and another. To do things behind each other's back. To pretend to accept what we really intend to rebel against. No, no." He shook his head. "I don't want to upset you, but I hope you'll think this over. Try to understand."

She was about to say something in reply, but checked herself, picked up her skirts, and ran up the stairs.

Five minutes later Brook found her in the bedroom staring out of the uncurtained window at the fine flakes of snow. He stood there uncomfortably for a moment, wondering whether and how to end the first silence.

She said: "What sort of a breakdown was it at the works today, Brook?"

He was startled. "What? What breakdown? Oh, that . . . I think it was a drum. Or a roller on one of the drums."

"When did it happen?"

"Oh—after dinner, I think. I didn't really see it, you know. I was out most of the day."

"Did your father say it was repaired when he came home?"

"I don't remember. What does that matter? Delia, I hope you won't be too upset about this business of the clock. I told you you didn't know Father."

She said: "He made it seem something enormous—almost criminal. He talked about bringing up; well, I was never brought up *that* way, to see things all distorted and exaggerated. Heavens, how *could* you live in a big family if every little disobedience was made into a monstrous crime to upset the whole family!"

Brook sneezed. "I tell you, dear, it's no good arguing like that. He doesn't mean to be unkind; that's not it a bit. He made it a matter of principle because it *was* a matter of principle to him. And discipline, of course. But he'll always win in an argument."

She wiped her cheeks with the backs of her fingers, an upward, small girl movement. "Not if you're in the right."

Brook said: "Well, somehow he always seems to put himself in the right."

"He can't do. He can't if you're in the right first."

Brook moved moodily over to the table. "I asked cook to do me a lemon and have it sent up. I'm going to have some hot whisky and camphor with it tonight." She did not speak. "Don't stand there, Cordelia, or you'll have a cold next."

After a moment she sighed. "Oh, well, I suppose it will blow over. He's been very kind to me in most ways. . . . Brook, did Margaret get on with your father all right?"

He said stiffly: "I think he was very good to her. It's no good listening to all the silly prattle you hear."

Tuesday was New Year's Eve, and in the evening Mr. Ferguson was giving a larger party. This was an important occasion; and Cordelia spent all the early afternoon preparing the flower decorations for the dining-table. While she was doing this a maid came in and said a gentleman had called and would like to see her.

The brush with Mr. Ferguson had left her lonely and flat. Almost more than anything in her new life she found she missed the chiming of the clocks. They had been a part of her birthright, her babyhood, her adolescence. All her home life had been lived to their regular commentary. At times in the afternoons this house was so desperately quiet that one was almost afraid to walk about in a normal way. The one chiming clock in the dining-room was like a pathetic orphan. Like herself. Lonely and lost.

So she was very glad to hear someone had called, and it was not until Patty had disappeared that she remembered Margaret's maiden name had been Massington.

As she went into the drawing-room a tall thin man turned from the window, tapping his gold-mounted cane in his open palm. He was in the middle thirties, with close-set prominent teeth and a black well-groomed head. Raffish, distinguished, ever so slightly shy.

"Ah," he said. "I asked for Miss Ferguson. That's a new maid you've got. And are you—the new Mrs. Ferguson?"

"Yes. Aunt Letitia's resting. I'm sorry. I expect Patty misunderstood you."

He had been eying her.

"No matter, my dear. It was a good mistake. You know who I am?"

"Some—relation of Margaret's?"

"Yes. Her brother. And you're Brook's new wife."

She coloured. "Will you sit down?"

"Thank you." But he waited for her.

They talked about the weather. Dan Massington had come on horseback and he complained about the slippery roads, said the frost would spoil the hunting. But all the time they were being polite he was weighing her up, glancing round the room, cocking a cynical eyebrow. There was something in his manner which made his courtesy insincere. Quite abruptly he broke off and put his lips together over his teeth.

"Brook didn't take long for his next choice, did he? Bereaved in March, married in October. But I expect it was mainly the old man's doing, wasn't it?"

Her colour came again but deeper. "Do you want to see me about something?"

"I didn't. But I'm interested now. Tell me, my dear, d'you like living here?"

"Yes, thank you. Very much."

"Do you come from somewhere out of the town? I've never seen you before. But that's not surprising; you're so young. Were you poor and did the gilded cage attract?"

She did not reply.

" 'Fraid you'll find it a whited sepulchre. That's what Margaret found it. If it hadn't been for her damned religion—I beg your pardon—she'd have walked out of here years ago and would have been alive and well today. Are you a religious gel? I hope not. What's the good of sticking to a man for better or for worse when the worse is of his own making? There's things I could tell you . . . But you'll find them out for yourself all in good time." He yawned. "I like the looks of you, you know. I hope you fly away before you get your wings clipped."

"Thank you for liking my looks," she said. "Now will you tell me what you've come for?"

"Not a nice subject, is it, the family of Ferguson. They're an unbalanced lot—all excess and deficiencies. You might expect it in the old rich but not in the new rich. Tell me, d'you ever go out on social visits? If so, remember the Massingtons. Come and compare notes some time."

She had never felt her inexperience so much as now. Have him shown out. Yet she was the newcomer, he the older relative.

She got up. "Perhaps you'd like to see Brook's uncle."

He rose to stop her. "Old Pridey? A monumental bore. There's nothing worse than an eccentric who's really only commonplace. Spare me that."

Flushing still, she hesitated, facing him. Looking at her, something kindled in his eyes.

"My sister used to give me tea."

46

"Oh?" she said.

"Perhaps you don't feel so well disposed."

"Yes, certainly."

She pulled the bell and ordered tea, hoping that one of the others might come in unexpectedly. Once there was another person there his guns would be spiked.

But no one came; and after he had sipped his first cup of tea he crossed his legs and said:

"It's queer to be back in this room again. And you sitting there, Mrs. Ferguson. Just where my sister used to sit when she was Mrs. Ferguson."

He had a knack of saying the uncomfortable thing. But the interval had given her back some self-possession.

"I wonder, Mr. Massington, that you can bear to come here."

He raised his eyebrows at her.

"I assure you, I shouldn't come here often if it was to see the Ferguson family. I used to come to see my sister. . . . And now perhaps I may come to see you."

"I'm sorry," she said, "I only want to meet people who want to meet my husband."

"All right, that's a bargain," he agreed. "I want to meet your husband—so long as I can call in the afternoon when he's likely to be out."

"I'll ask his permission for you to come," she said.

"Oh, that would be a bad move, my dear. I don't think he likes me. We've hardly been on speaking terms since the funeral."

"Then——"

"Tell me," he went on. "I suppose you've known the Fergusons a long time?"

"Quite a time."

"Then you knew my sister?"

". . . No."

"I see." Satisfied, he stretched forward for his tea. "Now if——"

"Would you tell *me* one thing?" she said.

"What?"

Her heart was beginning to thump. "Why do you bother to come into the Fergusons' home to insult them when I'm sure you must be able to do it so much more freely outside?"

He stared at her, tried to read her cool hostile expression.

He said: "Perhaps you're different stuff from Margaret, perhaps you'll be flattered into becoming a chattel, another slave in the old man's retinue, think it fun to dance when he pulls the strings and then be put away in a convenient drawer. Perhaps. But I don't think so now. The pretty pussy has claws."

She said: "Can I give you some more tea, Mr. Massington?"

47

"Thank you."

They sipped in silence.

"I really came to ask if Margaret's writing-case had been found. It has some family papers in it."

"I don't know. I'll go and ask Aunt Tish."

"No, don't bother. I'll call again."

"If it's found we could send it to you."

"Dear, dear, so the young lady is really on her dignity."

"Didn't you expect me to be?"

"Let's see, how long have you been married, two months? Well, yes, I might have done. . . . Have you any brothers and sisters?"

"Yes."

"Fond of them?"

"Yes."

"Would you like to see one of them marry and be unhappy and constantly at loggerheads with her father-in-law and have a weak-kneed shadow for a husband? And then would you like to see her taken ill and fade away? None of it for any good reason either?"

"No."

"The world's a wicked place, you know."

She said after a moment: "Are you married, Mr. Massington?"

He glanced at her again, uncovering his teeth.

"No."

"But suppose you were, and you were fond of your husband, happy in your home. And a man called one day—and said the things you have said. Would you be—offended?"

"Not if I believed him."

"Why should I believe him?"

"No," he said. "I see your point. But you will. Leopards don't change their spots. Neither will Frederick or dear Brook."

Tea was finished in silence.

He got up to go. "Well, thank you for your entertainment, Cousin. I suppose we are some sort of relations, aren't we?"

"I don't think so."

"Perhaps not. I think I'd rather have it that way." He smiled at her, looking her quickly over very expertly just once more. "Don't forget, it's the merest etiquette to return a call."

"Thank you. I don't often go out alone."

"I'm sure you don't," he agreed. "Nor will you if the old man has anything to do with it. You'll find that out, my dear. It isn't that he begrudges you pleasure, but that he doesn't like you to have any in which he's not concerned. He doesn't fancy anyone in Grove Hall having a separate life of their own."

CHAPTER EIGHT ✻ In the evening Mr. Ferguson was in one of his best moods. In preserving a balance, Cordelia noticed, Mr. Slaney-Smith's presence was a help.

Mr. Slaney-Smith was Mr. Ferguson's best friend. Mr. Ferguson esteemed him above all his other acquaintances, and sometimes deferred to his judgment—which alone put him on a pinnacle not reached by ordinary men.

He was a tea-taster by profession, but he lectured on biology two evenings a week at the Carpenter's Hall, Brook Street. *The Origin of Species* had been published only seven years and Mr. Slaney-Smith was in the forefront of the battle raging over the body and soul of man. But the gentle agnosticism of Darwin was not for him; he was a militant atheist ready to thrust a sword into the belly of any entrenched churchman who came in his path. There was in fact something almost religious in his irreligion. No priest or deacon could have brought a more unquestioning faith to Holy Writ than he did to Mr. Huxley's successive chapters in the gospel of scientific revelation. For him the principle of natural selection had got itself transformed into a self-seeking, terror-shot, bloody-handed struggle for existence in which only the basest attributes callously exercised could ensure survival. The universe was by its very nature evil—science, he said, had proved it so, logically and with good evidence. There was no hope. Man was alone in the jungle. Away with God and the hypocrisies.

To the furtherance of these views he brought a peculiar personal animus, as if any semblance of a religious idea was an affront to his soul. He was no longer on speaking terms with his own brother because one day he had met his brother's little girl coming home from Sunday School and had said: "Well, Annie, have you seen Jesus Christ today?"

Tall, thin, square-shouldered, and rather stooping, with dark, gold-brown eyes, he wore his sandy hair in a well-plastered quiff and had a long, smooth, drooping moustache. (As Aunt Tish was fond of saying in private: "Eh, it should be cut off. It should an' all. And him a tea-taster too.") He had nine children who were reared on a strictly rationalist diet and were never allowed downstairs when their father was at home. He also had a wife, but she stayed in with the children.

His welcome in Grove Hall, where he supped twice a week, seemed a little contradictory, since Mr. Ferguson was a stickler for all the religious observances and was unfailing in his Sunday churchgoing, gave money to the church, fed the rector, was a churchwarden and on the council. But Frederick Ferguson had an intellectual pride in his own openness of mind, and it interested him to hear the other side. It interested him to hear all sides. He was always taking up some new sub-species of religion and bringing its believers to the house or bringing books on it when the believers were all distant or dead.

What might have been a cause of the utmost friction was a curious link. They were both fascinated by the religious topic though they looked at it from different sides. They wrangled and said outrageous things to each other, but they never quarrelled. And on all other topics they saw eye to eye: liberalism, reform, hygiene, cold baths, gambling, municipal art, the menace of Russia, tripe, Swinburne, Garibaldi, and the water supply.

Mr. Slaney-Smith had a poor opinion of the female sex generally, and his advanced ideas curled back like the horns of a snail whenever they touched any suggestion of the emancipation of women. He usually ignored Cordelia, and she was not a bit indignant but rather grateful for this. His crushing intellectual armour overawed her.

Mr. Ferguson had recently been elected to the city council, and a dozen of the guests tonight were friends of his on the council or the aldermanic bench. The family doctor was also present, a man called Birch, a school-friend of Brook's, who had taken over the local practice recently. A tall gaunt young man with a reserved manner which made him difficult to know.

It was to be a musical evening. Uncle Pridey had got out his old 'cello, and he and Brook and Brook's friend Tom Griffin played a Haydn trio and one by Boccherini. Brook played two of Chopin's Nocturnes and Mary Griffin sang. Then a lady called Mrs. Thorpe recited a dramatic poem; and to give the evening its final crown Mr. Slaney-Smith allowed himself to be persuaded to sing: 'Oh, Give Me Back My Arab Steed.'

By this time it was nearly midnight, and the darkest man in the room was sent out to let the New Year in.

It had always been a happy time for Cordelia before. This year while Tom Griffin was outside she felt again that little twinge of melancholy.

"A happy New Year, Brook dear! A *very* happy New Year!" She kissed him. "A happy New Year, Mr. Ferguson." He kissed her cheek and she caught the smell of wine and broadcloth and eau de Cologne. His heavy hand was on her shoulder and she smiled up at him. "A happy New Year, Mr. Slaney-Smith. A happy New Year, Mrs. Thorpe." So it went to the end, and then Cordelia expected them to join hands and sing 'Auld Lang Syne,' but instead they stood with bowed head while Mr. Ferguson said prayers—all, that is, except Mr. Slaney-Smith, who was allowed to remain seated and represent New Thought by pulling at his moustache.

When they had all left—as they did very soon, with none of the jollity that the Blakes had afterwards—she found herself again in the hall with Mr. Ferguson alone. But this time, with no irreverent tongue-protruding clock to disturb his temper, he linked his arm in hers, a thing he had never done before, and steered her slowly back towards the drawing-room.

"Well, this is your first New Year with us, Cordelia. I trust it will be a very happy one for you and for us all."

"Thank you, Mr. Ferguson. I hope so." She was not a bit at her ease with him.

"I hope we shall be a happy and united household. If you're ever in doubt or difficulty, come to me—always come to me. We can discuss it in a friendly way. A problem shared . . ."

"Thank you," she said.

"I hear Dan Massington was here this afternoon. Did you see him?"

I told Brook and Brook has told you. "Yes," she said. "He stayed to tea. He came for something of his sister's, a letter-case or a satchel."

"I suppose he gave us a very bad name, eh?"

"He had a sort of grudge."

"I see you've summed him up perfectly. I shall come to respect your judgments, my dear."

Flattery, she thought. But *I* mustn't be unfair, *I* mustn't bear a grudge too.

Mr. Ferguson said: "Some day I'll tell you about the Massingtons."

They went into the drawing-room.

"Eh, but I'm proper tired," said Aunt Tish. "We've had a real good evening, Frederick. But I must say I couldn't make head or tail of that Mrs. Thorpe's reciting. What was she talking about: something in the snow?"

Mr. Ferguson said to Cordelia: "Have you ever had singing lessons, my dear?"

"No—except what Mother taught me and what I've learned in the choir."

"You must miss singing in the choir. Would you like to take lessons?"

Some pride in her would not allow her to be too eager. "I should like that very much."

"Brook!"

"Yes, Father?"

"On your way to Town in the morning call at Madam Herbert's Academy. Ask her to come here and see Mrs. Ferguson. Arrangements for singing lessons. She has a very sweet voice, and——"

"Much better than that Griffin girl," said Uncle Pridey, rubbing down his 'cello. "She draws breath like a tired horse."

"Kik—kik, kik—kik!" Aunt Tish sniggered. "That's true. That's true, an' all."

"Personally," said Mr. Ferguson, "before speaking of other people's imperfections I like to feel sure that I know my own."

Cordelia glanced at the other man, but Pridey had got his straggly imperial bent over the 'cello and he did not reply. No one in this house, it seemed, ever did reply to Frederick Ferguson.

A little later she stood alone and warmed herself before her bedroom fire. Dimly she sensed that she was being subjected to the same process which had reduced everyone else in this house: a mixture of intimidation and cordiality. Dimly she suspected that even the trouble over the clock was not so much a matter of principle as an opportunity he had seized for asserting and establishing a preliminary mastery. Now this was the second stage.

Yet, against her better judgment, she found herself responding. The value Mr. Ferguson put upon himself had its implicit effect on everyone he came in contact with; when he chose to unbend, one was flattered by his unbending. Cordelia was a modest girl; she had lived too much in the midst of a large and poor family to have any distorted ideas of her own importance. She was half unwillingly gratified and happy at her father-in-law's attitude tonight. If only Dan Massington had not made his disconcerting call . . .

How to judge, and where to find the truth? She wished she were older, more certain of her own mind. Sometimes these last two months she had thought despairingly that she had no opinion or judgment of her own at all but was a bundle of obvious responses, returning affection for affection, excuse for rebuke, anger for anger, gratitude for kindness, loyalty for esteem. She wished so much that she were the 'strong' character some of her family thought her.

Brook came in, but she did not at once look up. (Brook should be the quadrant, the compass by which she might see and steer. But Brook, she already knew, was affected by the magnet of his father's presence and pointed steadily in one direction only.)

Yet she was very fond of him. She had found no bad in him except the surface failings: they'd been happy together, listening to music, reading books aloud, walking in the fields, driving to church down the leafless country lanes.

He said: "I ate too much supper. I think I'm going to have one of my bouts of indigestion."

She got up at once. "Let me make you something to drink. I can easily run down to the kitchens."

He sat down looking depressed, and wiped his nose. "No, thanks, dear, I've already drunk too much. There's nothing much to be done about it. I often get an attack after a cold."

She sat beside him. Her carping mood of the last few days had gone and she saw nothing ludicrous in his complaints.

He said: "I didn't play the F Sharp Nocturne too well tonight."

It was a familiar gambit to her. It was not that he was terribly conceited but that his nervous self-doubting mind needed constant reassurance.

"I wish I could play it half as well."

He smiled at her, his thin-lipped friendly smile.

"Perhaps you'll soon be able to. I don't see why you shouldn't have piano lessons as well."

"I'd love that!"

"I'll ask Father about it in the morning."

She said quietly: "Couldn't we do it without asking your father? He wouldn't mind?"

A shadow crossed his face, and she instantly saw the same pit yawning. "Well . . . I don't suppose he would. It's only that——"

"I mean," she said, sticking to her guns, "we shall pay for the lessons, shan't we? You will, out of your salary?"

"Yes, of course."

"I don't want to offend him again. It's only just—you do see, don't you, Brook, that perhaps it isn't good for us not to have any independence of our own?" She waited.

"Yes . . . Of course you're quite right. I don't look on it that way, as I've lived with him all my life, but I see what you mean."

She hesitated. "Margaret's brother said that Margaret and your father were quarrelling all the time. He made it out that it was your father's fault she was unhappy here and ill."

"Uh! You don't believe that, do you?"

She touched his hand. "Not if you tell me it wasn't so. But either way it doesn't matter to me, Brook. I have to do with the present, not the past—it's my life, not hers. Whether she was happy or not . . ."

There was silence. She could see that he was unconvinced about the piano lessons. She had begun to say, 'Whether she was happy or not, I intend to be.' But if she intended to be, why this hidden revolt? She struggled with her own feelings, wrestled as with the devil, and won.

She said: "Perhaps you're right. Ask your father first and see what he says."

"I think it's the best way, Delia. It saves the risk of giving him offence, and it will amount to much the same thing in the long run."

53

She said impulsively: "Margaret *didn't* get on with your father, did she?"

"Well—no. Not altogether. There were times."

"Well, I intend to. I—married you. We have to live with him. He's got little peculiar ways; but we all have. I'm going to try and please him— why shouldn't I? It's little enough. That'll be my New Year resolution. I'll set myself out to do everything I can to please him. It shouldn't be too hard. Don't you think it a good idea?"

"I think you're sweet. And it's a splendid idea."

She got up, breathing out some of the emotions that had gathered in her. "All right. That's settled then."

He said: "You look lovely in that frock."

"Do I? Well, you bought it me."

He put his hands on her shoulders and kissed her, and she kissed him in return. She had a deep regard for him at that moment. He kissed her again and she put her hands up to smooth his hair. Affection for affection, she thought; gratitude for kindness; loyalty for esteem?

The following day Stephen Crossley arrived in Manchester.

BOOK TWO

CHAPTER ONE More than twelve months passed before he heard of the Fergusons or they of him, and then it was through Mr. Slaney-Smith that the contact was made.

The tea-taster's leisure hours were arranged to a set programme. On Wednesday and Friday evenings he lectured to earnest and anæmic young men on biology and evolution, on Tuesdays and Thursdays he supped with Mr. Ferguson, and on Mondays and Saturdays he visited one of the music halls of the town. (Sundays he spent with his wife and family and read aloud to them from Mill, Darwin, and Charles Brad-laugh.)

Music halls had an irresistible fascination for him. There was nothing more liberating to the spirit, he found, than to stand at a silver, shiny bar and sip a scotch and splash and listen to 'Villikins and His Dinah' or to discuss with his friends the merits of Tom Maclagan and Harry Liston. As he was unable to cut the habit out of his life because it was beneath him, he tried to elevate it to the same level as the rest by mak-ing a science of it, and there was no one who could talk more learnedly about the 'singing assemblies' and 'night cellars' of the eighteenth cen-tury. Many times he'd tried to interest Mr. Ferguson, but Mr. Ferguson was not to be lured away from righteousness.

Though he had been known to visit the Lancashire Stingo, a low place hidden in the wilds of Deansgate, Mr. Slaney-Smith's usual haunt was the old Variety Theatre, at the corner of York Street and Spring Gardens. This had recently come under new management, had been redecorated and reseated in a very genteel style; those walls which seemed likely to fall down had been propped up, and the place was mak-ing a bid to attract the aristocracy of the profession, both on the stage and off.

Mr. Slaney-Smith soon got to know the Crossleys, father and son. The father, a plump, short-tempered, business-like little London-Irishman, had interests all over the provinces and lived in London; the son man-aged his father's local affairs. He was twenty-six.

One did not stay long in Mr. Slaney-Smith's company without the

Jolly Roger of atheism being hoisted. Stephen Crossley was too young and happy-go-lucky to care a great deal either way, but he listened with amusement to the older man's embellishments, which seemed to suggest a campaign for going into every church in England carrying the spear of pure reason and winkling out the fat clerics who skulked there.

The name of Frederick Ferguson came up.

"There, my dear boy," said Slaney-Smith, pressing his long moustache downwards on each cheek with a yellow silk handkerchief, "there you have the perfect example of an intelligent man ruined by Christianity; this age-old superstition, this monstrous survival of the totem pole, what? has so got hold of him that one comes to suspect all his ordinary behaviour. Is he enlightened, does he do good deeds, does he help his fellow men, because his mind so directs him, what? or because he is driven on by fear—fear of hell-fire, fear that if he does not do so he won't earn a future life and sit among the company of angels in sublime and asinine vacuity?"

Stephen Crossley laughed.

"Does it matter why he does it, so long as he does do it?"

Mr. Slaney-Smith was shocked and said so. For him the springs of conduct were more important than the conduct itself.

"Aside from this," he said, "my friend Mr. Ferguson's whole life is dominated by religion, by prayers, by Sabbath observances. It's unwholesome. He's a slave, not a free man at all. I tell him so. Superstition and fear rule him as surely as they do the African Hottentot." Mr. Slaney-Smith took another sip. When he had finished with his handkerchief he added: "Lamentable."

"Bring your Mr. Ferguson along some time," said Crossley goodtemperedly. "There's no doubt we should be able to broaden his mind."

"Ah. Quite impossible. He wouldn't enter a music hall. Again I've tried."

"Tell him to come along any day the week after next. The Great Clodius will be here then. I'll get him to read his fortune. Couldn't be fairer than that, could we, Char?"

"I should think not," agreed the barmaid, leaning her thick body against the bar.

"I wish it was possible," said Slaney-Smith. "Ah, yes. Ah, yes."

"What's 'e like, this friend of yours?" asked Char, polishing a glass.

"Some time I'll give you a precise description," said Slaney-Smith. "He owns Ferguson's Dye Works and lives south of the city in a considerable house. I visit there regularly. He depends on me for advice in most of the important decisions he has to make."

"But you can't cure him of religion?" Stephen said.

"I confess the failure. Was that the bell?" asked Mr. Slaney-Smith.

"Don't worry. Morris will come and tell me before the curtain goes up."

"One evening," said Slaney-Smith, "one evening also you should come to one of my lectures at the Carpenter's Hall. I flatter myself that at this important moment in the history of man I am helping in the battle to defeat ignorance and prejudice. One sees ahead new vistas of education and progress. Even though the over-all picture is dark. It is inspiring—far more inspiring than a slavish reliance on the age-old superstitions—to visualise the mind of man progressing through a darkened universe unaided and alone. One doesn't need to be interested in biology. I take the broader issues——"

Major Morris put his head round the door.

"All ready at the starting post, Stephen. Shall I keep your seat?"

"No, let Mr. Slaney-Smith have it," said the young man, ready enough for the interruption. "I'll not be coming in tonight."

But a week or so later he went with his new friend to the Fergusons' to supper. Mr. Slaney-Smith meant nothing to him and he wasn't much interested in the owner of Grove Hall, but he knew the value of goodwill in the right quarters.

So he went prepared to be agreeable in a good cause and came away caught in a net of his own weaving.

It was nearly all his own fault.

The house was much what he had expected, but the people came as rather a surprise. Slaney-Smith had not prepared him for Mr. Ferguson's size and presence, and for a little while it put him off his balance. The man was so big and imposing and so vigorous with it that Stephen forgot that cool inner detachment he usually held to when meeting people less cosmopolitan than himself. He found himself unwillingly submitting to an influence so obviously regnant in its own sphere. The other old people were nonentities and the son an anæmic shadow of his father. But the daughter-in-law . . .

She came in just before supper, wished him good evening in a pleasant voice, but hadn't much to say during the meal, though once or twice she spoke to the servants.

He carried on a conversation with Mr. Ferguson and Mr. Slaney-Smith; but his eyes kept straying in her direction. Forgetting the past, he thought: I've never seen anyone so beautiful. She was like a pale golden glory that had suddenly come into his life, into the room, into the dull talk, the dreary business of making oneself agreeable, someone totally unexpected and exciting whose presence caught at your throat and made your heart beat again. He began to talk better, to talk with greater gusto and charm and with something of the wit of his Irish forefathers. Afterwards he could hardly remember all that had been going on, but Mr. Slaney-Smith said that a meal had seldom passed so quickly. When the girl left them things lagged. Stephen wondered if he would have the luck to see her again. Two or three times he'd caught her listening intently, and once specially when the future of the theatre was in question. But he'd had to change the subject because he saw that Mr. Ferguson didn't approve. And if he was to be invited here again he couldn't afford to offend his host.

Mrs. Ferguson, to his delight, later rejoined them; and he had a better chance of seeing her as she moved across the room and took a seat before the fire. He couldn't imagine where she'd come from or, for that matter, what she was doing here. He tried to draw her into the conversation, but his efforts were usually side-tracked by one of the others. The two older men did not expect her to talk at one of *their* evenings. He itched to hear her voice more, to find out what she was really like.

Partly out of curiosity, he turned the talk towards religion, wondering if the two men would fly at each other's throats. But it didn't happen that way. He saw that they were like two old hands at fencing; they had fought together so often that they parried thrust for thrust, knowing each other's moves so well. With one eye on the girl, he fed them with semi-innocent questions, trying to provoke them, but finding only himself provoked by the importance they attached to their own views.

Presently Mr. Slaney-Smith deviated to speak of the woman who had given an exhibition of thought-reading and telepathy at the Variety a month ago. This was on Stephen's own ground and he gratefully accepted the opening. But again he was talked down.

Brook said: "It was interesting at the Athenæum last night. A pity you couldn't come."

"Oh, this new-fangled spiritualism——"

"This new-fangled spiritualism," said Mr. Ferguson. He explained to Stephen Crossley: "A *conversazione* was held to—ah, what were the terms of reference?—'for the purpose of arriving at some safe conclusion about table-turning.' The whole discussion was on a high intellectual level, and some experiments were tried."

"With success?" said Slaney-Smith.

"With some success. Not sufficient to convince me of the claims put forward by the advocates of the movement. But with *some* success."

"What happened?" Cordelia asked. "Brook didn't tell me."

"Oh, well—I confess—the table certainly moved, and moved quite vigorously, but the conclusion the meeting came to was in agreement with Dr. Carpenter's theory. That is that, when a number of people are gathered round a table, a force he calls idea meter power comes into being and can move a lightly portable table about the room."

"Idea meter power!" said Slaney-Smith with scorn even in his moustache. "That's not scientific."

"What is your explanation then?"

"Charlatanry, pure and simple. Someone was hoaxing you. I know that Athenæum! Full of young shavers up to their pranks."

"Oh, no," said Brook. "That's hardly fair, Mr. Slaney-Smith. The whole thing was done most seriously and Dr. Powell presided. You know he wouldn't countenance anything."

The girl said: "D'you mean the table actually moved about because you had your hands on it? Would *any* table do?"

"Almost any," said Stephen. "But a round small table is best, with a top not too highly polished. Of course, table-turning is the simplest of all the phenomena. If you've a medium present—why, then it's real shocks you may be getting."

"Have you had a lot of experience?" she said, addressing him directly almost for the first time.

"Well, yes, quite a little." He'd tried it once, with the Bailey Sisters and Max, the comic, in a lodging-house in Nottingham.

"To do with your music-hall work?" said Brook.

"Not at all." Stephen was irritated. The question implied the wrong sort of interest. "The spiritualist side. Why, there have been all sorts of experiments in America. I have contacts with America, and one hears about them."

"One also reads about them," said Mr. Ferguson dryly.

"You're not a spiritualist, are you?" Mr. Slaney-Smith said, with pity dawning.

"No, no. But I'm interested—as an inquirer, you know. I've travelled. One keeps an open mind."

It was a good line to take, if a little obvious. But he was so intent on holding her attention and interest that it hardly occurred to him he was now also interesting the others.

They talked on, Stephen getting ever deeper. His tongue ran away and he did not care. Inspired, he confessed to knowledge he hadn't got, knowing his listeners knew less.

Then half-past nine struck and family prayers were said and followed by refreshments.

"Some time," said Mr. Ferguson, "when one of these mediums you're acquainted with happens to be in the neighbourhood, let me know and we'll invite him to the house. I should be interested to know more."

"We'll arrange a séance," said Mr. Slaney-Smith, showing his false teeth. "See what the spirits can bring us."

Cordelia said: "It wouldn't be fair to Mr. Crossley to invite someone here and then not treat it seriously."

"By all means seriously. Nothing else entered my head. I shall be glad to regard the experiment with an open mind."

"Any time you like," said Stephen recklessly, gazing at her.

"Do you mean you have someone in view?" said Mr. Ferguson.

Withdraw now or over the brink. But to withdraw before her was impossible. "It's not an absolute promise I could make for someone else. I would let you know."

"Naturally. That would be agreeable."

"May I call and tell you when something is arranged?"

"By all means. We shall be very pleased."

In the flush of his sudden folly he felt not displeased at the outcome. He had at last interested her; and his next visit was secure. It was not until the following morning that he began to wonder why he had made an idiot of himself over a pretty girl. He had no idea where any suitable medium was coming from.

CHAPTER TWO   The next morning at the theatre Char began to question him about his visit, but after a few minutes he cut her short and went into his inner office. He was not in the mood for light conversation.

There he began to pace up and down, going slowly over the events of the night before. She's fair, he thought, but not insipidly or ordinarily fair: corn fair with blue-grey eyes that have a sudden surprising glint in them from time to time; darkish brown lashes; more like a girl than a wife, yet now and then you get a sudden sense of maturity: it's that glint, I suppose. Half way through the supper he'd begun to wonder what her relationship was with her delicate-looking husband. They were at ease in each other's company; there was friendship between them but not real intimacy. He'd swear to it. Nor was it indifference following estrangement. She did not love him, that was what emerged.

Morris came in to ask some questions about the evening. After a few moments he said:

"What's the matter? You seem off the mark this morning."

"Do I?" said Stephen. "Oh, it's nothing."

"I want to tell you about that idea of mine for taking Johnson and a few others over to the Pomona. It might help as an advertisement."

"Well, tomorrow perhaps. I've got one or two things to do now."

Morris glanced at his cousin curiously. "I'll see Clodius then. He's just come."

60

When Morris had gone, Stephen tried to read, then resumed his pacing. Perhaps it was just the setting, the surprise that had put him off his balance, the surprise of finding her in such a house. Put a camellia among the privet and it draws more attention than it would at a flower show. Yet he must see her again, must rise to his own challenge, as it were. Impulse had always been a ruling factor in his life—it was part of his charm. Steadying reason, never his strong suit, did not interfere until he was committed. As now. If he backed down the memory would give him no peace. He went out into the private bar and was rather relieved to find that Char had gone downstairs. Char knew him too well—or thought she did; and that could be irritating.

He fiddled about going through the changes of programme, but felt impatient with it all. Morris came in again.

"Stephen, I've been thinking: it would be best to change Morley's song——"

"Charles," Stephen said, suddenly swinging round, "did you say Clodius was here?"

"Yes, he's just come. He's complaining the lighting from the wings is still too bright. I thought——"

"I want to see him."

Morris stared. "About the lighting?"

"No. Just tell him I want to see him."

The Great Clodius was sent for. On the stage under the glamour of the lights he was an imposing figure. By day he was sallow and thin and bald and untidy. Without the distinction of his black wig and his high-heeled shoes he looked like a seedy Italian waiter. In fact he was a Gascon.

"Oh, come in, M. Clodius," Stephen said. "Let me get you something to drink. Port? Brandy? Good; I'll have the same. Sit down, will you? Take the seat over there. It's a good seat. You'll find it fits the back."

"Thank you," said Clodius. "I drink your health, Mr. Crossley. . . . This is very good, this brandy. I am glad to choose it."

"I see you're a connoisseur. But I should have expected it. A distinguished artist, I was only saying. Do you like your first week in this city?"

"Yes. I am very happy to come. But about those lights. I have the fancy . . ."

They talked business for some time. Stephen said:

"Oh, by the by, I'm sure you will have had experience of the occult? D'you, for instance, understand this new spiritualism?"

"Oh, poh, I understand as much as is understood," said Clodius with dignity. "That it is trickery. I once had a dog who was good at trickery. Little Togo——"

"This new American craze, now, this business of table-turning and spirit rapping. Everybody's trying it. It catches the interest. I was discussing it only yesterday, and while we were talking I thought: If anyone understands this business thoroughly it will be M. Clodius."

"Do you not think, Mr. Crossley, that I make greater mysteries every evening?"

"Oh, I do indeed. In fact I never remember being so much impressed by an act before as I have been by yours. I was mentioning it only yesterday in a letter to my father. But it's quite a fashion, isn't it, this new craze? It isn't looked on in the light of stage magic but as something high and superior—you're in touch with the spirit world, they say."

"And your view, Mr. Crossley—what would it be of such a claim?"

"Very much what yours is, I'm thinking. Another of the same?"

"Thank you."

Stephen went with the two glasses to the bar.

"Little Togo," said Clodius. "He had much dignity. Quite the *grand seigneur*. And such pretty habits——"

Stephen said: "Have you ever been to one of these séances, as they call them?"

"*Comment?* Oh, the séance. Well, not so in person. But a friend—you understand, a friend is describing it all for me. I am not impressed. If it was put on the halls it would not impress. They would say—you would say: 'This is poor stuff, give me something fresh, exciting. . . .'"

"Ye-es," said Stephen. "Ye-es. But of course it must be much more difficult to perform these tricks—being in a room with people everywhere. One hasn't any of the advantages. If these people are charlatans they must be very clever."

"Clever? Not at all. A few table-rappings, a few spirit voices."

"But without properties," said Stephen, "and in a strange house."

"Simplicity. But why should one copy these frauds? My act is ten times more sensational."

"And far more challenging and intelligent. But this is very interesting to me, M. Clodius, for a special reason. It's your advice I should like."

"Anything I can do."

"Well—to be frank, I'm in rather a quandary. It happened—I went with a friend to a gentleman's house last night and the conversation turned on the spiritualist craze. In the rush of the moment—quite on impulse, you know—I said I knew a spiritualist—a medium, they call them—who would demonstrate his powers before them. In fact I didn't—far from it—but having said as much, it wasn't in me to climb down. And in fact I have no one to take."

Gustave Clodius had finished his second brandy, but he refused another. Instead he went and stared out into the street, breathing his thoughts upon the window-pane. He fingered the ends of his big bow tie.

"Well, m'sieu?"

"Well?"

"You are saying that you have no one to take?"

"I've no one to take."

"Am I understanding it that you suggest me to be that man?"

"Well, I would hardly have liked to suggest it. But certainly I should be greatly obliged . . . Naturally I should be prepared to pay—say double what you get for a performance here. It would solve my difficulty entirely."

"But let me understand it quite, if you please. I wish to have this put more plain. You take me to this house of your friend. You say to him, 'Here is the great medium Clodius who will now proceed to show you how the spirits work on him.' And Clodius will then sit down at a table and produce spirit-rapping for you. Is that right?"

"That would be fine. As a matter of fact, if necessary, perhaps I could help you. I should be there at the time."

The Gascon regarded the ends of his finger-nails and fastidiously dabbed them with his handkerchief.

"My friend, forgive me, but you go too fast. Do you understand what you are asking? No. No. Will you let me speak for a minute? I am Clodius, the Great Clodius. I come to your city to perform, having so performed in London, Paris, Vienna. But I come as a conjurer. I say in effect: 'All this magic that I do before you is tricks. I vanish a lady; it is a trick; but catch me if you can. I stab a boy in a box; the blood runs out; it is a trick, detect me if you can.' That is honest. I am an honest man. But now you ask of me to go with you into a friend's house and say in affect, 'This is the truth: I speak with the spirits: I am undetectable, for there is nothing to detect.' That is dishonest. I am to become a dishonest man. And for that you offer me double the payment for one performance!"

"As to payment—well, it was a mere suggestion. I'll double that again if you think that would make it worth while. But it was you that was saying the tricks were easy. If there was risk of exposure, now . . ."

"That is nothing. I have told you. But that is not the issue."

"Well, we agreed, didn't we, that these people are frauds. It is not as if we were profaning something any grown-up person believes in. . . ."

"Because I think a man is a fraud, is it that I wish to be a fraud like him?"

There was silence.

"Oh, well . . . I have a week or two yet."

Clodius hesitated. The Crossleys, he knew, controlled a half dozen music halls in the provinces, and Crossley senior had some sort of an interest in the Alhambra in London. Clodius had performed in London but not yet at the best places. He did not know whether young Crossley was a vindictive man. One could be deceived.

"Is it not the same," he said, "if I am announced as an impostor and thereupon do all that the best spiritualist will do? That I would willingly perform—and astonish you."

"No, no, I'm afraid that wouldn't suit them at all. Whoever comes with me must come as the real thing. We shouldn't even be admitted."

"And your friends are genuine inquirers, is it?"

"Oh, well, they're genuine in being curious. But you're not at all imposing upon believers; they're not even would-be believers. It's a bit of a joke, if you look at it right. Believe me, I don't want to offend these men. And if anything went wrong I should have the blame, make no mistake: in a fortnight's time you'll be in Liverpool, but I've got to *live* here. I'm doing this because I want to strengthen my friendship with them, not break it."

CHAPTER THREE The 'séance' was held at Grove Hall on the first Monday in February.

Stephen had been a little concerned at the risk of Clodius being recognised by Mr. Slaney-Smith. Fortunately, Slaney-Smith had not been at the Variety on the first Monday of Clodius's appearance and Stephen kept him away on the Saturday by inviting him to the Pomona Pleasure Gardens which the Crossleys had recently bought. In any case, the risk of recognition was not too great, for Clodius looked very different on the stage.

On the Monday evening Stephen called for Slaney-Smith in his carriage, and found the tea-taster slightly less sure of himself in his own home than out of it. In the trim, prim, ornate little front room, surrounded by the furniture and curtains and antimacassars of his young married life, the spear-head of modern thought was somehow not so sharp or so iron hard. In spite of his best efforts to be otherwise there clung to him some traces of that naïveté he so fiercely despised.

"Where's M. Gustave?" he snapped, as they walked out to the carriage, watched by ten pairs of eyes through the lace curtains of the upper windows.

"He's coming later," said Stephen. "He'll never eat before a séance."

"Ha!" said Mr. Slaney-Smith.

As they jogged along over the uneven sets of Hyde Road, Stephen had a twinge of misgiving. All this trouble, expense, preparation. To his intense chagrin Cordelia had been out when he called on Thursday to arrange this visit. So, to gain only one more sight of her, he risked a minor scandal and his father's very forcible annoyance. Well, who cared? There'd been no other person in his thoughts for ten days.

Anyway, the evening was not without its sense of comedy. Confront two sober hard-headed men of affairs with precisely what they asked for —and see what they would do. He had no fears for Gustave Clodius. His first scruples overcome, the Frenchman had entered into the thing thoroughly—it was necessary to do so for his own sake.

They reached Grove Hall, were deprived of their cloaks by Hallows, and Stephen made his apologies for M. Gustave's non-appearance. He would, he said, arrive without fail before nine. (Clodius was to be put forward in the bill for one night, and came on at eight.)

Other guests had been invited for the occasion: a young couple called Griffin, brother and sister, insignificant, amiable people; Mrs. Thorpe, a monumental woman dressed in cascades of beautiful home-made lace; a young doctor called Birch, tall and ugly.

At supper Stephen found himself at the opposite end of the table from Mrs. Ferguson and had no chance of speaking to her. Afterwards the men sat for an interminable time until he broke up the party by saying he thought he heard someone arriving and wondered if it was M. Gustave.

This being unfounded, they went to join the ladies, but Stephen, catching sight of a wisp of white frock through another door, hung back examining a picture. Sure enough, in a few moments Cordelia came out, having been to see Mrs. Meredith about later refreshments, and as she crossed the hall he turned and spoke to her. She came towards him pleasantly enough, saying she knew very little about the painting except that it was by Richardson, and offering to call her father-in-law.

As she turned he said quickly: "I should be obliged for you not to do that. I'd rather have *your* help in my stumbling appreciation."

She glanced at him in the shadowy light, and in that moment he knew he was lost—more lost than he'd ever been before in his life. At such close quarters . . .

She said: "It's a picture of the Lake of Brienz in Switzerland. I don't know if it is a good painting."

"Yes, I think it's fine. Brings out the depths of the lake."

"Is that the Matterhorn?"

"No. Most likely the Jungfrau."

"I like it best," she said, "because it's a water-colour and most of the oils here are dark."

"Do you know Switzerland, Mrs. Ferguson?"

"No. I've never been. As you must have guessed."

"I've been once," he said, "but not to this district. Do you know Paris at all and the paintings there?"

"I'm afraid not."

He hesitated. "I asked for a special reason."

"Oh?"

"Yes . . . You'll be thinking me impertinent, no doubt." He turned, and to his own annoyance stumbled over the next words. "It's that white dress. You remind me of some picture I saw there. If they put a frame round you I'd take an oath you'd been stolen from the Louvre."

The grey of her eyes deepened as she turned to look up at the water-colour. She was getting used to occasional half-furtive glances of admiration from strange men, but she had not been paid a compliment like this before. For a moment she didn't know what to say.

"Your friend hasn't come yet, has he? Do you think he will be late?"

"I'm sure he will not. I impressed on him not to be after nine."

"My father-in-law is looking forward to this evening very much."

"I think," said Stephen, speaking rapidly, "that was a rash liberty I took. Indeed, perhaps you're insulted by the comparison. Living beauty—like yours—well, beside it the most beautiful painting is dull. Please say you'll overlook the impertinence."

She began to walk slowly towards the door of the drawing-room, across the open threshold of which the enormous shadow of Frederick Ferguson had fallen. At that moment there was a ring at the front door.

"Perhaps this will be your friend."

They had only a moment or two more together. He was determined to force some reply from her. As she turned again he put two fingers deferentially on her arm.

"I hope, now, you'll be good enough to forgive me."

She looked at him. "Of course, Mr. Crossley. There's nothing to forgive. Thank you for being so kind."

Hallows crossed the hall on his way to the front door.

CHAPTER FOUR Gustave Clodius said: "I wish you to be quite calm and quiet about this thing. There is no need for excitement. It is a simple, natural, good thing we are attempting, though that does not mean it will be easy. Just, please, as if you are relaxing your muscles and waiting."

All twelve of them were round the carved table in the drawing-room. Clodius, looking like a shabby professor from the Sorbonne in his sham pince-nez, was held by leather straps and buckles to his chair. He had insisted on this because, he said, his hosts were sceptics. After some polite protests they had given way, and Stephen and Dr. Birch had fastened him.

When they were all seated, Stephen's luck suddenly turned. Cordelia had seated herself between her husband and Mr. Slaney-Smith, but Slaney-Smith, wanting to be near the medium, asked Stephen to change with him. To be sitting next to her was good enough, but then 'M. Gustave,' by some inspiration, commanded them all to clasp hands firmly as they sat round the table. So with her cool left hand closely held in his right he knew that even this much made his scheming worth while.

Frederick Ferguson sat on the Frenchman's right and Slaney-Smith on his left; the sceptics at hand; but Clodius was not intimidated. They had made their attitudes so perfectly though politely clear that his Gallic nature rose to the challenge. He didn't want to impose on orphans and widows, but this was different. These two represented types of Englishmen he was not fond of: Mr. Ferguson the successful, busy, wealthy, slightly smug man of affairs who looked on music halls and Wagner and love and all foreigners with slight patronage and distaste; and Mr. Slaney-Smith, the stringy, intellectual, scientific idealist whose duty it might well be to instruct a poor Frenchman, but who could not conceivably ever be instructed by one.

The gas had been turned out, but four tall candles Clodius had brought burned down the length of the table.

"You will understand," said M. Clodius, "I can promise nothing. It is always so much more difficult when there are unfriendly influences in the room."

"Don't call them unfriendly," said Mr. Ferguson, and brushed his coat with soft confident fingers.

"With you that may be so," said Clodius. "Quite so. But I am conscious of the unfriendly influence also. I do not say more than that."

Slaney-Smith coughed dryly. "I'm sure I shall be most affable to any spirits I see, what? I should like the choice of meeting some of the dear departed and asking what they think of Heaven. I want to know whether my two old aunts are harpists or trumpeters. They were always wondering themselves."

Mr. Ferguson frowned at his friend and silence fell. The ring was not complete because the medium's hands were not free, but he said this was as it should be. He asked for concentration and bowed his bald head as if in prayer. Mr. Ferguson breathed in the quietness.

A long wait. Aunt Tish's head nodded, but one of her corns gave a twinge and she wakened with a little irritable jerk of the leg. A great lion, old Ferguson, Stephen thought, with his fine curly hair and his heavy pale face with that distinctive crease above the bridge of the nose. Outside his own home he was known as rich, religious, of unimpeachable reputation. The perfect shop window for the hypocrite.

And his daughter-in-law . . . Hidden here in this heavy dark house, among these heavy unimaginative people, she was never seen at all. 'Full many a rose . . .' Come on, Clodius.

Above the uneasy creaking silence of twelve waiting people a faint sound made itself heard. One moment it was rejected by the ears as imagination, then it was too clear to be ignored. It was a small bell, an elfin bell, ringing insistently, distant yet somewhere in the room. Stephen glanced at Clodius, but he had not moved. Well, it was a good beginning. If he had not known the truth he would have felt a little superstitious jump of excitement.

It went on and on. Slaney-Smith turned his head and tried to see where the sound came from. But it seemed to have no source. It was buried too deep.

Clodius lifted his head and half opened his eyes, showing the whites. "Is anyone there?" he said.

The ringing stopped. There was dead silence now.

"Is anyone there?" asked Clodius.

There was a sudden loud knock on the table. Stephen felt the girl beside him make a little nervous movement.

Mr. Slaney-Smith stared closely at the little foreigner and then turned his head to look piercingly down the table, where the knock seemed to come from.

"Is someone playing a joke?" he demanded.

They denied it.

"Ssh, ssh!" said Clodius. "One for yes and two for no. Is it that you are friendly towards us and intend us no harm?"

One knock.

"Are you an elemental?"

One knock.

"What does that mean?" Mr. Ferguson asked.

The medium did not answer him. The ringing began again.

"Will you please answer our questions?" Clodius said loudly.

Two knocks.

"Why, is there something wrong?"

One knock.

"Are there too many people here?"

Two knocks.

"Is there too much of light?"

One knock.

"Oh, then . . ."

68

Dr. Birch, who was opposite Stephen, lifted his hand questioningly towards one of the candles, but Clodius said sharply:

"Please not to break the circle."

Someone gave a gasp. One of the candles was beginning to smoke and flicker, and as they watched it the flame dwindled and went out.

After a moment a second did the same. In the encroaching darkness everyone's eyes were on the remaining two. One of these suddenly dipped and ducked and the flame was gone.

"Leave us some light," said Clodius.

The fourth and final candle was also flickering, but, it seemed, as the result of his words, it partly recovered and grew until it was like a tiny feeble eye in the darkness. All the shadows of the room had come up to the table.

Stephen felt her hand move slightly in his as if trying to slacken its hold. He instantly released her, and then after a moment or two sought her hand again and took it. He glanced at her in the semi-darkness but she kept her own gaze on the remaining candle. The faint light reflected little amber glints in her eyes.

When he came back to himself the ringing had stopped and he heard Clodius saying:

"This gentleman here on my left? Mr. Ferguson?"

One knock.

"Now wait a minute. I hope I shall be describing you. I think I can see a little faintly. I see you as a tall elderly man with gold-rimmed spectacles and a white beard. You have a rose in your buttonhole and wear a silk handkerchief instead of a collar. Am I right?"

One knock.

Well might you be, thought Stephen, since his picture is in that book on the velveteen trade I found for you.

"Is that anyone you know, Mr. Ferguson?"

"It could be," said Frederick Ferguson steadily.

"Eh, yes, it's Papa!" came a thin voice from the end of the table, girlish in its excitement. "Well, dear Papa, how are you? Your little Letitia is here!"

"Hush your noise, Tish!" snapped Uncle Pridey. "You're jumping to conclusions. We don't want to hear your chattering."

"Nay, but Papa does, Tom. Dear Papa! And him gone all these years."

"You have a message for them?" said Clodius, now in conversation with the spirit. "Can you give it to me?"

One knock.

Clodius started creaking and shifting in his seat.

"Hold me!" he said suddenly in a whisper. "Hold my chair, or I shall go!"

They held his chair, the sceptics, one grasping each arm, while he turned and twisted impressively in his seat and wrestled with the leather straps. Mr. Ferguson admitted afterwards that there seemed to be some power drawing the chair away from them. Then abruptly he was quieter and he told them to let go.

"No, there is no time for more, I say. Yes, I will give it so. He says, this old gentleman says to his children, prosperity is founded on trust. He says always to remember the flowers that grew on the banks where the works were built: you must not destroy all the flowers. . . ."

Silence fell.

"Eh! . . . That's just what he used to say," moaned Aunt Letitia. "He's gone now. I can feel it. Eh, dear! Eh, dear! Eh, dear! . . ."

There was a grunt from Uncle Pridey, but Frederick Ferguson made no sign. He was not to be lured into easy admissions. Two or three messages came through which did not seem to make much sense.

But Clodius had not finished yet. Clodius was an artist, with a poetic sense of what was suitable for the occasion. He knew what he knew. And he had no intention of overplaying his hand. Slaney-Smith sniffed several times, and now they were all aware of a distinctive scent—something like the smell of tonka beans. Suddenly the last candle flickered and went out. The darkness was almost complete.

"Oh, dear," said Clodius. "You will pardon them. They do not like the light. . . . Yes. Very well, I will. It is as you say. There are two people here, two who have passed over. They are for different ones, they are not connected. One is a young man. He is carrying a little painted wooden figure—yes, it is a crucifix—and a candle and he is dripping wet. He has a message for someone here. Is anyone recognising him?"

There was no reply.

"I think there is little more to say to describe. He is, I think, in the middle of the twenties and wears a black cape. He is very wet and very unhappy that he is not recognised. Does anyone know him?"

There was still no reply.

"He has at least then a message which he urges me to give out. It is this, he says. He says to read, please, the Acts of the Apostles, chapter nine, verse four. That is all."

"Eh, dear!" said Aunt Tish. "Eh, dear! Eh, dear! . . . We was wrong to have started. . . ."

"Can't we have more light, please?" said Mrs. Thorpe in a tremulous voice. "Something touched me then."

"Now, I fancied exactly the same a minute ago," said Miss Griffin. "Yes," she added, "there it is again."

"And the other," said Clodius, "is a woman. I do not see her so very distinct, but she too is young. She has dark straight hair parted in the middle and a straight thin nose. She has had a long illness. . . ."

"I think," said Mr. Ferguson, "we have had quite a satisfactory sitting. On the whole, M. Gustave——"

"Please to be calm; for my sake be calm," said Clodius breathlessly. "You have frightened the woman away and she had something that she wishes to say very important. It is a pity. Please to be calm."

Surprising how nervous one got. Panic was contagious—one did not reason. The smell of tonka beans was still strong.

"So far," said Clodius, "it has been very satisfactory—as you say. We have had all except materialising, and that is very difficult. With people like yourselves it is so difficult, for you do not keep silent."

"Well, you can't expect too much from beginners," said Slaney-Smith.

"I fancy we've all had enough," said Brook, speaking for the first time. "It's been rather a joke. Shall I ring for refreshments?"

But he said just the wrong thing for his father, who was always alive to the courtesies.

"M. Gustave will have quite the wrong impression of us if he accepts that view. And so will Mr. Crossley."

"Thank you. I'm sure that's how we understand it," said Stephen.

Thwarted in his desire to break it up at once, Brook sat there sulkily, his heart still thumping. He could tell though that his father would end it soon.

"It would be useful," said Mr. Ferguson, "if we could question you later on one or two points. . . ."

Clodius did not reply.

"For instance, can you induce these conditions to order? I find it very difficult to understand how it is that——"

Clodius said: "There was eight years' difference, the wrong way round, though it shouldn't have mattered, if he'd been what I thought, but he wasn't, he hadn't a chance, to have grown to a man and yet have no life of one's own. . . ."

The voice died away into an unintelligible babble, but the unpleasant thing was that it wasn't his voice but a high-pitched sort of squeak. Then he began again:

"It's all wrong, the arrangement was wrong, from the start you can't have it, from the *start* we were quarrelling daily! His fault, *his* fault, *his* fault!" They heard Clodius begin again to struggle in his chair. "Quiet," he said abruptly, in his normal voice. "I think something will be coming."

One of the women at the end of the table gave a gasp. In the darkness, two or three feet above where Clodius was sitting, could be seen a faint light. After a moment it assumed shape, became circular, wavered, and moved an inch or two. Then out of the darkest darkness came the sound of a discord on the piano. No one was near it. There was another sound as of someone speaking, but this was lost in a sudden jerk and scrape as Brook thrust his chair back and got to his feet. They heard him stumbling across the room towards the fire. The circular light had disappeared. Clodius was panting for breath.

"Eh, dear, we should never've done it," said Aunt Tish in a moan. "It were a silly game to play, a proper silly game to play."

A flicker of light as Brook lit a spill; then the hiss of gas as he turned it on. Trembling, he lit a globe and slumped into one of the black horsehair armchairs.

The light grew. They stirred at the table, staring about the room, screwing up eyes, partly to keep out the light, partly to hide expressions the light had surprised. They had all been scared. Clodius's head had fallen forward on his chest and he seemed unconscious. Stephen reluctantly gave up the hand which had suddenly become moist within his, went round and helped to unbuckle the straps. The Frenchman began to sigh and shake his head as if lifting it out of water.

All the music had been knocked off the piano, and lay scattered on the floor.

Everyone was self-conscious and avoided each other's glances. Miss Griffin looked very pale, as if she might faint; Dr. Birch, the quietest of the sceptics, had passed her some smelling-salts.

The moment Cordelia's hand was free she got up and went to her husband at the fire.

"Are you all right, Brook?"

He turned his face up to hers.

"Yes, of course. Light the other gases, will you, dear?"

She moved to do so, but Stephen was before her.

"Thank you," she said.

Clodius was being helped from his chair.

"I am afraid," he said shakily, "I am afraid I did not know what happened just then. It was broken—at the wrong moment the link was broken. Does anything come? Has everything been quite right?"

They reassured him while Mr. Ferguson rang for refreshments. Everyone knew what Clodius's last spirit messages referred to. Everyone was sympathetic with Brook's sudden move. The matter was better dropped. What they needed now was some solid commonplace talk—about the Fenian outrages or the Ladies' Literary Society or the bad weather—to re-establish their security and comfort. Spirits—spirits were all very well so long as they were confined to a few raps on the table. . . .

Refreshments helped a lot. Although it was only two hours since supper, they were expected to drink port wine or stout and eat egg sandwiches and chicken patties and cold pastries and jam rolls and plum cake and biscuits.

Clodius was conscious of triumph and not yet of remorse. He had gone a little further than he had intended, but the drink kept his conscience at bay. The young thin man was very pale and there were dark rings under his eyes; and his beautiful but deceitful young wife was pretending to be much concerned for him. (Deceitful, for why else, Clodius asked himself, had young Crossley gone to all this trouble if not for some overwhelming cause, and what more obvious cause than a young married woman with all the looks to inflame a man?) And the thin, sandy-haired, pomaded philistine was nearly chewing the end of his thin, sandy-haired, pomaded moustache—and only the fat man carried it off well, and that merely because he had the best nerves—iron nerves.

Stephen began to get uneasy as Clodius grew expansive. It seemed as if it might be only seconds before he opened his reminiscences of the music-hall stage. He talked about France and the Second Empire and his dog Togo, and everyone was surprised what an affable little man he was after the sombre beginning. Stephen dropped him several hints, but there was no shifting him until all that could be eaten was eaten and all that was offered him was drunk. Then, just as there seemed nothing more he could stay for, Mr. Ferguson returned to the question of his first connections with spiritualism and Clodius was now too much at home to refuse. While Stephen sweated and gritted his teeth the Gascon went off into a completely fictitious history of his childhood which lasted another quarter of an hour.

When at last he had graciously bowed himself out of the front door, silence fell. Stephen knew they could have expressed their feelings much more frankly had he not been there, but he wasn't leaving yet.

"A remarkable little man," said Mr. Ferguson in his most broad-minded tone. "Of course one is inclined to jump to conclusions, to meet any psychic suggestion more than half way. I am rather sorry that Brook interrupted at so interesting a moment——"

"But the piano!" said Mrs. Thorpe with a shudder. "Did you hear the piano?"

"—at least we are greatly indebted to you for the experience."

"There, it was nothing," said Stephen. "Thank you all for being so patient. He *is* a remarkable man."

"Quite astonishing," said Slaney-Smith dryly.

Stephen glanced up, but was reassured when Slaney-Smith added: "Of course there's a scientific explanation for it all. Telepathy in the main. Telepathy and some trickery."

Pridey said: "Well, I hope you're all satisfied. Why didn't you stick pins in him to see if he was a witch?"

73

They ignored him, but began to argue, three or four of the other men, as to how it had happened, how it could have been done.

Stephen said in a low voice: "Thank you for having me in your home, Mrs. Ferguson. It's been a rare privilege; it has indeed. I have been lonely since I came to Manchester."

"Do you live here all the time?"

"Not quite all the time. I travel about. My father has bought a house in Moss Side. But of course it's in the city that I spend most of the day."

There was a pause and she seemed about to turn away.

He said: "Although I'm always meeting people, I am really very slow to make friends. But I've the feeling I have made friends here."

"Yes," she said. "Yes," embarrassed by the admiring zestful sparkle in his eyes. He would be good company anywhere—one didn't imagine him slow at anything.

Frederick Ferguson said in an undertone: "Well, I am interested that the evening has brought one convert."

"Convert nothing," said his brother, who had heard. "You can't convert a man to what he already believes in."

"You've believed in spiritualism? I didn't know you were even interested."

"I don't believe in spiritualism, man. I believe in the existence of spirits —as you would if you read your Bible as much as you claim."

Cordelia glanced across with a troubled frown. It was rare for Pridey to stand up to his brother—and in company. Stephen said quickly:

"Some time I would like you and your husband to visit me at the Variety. We are trying very hard to raise the standard of the place and to provide respectable entertainment for all."

"Thank you," she said.

"Do you go out in the evening much?"

"No. Only sometimes to concerts."

"In Town? I go regularly," said Stephen. "Let me see, when will the next concert be?"

"Next Monday, isn't it?"

"Of course, yes. I have tickets. Would you join me—you and your husband, Mrs. Ferguson?"

"Thank you," she said. "But usually my husband's father goes with us. . . ."

"Of course, please include him. May I call for you here?"

The word 'you' on his lips still seemed to mean only her.

"Please don't take it as a definite engagement, Mr. Crossley. I can't accept for Brook or Mr. Ferguson."

Partly to stop the storm that was developing, Miss Griffin had risen to go. It was a signal for a general move. Although he did not persuade the Fergusons to accept an invitation to the Variety, Stephen went away content that they were to be his guests at the concert on Monday, content that he would see her at least once more.

Slaney-Smith was silent on the way home, and Stephen could almost see his astute logical brain working out the mysteries of the evening. Before they separated, Stephen had invited the older man to go with him on the following Saturday to the Pomona Pleasure Gardens again. It would be the last opportunity Slaney-Smith would have of seeing the Great Clodius before the Great Clodius took his vanishing lady to Liverpool.

CHAPTER FIVE ❧ He called again on the Friday. It was an incautious thing to do, but he just could not get her out of his thoughts.

A maid let him in, not the side-whiskered butler, and she said she would see if Mrs. Ferguson was at home. He twiddled his hat for a few moments and then, hearing voices in the drawing-room, he moved across and half through the open door, to come upon the maid with her back to him speaking to Cordelia, who was by the middle table. The maid stepped back and nearly bumped into him.

"I do beg your pardon," he said, not to her but over her head to Cordelia. "It was all my fault, Mrs. Ferguson, but I quite understood your maid to say I was to follow her in."

"Oh, then . . ." Colouring a little, Cordelia said: "It doesn't matter, please come in, Mr. Crossley. All right, thank you, Patty."

Smothering her indignation, Patty left them. Stephen said again:

"And I swear I'd no idea of intruding. But I thought your husband looked upset after the séance; I called to ask about you, to know if you were all well."

At sight of her he was in fact angry that his thrustful impulses had betrayed him into a show of bad manners. He would not win her approval this way. A dust-sheet had been spread over the plush tasselled table-cloth, and on the table were brass wheels and pinions and an upended case. Over the spreading skirt of her cashmere frock she had tied a small black silk apron with a fringe.

"Thank you, we're all well." She was going to say that Brook had a sore throat, but something stopped her. "Please sit down, Mr. Crossley."

"I'm interrupting you. I feel guilty."

". . . It's only a clock."

"So I see. What are you doing with it?"

"Cleaning it—now."

"A very unusual pastime. Very original."

"Not really. I'm used to clocks. Is it raining?"

"Just a few spots in the wind. You know, I haven't a mechanical bent at all."

She said: "Uncle Pridey went out without his coat." Her eyes glinted as she looked towards the window.

"Now, Mrs. Ferguson, if you don't go on I shall be forced to leave again; I shall indeed. It was bad of me to interrupt you."

She picked up one of the cog-wheels and looked at it, glad of something to occupy her attention. She knew now—had known since early on Monday evening—that this handsome, widely travelled, and curiously vital young man was 'in love' with her. (Or he thought he was in love, which was more likely, she felt.) It was impossible for her not to know it, and she was flattered and excited and a bit uncertain of herself.

"I found out what was wrong," she said; "but then I went on taking it to pieces because it was so dirty. A pity to neglect a nice old clock like this."

"And what was really wrong?" He moved over to the table and stared down at the oak case and at the mêlée of nuts and wheels and cogs.

"The escapement," she said. "It's one of the old anchor escapements, and the teeth have worn tiny places in the pallets so that the pendulum isn't true any longer."

"Where?" he said. "Well, it's all double dutch to me. Can you show me?"

She showed him. He bent to look and their heads were close together.

He took in a slow, deep, fascinated breath. "Those tiny dents, now. Do you mean they make a difference in time-keeping? How are you to stop it?"

"It needs a new part for the clock. A dead escapement doesn't wear like this—or if the pallets are shaped differently."

"But why should a trifling flaw make all the difference?"

"It affects the swing of the pendulum."

"And what are all these things?"

"That's one of the pinion wheels. And this is a cam. Er—this is the hour-wheel. And that's what they call a snail."

"Why?" he said in amusement. "It's not at all like one to me."

"Perhaps it's because it moves slowly. . . . This is the striking train, as you can see, and this is the fan-fly." She glanced at him, suspecting that he wasn't listening. He met her gaze and she straightened up.

There was a second's pause.

"Clever of you to know all this! Where did you learn it?"

"From my father. He makes clocks."

"For a hobby?"

"And a living."

"I'll swear he must be an interesting man."

"Yes, I think he is."

"Does he live very far from here?"

"About a mile."

"Do you visit him often?"

"Yes—quite often. Why?"

"I should like to meet him some time. I wondered if one day you would take me with you?"

She said: "Yes, I—shall be very pleased." She'd never met anyone like Stephen Crossley before. With a charm that made one forget his impudence he went on attacking and attacking.

"Is your husband out?" he asked.

"Yes. He doesn't usually get home until about six."

"Ah, I'm sorry. I didn't realise he would be away every day. But I hope we shall be meeting on Monday." He moved slowly over to the window. "What a gem of a garden this will be in the summer, Mrs. Ferguson."

"Can I offer you tea, Mr. Crossley?"

An instinct of timing made him refuse. "But it's good of you. Perhaps another day when you are more prepared for me and I shall feel less in your way." He turned. "Did you like M. Gustave?"

"I was very impressed." ('It wasn't *her* voice,' Brook had said, 'and it wasn't what she *would* have said if she could have come back; I swear it, Delia. And as for that light . . .')

"Do you feel interested enough to go on with it?"

"I don't think so."

"M. Gustave has left the district. But I had hoped we might have tried a private séance among ourselves."

"You'll have to ask Brook. But I'm nervous. It's too uncomfortable a feeling for me."

Stephen nodded. "I felt it the same at first." He added: "M. Gustave was greatly impressed by you."

"By me? I hardly spoke to him."

"No, no; it wasn't what you said. But he's a student of character, you know, and his view was that you were—wasted here, that you were really meant to go far. He wasn't at all meaning it against your family, but he said you'd exceptional powers that needed exceptional scope to develop."

". . . Did he say all that?"

"Oh, yes, and more. He spoke about your great beauty—which of course is not to be wondered at. . . ."

"I'm very happy in my life here, Mr. Crossley."

"Oh, I've no doubt of that. Why shouldn't you be?"

"Also," she said, "I haven't got exceptional capacities."

"But it may be you don't realise them yet."

"Even if I had I shouldn't want to use them at the expense of—of other people." She smiled at him. "Thank you for your kind inquiries about us. We shall meet again on Monday, shan't we?"

"Of course." He took her hand rather gravely. "Thank you for seeing me, Mrs. Ferguson. Thank you for your kindness in having me here at all. Good-bye, now, and I shall be looking forward to Monday."

He went out, quietly and pleasantly but with a slightly hurt expression, before she could ring the bell for the maid.

In sixteen months, I've tried to become a Ferguson. Good wife, dutiful daughter-in-law. To be kind, keep my temper, be obedient gracefully. Fallen in with all Mr. Ferguson's preferences, habits. Church three times on Sundays, once on Wednesdays; prayers in the house when held, my own prayers privately at night. Queer feeling to be looked at like that. Knees weak after he'd gone—and my tongue dry. If there's spiritualism, there's magnetism too: when I was explaining the clock it was as if I were being infected by something. Oh, rubbish, more likely it is Brook's sore throat.

Mr. Ferguson's cold bath not quite ready this morning, at breakfast as if we had all committed some crime. (Do we live, do we breathe, except through him?) Anyway, why must he insist on having it so early and in the cellar, making everyone else feel uncomfortable, pampered? Yes, I've given way to him all along, but I've done it freely, so why should I feel resentment? Tell them of Stephen Crossley's call? No one saw him except Patty. But of course I must; absurd not to.

She said: "I think you should send down to the Polygon, Brook, if your throat's so bad." (In Grove Hall one never called in the doctor, one always 'sent down to the Polygon' where Dr. Birch lived.) "These patent gargles and things."

"Oh, I shall be all right," said Brook indistinctly. For all his succession of minor ailments, he never wanted to be thought really ill. He was frightened of the medical profession, even one who had been a school friend.

"Well, do go to bed, then; you may be so much better in the morning."

A good daughter too. Mother has lots of nice things for the children, Teddy no longer in grey cloth but in insurance, Essie engaged to Hugh Scott. Papa . . . Well, if he will not come here he at least can't deny

78

what I've been able to do. And for myself. Happy. I told Stephen. Not excited perhaps, but happy. I *am* excited now. . . .

"Mr. Ferguson," she said. "I've persuaded Brook to stay in bed. I'll take a bowl of gruel up to him after supper."

"You've done right, my dear. Oh Lord, we commend this food to Thy blessing and give thanks for the bounteous gifts granted to us this day. . . ."

Unkind at the end? But it wasn't what I *said*. Perhaps he has taken offence. It can't be helped, he was saying too much, going too far. Well, perhaps I shan't see him again, after Monday. Should I care? . . .

"Amen. Arrowroot's more use," said Aunt Tish. "A nice bowl of arrowroot delicately made, that's what the poor lad needs. Eh, Frederick, you shouldn't work him so hard; I know your own son better than you do yourself."

"He coddles himself, that's half the trouble. I don't like to say it of my own son, but if he took as much exercise as I do he would be much healthier."

Cordelia had noticed recently something acid in the old man's voice when he spoke of Brook. Sometimes now he was nicer to her than to Brook.

Aunt Letitia had no tact. "He's not been well, not since Monday and that darkness game. It wasn't right to have it here; he's a nervous lad, Frederick, you should remember, Frederick."

"If I'd been Margaret," said Uncle Pridey, chewing, "back from the spirit world for a minute or two, I shouldn't have wasted my time telling us all the things we already know. But she always was a bit cross-grained. Didn't like music," he said to Cordelia, waving his knife. "It's a sign of something wrong in the character. Something atrophied. Like a wall-eye. Only it doesn't show. Now——"

"I'm sure," said Mr. Ferguson, "that Cordelia is not interested or elevated by your conversation, Tom."

"Oh, I almost forgot," Cordelia said. "Mr. Crossley called this afternoon."

"Did you receive him?"

"For about ten minutes. He called to see if we were all well after Monday evening."

"That was very obliging of him," said Mr. Ferguson in an equivocal voice.

"He insists on coming for us in his carriage on Monday evening. It seems a little unnecessary."

"Some gentlemen like to pitch their hospitality at a high level. I regret I shall not be there. I find I've to go to Oldham on Monday morning and shall spend the night there. No doubt Brook told you."

"No. His throat was so sore when he got home." She glanced at her father-in-law to see if this was one of his diplomatic absences.

He said: "I expect Uncle Pridey will go in my place. Do you wish to, Tom?"

"Already going," said Uncle Pridey. He plucked at his imperial. "But my seat was a cheap one so I may as well have yours. Pass the cake, Tish."

Mr. Ferguson had never been to these concerts until she and Brook started going. A relief, this change, she thought; Uncle Pridey is unpredictable but he is a person by himself. We'll be free to forget him and to enjoy the music. Had Mr. Ferguson taken a sudden dislike to Stephen? He so often did if a friend of his was becoming a friend of theirs. He didn't really like them to have personal friends.

To test her suspicion, she said after supper:

"Is it an unexpected call to Oldham, Mr. Ferguson?"

He put down his paper and looked at her over his reading spectacles.

"Some trouble with the unions. The employers are threatening to lock out the men if they amalgamate further. I am going to see if I can prevent a deadlock."

"What do you hope to do?"

"I may be able to persuade the employers. There may be a time when it is necessary to make a stand. Then we must be sure we are right—as Christians. This is not the time."

"Do you think you'll be able to make the others see it that way?"

He smiled tolerantly, conscious of his power, his influence. Councillor Ferguson.

She would have gone then, but he said: "Why do you always ask these questions?"

"Because I'm interested."

"I really believe you are." He took off his glasses and polished them. "It is a contemporary mistake to confine the interests of our womenfolk too closely. Those few who have broken free of the shackles have given ample proof . . . Let me see, where did you go to school?"

"At Miss Griffith's."

"Not very good, was it?"

"It was better than my father could afford."

"Quite. But your talents are natural ones. No teacher could give you the ability to order this house the way you have done."

She smiled. "Oh, it isn't really hard, doing what you like doing."

He nodded slowly. She was embarrassed now, pleased with his praise but anxious to be gone.

"Have you ever seen our works?" he said.

"No."

"Is that something that would—interest you?"

"Yes. I'm sure it would."

"We must take you over some time. Tell me. How do you find young Crossley?"

"I think he is—agreeable."

"Very agreeable indeed. Personally I like him. I have one fault only to find with him—and that is that he comes from the theatrical world."

"Yes," she agreed, and waited.

"There is a certain brittleness—a superficial warmth that is to be guarded against. I feel that friendship in that sphere means a little less than it does in ours. Don't you agree?"

"I've really had nothing to do with people in the theatre before."

"Quite so. Our relationship will continue, I trust, on a friendly basis. It is just that we come from different worlds. Ours is real, solid, perhaps a little hard-headed, down to earth. His is a little brighter but a little falser. You understand what I mean?"

CHAPTER SIX Brook was worse, and they 'sent down to the Polygon.' Brook had quinsy, he was told, and must stay in bed for two days. With a rising sense of excitement and panic she saw Monday approaching. On Monday morning Brook was a lot better, and, the concert being a Chopin concert, he was anxious to make every effort to go.

Mr. Ferguson left for Oldham with the issue undecided, but Robert Birch arrived and was so definitely against the idea that his patient began to feel worse again.

All day she was quite exceptionally attentive. A peculiar feeling, a sort of guilt without reason. She must cosset him. It was a defence against her own gathering excitement.

After dinner she read to him. All day he had been both patient and grateful. They were on the last chapter of *The Warden,* and when she finished it Brook said he wanted to know the sequel. He had had *Barchester Towers* given him once as a birthday present but had never read it. It might possibly be in the lumber-room with all his school books and children's things. She jumped up at once and, taking no notice of his hoarse protests, she fluttered her hand at him and went out.

The lumber-room was on the next floor, a great attic with a sloping roof and small dormer windows set too high. She picked her way with raised skirts, treading delicately like a cat among the dust towards some book-shelves and a pile of ragged books on the floor. Having glanced over the first, she knelt down and began to look through the pile.

It was here. 'To dear Brook from his loving Mother, on his eighteenth birthday.' Open it gingerly. Even the leaves uncut. So the boy had treated his birthday present. Had *Mr.* Ferguson disapproved of it? She often wondered about Brook's mother, whether she had been downtrodden by her domineering husband or whether she had somehow escaped the influence. A single remark made by Uncle Pridey once suggested that she had willingly accepted her yoke.

By her knee was a small blue leather case and she picked it up and clicked back the catch. Two or three letters fell out, but the main content was a slim book which she opened. 'Diary for the year 1865.' Household accounts in a small neat hand, and here and there were pages of writing. No names, only initials, and she turned it idly, almost incuriously, until a few words went through her and she thought: This is the writing-case. He had called for it once, a month later, but on Mr. Ferguson's instructions she had diplomatically been 'out.' Since then she had heard little or nothing of the Massingtons. Margaret was never mentioned in the house. After Dan Massington's visit curiosity had flared up in her, but it had not been satisfied and had gradually died away in the day-to-day preoccupation of living.

The page was January the fourth.

If it were not wicked to do so I should ask God to punish him for his everlasting *prying* into religion. He claims to be deeply religious but he doesn't understand anything about *faith*. He thinks it a sign of modern enlightenment to be able to argue out the Biblican stories with that evil man S.-S. who takes pleasure in speaking blasphemy in my presence. For weeks now they have been talking of Plato and metempsychosis and whether we live again after death in the body of an animal. What wickedness! To bed early and waiting for B., who as usual sits there listlessly saying nothing. What I would say if I were in his place!

Cordelia closed the book guiltily and then, driven on, she flipped it open again.

February 12: The third day and still no inclination to get up, but I suppose I must make the effort. Mr. F. has pretended to be kind and I have pretended to appreciate it for Brook's sake; perhaps for my own sake. For five weeks Mr. F. and I have not quarrelled, never an ill word. Nearly the longest ever. He has been to my bedside and brought me grapes, and a young capon specially ordered from Sharpe's of Smithy Door. Have thanked him adequately. But under it all is caution, tension, enmity buried an inch deep. There is not a second of naturalness between us. I wish he would *die*. God forgive me, but I feel he's squeezing the blood out of my veins. Sometimes I think it is his life or mine.

Shut the book. She felt as if she had been reading something wicked and forbidden. The first wife had at last spoken to the second, and would, if one wished it, speak again and again. More surely than through any medium.

She could see it all, see Slaney-Smith's jarring irreverences and how a woman with a less easy temperament than hers would find Frederick Ferguson's manner quite unbearable. Indeed they were the sort of notes which, in an exaggerated nightmare, she might have come to write herself. She picked up the copy of *Barchester Towers* and ran from the room.

When she went back into the bedroom, Brook was too occupied with his own complaint to notice any change in her face and manner. Reading soothed her as well as him this time and brought her reassurance. Margaret had evidently been a bit unstable. She was a normal girl, feeling undoubtedly the sort of feeling Margaret sometimes experienced but in so much less a degree that it could be cheerfully borne.

Evening came and she tried not to dress with special care. But she did her hair three times in three different styles before she finally put on her evening gown, which was of a light rose-coloured velvet with Valenciennes lace on the sleeves and petunia-coloured ribbons at the throat.

The fortunate possession of a dressing-room saved her from Brook's eyes, and when she at last came in he was writing in bed. She sat beside him and kissed his forehead.

"I am so sorry you're not able to come." She bent to read what he had been writing.

> Once on a time came Sorrow
> Saying,
> "Stay with me and be my bride."
> I answered him "good morrow,"
> Praying
> He would leave my side.
>
> For Sorrow's love is grief,
> Unwanted,
> Grief before the morn;
> Joy and pleasure's thief
> And haunted
> By a crown of thorn.

"I like that," she said eagerly.
"Do you? Yes, I think I do. It's simple. Would you add to it?"
"No, it seems complete to me."

83

"Three verses are more usual."

"Well, why not be unusual?"

He bit at the pencil. "Perhaps you're right. Tell Crossley I'm sorry I couldn't come. Be sure to explain what's the matter. Don't let him think it's something to do with the séance."

"Of course not. I'll see he understands. Good-bye, dear."

Uncle Pridey, of course, had not dressed. Unlike his brother, he set no store by clothes, and his dowdy suit, grey with age and dust, would be conspicuous in the front rows. The bell went almost as soon as she got down, and Stephen Crossley was announced.

He came in, she thought, trying to control his exuberance, the characteristic unstudied swing of his shoulders and head, trying to adjust himself to the manners of the people he was visiting; but his lively brown eyes lit up as he saw her, and when she apologised for Brook's illness and Mr. Ferguson's absence he looked as if he could hardly believe his ears.

"Brook's uncle is coming if he may," she said quickly, turning to Pridey. "I have been specially asked to apologise on their behalf."

"Of course," said Stephen, making a little bow in Pridey's direction. "Thank you for coming. Thank you both for coming."

In the carriage on the way to Town the gaunt old man began to talk about his book, which was to be called *Habits and Heredity in Mice*. She had never heard him talk about it before. She hadn't even been sure that there really was a book. Stephen encouraged him. He kept looking at Cordelia, as if not yet able to believe his luck.

Carriages were thick outside the Gentlemen's Concert Hall, and the fashions sombre and impressive within. Blavatsky, fresh from American triumphs, was playing the twenty-four preludes and the nine scherzos. Stephen had had to pull all the strings he knew to get such good seats at such short notice.

As they sat down and Uncle Pridey began to read and to disagree with the Programme Notes, Stephen said in an undertone:

"I've had a miserable week-end!"

"Oh?" said Cordelia.

"D'you realise how it is when you feel you've hurt someone—someone whose goodwill, whose good opinion, you know, means more to you than almost anything else?"

"Oh?"

"I suspected my call on Friday had been misunderstood. I suspected something I said had given you offence. I went away fit for tears."

"Oh," she said, feeling happy in spite of herself. "No . . . I don't think so."

"Well, now, you don't know how relieved I am to hear it! On

Friday night I kept thinking it over in my head; round and round it went like a cat in a cage. Was it this, was it that? Did I tell you too much of Gustave's opinion of you?"

"Please don't think any more of it."

"I might have expected such kindness from you. But there *was* something?"

"No . . . I am glad to be here tonight. Which are the critics, Mr. Crossley, do you know?"

"Would you do me the honour," he said, "of calling me Stephen?"

"We have only met three times."

"Three times, is it? I thought it was once."

"Once?"

"Yes. It's once that I've met you—and that once has lasted since the first time we set eyes on each other."

"Well, that's only a fortnight ago."

"What a head you have for figures. Could you not call me Stephen just to try your tongue on the name? Some people find it hard to say."

She said: "I shouldn't have thought that."

Uncle Pridey put the programme in her lap. "Could write better notes than that myself," he said. "Some day I'll do so. Such milk-and-water stuff. Enervating! Enough to put you off any music."

She smiled. Life was no longer quite the serious thing it had become these last months. It suddenly occurred to her that perhaps Uncle Pridey was different because he was away from Grove Hall.

"Do you always come to these concerts, Uncle Pridey?"

"Only missed two in fourteen years. That's not bad for an old man. Have a sweet." He passed the bag along.

"Do you come alone?"

"Of course. You don't need four ears to listen to music, young woman."

"We never see you here."

"I sit at the back. Can't afford these velvet seats. And the company's too frivolous."

She glanced at the people about her, sober merchants and their wives, hard-headed bankers, wealthy Jews and Germans, bearded doctors, town councillors and clergymen. The cream of the city's sobriety and respectability. She glanced then surreptitiously at Stephen Crossley, noticed for the first time his well-shaped head, his long capable hands.

A burst of applause greeted the appearance of Blavatsky. The great man acknowledged his welcome and sat down. There was a pause while he adjusted his seat and while the noises of the audience died away. In it Cordelia turned to the young man.

"Would you like to see the programme . . . Stephen?" she asked.

You couldn't rely on Uncle Pridey. That was what Brook always said. Most of the time he was reasonable and well behaved; but every now and then an eccentric impulse would betray him.

At the end of the concert his conduct was monstrous. There was not a respectable woman in England who would not have condemned him.

On the way out he caught sight of a crony of his called Cornelius who played the oboe at the orchestral concerts, and he muttered his apologies and pushed his way across the stream of people moving towards the door. There he found himself involved with six other self-opinionated excitable old men in a discussion on the merits of Verdi and Meyerbeer. Stephen and Cordelia waited in the carriage for some minutes before he reappeared. Then it was to thrust his head in at the window of the coach and say he must go back to the Club with Cornelius and could Crossley see his niece home?

Stephen cleared his throat. "Of course," he said. "Yes, I can. And afterwards? Shall I send the carriage back for you?"

"No, I'll walk home. It's only two miles. Always do."

Before they started, Stephen got out and spoke to the coachman. Then he turned to look after the shambling figure of the most blessed Uncle Pridey before climbing in again.

In the darkness of her corner Cordelia was wondering what might be the effects of Uncle Pridey's appalling breach of taste. Stephen sat down beside her. The lights of Peter Street flickered and glimmered as the horses broke into a gentle trot.

After a moment or two she turned to look out of the window at the passing scene, at the people streaming away and crowding for buses, at the old woman still selling hot potatoes on the corner, a shawl round her head and a battered umbrella at her side.

Stephen said: "You'll be taking supper with me first, of course."

"Oh, no, thank you. . . . What a wonderful pianist. I feel full of music."

"But I've already booked a table at Cottam's. The evening would be cut off in its prime without it."

"I think it's been a lovely evening. Thank you all the same."

"It is a quiet place."

". . . I'd rather not, Mr. Crossley."

"Stephen," he said.

"I'd rather not . . . Stephen."

He tapped on the trap door and spoke to his coachman. They turned another corner and jogged off in silence. Some drunken men were coming out of a public house singing and shouting.

"You're thinking we should not be alone together," he said. "Well, it's happened and I'm grateful it's happened. I am going away tomorrow and it may be months before I come back."

"I'm sorry."

"I hope you are. I *hope* you are."

She felt suddenly flat.

"Cordelia," he said. "May I call you Cordelia?"

"Yes—if you wish to."

"Cordelia," he said. "Cordelia, Cordelia, Cordelia . . . Cordelia . . ."

It was strange. Every time he spoke it he seemed to increase the intimacy between them.

"Cordelia," he said. "Cordelia . . ."

"Yes?"

"Do you know how I feel about you?"

"I think you like me."

"Oh, pah, it's not that! It is nothing small and plain and level and commonplace and mediocre. Upon my soul it is not!"

"I'm sorry . . ."

"I love you," he said. "That's what it is, as you know."

Her heart was thumping now. "No," she said, denying it wildly. "I didn't know. How could I know?"

"By the grace of Heaven, and everything I said and did and looked. There now, I shouldn't have spoken so soon."

"How can you know yourself? It's—not possible."

"Not possible!" He was indignant. "What's time to do with it? Can't you die in an hour? I *knew* in an hour and the half of an hour. I knew when I saw you. I'd not dreamed of the likes of you. By God, I've tortured myself, thinking, If I'd known this woman earlier might she not have become my wife instead of his? *Would* it have been possible? Tell me that before I go."

"I can't answer you, Stephen. I don't *know*. Please don't ask me."

"Your answer gives it all away. If it had not been possible, wouldn't you have said so on the instant of speaking?"

"I can't answer either way. It isn't fair to ask me. You're not being fair at all. Please don't say any more."

It was much darker here in the first suburbs. They passed the warm gleam of a coke fire where a watchman sat huddled in the shelter of an upended cart.

The brief respite gave her back some control. What *had* she said!

"Thank you for the compliment you've paid me. But you've mistaken what I meant when I——"

"Compliment! *I've* paid you no compliment. The honour is mine, for I've known you a while and you've been kind as a saint."

"No saint, Stephen."

"No, and I'm glad, come to think of it."

"I've got a ring on my finger, not one round my head."

"Well, I'd rather have that, though it's bad enough. Tell me, are you happy with Brook?"

". . . Of course."

"And do you love him? Answer honestly."

"Why should I answer every question you choose to ask?"

"How long have you been married?"

"Nearly a year and a half."

"Your feelings are so obedient that they do what duty tells them, eh? Like a regiment of soldiers. I wish mine were. I can't believe anyone is so well behaved. . . ."

For a while there was silence. They had been talking in quiet pent-up voices which only just reached the corners of the carriage.

Stephen said at last: "Well, you're bound. I grant you that. I grant you it all. But does it mean you must say no to a friendship between us? Good Lord, I doubt that! But then it doesn't arise since I'm leaving Manchester tomorrow and may not return. Oh, well, what *you* feel can't stand in *my* way, can it? And you can't stop me from loving you, your voice, the lights and shades of your hair, the glint in your eyes, the inmost you, call it any name, that's known as Cordelia. No, not if I were married fifty times and you a hundred. And I shall love you until there's no more of me. There, that's another vow for you—and I swear it's as strong and hard-wearing as any made in church. You're the witness to it. It's not in ink so it won't fade with time."

"Please, don't say any more."

"I'm sorry. I feel I've spoiled your evening. Have I made you un-happy?"

"Yes, in a way."

"Why would you be unhappy if you didn't care anything for me?"

"You make me feel I don't know *what* I'm saying!"

He stopped. "Well, you must forgive me. I know I'm the one to blame. I'm an impulsive sort of person and always say what's in my mind. I know I should never have spoken. Say you'll forgive me?"

"Yes . . ."

"And forget I ever uttered a word of it?"

". . . I'll try."

"It would make my life more endurable while I was away if I felt your door wasn't closed tight against me."

"Of course." They were nearly home.

"Let's talk of other things," he said. "It was a very pleasant concert tonight. A beautiful concert. I heard nothing of it."

"You applauded with the rest."

"It was not that hairy old man I was applauding, it was you."

"I thought we were talking of something else."

"The weather's turning cold again. I expect we shall be having the fogs. Will you think of me sometimes, Cordelia?"

". . . Yes."

"My coachman's name is Marcus Heather. He was born in Newcastle and has twelve brothers and sisters. Where were you born, Cordelia? I don't even know that yet."

"Quite near here."

"Have you any brothers and sisters?"

"One brother and eight sisters."

"Do you think if I went to your father and said, Mr.—— What would his name be?"

"Blake."

"Blake. Cordelia Blake. I like that. I like it very much. If I went to your father and said, 'Mr. Blake, I am in love with Cordelia, but she has no thought for me; have you *one,* only one daughter in the other eight who has a quarter of her beauty and a tenth of her charm and can smile a little bit the same and bite her lip when she's puzzled and frown with one eyebrow and might look on me favourably'—do you think he would help me?"

"I think he would recommend Virginia."

"H'm. It's a pretty name."

"She's a pretty girl."

"Is she younger than you?"

"Yes. About nineteen years."

For the first time he touched her. He put his hand on her gloved hand.

"I can't wait," he said. "I can't wait nineteen years till she grows like you."

They turned in at the gates of Grove Hall. He bent and lifted her hand and pulled back the edge of her glove. He kissed her wrist.

"You don't like me, do you?" he said. "No, no, don't dare to deny it. You think I'm theatrical and overpressing, and've got a fickle Irish way with me. Well, you're right. All the bad things you can say about me are right. I don't deserve your kindness. But believe one thing. I loved you. I did indeed. Throw the rest away if it pleases you, but keep that. Good night, my very dear, and good-bye."

CHAPTER SEVEN Stephen Crossley was a young man to whom fortune had given money, good looks, and an uncommonly liberal education. He had been in love a good many times since he was sixteen, and this had begun not very differently from numerous other such affairs. But already it was taking a character quite its own.

His absence from the city could not be prolonged beyond a week, but his tongue had run away with him again. When he returned, therefore, he was careful to be inconspicuous about the town, to avoid his club, and to keep away from the Variety Theatre when Mr. Slaney-Smith was likely to be there.

The right thing was to keep away from Grove Hall for two or three months. But all this fretted his impetuous temperament. It was a constant provocation to know she was living only a couple of miles away and was alone nearly every afternoon, to feel that only his own restraint kept them apart.

At times he was moody and morose, very rare for him, and he had spurts of energy, driving everyone before him and making life a misery. Then he would lose interest and not go to the music hall or the pleasure gardens for several days. He stayed at home for long periods and read too much and drank too much and could settle to nothing else. In the end he forced himself to go away again for a few days. He went to London and made a round of the lesser music halls spotting talent, but there was no zest in the enterprise.

Cordelia had spent the first week in an uncomfortable daze. She did not know if she was in love with Stephen Crossley, but she knew she had not often before been so unhappy and never before so discontented. For almost the first time in her life she found herself quite unable to take pleasure in small things. Unconsciously she looked at her surroundings with a new and critical eye.

Mr. Ferguson came back from Oldham with a cut on his cheek which no one dared to ask about but which might have been caused by a flying stone. He did not inquire about the concert but was very agreeable all week, and on the Saturday morning survey of accounts, when Cordelia's weekly expense sheet was scrutinised, he again congratulated her on her work. He thought she must have a talent for business affairs.

The image of Stephen somehow came between her and her gratitude and made it short-lived.

Towards the end of March, Brook said at Saturday dinner:

"By the way, I met Stephen Crossley this morning. He's back again and was asking how we all were."

Cordelia's heart made a curious acrobatic movement.

"I didn't know he'd been away," said Frederick Ferguson.

"Yes, he's been in London. He says he usually stays at Verney's Hotel. I thought I might try it when I go in October."

"I'm not sure that the sort of hotel Crossley would favour would necessarily be the ideal one for you, Brook."

"We could inquire. But Crossley isn't at all the ordinary theatrical. One feels he's very much the gentleman."

"Of course. I ascertained that from Mr. Slaney-Smith before he was invited here. But I feel that anyone who has a connection with the music halls . . . I should accept his recommendations with a certain caution —especially in the matter of hotels."

"He was talking about his music halls," said Brook. "He's trying to raise the standard of the places under their control so that in the end ladies can be invited and it can be more like an ordinary theatre, with refined entertainment suitable for all."

"I'm very glad to hear it."

"In fact he's asked me so often to spend an evening at the Variety that I hardly like to go on refusing. I don't see very much harm would come of one visit."

"My dear boy, harm seldom comes of a first visit anywhere, except that the first visit usually becomes the first of many. I don't want to restrict your movements—go and see for yourself and be satisfied. Personally I should not want to go—and if I were Cordelia I should not want you to go—to a place where women of the unfortunate class frequent the bars and lobbies."

"Mr. Slaney-Smith seems to be all right," Brook said sulkily. He was always more restive under his father's hand when Cordelia was present.

"Mr. Slaney-Smith," said Mr. Ferguson, "is a man of mature years who studies deeply on certain scientific subjects. He finds—I am at a loss to understand how—some interest in the music hall. It is a relief from his serious work. But what he does with his time out of this house is not our concern."

"He hasn't been to see us so often recently," said Cordelia, trying to turn the conversation.

"He is preparing a new series of lectures."

Later, when they were alone together, Brook said:

"I think Crossley's a nice fellow. Anyway, I've promised to go to his music hall next Wednesday. I was going to tell Father, but I funked it at the end."

"What are you going to do?"

"Oh, make some excuse. Couldn't I say your father wanted to see me about—about something—Teddy or something?"

"Why not tell your father the truth? After all, he can't eat you."

"Oh, no; but he'd make things so uncomfortable that I'd go feeling like a worm. And then the fact that I'd gone against his wishes would be hanging in the air at least a week after."

"Yes . . . Yes . . ." She took a sudden desperate resolve. "Brook, I don't think I should ask Mr. Crossley back here if I were you."

Brook stared. "What? But I've already asked him. Why, don't you like him?"

"Oh, yes, I like him. I like him very much. But I just thought your father might not want us to make a friend of him."

"I don't think he *minds* that. I've asked him for Friday week. Father's got that woman coming. You know, she's lecturing on Oriental Theosophy or something first and then coming on here to supper after. Crossley seemed very interested so I asked him to join us."

Friday week was a long way ahead. Counting Sunday as one, it was thirteen days. But thirteen days are not long enough to make a plan of behaviour that cannot be upset. You can't plan against the unpredictable.

Mrs. J. Spenser Crabbe, who was journeying round England lecturing on "The New Theosophy," was an untidy woman with a big bust and pearl ear-rings to match. This much Cordelia took in before she saw Stephen. He had just slipped off his cloak and was handing it to Hallows and speaking to Brook, who had been to the meeting. In a minute he came through the door and greeted her.

So it was going to be all right. Not by any sign, even one imperceptible to the others . . . What else had she expected? At supper she found her glance constantly straying in his direction. He was much quieter than at other visits, no longer, it seemed, drawing her attention but trying to be inconspicuous. His whole manner was subdued and rather sad. Mr. Slaney-Smith, his quiff and his nose shining in the gaslight, wrangled gallantly with Mrs. Spenser Crabbe, and Mr. Ferguson murmured occasionally in the background like summer thunder which might any time move up and occupy the sky.

After supper someone mentioned spiritualism. Mrs. Crabbe had never heard of M. Gustave. Stephen was asked if he could arrange a meeting, but he replied in a quiet, serious tone that M. Gustave had gone back to France.

He stood out among these people. Not only was he younger and better-looking but he seemed to her more normal. 'We come from different worlds,' Mr. Ferguson had said. Was their world more real and solid or merely more pompous and drab?

Theosophy had many side issues. Eventually Stephen rose to go. He bent over Mrs. Spenser Crabbe, who shook her plump pearl ear-rings at him and smiled. With a politely correct expression he took leave of the other ladies, of Cordelia.

"Thank you, Mrs. Ferguson, for your hospitality. A delightful evening. Good night."

Something in her hand—she'd nearly dropped it—a crumpled piece of paper, in front of them all as they shook hands it had passed; she tried to keep back the colour. Fortunately they were looking towards the door.

"An estimable young man," said Mrs. Spenser Crabbe. "I was gratified at the smattering of youth in the audience tonight. Is he a neighbour of yours, Mr. Ferguson?"

"Just a friend. His father is the proprietor of one of our music halls, and young Crossley manages it for him."

"Strange. I should have placed him in almost any milieu but *that*. He has a studious manner."

"I was agreeably surprised by his quiet behaviour tonight."

Brook said: "I think—as a matter of fact, there is an explanation. He's been crossed in love, as they say."

"Really? How engaging! Do tell us about it," said Mrs. Spenser Crabbe, betraying a sudden feminine disregard for the higher things.

"Well—er——" said Brook, self-conscious as always at having the attention of everyone. "He said he was in love with some lovely girl who didn't care for him. Apparently he—er—fell in love with her at first sight but she wouldn't have anything to do with him. He was in a desperate state. She only saw him about half a dozen times and then she wouldn't see him any more."

"Well, I think she showed very poor taste," said Mrs. Spenser Crabbe. "Don't you agree, Mrs. Ferguson?"

". . . Yes," said Cordelia.

"When did he tell you all this?" Mr. Ferguson asked suspiciously.

Brook said: "Oh—a fortnight ago, when we met. You remember I told you."

"Young girls of today are very silly," said Mrs. Spenser Crabbe. "They think it fashionable not to know their own minds and often ruin young men's lives."

The piece of paper was in her hand for nearly an hour before she had a chance of opening it. It got hot and sticky from being held so tight. It was there like some fearful admission of guilt. She could have put it away, but she was afraid of someone going directly, as in a nightmare, to the place where she'd hidden it. At length the party broke up. She went upstairs ahead of Brook and lit the gas in their bedroom and smoothed out the paper hurriedly under the light.

He had torn an old envelope and written it hastily some time after supper. His writing scrawled across the page.

Can you imagine the agony I've been in tonight sitting here watching you and adoring you and knowing that you care nothing for me? I can never come to your house again.

STEPHEN

Pain and alarm and compassion as she screwed the envelope up into a ball again. It hurt to feel that one was hurting someone one liked.

"What are you burning?" Brook asked, coming into the room.

"Oh—I—have just been lighting the gas with it."

"Why strike a match to light a paper to light the gas?" he asked, amused.

"Well—I don't like the pop so close to my fingers. The matches are too short."

He moved across the room. "It was interesting over supper, but, Lord, it got tedious before the end. I don't see what good it does, all this talking. I nearly let out about going to the music hall, didn't I?"

"No one noticed." Brook, Stephen, Stephen, Brook. No, it wasn't fair —it wasn't fair to make comparisons. Brook was her husband, Stephen an interloper. He had no right to thrust passionate messages into her hand, to presume upon a few casual meetings.

"Brook," she said, "you do love me, don't you?"

He turned and stared a little blankly. "What? . . . Oh . . . Yes, of course I do." He picked up a book then to avoid her eyes because he was embarrassed by the question. "What a funny thing to ask." Their relationship over long periods was very matter-of-fact.

She put her hands on his shoulders, looking into his face, claiming his reluctant attention. "And am I a good wife to you?"

"Of course, dear. Don't you think you are?"

"I don't know. Not always, perhaps. But I like to be told. Am I as good a wife to you as Margaret was?"

He flushed. "Have I ever said you're not?"

"No, Brook. But don't answer my questions with other questions: just say yes or no."

"Yes, then. You are as good, and better."

"Better." She kissed him. "I'm glad. In what ways am I better?"

"Oh, why bring Margaret into it now? You've hardly mentioned her for months. Let her rest in peace."

"It's funny, isn't it," she said, "that her letter-case was never found?"

"What letter-case?"

"The one Dan Massington inquired for. Don't you remember?"

"Well, the thing was thrown out, I expect. But it was nothing important: a few household accounts."

"You know," she said, "somehow I don't often think of you as having been married before."

"I'm glad. Why should you?" He patted her cheek, tending to move away, impatient because *he* had not sought the intimacy. "After all, you never knew her."

"I never knew her. . . . Brook, it must be—strange to have been in love with two people."

He looked into her grey eyes a little furtively, as if trying to read her thoughts. "There's nothing very strange about it. Plenty of people marry twice."

"Do you ever think of her, Brook—of the happiness you had together? When you put your arms round me, do you ever think that—perhaps it is Margaret? Do you ever forget, I mean?"

"Good Heavens, of course not! What an idea! Come along, let's go to bed. It's late and we have to be up as usual."

"But when you've loved two people, don't you *ever* compare them? I'm not trying to catch you, or anything, but mustn't it be so? Don't you ever—don't you put your hand on my hand and think: Margaret's was thinner—or plumper—or softer or harder? Wasn't my hand ever strange under yours?" He didn't answer, waiting, petulant now, for her to finish. "I'm sure I should feel that way," she said lamely.

"One thing I like about you better than Margaret is that when she was ill she used to get all sorts of miserable and morbid notions. I don't see any reason for you to start, I don't really. It's just silly to talk like that. I'm going to bed, my dear."

There was silence for a long time. Cordelia thought: That diary's still lying upstairs. Is Brook right: am I being prying and inquisitive, asking so many questions, being so curious about Margaret's life here? But have I? Have I? It's only tonight. And why tonight? Because a handsome and nice man . . . And is my curiosity really about Margaret? I don't think so. I don't know. I *don't* know. Brook *is* right. I must go to bed, go to sleep.

She said quietly: "Brook."

"Yes?"

"Am I inquisitive?"

"Oh, it doesn't matter. It's natural to wonder, I suppose."

"Brook, after your mother died, did your father never think of marrying again?"

He stirred restlessly. "How can I tell? I don't know all his thoughts. He never seemed interested in anyone. He was fifty-six, you know."

Presently she lay back on the pillow, knowing she would not sleep for a long time. She had said her prayers, praying for common sense and peace of mind, but the second at least seemed very far away. Thoughts were racing round in her head. She had also said a short prayer for Stephen, praying that he should be given the strength to get over his infatuation and that he should be able to leave her alone and marry some nice girl and that they should be happy all their lives.

Her mother had always taught her to end her prayers with the words: "Nevertheless let not my will but Thine be done." It was usually the hardest prayer of all to say. Tonight, with a peculiar sense of discomfort, she found it easier to say—and that ease of itself seemed an irreverence of the worst kind.

CHAPTER EIGHT ⚘ In spite of Mr. Ferguson's silent disapproval, she still continued to pay her family about three visits a fortnight. The distance from Grove Hall to the shop, if one cut through the lanes, was not great, and often she would walk, another act that Mr. Ferguson disapproved of. But she found it ostentatious to draw up at her old home with a coachman to hand her down.

Today was fine and rather warm for April, and she looked forward to being able to detect the first stirrings of spring in the gardens and among the trees. Only just a little way along the Grove he was waiting for her.

She half hesitated with the shock, considering how to avoid him, until he turned and took off his hat and she knew then this was not a chance meeting.

He looked thinner and less buoyant. There was no contrivance in that. In a queer way it suited him. His was a face with good bone structure; plumpness would mask it, leanness gave it strength.

"May I walk with you?" he said.

"Yes, if you wish to."

He turned with her and they went some way in silence. It was an ominous, explosive silence.

At length he said: "Do you dislike me all that much for loving you?"

"No," she said.

"Then I may go on loving you?"

She moistened her lips. "How can I stop you?"

"Do you want to stop me?"

"It would be better for us all if you did."

"Why would it be better?" he said obstinately. "I don't see that."

"Well, it is only making you unhappy—and me unhappy—and it would upset Brook if he knew."

"Doesn't it depend how you want to live?" he said. "How intensely you want to live. Is it drifting along in peace and comfort you want or the excitement of swimming against the stream? Yes, I'm unhappy but I wouldn't change it. I'll take the rough with the smooth. Even if there's only frustration in it, I'm the richer for knowing you."

"Why do you say things like that?"

"Because they're the very truth."

"You don't—know me, Stephen. And if you did—none of this is—going to help."

"You've just said you're unhappy because of me. That means you're not indifferent. Are you? Cordelia, are you?"

"I'm married to Brook. That's all anyone can say. . . ."

"Whatever I feel? And whatever *you* feel?"

"Yes. I've told you so before."

"Supposing you were deeply in love with me. Would you still stay married to Brook?"

"Yes. . . ."

He took a deep breath. "I don't believe it!"

"You must. . . ."

He was silent for some seconds. "Very well."

Some of the young trees were showing green and the birds were twittering in the mild afternoon, but she saw none of them.

He said suddenly: "You're sorry for me, aren't you?"

"I'm—sorry this has happened."

"No more?"

"Well, I can't seem to—condescend. Not to you, of all people."

"Thank you. But you're grieved all the same?"

"Yes."

"Then will you do something to help me?"

"If it's—reasonable."

"Will you let me meet you sometimes when you go to see your family and let me walk with you part of the way?"

Say no. Say no.

"But if I do that it will only make things far worse."

"Who for?"

"For you."

"I'll take the chance on that. I'll bear the risk. I don't think it will. Just to see you is what I'm needing."

"No. . . . If we met and you talked like this it wouldn't be fair."

"If we met I should promise not to talk like this."

"And would you keep your promise?"

He smiled slightly. "I would."

"You want me to begin to deceive everyone? From the first I should have to tell lies. Heaven knows where it would lead."

"Why should it lead to anything at all? It's your family you would be visiting in the ordinary way. I should have business in this district and should come across you and stroll a few yards in your company. No wickedness in that. Tell Brook you've met me, if you like. Would there be anything improper in being gracious to a friend?"

She puckered her brow in an effort to see it in a detached way. Yet she knew she must refuse.

"Lord," he said, "it is a small thing, this. Isn't it? If I were a beggar, would you deny me a crumb? There are twenty-four hours in your day, seven days in your week. If you don't dislike me and you're sorry for me, as you say you are, d'you think it overgenerous to give me your company for twenty minutes in a fortnight?"

"You make me seem narrow-minded and mean."

He touched her arm. "It's only my way of putting the thing. I over-state the case to make you see it the way I want you to. Maybe it's bold of me to ask it, but I ask it all the same."

They had walked so far that in a few moments they would be at the shop.

She said: "I don't *want* you to think me narrow-minded and mean."

"I don't, Cordelia. How could I, now? How could I love you if the thought ever entered my head?"

She said: "You mustn't come any further. I'm nearly—— Good-bye, Stephen."

He hesitated a moment, looking at her, peering at her for indecision. "And is it really good-bye?"

"I usually," she said, "I usually come to see my family on a Monday and every other Thursday. On fine days I walk. If you do—care for me, as you say you do, please don't come too often. . . ."

He took off his hat. "*Thank* you. Good-bye."

The older Crossley had been in the town over the week-end and was dissatisfied with his son's stewardship, which had been adequate but not exceptional. Knowing what talent Stephen had, Patrick Crossley was angry and disappointed.

"Mother of Heaven!" he said. "I can't follow you, Stephen, that I can't. Haven't you had enough to do with women these ten years past to know by now that one's much like another when you take away the frills they disguise themselves in; and if one won't have you, then bad cess to her and take up with the next! This muling and puking isn't sense for a grown man at all. You were always a spoilt boy, and that's my doing and

I know it and I take the fault; but sure at twenty-six it's time you stopped crying for the moon and came down to earth for a while!"

Stephen lit a cigar and looked at his father with an even gaze.

"This one's different."

"So you've said before. Louisa was different. Caroline was different. And what about Virginia? Wasn't she different, now?"

"Oh, so I thought. So I thought. But now it's not a question of thinking: it's a question of *knowing*."

"Very well; very well. You know this one is different. This one . . ." Mr. Crossley scratched his fat neck in irritation. "I've forgotten her name."

"Cordelia."

"This one is different, but unfortunately she's already got a husband and she's a prude. So you're beaten. Confess it: you're beaten."

"I'm nothing of the kind."

"Well, you will be beaten. I know the type. I recognise the type, me boy. You'll play her for six months, for twelve months, and in the end, just when you'll be thinking you're going to land her, away she'll slip off the hook and you'll be left high and dry on the bank cursing the day she ever was born."

Stephen drew at his cigar. His handsome brown eyes had a staunch look.

"I happen to be in love with her, Dad. Why won't you accept the words when I tell you them?"

"Oh, faith, well, suppose ye are——"

"There's no supposing about it. But even supposing I wasn't, I'd still go on."

"And where's it going to lead, tell me that."

"I don't know."

"No. That's it. All this year you'll be fussing and fretting over it, while my interests here go to pot, and then at the end you'll be up in the divorce court with all the notoriety and bad odour. All the respectable people of the town will turn up their noses and our business will go back to what it was when we bought it."

Stephen stared moodily at the fire. There was a good deal of conflict in him this morning, and the feeling of unresolved stress made him irritable. His father's words spoke direct to that hard sense which the show business had bred in him. But his association with Cordelia appealed to a side of his nature which, despite his other love affairs, had not fully emerged. Against it the old loyalties beat in vain.

"Now look, boy. Why not cut free at this stage? There's a chance of acquiring a nice property in Birmingham—belonged to the Taylors; it's got a fair reputation and could be worked up in a very pretty way. I've had me eye on it for some time. Supposing now I bought it and made it over to you, lock, stock——"

Stephen shook his head. "Sorry, Dad, I couldn't find it in me to go. Thank you for the offer."

Patrick Crossley's neck grew redder. "And if I gave you no choice?"

"It wouldn't work. You've given me my way all my life and now it's too late to change. I could always get work in this town if you turned me out."

The older man threw the butt of his cigar irritably into the fire.

"I don't know what's the matter with you, boy; I was never such a fool about women. Or only once maybe. . . . Well, go on. But do what ye can to hurry the thing on and get it out of your system. And if you've no other consideration for me at all, try to keep it dark for the sake of our good name. Will you promise me that? No scandal."

"I'll do my best."

"And try to spare a little attention each day for the work I pay you for. Look on it as a filial duty."

"I will," said Stephen. "I'll see to things all right. I promise to do that."

Another father was feeling a sense of disappointment in his son, but its expression was more devious. Frederick Ferguson was not so blunt in his frustration. He criticised his son's velvet coat, telling him it was time he got a new one and that the foremen at the works were tidier-dressed. Then when Brook mentioned a poem he was writing on Spring, Mr. Ferguson said didn't he think the subject overdone and it would have been more original and to the point if he wrote one about a dye works. When Brook spoke of Blackpool, Mr. Ferguson corrected him sharply on a matter of detail. Cordelia, who usually smarted for her husband, was in a brown study of her own, and she came out of it only in time to find an open conflict.

Brook, very white, was standing up to his father for once and answering back.

"It doesn't matter what you meant, it was a very unpleasant thing to say, Father. I—I'm sick of it all. Leave us alone, can't you? Things will turn out all right in the end. And if they don't—well, they don't, that's all I've to say. I can't stand—sarcasms!"

"My dear boy, there's no need to raise your voice. And if you read sarcasm in the merest pleasantry to your wife . . . Even Cordelia must agree with that."

"I'm sorry," she said. "I didn't hear what you said."

"I said I was coming to have a regard for your administrative talents. It seemed to me a not uncomplimentary remark, even if partly in jest."

"That wasn't all you said," Brook muttered, and left the room with a slam of the door.

Frederick Ferguson raised his eyebrows. "Juvenile and ill-mannered. I thought Brook was above it."

"Eh, Frederick," said Aunt Tish, putting down her crochet work. "The lad's sensitive, that's what it is. He was always a touchy lad, was Brook."

Mr. Ferguson said: "I was telling Brook I had promised to take you over the works, Cordelia. You will find them well worth a visit."

"Thank you. I should like to go."

She was aware of his continuing look. Sometimes he would so brood on a person, embarrassing them without any self-consciousness on his own part.

Presently he said: "To anyone with business acumen it should be specially stimulating. A pity that because you are a woman you have had no opportunity to develop."

When she and the old lady were alone for a few minutes Cordelia said:

"Aunt Tish, what was it Mr. Ferguson said that upset Brook?"

"Why nothing all that bad. He was giving praise to you and saying what use you'd be to him down at the works. Then he said maybe Brook would stay at home instead of you and look after the cooking."

"Oh . . . That wasn't very nice. . . ."

"Frederick's been on to him lately. Like what he was with Margaret sometimes. But he'll suffer for it—Brook, I mean. Frederick always pays him out somehow."

Tish's weak, placid, pouchy face seemed less inert than usual. She was devoted to Brook.

"Aunt Tish, do tell me more about when Margaret was alive. I've been living in this house eighteen months now and sometimes I still think I don't know any of you—*really*—except Brook, of course. Sometimes I think if you'd talk to me more, tell me more, I should be—should be more useful to you all."

Aunt Letitia fumbled with the white embroidered muslin of her old-fashioned over-jacket. All her face was puckered up in an effort of concentration to answer what Cordelia had said. Then abruptly it cleared and relaxed into its accustomed lines.

"Frederick told us not to," she said.

"Told you not to what?"

"Not to talk of Margaret in front of you. Eh, I remember, he said it would upset you."

"But what is there to hide? What is there to upset me and what is there to hide?"

"Nay, that would be telling, wouldn't it?" She stopped and scratched her head. "But true enough I don't know myself. If you asked me I wouldn't know. Except that they were often squabbling. Except for that I wouldn't know the difference from now. Except that things are better seen after now. Except that at the end them and the doctor were arguing. And Margaret's ma came and there was a set-to." She glanced at Cordelia with her round blue eyes, and then they went flickering off to the easy, familiar, comforting things: the fire, the crochet work, the armchair, the footstool. "But I didn't hear it. I didn't hear anything for I was crocheting and didn't have the time to listen. But don't tell Frederick I told you, mind. He'd be ratty if he got to know."

She found Brook upstairs, lying on the bed, scribbling couplets on the back of an envelope. He started a little when she came in, and she wondered if he expected his father.

"It's cold up here," she said. "Why don't you go down to one of the fires?"

He grunted but did not reply.

She pretended she had come for something and pottered about the room for some minutes. Then as she moved back to the door he crumpled up the envelope and flung it across the room.

"Oh, God, I wish I were dead!"

She paused, hesitated, thinking that at the merest suggestion of death or illness . . . Yet that was unsympathetic.

She came over to the bed. "What is it, Brook?"

He turned over, showing his wretched face.

"You think I love my father, don't you?"

"Mm . . ." She nodded.

"You think I like being treated like a child and told what to do and what to eat and nearly what to say?"

She was silent.

"Well, I don't. Sometimes it's all right. I know I'm weak—I live off him, I haven't the initiative. I tell myself he means well. But it doesn't always work. I wish to God I could get away. If I could be sure of making a living with my pen—even working for a newspaper like Hugh Scott—I'd go! I'd clear out tomorrow. There's not room for us both."

She sat on the bed and began to stroke his hair and she noticed that his forehead was damp. She was sorry for him, but she did not take his words seriously. She knew him better than that. In the morning he would be the usual docile son.

CHAPTER NINE 🌿 Stephen began to meet her alternate Mondays and Thursdays. He wanted it to be a weekly arrangement, but illogically she felt that an interval of ten days made it less flagrant.

Otherwise he kept to his side of the bargain, never pressing his attentions and always accepting her decisions with the greatest respect. Veils were fashionable, and she took to wearing one. She was conscious of carrying a tremendous burden of guilt.

Yet in spite of this she looked forward to the meetings and soon could not hide it from herself. Now that he was not to be completely cut off from seeing her he was so lively and full of animal spirits that it was a stimulus to be in his company. They came to laugh and joke and tease each other. Laughter was one of the things she so greatly missed in Grove Hall, and in a very short time they had found a new and more friendly understanding of each other.

But although he took his cue from her, it was often hard for her to know where to draw the line. The simplest fun between them had a tendency to slip imperceptibly into something like a flirtation. Twice her mother asked her what the news was because she looked so flushed and excited when she got there.

He asked that he might come with her and meet her family, but she said no, thinking it safer; until one day Teddy came upon them a few hundred yards away and, to cover her hesitation, Stephen introduced himself and explained that he knew Mrs. Ferguson slightly and that he had met her by accident when he was on his way to call on Mr. Blake, to whom he had been recommended, about a valuable clock which needed attention.

All this went over so smoothly that in a very short time Stephen was being asked in and was taking tea in the kitchen and discussing the cooking of Eccles cakes with Mrs. Blake as if he'd known her all his life. Because of Stephen's quick-thoughted explanation and because he had come in with Teddy as well as Cordelia, he was accepted as a new friend common to all.

When he left they all asked Cordelia questions about him but with perfect innocence of manner which showed they suspected nothing.

At the end of May a soirée was to be given at the Free Trade Hall by the Philosophical Society. Stephen was making up a party to attend. He invited Mr. Ferguson and Brook and Cordelia and a number of others.

Once a fortnight Cordelia stayed to supper with her family and Teddy took her home. On the middle Thursday in May she came as usual about four and was told that they had invited Stephen to supper.

The supper was a lively one. Hugh Scott, Essie's fiancé, was there, and he and Stephen kept them all amused, Hugh telling Scottish stories in a rich brogue and Stephen capping them with Irish tales. It was a surprise to hear the chorus of clocks wrangling together through nine o'clock. Cordelia got up.

"Let me save you a walk, Teddy," Stephen said. "I can see Mrs. Ferguson home."

"Oh, no, please don't bother," she said. "There's no reason for you to leave so early."

"On the contrary, I must leave soon as I've an appointment in Town at ten. I think that is Marcus now. And Teddy is very comfortable and has his slippers on. I'm sure you'll trust me with her, Mrs. Blake."

"Why, yes," said Mrs. Blake, though a little uncomfortable. "If Mr. Crossley is so kind, Cordelia . . ."

They left with gracious good-byes all round. In the carriage there was silence as they drove off.

At length Cordelia said: "It wasn't wise of you, Stephen. Hugh Scott knows Brook and——"

"I couldn't resist it. I see so little of you. It gets on my mind and I can't get it off. Are you listening to me?"

"Mr. Ferguson will hear the carriage and ask who has brought me."

"We can stop outside. Or better still . . . It's a rare and lovely evening." He leaned forward and told his coachman to stop. "The lady and I will walk, Marcus. Meet me at the end of the Grove in half an hour."

Cordelia got slowly out. The last daylight was fading out of the sky and stars were glimmering through a faint summery haze. Northwards over the city was another faint loom of light, and the uneven buildings of the Oxford Road showed grey through the darkening trees. The victoria drove discreetly off, creak-creak, clop-clop, diminishing down the road, clop-clopping away into silence.

"Marcus is very close," he said. "He wouldn't open his mouth to a living soul."

They began to walk. Oh, well, what does it matter? she thought wearily. Perhaps this is part of the fun of life, taking risks. All the evening has been lovely.

She said: "What a wonderful mimic you are, Stephen."

"It comes as second nature, and can you wonder?"

"Were you brought up in the theatre?"

"The first thing I remember is a dressing-room back stage. My mother was an actress, you know."

"No, I didn't know. You never told me."

"Oh, well—it's precious little to brag about. She was a very good actress, but a poor sort of wife and mother."

"Tell me about her."

"Why should you be interested?"

"Well, I am."

He looked at her. "Lift up your veil. It's wicked to cover your face."

"D'you want me to be recognised?"

"There are few enough lamps this way."

"All right then." She did so. "Go on."

He looked at her face for some seconds in silence. She was conscious of his gaze and conscious of the pleasure that it gave her.

"Go on."

"She was a beautiful woman. Not so beautiful as you but——"

"Oh!"

"I mean it. But she had the makings of a rare good actress, so I'm told. She married Dad when he was assistant stage manager in a little sort of a theatre in Bristol. After a few months they took up their stakes and went to London. It was bad in London and they nearly starved. Then she took a walking-on part at the Lyceum, and he found work at a place called the Grapes, one of the early music halls, it was. Thanks to his backing and training, she began to get on—and then I came along with my screeching and squalling to spoil her first good part. After that it was not so long before she decided that Dad had taught her all he knew and that I would be a pack on her back and a burden to her career. So she left us flat and went off on her own like the self-seeker she was. She had two or three big hits and then went to New York and stayed there."

"How old were you when she left you?"

"About three."

"Have you seen her since?"

"No. She died ten years ago."

"I'm sorry."

He was silent a moment. "I don't know. Perhaps it was all for the best. Do you think she would be a very nice person?"

"It must be strange not to have had a mother—ever. It must make you look at life differently."

"I think I should have forgiven her more if she'd gone off with another man."

She was silent, thinking it over, trying to visualise growing up like that. In a way she understood him better tonight than she had ever done before, the different claimant influences upon a nature not yet perhaps fully integrated. At times his easy tongue offended her. At others the warmth of his generous admirations seemed to fill her veins with a responding warmth, heady and throbbing and sweet.

He said: "Isn't it more human, more natural, a failing we can understand and forgive if a woman chooses wrong and finds she's married the
wrong man and falls in love again and goes off with her second choice?
There, that's weakness and we excuse it. But if she throws off her husband and child because they stand in her light and might spoil her
career? That's meanness, I'd say, and good riddance."

"I suppose it depends whether your career means more to you than
anything else in the world."

"Well, it shouldn't, that's all I can say."

"You mean it shouldn't in a woman."

"It's worse in a woman, I admit. . . ."

They were silent for some time. It was growing darker and the birds
were giving up their evening songs.

"I like your family," he said suddenly. "All of them. They're grand
people. And I like to see you in the middle of them. That's where you
belong—so much more than at Grove Hall."

"Why?" she said, curious to know what he would say.

"The Blakes are alive and kicking—more like me; and you were born
and made by nature to be more like me. I can sit there and watch you
expand. Cordelia, I'd like to invite your father and mother to the soirée
next week—and Esther and Teddy and Hugh Scott."

"Thank you, Stephen." She was genuinely gratified. "But I don't
think it would work. Mr. Ferguson looks on them as not quite good
enough for him."

"What? Why ever not?"

"Anyway, I don't think Papa would come," she said. "He hasn't been
to Grove Hall for nine months. Perhaps you could ask Essie and Teddy
and Hugh only? I hate to see Mother deprived of an evening, but——"

"Very well, it's as you say."

"Thank you for the kind thought. And do invite them again, please,
when you can take them alone and when perhaps I can make an excuse
to join you."

She had enjoyed the walk, and they had been serious and not flirted,
and she was sorry it was over.

He said: "Shall I not see you again before the soirée?"

"I'm afraid not."

"Cordelia," he said.

"Yes?"

"Oh, it doesn't matter."

They turned in at Grove Hall. There were three lights on the ground
floor and two on the first floor.

"Uncle Pridey's at work on his book," she said.

Their feet crunched on the gravel path. It was very dark here except

106

where the lights from the windows fell upon the shrubs and the lawns. About them was the scent of lilac and laburnum.

He stopped. "Cordelia."

"Yes?"

"I'm crazy about you."

"You mustn't say that, Stephen."

"I'll not say it again. I promise. Or not very often. But sometimes it's—well, it's necessary."

"I understand."

"Do you? I wonder."

"Of course."

"I doubt you can understand when you're so cool and so calm."

"Not always so cool and so calm," she was forced to say.

He put a hand on her shoulder. Aware of crisis, she took a step backwards and found her back against a tree. He kissed her. It was rather a clumsy kiss for it was very dark. At the second attempt his lips found hers. And that wasn't so clumsy.

For a few seconds they did not move. Then she started from him and turned her face away.

"Now the promise is broken all ways at once," he said. "And I don't care. Let it break. I don't care."

"Please go now."

"Are you offended?"

Offended? That wasn't the word.

"Cordelia, I can't leave like this. Tell me, it isn't going to make any difference, is it?"

"Stephen," she said. "Please, please go."

CHAPTER TEN ❧ Not at the soirée—so soon after—as if nothing had happened. Be ill. Haven't had an illness since I was married. My turn to catch a cold instead of Brook's. A chill. Something that makes one feel ill and nothing to show. Another week to think things out. *Must* think. I can't just drift, especially now. I might have known something like this . . . Closed my eyes to it, pretending, pretending . . .

"Cordelia," said Mr. Ferguson. "I find it would be convenient for you to pay your visit to the works this morning. I happen to have an hour or two free—very rare—and the promise is of long standing. Brook won't be back from Oldham until this afternoon, but we can take care of you without him."

"I should love to come, but I've a headache this morning. I think perhaps another day . . ."

"The drive will do you good and the air will blow it away. Another day I will almost certainly not be free."

"There're some things I should see to in the house. Mrs. Meredith says——"

"Let Mrs. Meredith take care of them. The house can spare you for one morning."

Might have known better than to argue. Is my nature weak, weaker than Margaret's, that I'm always giving way to him, or is it my duty to do so? Is it weakness or strength to stand up for your own way in all the small things, the petty things?

A lovely May morning with not a breath of air to stir the young leaves, and a great bank of white clouds motionless in the north.

They took the phaeton and drove at a fine pace into the town, past the plodding buses and the horse-drawn drays and boys pushing handcarts and the tattered beggars; past the tall old houses of Ardwick Green and up the London Road; and there they turned sharply off and broke through the fine crust of trade and prosperity and plunged straight into poverty and slums.

In a few moments it was no longer possible to drive at anything but a slow pace through narrow streets in which ragged children played and naked babies crawled. Rickety houses, four storeys high, shut off a day-light which was already filtering through a smoky cloud in the upper air. Thin dirty women in clogs and shawls sat in doorways clutching babies, or screamed at other women across the road. Side streets showed glimpses of narrow alleys with washing stretched across and cobbles sloping down to a middle gutter. Factories clustered behind with tall black chimneys wreathed in smoke, amid acres of battered hoardings and murky brick. Cordelia had seen poverty before, there were bad patches not far from where the Blakes lived, but she had never seen anything like these tenements, this universal squalor.

"It is better near the canal," said Mr. Ferguson, noting her expression.

Her own problems seemed suddenly trivial beside those of the people who lived in this district. Here men and women had no time to be concerned with flirtations: they worked to live and when there was no work they starved. Very recently they had been starving in their thousands—literally starving, and dying off in their weakness of typhus and cholera. She could not understand how the rest of the town continued to live in peace while this great community festered in its heart. Yes, there had been riots during the cotton famine; she remembered them when she was at school; but they had been quite small compared with the distress there must have been. And there were no riots now.

She felt herself intolerably fortunate living in opulence and comfort—and intolerably wicked to be expecting something more. Did she live off these people? Was her opulence and comfort gained at their expense?

Mr. Ferguson said: "You haven't been here before?"

"No."

"It would do everyone good to come this way once or twice a year."

She glanced at him in surprise. "Yes . . . I was thinking that."

They turned under a railway arch plastered with tin advertisements, passed a shunting yard and a cemented playground where children were running and screaming.

"That used to be an old cemetery until last year," he said. "It was at my instigation that it has been made use of. Better to have some care for the living than too much respect for the dead."

"Yes," she agreed, reluctantly finding common cause.

"Are you quite happy at Grove Hall?" he asked.

"Yes!"

"Brook is a queer young man. But he has many sterling merits."

"Oh, yes. He's very kind. I'm very fond of him."

Fond of him? Was it fondness that made your heart beat and your blood go racing?

"Well, we are here." Mr. Ferguson helped her down. He was being more agreeable than ever today, and she was a little uncomfortable under it.

They went in at wide iron gates, and were at once among the reek of chemicals. They passed some sheds and walked along the cobbled way towards the counting-house at the end. There were several men in here who rose and said respectful good mornings as Mr. Ferguson made his lordly and benevolent way through. She was conscious of their eyes following her.

They came out again into a yard where water was dripping. The rumble of machinery was close at hand.

Mr. Ferguson said: "This is the section devoted to calicoes. You'll find it perhaps the more impressive."

In a dark shed were several huge machines. They were like great crabs, lifting up bales of material with hundreds of cogs turning, the men tending them dwarfed and shadowed by their size. It was not a pleasant hum or a steady buzz but a clanking, clanging metallic noise, jerky and awkward and laboured.

"This," said Mr. Ferguson in her ear, "is known as mordanting. With these machines a mordant is fixed on the cloth to prepare it for absorbing the dye. You see . . ." He turned up a corner of a roll of calico lying near. "This is the untreated cloth. Here we are printing this cloth with six colours. Each of those machines has six rollers which, as you see, engrave their particular colour upon the calico as it passes round the drums. You'll appreciate how intricate an arrangement of the machine is necessary to enable each colour to adhere exactly to its own part in the design."

A man had followed them from the office, a tall thin anæmic man with a prominent adam's apple; and Mr. Ferguson introduced him as Simnel, the head foreman.

After a while they moved on and out of the shed, and Mr. Ferguson stopped a boy labouring to push a truck into the next shed. He lifted up a piece of cloth to show her.

"This is the same calico, etched with the colours as you have seen. It has now gone through processes to get rid of the acetic acid; you'll notice how little at present is to be seen."

The calico was barely different from the piece she had seen before except that by peering at it a faint design could be distinguished.

"Wait. Let us go on a little way." They entered another shed in which the smell of chemicals was overpowering. Here there were great metal baths full of yellow-brown fluid. Following the boy with his load, they watched two men prepare to drop the calico into one of the baths.

"That is a chemical called alizarin. Watch the effect."

The men plunged the calico into the bath, and she stared as it was presently brought out. It seemed as if magic had suddenly imprinted on it a vivid flower design of reds and yellows, pinks and lilacs and blues.

"Wonderful, isn't it?" he said, pleased with her astonishment.

"Yes, wonderful!"

"The action of a single chemical. Yet it is not a new thing. The machines are new, but the process was known to the Egyptians."

They went on through the starching room to watch the calendaring, and then across to the designing and engraving rooms, where the rollers were prepared for the printing machine. At the other side of a cobbled yard the dyeing was done. Long rows of women in grey calico frocks were cutting the threads of the velveteen by hand. With big knives they cut along the weft of the material, in magnificently expert undeviating lines, backwards and forwards, over and over again, endlessly active, endlessly patient. He said that it took an hour to cut a two-yard length.

Beyond were the open sheds with their damp flag floors, the heavy cross frames of the roof low on their heads, where men were tending the dyeing rollers, working them by hand, squat, sparsely built, grey-faced men who did not look up as they passed.

Out at last at the end of the sheds, and she found herself on the banks of a small stream. The sun was trying to break through the drifting smoke overhead.

"There is more to show you," he said. "But perhaps you are fatigued and would like to leave the rest."

"No, thank you. But I'm glad of a breathing space." The smell of the dyes and the noise of the machines were overpowering. Yet she was fascinated, felt the lure of it.

The water of the stream was a rusty red colour and smelt vilely.

"Do you drain your used dyes into here?" she asked.

"Yes. But we are above our outlet. The colour is from Henshawe's— the two chimneys by the railway bridge."

"Oh, yes, I see."

Mr. Ferguson stared reflectively at the muddy bank, the cemented gulleys.

"My father built these works. I remember while they were building it the workmen used to pick the primroses on the banks of this stream. It was strange and remarkable, that reference of the medium. You remember—in February?"

"Yes."

"At the time it gave one the feeling of some supernatural influence. But now I'm not at all sure. I believe that my father recorded it somewhere, in one of the pamphlets he wrote. I haven't traced it. It was very strange. Even Mr. Slaney-Smith was impressed."

They went on.

"Where is Brook's office?"

"We passed it on the way in. But there is nothing to see there."

She glanced at him, noticing the tone of his voice.

"I suppose when you are away Brook has charge of all this?"

"In principle, yes. Unfortunately he has very little talent for management or supervision."

She was silent. "Brook is always doubting himself. If he could get out of that, Mr. Ferguson . . ."

"I have to confess," he said, not listening, "that Brook has been a great disappointment to me. I had always hoped and prayed for a son with the same sort of capabilities as my own. Brook is a highly intelligent young man, but his abilities are literary and artistic, not practical. I wish he had some of your talents, Cordelia."

"Mine?" she said. "Oh, running a house—that's different from running a great business."

"Different, but it needs the same capacities. I have mentioned it before. We have never had so little trouble with the staff of Grove Hall. It has never cost me so little to run, yet the quality of everything has improved."

She said: "Perhaps that's because I've never been rich before."

"I wasn't rich once. Like you, I know the value of money. I like to spend it, but I like it well spent."

"I'm glad I please you."

"Sometimes recently," he said, "I've quite seriously been considering whether your talents are not wasted at Grove Hall."

She met his gaze inquiringly. He looked down at her and she felt the power of the man. An all-seeing Heavenly father, almost.

"All my life I have had one failing: a reluctance to delegate responsibility. I like the reins in my own hands. I know I only can drive as I wish. But the result has been to limit. Inevitably. The people under me are unused to responsibility, and in the main are incapable of it. I lack sons and daughters, people I can rely on because they know my interests are their own. For some years now it has been the one thing holding me back from the things I want to do, from taking a larger part in public things, in the life of the city."

She said: "But Brook——"

"You are Brook's wife, not mine—and you are your own mistress. This is no more than a passing thought, a casual suggestion thrown out."

"Do you mean you have something seriously in mind?"

"If you choose to look at the thing seriously."

"But what?"

He frowned at his coat. "Especially when I am away for several days it would be of advantage to me to have someone with a general grasp of the business here, my *personal* representative, repository of my instructions yet capable of initiative of their own. A few hours a day. Not as a manager or as an employee. Of course, it would be many months before anyone could act in that way. It would mean study and trouble. But think it over. No more now."

They walked on in silence, approaching some other gates through which several horse-drawn tarpaulin-covered carts were coming.

She felt a little overwhelmed. She was also embarrassed. It is always embarrassing to be shown some special gesture of liking and trust by a person one has, however reluctantly, come to dislike.

"I don't know what Brook would say."

"No more now, please. We have said enough. We'll both think it over just for a week or two. Now look at those. I am fond of experiments. That is another experiment for you."

Beyond the gates was a narrow dismal street, unevenly cobbled, with a piece of blackened rubbish-strewn wasteland at one end, sloping to the stream. Opposite them was a three-storey building newly built of brick with a lot of windows and balconies.

"A tenement for some of my workers," he said with complacency. "Finished last year. Not a palace, but little less compared with the places they had before. More than half of them lived in cellars or a whole family to a single room. Here they have a little breathing space. It is not built as a profit-making venture but as an experiment in welfare. You've heard of Robert Owen?"

"No."

"A great innovator in this field. But he went too far. The prime essential of any experiment is that it should succeed."

An hour later she drove home alone, and that evening she had her first real quarrel with Brook.

He instantly resented her visit to the dye works, that he had not been there, that he had not been even told; but this was nothing to the explosion touched off when she told him of his father's extraordinary proposal. He saw it as a deliberate insult levelled at himself, and pretended to think that she had connived at or even invited it.

When she suggested he should go and see his father and have it out with him, he said he would indeed and left the bedroom, slamming the door behind him.

It was all rather petty and upsetting, the more upsetting for her because she found herself for once ranged on what she instinctively knew to be the wrong side. She was flattered by Mr. Ferguson's change of front and the tremendous compliment he was paying her. But this quarrel took her gratification away. She had set out to please Mr. Ferguson. She had told Brook she was going to do so, more than twelve months ago. She had done it for his sake—often it had been hard and bitter and against the grain—yet now her success had somehow taken on the appearance of treachery. In the subtle stress and counter-stress of family life they had all shifted their positions relative to each other.

Yet she knew that, even to begin to preserve some sort of balance in the house, she must side *always* with Brook against his father. While he was out of the room she tried to school herself to see this from his point of view. What upset her was that he seemed to suspect her of motives which had never entered her head. She was in the awkward position of: 'This animal is dangerous, when attacked it will defend itself.'

In the meantime she remained, most unwillingly, in Mr. Ferguson's camp.

CHAPTER ELEVEN ✿ She went to the soirée.

Her efforts at illness had been a failure. On her Monday visit to her family she thought to prepare the ground by complaining of feeling unwell, but this roused such curiosity in her mother as to the exact symptoms that she was feeling better before she left for home. She realised that if she had two days in bed at Grove Hall with the most obvious sore throat in the world, every woman in the district would jump to the wrong conclusion.

The soirée was to be presided over by the mayor and would be addressed during the course of the evening on 'Scientific Signs of the Times' by the Rev. Claude Boxley, D.D., a notably forward-thinking member of the church militant. When Mr. Slaney-Smith heard this, he wrote to the committee in protest and refused to attend the soirée, as no member of that degenerate class could be forward-thinking enough for him.

A fashionable evening, with dancing, refreshments, and the Cathedral Glee Singers. Stephen had made up a large party.

Cordelia was wearing a new dress of green and black checked taffeta, with a silk underskirt of a paler green. She persuaded herself that the event of a week ago did not mean as much to her as she'd thought. Seeing Stephen at a distance, she was able to admit his good looks without qualm, to slip quickly over the memory and feel it was not important.

The Glee Singers gave 'By Celia's Arbour' and 'When Winds Breathe Soft,' and before the clapping had died he turned to her and said:

"May I have the pleasure of this dance, Mrs. Ferguson?"

Brook was listening to a captain of the Lancashire Hussars. Other people were near: she couldn't think how to say no to her host.

"Isn't there to be another song?"

"No, not at present."

The band struck up. A waltz. She allowed herself to be led towards the floor.

He said: "I've been looking forward to this for six days. . . . Good evening, Mr. Tracey, good evening, ma'am. . . . I was scared to death you might not come."

"I shouldn't have come if I could have found a reasonable excuse."

"Praise the Saints for reason then."

"Don't talk of it now."

"When I got home . . . Oh, I took unfair advantage, and I know it."

"I think it was I who was unfair."

"You lift the weight off my mind. You're always so kind and for-giving."

Was that what she had come here to be?

"No, that isn't what I mean. . . ."

He had taken her on to the floor and with his arms about her had steered her into the dance.

"You must listen," she said breathlessly. "It isn't that I'm forgiving but that I realise the blame was partly mine. I shouldn't ever have agreed to meet you. It must end now."

"Do one thing for me," he said. "Say no more of it till we've ended this dance. We're committed to waltz together, even if it's for the last time, so let's have the pleasure of it and leave farewells till after. What do you say, now?"

". . . Yes," she said.

They were both good dancers and the floor was not crowded. For a minute or two they were just two figures among many, adapting themselves to the floor and to each other, troubled in mind, conscious of their separateness. Then the rhythmic movement began to have its effect on their bodies and their minds. They went round and round in unhurried gyrations, reversing and twisting among the other figures, finding perfect balance and union. After a time the weight of their bodies coming at the end of each swing seemed enough without effort to carry them through to the next; the music swung them on, not their own wills; their track was an endless spiral woven and interwoven among the rest. In a little while her stiff body grew softer and bent a little on his arm, her thoughts relaxed, she felt faintly but pleasantly dizzy and was only aware of his face looking into her own. They were not two people any longer but one.

Oh, God, she thought, I love him. Oh, God, what is to become of me? I love you, Stephen. I love only you. No one else matters, nothing matters but this dance, let it go on for ever; drift away, close my eyes, don't let it ever stop. . . .

And when it did stop they were fortunately in the centre of the room, for her face was so pale that he took her arm and said was she quite well? And she said yes, she was quite well. And when the band struck up for an encore, he said would she prefer to sit down? And she said no, she wanted to dance.

So it all began again, like a sensuous experience deliberately sought for a second time, as if she disbelieved it had happened and wanted the reassurance of knowing it afresh.

And this time when it was over she walked dizzily back with him to her party. Fortunately a man was talking to them, occupying their attention; she was sitting down before any of them knew she was back.

The man was Dan Massington. She hardly saw him.

"Mrs. Ferguson. Mrs. Brook Ferguson. As pretty as ever, I see. And Mr. Crossley. Good evening, Crossley."

"Good evening, Massington."

He was drunk. Something objectionable or embarrassing had been taking place. Frederick Ferguson, very handsome and imposing in the great bulk of his evening dress, was standing behind his chair frowning at Massington; Brook angry and pale.

She saw hardly anything of this, sat back frightened and shaken, trying to hold her thoughts, trying to realise what had happened to her.

Massington said to the Captain of the Hussars: "There's no telling, Frith, whom you'll meet anywhere these days, is there, Frith? It's a breakdown of society, Frith. I dreamt last night that I went into my club and who was sitting there with her feet up but our old cook. It shows, Frith. It's broken my dream, Frith. I shall be afraid to go anywhere soon."

Captain Frith said uncomfortably: "Yes, old man. Now supposing you go and sit down somewhere. It's time for the address."

" 'Scientific Signs of the Times,' " said Massington, shaking his long thin head. " 'Social Signs of the Times,' that's what it should be about, Frith. The social collapse of North Country society, Frith."

"If," said Mr. Ferguson, "it was worth arguing with you to correct your manners, I should do so. But drink is a poor help to logic. Will you please go away as Captain Frith has asked you to?"

"Drink?" said Massington. "Drink? Have you had too much? Well, it's no more than I might have expected. People who've come up often don't know how to hold their liquor. 'Jumped-up uns' is the ver-vernacular term. They ape the gentleman but you can't bring out what's not bred in the bone. Drink makes 'em soft, makes 'em rotten. . . ."

There were so many 'shushes' all round him now that he became aware of them and, seeing general disapproval, he turned and mean-dered off to a vacant seat. There was applause as the mayor came on the platform, followed by the Rev. Claude Boxley, D.D.

Nothing of the address, which seemed to last for hours. It meant nothing to her at all. After it she did not look at Stephen but went to Brook. For the first time in four days Brook and his father were at one. Adversity had united them. Mr. Ferguson would not discuss Massing-ton's insults—it was beneath his dignity to do so in public—but she could see how he felt. She listened to Brook's bitter comments without taking in what he said.

She nearly said to him: 'Something more important has happened than an insult to your dignity.' Was it more important, to him, to them, father and son? She didn't know. She didn't know anything tonight.

There was another dance and this time Teddy asked her for it. She was glad. She could relax with her brother—need not think, need not talk. But Teddy had other ideas.

"Who was that frightful bounder who came up just now?"

"Dan Massington," she said absently.

"Who's he?"

"His sister was Brook's first wife."

"Oh . . . I wonder if that's who he was talking about. No, I suppose it couldn't have been."

"About Margaret?"

"Yes, Margaret was the name. I think he was a bit drunk, wasn't he? That couple can't dance; look at the way they bob up and down. He was talking about somebody called Margaret—her death. But I thought from the way he spoke it had happened quite recently."

"She's been dead over two years now. . . ." For the moment her interest was caught. It held, a thin thread in a rushing stream. "What did he say?"

"Oh, something about it being all hushed up. And about things only being hushed up when there was something to hide. And if he'd had his way, he said, there would have been an inquest."

She did not reply. Now at this moment in the midst of all her confusion of mind . . . She could not face it fully but she knew something ugly was there. Now at this moment when above all others she needed every help to buttress up her loyalty to Brook—that loyalty which, whatever her feelings for Stephen, must go on and on and on. She had a sensation of sickly hurt but was too dejected and confused to be sure of its absolute source. Stephen, Margaret, Brook, Dan, Teddy, Stephen—they whirled round in a crazy kaleidoscope of doubt and loyalty and emotion and fear.

"I say, d'you think there's some truth in it?" said Teddy.

"No, of course not. He'd had too much to drink, that was all."

"But what did she die of, Delia? Do you know?"

"It was quite ordinary. There was nothing sinister about it."

Teddy looked faintly disappointed.

"Is this Massington man an aristocrat?"

"He's a gentleman—or supposed to be. It's an old family."

"I must say I was amused."

"Amused?"

"Yes. I expect you missed most of it. Brook and his father—well, I must confess I thought it funny how indignant they were when someone started looking down on *them!*"

"I thought they'd both been very friendly tonight."

"So they have. I say, that's a pretty girl in blue! Delia, you're not offended with me?"

"No, of course not."

"I forgot to tell you, Mother sent her love and told me to say you were not to overtire yourself. And I was to hope you were better from Monday."

"Yes, oh, yes, thank you."

"You look all right. You look fine, as a matter of fact. You've not been painting your cheeks?"

"Heavens, no!"

"Hugh and Essie are enjoying themselves. It was nice of Stephen to invite us. I think he's a jolly good fellow, don't you?"

"Yes," she said.

There was quite a lot more of the evening. Refreshments and polite conversation; the Glee Singers came on again, and more dancing. Stephen, not free from his own confusions of spirit, left Cordelia alone. He didn't want to press his attentions unduly while Brook and Mr. Ferguson were there; and also he couldn't fathom her state of mind. He knew it to be touch and go whether she carried out her threat not to see him again, and he didn't want to frighten her into it.

But then at the end of the evening, moth to flame, he could stand it no longer and, hearing another waltz, he slid up behind her chair and asked her to dance. This time, to his surprise, she made no attempt at excuse but rose and went with him to the floor.

He said: "I'm sorry, now. I know we'd agreed that other was to be the last."

"Yes," she said as he took her in his arms.

He said: "I'm always breaking my agreements, though I try so hard to keep them."

"Yes," she said.

There was silence for some moments.

"You don't want to talk," he said. "Well, let it be. Let us not talk."

The dance went on. He knew that there was some change in her, in her silence and acquiescence of mind. They were dancing as one person again: there was no stiffness in her body now, it was relaxed, pliant, defeated. They swung in absolute harmony to the slow throb of the waltz, unthinking, the music and the rhythm inside them, a pulse in their blood.

On my oath and soul, he thought suddenly: I've won. It came on him like a great flash of light, like a beacon flaring in the darkness. I've won.

CHAPTER TWELVE She changed the household arrangements so that she could visit her family on different days. When she went she took the carriage and left an hour earlier. That way she avoided seeing him. She could find no genuine interest; not in listening to Brook reading his poems, not in managing the house, not in Uncle Pridey's mice, not in Ferguson's dye works, which she visited again. Nor in the many books on dyeing Mr. Ferguson gave her to read.

In the end she resorted to Margaret's diary—as to a vice which had been tempting her for a long time.

She couldn't bring herself to read much at a time. It was not only prying into a dead woman's thoughts, it was prying into her husband's past.

On February 20, came this:

Dan here today. He's the only one I can really talk to freely and frankly. Dear Dan, how I love him! though I know it is wrong to condone his way of life. If he would only abandon his loose living he could yet become a brilliant success in some suitable profession. He feels about the Fergusons just what I do. Today he comes with a new discovery. His Lawyer friend, Mr. Fry, tells him that when Grandfather Ferguson died he left the dye works and all his other possessions equally among his three children, and that Frederick Ferguson, *my* father-in-law, has cheated the other two of their fair portion! It's a pretty story, and one I confess I believe, God forgive me for my uncharitableness. It just fits in with his character. And they, the simpletons, now live on *his* charity, and he puts on the smile of benevolence to dole out a little of what is rightly theirs!

For a time Cordelia could not read on. She sat there idly flipping the pages, trying to reject this thing as a great calumny.

February 27: Insomnia so bad that I asked Dr. Birch for more sleeping tablets. He asked me if I was worrying over anything. I said no, for what is the good of telling outsiders of these things? And they are so little when told, so big when experienced. My Bible is my great consolation. The prayers downstairs are nothing, little better than an empty sham.

March 22: Mother and Maud came. They are worried about Dan, who is spending above his income. They talk nearly all the time about their petty troubles, as if thinking I have none. Just before going Mother says I am losing weight and she shouldn't have expected it in a house where so much is spent on food!

April 6: A big fuss last evening because B. gave a reading of his poems. I wish I could think more of them. To many of these people the very faculty of being able to compose verse at all is quite a matter for wonder, but to me, brought up on Milton and Wordsworth . . .

April 12: That hateful creature S.-S. has been here laying down the law and making fantastic statements. It is queer what pride, what wicked intellectual pride there is in this house. It goeth before a fall. Last night Brook's uncle was at loggerheads with the others because S.-S. made some disparaging remark about a horrible dead rat he had stuffed. They are like children, *children*, pretending to play at some adult scientific game. They have a little trumpery knowledge, but *no* wisdom. I should pray for them, it is a confession of failure that I cannot.

That was as much as Cordelia could face in one day. She felt as if she were getting to know Margaret, as if she had met her and was becoming her intimate. She didn't think she would have liked Margaret if they had really met, but the diary, although it did not show the writer up in a nice light, showed up the Fergusons in a worse one.

It was dismal sitting up in the attic amid the dust and the old books, but she could not bring herself to carry the diary downstairs.

The second day it was raining and the light from the dormer windows, coming through the dirt and dust, was very poor.

April 19: Not seen Dan for two months until today. Had a quarrel with him which much upset me. I taxed him with what Mr. F. had told me: that he was throwing all his money away on the Porteus woman. He denied it, but I don't know which of them to believe. A pretty confession, that I don't know whether to believe my own brother or this man who has ruined my life. Before he left we made it up, and to save me getting up I asked him to pass me my iron pills, which I had hidden in the corner cupboard. He called me 'Old Jackdaw,' and the old familiar name struck strange echoes in my memory. Those happy times!

May 12: All this undercooked meat that Dr. Birch prescribes revolts me. Besides, I can't digest it. Think I shall demand my own doctor. Dr. Vernon is so different.

May 20: Mr. Ferguson and Brook both away. Made great effort and went downstairs. Think I was better for it, only at the end . . .

As Cordelia turned the page she heard a light footstep in the shadows behind her.

Before she could stir a voice said:

"Pretty pastime for a young woman!"

She turned and stared up into the face of Uncle Pridey.

. . . Her heart began to beat again, her circulation to move. She swallowed something in her throat but could not speak. She groped on the floor for the book she had dropped.

He grinned. "D'you think it was one of those ghosts we raised at the séance?"

The best defence. "What are you doing here, Uncle Pridey? It's horrible to creep around like that!"

He squatted beside her. "Didn't *really* frighten you, did I? Sorry. It seemed a good joke when I saw you creeping up the stairs."

She picked up one or two books, contrived to hide the tell-tale diary among the others. It could only be a clumsy movement, but it might serve with Pridey.

" 'S a matter of fact I've just finished my book," he said. "I was coming to tell you when I saw you moving this way. Care to see it?"

"Yes, I should."

Shyly, a grey old man producing the toy he had fumbled over for years, he took a manuscript from under his arm. It was a thick wad of paper neatly but amateurishly bound. On the front was written in fine script, *Habits and Heredity in Mice, with Some Observations on the Anatomy and Behaviour of the Common Shrew, by Thomas Pride Ferguson.*

"May I open it?"

"Yes, yes, of course, go on, go on."

She opened the manuscript at random, trying to read a paragraph here and there. It was finely written, and there were diagrams. As her mind unfroze, allowing normal thought, there came a sensation of pity for this queer old man who had been deprived of his true place in the world and had turned his attention, his time, and all his thoughts to the study of vermin. Perhaps he, too, in his youth had been an idealist like his brother, dreaming of social progress and reform but lacking his brother's domineering spirit. So he had allowed himself to be pushed out of his true place, and his idealism had turned inward and become eccentricity.

Now was to come this last test in which all his mind's wandering speculations were to come out into the open and be measured against the standards of ordinary men. She wished he had never completed it, so that it could remain for his private happiness and could never be ignored or derided.

"Have the others seen it?"

"Heavens, no!"

"I'm very flattered."

"You've no need to be. Would *you* show it to Aunt Tish?"

"Well, perhaps not to her."

"Unless it was a book on corns. Or to Brook unless it was on Shelley or Chopin?"

"I think he'd be interested."

"Or to Frederick unless it was about the religious practices of the lost tribes of Israel? Or to Slaney-Smith unless it had 'Evolution' written on every page?"

"What are you going to do with it, then?"

He was cracking his knuckles. "Biology's in the news, thanks to this Huxley fellow. Might do worse than get it published, make a bit of money. It won't be fashionable, mind, but I haven't watched the little beggars for nothing. Oh, that reminds me; hope I haven't squashed 'em. . . ."

He felt in his coat pocket and produced three tiny wriggling baby shrews betweens his fingers. They were revoltingly small and hairless and scrawny. He put them on the floor and took out another handful. As he put these down Cordelia drew back her skirts with a gasp.

"Just born," he said. "Just born. Don't be scared of them. They're quite blind. They can't run after you, so you won't need a carving knife." He drew out an odd couple he had found in the corners of his pockets. "They'll snap soon enough but they can't snap yet. Notice anything peculiar? No, you wouldn't. Two of 'em are normal: five have only got four toes on each foot. Interesting, isn't it? Their father and mother have each only got four toes: very rare: I've inbred it for seven generations from one freak. Curious thing is I can't get a complete four-toed litter: this is the most freaks I've got; very encouraging; but the normal keeps pushing its way up. Drat the normal, I say. What's the good of the normal even in human beings? There's too much normality. We should get away from it."

"They look as if they all need overcoats," said Cordelia.

"You sound disgusted: is it the shrews or the theory? Don't you believe in inbreeding? What's wrong with it except that it breeds peculiarity? What's wrong with peculiarity? Look at our family. A bit out of the ordinary but the better for that. Two good brains and one bad one: it's a fair average; better than three nonentities. Have a sweet. No: you'd better not; Mr. Gladstone's been at 'em."

"Our family?" she said.

"Yes, in a small way. My father and mother were first cousins, didn't you know? Both Fergusons. I'm all in favour of it. If I'd married I should have tried to find a cousin too. It doubles the pluses in your children—and the minuses as well, but it's a fair risk. Look at Frederick. Look at me. Don't you think it's worth the risk of an occasional Tish?"

". . . Did Mr. Ferguson marry a cousin too?"

"Frederick? Heavens, no. Married a Miss Potter from Stretford. A dull little woman, but she suited him." Uncle Pridey began to pick up his shrews. "Don't worry, there's small risk of four-toed freaks in your children."

She moved away from him, moved to the window and stared up at the rain. She heard Pridey pick up his manuscript and flip lovingly through the pages. Two good brains and one bad one, she thought. Or should it be one good brain and two bad? . . . Or three bad? Where did brain and character overlap?

"Have you always been interested in mice, Uncle Pridey?"

"I kept them as a lad. But not scientifically. One time I wanted to be a doctor, but it didn't work out. They began to breed, but not in cages, so they had to be destroyed."

"I think I'll go downstairs."

"Always had a liking for cutting up," he said, chewing. "Might have made a surgeon. Couldn't be, so I cut up mice. When they're dead, of course. What? Oh, yes, I'll come with you."

"Thank you for showing me your book."

"Oh, tut. I'll give you a copy when it's printed. More than Slaney-Smith will get. Or Frederick unless he recants his heresies."

CHAPTER THIRTEEN Brook was away for a week in Oldham. She had suggested going with him, but Mr. Ferguson had not wanted it. She was afraid of being left alone, but the old man's objections had their way.

While Brook was absent, in fact, she was more occupied than usual, for Mr. Ferguson took her down three times to the dye works and showed her everything in great detail. Against Brook's wishes, and with no formal consenting decision from her, Mr. Ferguson was pushing ahead with his plans.

It was a fine June, and the only real balm to her turbulent loneliness was the garden. Beyond the lawns and the lilacs was a walled garden with roses and peaches on the walls and raspberries and blackberries in cages. Used to the restricted untidiness of the long strip behind the shop, she found all this a delight. As often as possible she worked in it herself, especially during the long evenings after supper when Farrow and Bollard had finished for the day and she could potter about undisturbed. It was a peaceful loneliness then, to be borne without too much discomfort.

The sun set over the wall just before eight and she was cutting some Gloire de Dijon roses, glad of the long shadows and the cooling air, sniffing each rose as she picked it and regretting they would soon be over, when she heard the crack of a twig at the other side of the garden and saw that a man had just come into the garden through the arched doorway at the far end. It was Stephen.

She stood quite still, roses in hand, not breathing until he came up with her. He looked severe, and desperate.

"Why have you been avoiding me?" he said.

She didn't reply.

"Why have you not been meeting me?" he said.

"Does anyone—know you're here?"

"No," he said. "I came over the wall."

She glanced round. "Come this way."

She led him into a corner made by the wall and the larger greenhouse.

None of this garden was overlooked by the house, but here they were not so plain to be seen if someone came to the gate.

He looked at her closely, at her young face lowered, at the fine rich hair, the white muslin frock. Her brown lashes hid the quick vitality of her eyes.

"Why haven't you met me, now?"

"Isn't it plain?"

"That you've no heart at all?"

"No."

"That it's all ended between us?"

". . . Yes."

"Because you don't care?"

"Do you think that?"

"Is your feeling for Brook what you feel for me?"

"Oh, Stephen, don't ask me. . . ."

"Cordelia."

"Yes."

"I've been crazy for you so long. I'm tired and—hungry."

She looked up at him again. And she didn't say anything. He put his arms about her and drew her to him. He looked down closely into her face.

"Cordelia."

"Yes?"

"You love me, don't you?"

"I . . ."

"Tell me."

". . . Yes, Stephen."

He kissed her—at first hesitantly and then more surely. The salmon-yellow roses twisted and turned in her hand, fell to the ground, lay in a trickle of water which had run from the plants in the greenhouse. She took a step back and his foot crushed one of the roses, soiling its fine petals in the mud. He put his hands to her temples, raised her face and stared into it, kissed her eyes and her cheeks and her mouth.

At first she was quiescent, yielding defeated in his grasp, but after a time she put her arms round his neck, the rough gloves still on, and then she clung to him so that he could kiss her no more.

He pushed open the door of the greenhouse and they were inside; he found a wooden seat for her, knelt and wiped her eyes.

"Don't cry. There's nothing to fret about, my sweetheart."

"I'm not crying. Just leave me a minute. I'll be all right."

"I can't leave you now—when I've just found you."

They stayed quiet for a while. About them there was the smell of grape vines and heliotrope and the damp earth.

She looked at him with glittering eyes, dabbed them and half laughed. "I'm sorry. You shouldn't have come on me so suddenly. It was the shock."

"Did you think you would keep me out for ever?"

"I didn't think that far."

"Do you often come in this garden?"

"Most evenings when it's fine."

"What a fool I've been! Night after night I've waited outside, for some chance—and all the time there was this. We must meet here often."

"No . . ."

"Why not?"

"We're sure to be seen, for one thing."

"Not after dark. People can't see in the dark. Can't you slip away?"

"Only while Brook's not here."

"Well, while Brook's not here. And we can meet in other places. If you'll promise to play fair and not keep avoiding me, we can soon fix something up."

". . . Why hadn't you the courage to keep away?"

"If that's courage," he said, "then I'd not be wanting it. Why are you always fretting yourself? Tell me now at this moment: aren't you happy? Be quite honest and tell me."

Happy? She didn't know. She was shaken, transported; her heart was thumping.

"Ah, well, if you won't say it," he said, "I will. *I'm* happy. There's nobody got the advantage of me in the British Isles. You've told me you love me. You can't get away from that. Whatever fences you raise or walls you build, you can't escape from that."

"*I* haven't raised the fences," she said. "They were there when we met."

"Then I'll trample them down. By all the Saints, I'll trample them down!"

He kissed her again, till she broke from him and groped a way down the darkening greenhouse. Then he followed her and caught at her arm and asked her pardon, and she gave it and they sat together on the stone wall under the vine.

They talked in whispers. She was glad of the chance to talk, though at the back of her mind a voice cried that it was asking for trouble staying so long, and her white frock would be stained with tell-tale marks and her roses were lost.

He wouldn't let her go until she'd promised the time and the place tomorrow.

Then she left him and tiptoed through the garden and across the lawn, up to the door of the french windows to the library. The room was in darkness as she slipped in. She bumped into a chair unexpectedly in her path, reached the door, which was ajar.

The hall, of course, was lighted. She was about to pick up her skirts and run to the stairs when Mr. Ferguson came out of his study. She slipped back from the door, listened to his footsteps, his breathing coming nearer.

Then they passed, the drawing-room door opened, and he went in. This time she came out more boldly, trying to hide her trembling hands, and safely reached the stairs.

It was mad to promise to meet again, but somehow now this was beyond her. She was in love for the first time in her life. All the old alarms were jangling; and conscience and deeply grown beliefs, her own reason; but the voices were muted, for the moment they could not get *at* her in the old way.

And supporting the new rule were all the little niggling insurrectionary thoughts: Brook, Mr. Ferguson, Margaret, Dan, diaries, doctors, whispered scandal.

As she sat the next night in her bedroom by the light of a single shaded candle watching the clock creep towards eleven, she knew that this next meeting was a sort of watershed in their affairs. She'd no thought of immorality; but to go down to meet a man in the garden late at night would be accepted by everyone as the equivalent thing.

The clock, her father's clock, reached the hour and faint whirrings began in its inside, the tongue on the face quivered, but it all ended in silent frustration like a man trying to speak who has lost his voice.

She got up and put a velvet dolman over her dark dress, snuffed out the candle. Then she opened the door, which creaked slightly, and peered out. All in darkness except a faint light under Mr. Ferguson's door. Reading in bed.

Slide out, closing the door, silently down the stairs. In the library the french windows were bolted. Stand on a chair to reach the upper bolt. A sibilant rusty screech. When she got down she sat breathless on the chair a few seconds, listening. All quiet.

She opened the windows and squeezed out, pulling them to behind her. The night was overcast and very warm. The clouds were right down on top of the house, and it was so still she could hear a night moth fluttering somewhere among the leaves. She took two steps down, and a few across the short-cropped grass. Then from among the shrubs a figure rose, and in a second she was in his arms.

Just the fact of his being there seemed to set her at rest.

"You're trembling," he whispered in her ear. "Are you cold, my sweetheart? There now, we'll change that."

"No—it's not that—— Let's get further away."

She led a groping way towards the walled garden. There was no need to hide in the greenhouse tonight. It was so dark they could scarcely see each other.

They sat on a garden seat under one of the cordon pears.

Something restrained him tonight, made him hold off. In five months he'd come to understand her a little—and had grown himself in the understanding. This thing that he had embarked on so lightly had run him on to unexpected shoals. Last night he had been beside himself with joy that he had carried the strongest defences. Tonight an unusual self-doubt prevented him from pressing the victory.

They talked in low voices and again she was glad to talk. He told her more about his life, and she told him more of hers. For the first time in eighteen months she had a confidant. Pride had kept her silent with her own family. But Stephen she was able to tell about Frederick Ferguson, about Margaret's death and the secrecy surrounding it, about the peculiarities of her daily life in Grove Hall. Merely to speak of them was half the battle.

He kept holding the dolman round her, but there was no chill in the air. They talked on and on, content to exchange confidences, not aware of the passage of time.

After a while the night seemed to lighten and they saw each other more clearly. When at length she asked the time he peered at his watch and saw it to be nearly one. He quickly lied, telling her it was just after twelve, but that was bad enough, and she rose at once to go. So after a while she left him, giving a promise to meet him again the following night.

She crept back and into the library; a last touch of fingers and he was gone, irretrievably gone, and she was alone; the upper bolt of the french windows gave a faint screech; then through the library and stealing up the stairs; no breath but the lightest, her heart thumping; to her door; the light under Mr. Ferguson's was out; asleep, that great figure in bed; and Uncle Pridey and Aunt Tish and eleven servants; only herself creeping, and outside in the darkness Stephen walking, walking back across country to his own home.

CHAPTER FOURTEEN ❧ The next morning she had a letter from Brook, one of the first he had ever written her. It was unexpectedly affectionate. Brook's life was the life of the imagination;

being apart from her gave that imagination scope and he was happy in expressing it. She felt like a thief.

In the afternoon she was due to visit her family, but Mr. Ferguson wanted her. The old man was home for dinner at twelve-thirty and drove her back with him to the works. There for the first time she attended one of the meetings at which the heads of all the departments were present. Mr. Ferguson introduced those she had not already met and she sat between him and Simnel at the table, listening to all that was said. Stolid, broad-spoken men in shabby velveteen jackets, they were all a little self-conscious in her presence, as she was in theirs, but he took no notice of that. At the end he told them his reason for having her there, that sometimes in the future it might be necessary for both Mr. Brook and himself to be absent, and if that was the case Mrs. Brook Ferguson would be his personal deputy. He praised her very highly and she was acutely uncomfortable under it. What, she thought, if I got up and said: 'You may think I have a head for business, but do you happen to know that I've lost it over Stephen Crossley; I'm infatuated like any other silly woman; you see all the other people are right and you are wrong: women are not to be trusted'?

She was angry with them both because they had chosen this day of all days to state their affection and trust.

In the evening Mr. Ferguson was out at a lecture. This was something she'd not expected and it was ten-thirty before he got home. As always the house must wait up for him, so that servants were moving about until half-past eleven, and Mr. Ferguson did not close his door until a quarter to twelve. Midnight came before she stood on the lawn wondering, half hoping, half fearing that Stephen had gone.

He came up like a shadow behind her as she crept past the laurels. "Delia."

"Oh . . . I thought . . ."

They moved off again towards the walled garden.

"I daren't come before."

"Something went wrong? I could tell by the lights."

She whispered explanations as they went. Rain was dripping from his hat and cloak; he said he had been afraid to stir from near the window lest he miss her; it must have seemed an endless ninety minutes, but he was not in the least perturbed about it, as Brook would have been. She loved his high spirits, his unreserved welcome. Obstacles didn't seem to depress him; he took them all as part of the fun.

Tonight they sheltered in the greenhouse, and something about the situation brought them closer to each other at once. They laughed together at the discomfort, and he kissed away her laughter and put his arms under her arms and held her tight so that he could feel the

128

beating of her heart. Later they talked, and he told her easily that he had sought out Dan Massington at his club that day and pumped him about his sister. (He didn't confess that he'd done it once before.) It all came down to something about sleeping tablets. She'd died quite suddenly, and the doctor had asked some questions about the number of sleeping tablets she'd been given. That much Dan knew but no more, but, Stephen gathered, he hadn't learned even this until after the funeral.

"Dr. Birch is a great friend of the Fergusons," said Cordelia. "I can't understand it—why should he say anything unless there was very good reason?"

"Why bother your head, my sweetheart? Aren't we wasting time on it when we could be talking about ourselves?"

"It's important to me, Stephen," she said. "In a queer way I can't quite explain."

"Well, shall I go and see the old man about it for you?"

"Heavens, no! Not on any account."

"I'm glad of that, for I shouldn't have liked the job."

Used by now to the endless cosseting of Brook, she was afraid he would catch a chill from his damp clothes, but he laughed at her. Brook was due back on Saturday; they had one more evening like this if they chose to take it; then it meant every sort of contriving.

When at last she rose to go it was with the promise that she should see him again tomorrow in the garden at eleven. She said she would pray for a fine night. He patted her hand and said far better pray for a dark one.

They reached the french windows and kissed and separated, and she turned and gently pushed the window. It did not move. She pushed again. A dreadful sick fear turned in her heart. She put her finger-nails to the nick in the wet wood.

He came up behind her. "Well, and what's the matter?"

"Its—locked. . . ."

She stood there while he tried the door cautiously himself. She stood there with the cold perspiration breaking out on her face and hands. She saw that he couldn't move it. She looked about and saw the stone steps and sat on one of them. The dark night suddenly began to move round her.

He was again beside her.

"Don't give up. It's a mere detail. We shall find another way in." She put her face in her hands. "So someone saw me. . . ."

"It doesn't follow at all. Someone will have come round and found it open. D'you know of another way in?"

"No."

"What about the ordinary windows?"

"All the ground-floor windows are closed and locked at night by Hallows."

He stood up and stared through the rain, his hands on his hips.

"It's a big house to be secured against a burglar. I would take a bet it'll not be hard. Aren't there pantries and things?"

"I think they all have gratings."

"Well, we can see. Tell me what other doors there are."

She tried to take a grip on herself. She could see it all: Frederick Ferguson's stony face, Brook's incredulous hurt, the whispering servants, her father and mother, Hugh Scott, Teddy, all her new friends. Her love for Stephen was suddenly tainted by the peering eyes of the world.

She told him about the back quarters. But she warned him of the servants sleeping overhead and of the horses and of Bob and Mrs. Tomkins sleeping in the room above the stables. He urged her to go back to the greenhouse while he looked around, but she wouldn't move.

While he was gone she took the shawl from round her head and let the rain fall on her face and hair. It helped, cooling the warmth which had followed the sickly sweat. Her steadying reason began to work. If someone had seen her, then she was lost in any case—unless one could invent a string of lies to fit the case: and at once her brain set about inventing them. No one had seen Stephen; she had felt ill and gone out into the garden—— She pulled her mind away from its ready deceits. If no one had seen her, then might she not be able to spend the night in the greenhouse and slip in unobserved in the morning?

He came back frustrated, and at once she put her idea: that he should go home and that she should—— He shook his head.

"The very last thing. Far better for you to come home with me and then we could face it out together."

She shrank from this proposition, which he put on impulse, and he was privately relieved that she did so. The last thing he really wanted at the moment was a resounding scandal and a blow-up with his father.

It was a pretty problem but he was not downhearted yet.

"Which is your room?"

"It's on the first floor round the corner."

"Is the window open?"

"Yes, but there's no way up."

"Let me see where it is."

He led her round to the west side of the house. Her bedroom was above the dining-room. "Glory be, that's easy! There's ivy and a drain-pipe—— I used to climb twice as far as that at school every Saturday night of my life. Are all three windows yours?"

"Yes. Well, the far one is our dressing-room." She caught his hand. "I'd rather take the other risk."

"Away with you. It's nothing. Which is the best window to open?"

"The dressing-room, I think. The sash works easiest."

He asked her for particulars of the plan of the house and then he was gone. She saw him take off his shoes and put his cloak and hat over them. Then he tested the drainpipe and began to climb.

He seemed to take it for granted that the french windows had been locked by someone unsuspectingly. She, knowing the household better, did not believe anything of the sort.

CHAPTER FIFTEEN It was not difficult for a young and energetic man. The ivy was thick at the bottom and the thin exploratory strands at the top were just tenacious enough to give him hand-holds. In three or four minutes he was at the dressing-room window, one hand over the ledge, and groping for a firm grip inside the room.

He found it and was able to release his other hand; with that he slowly slid the window up far enough to get in.

Now the difficult part. His eyes were used to the dark, but even so there was the danger of knocking over a table or sweeping something off a chair. She need not have told him this was her room; some perfume she used hung faintly in the air.

He crept across it and found the door of the bedroom shut. It creaked when he opened it and he stared round the larger room. A dark object lay nearly at his feet and he picked it up: it was her dressing-gown which had fallen from behind the door. He fingered it affectionately before dropping it on a chair.

But there was some alien presence here too. Things about the room bespoke the accustomed presence of a man. Stephen didn't like that so much. Brook had somehow been a nonentity in his mind.

With this in his thoughts he was not so careful as he might have been opening the outer bedroom door, and the catch clicked with a noise to wake the dead.

Half in and half out of the room, he stared round the square landing, half expecting a light to go on under one of the other doors. But the landing remained in darkness. There was a little wind, and he did not dare to leave the door unlatched. He felt behind it and down came something which felt like an underskirt to drop on the floor and prevent a bang. Then he groped for the stairs.

Somewhere not far away someone was snoring. He couldn't tell the sex of the snorer, but the sound was reassuring and brought a mischievous picture to his mind. The English commercial baron in his provincial castle, snoring his head off, secure in the knowledge of locked and bolted doors, while the despoiler, the worm in the bud, the thief in the night—he didn't underestimate the names he would be called—crept at his leisure about the stronghold.

Once on the ground floor, he felt more sure of his way. No one slept downstairs, and he knew how the house was planned. They had arranged to meet at the french windows, but now, over-confident, he made his first mistake and chose the wrong door.

It was a much smaller room, and he guessed at once it was Mr. Ferguson's study. He was about to back out again when he heard someone breathing.

Frozen, expecting to hear a voice or to feel a hand on his shoulder . . . But the breathing went on. He hesitated, peering, not able to see anything. Curtains drawn. Mr. Ferguson's breathing; its heaviness unmistakable. He was asleep.

But for how long asleep and how soundly?

The door had made no noise as he opened it: now with infinite care and patience he began to close it again, holding it to with his nails while he slowly released the handle.

It was shut.

He turned and moved to the other door, sweating a little now, but did not open it. There might be some other trap in here. Quick thinking and new thinking.

He moved across the hall to the front door, feeling with his fingers. Two accursed bolts and a key. They would all screech like devils in torment.

Into the dining-room. Here, he remembered, was a low window looking on the lawn. He tried the catch and it moved easily. He opened the window and vaulted lightly out.

Then he ran round the house.

He found her where he had left her.

"Thank Heaven!" she breathed, standing up. "But did you get in? I've been trying to think, to——"

"In easily. But there's one little small sort of complication." He explained it.

She was steadier now. While he was away she had steeled herself to meet the worst. This very nearly was the worst. He had evidently heard her leave and followed her down.

"No, no; who says so? Anyway, for the moment he's asleep like a babe. Can you get in through a window? The dining-room window."

"Yes."

They reached the dining-room. He climbed in first. She followed. It would have been easy if they had not been so afraid of the smallest noise.

Inside he caught her to him. "Listen, sweetheart. Rely on me. Don't be afraid. Go straight to bed and get up tomorrow as if nothing in the world had happened. I'll be round in the evening before dark. Can you arrange a signal?"

"Yes."

"If you can get out as usual make no signal. That clear?"

"Yes."

"If things are all right but you can't get out, what then?"

"I'll put a handkerchief—my dressing-room window."

"Right. And if things are *wrong* and you can't get out, two handkerchiefs?"

"Yes." They repeated the arrangement. Then he kissed her and left.

His last words were: "Don't worry your head, now. There'll be no footprints on the flower-beds. I've all night to do it. Get out of those wet things and go to bed. Good night."

He was gone. She turned as in a nightmare, climbed the stairs, trembling, and reached her room, shut the door, stood with her back to it, taking deep difficult breaths. There were still four hours till morning.

She slept a little, like a storm-tossed ship rent by the gales of nightmare. Faces peered at her, great voices whispered, she was discovered or nearly discovered a dozen times, she crept away from following footsteps, she tried to lock doors against insinuating hands, she fell out of windows and started into wakefulness to find the darkness as intense as ever and the rain drumming steadily on the roof.

Dawn was an age, and when it had fully broken she got up and washed her face and hands and then lay quiet for a time listening to the noises of the slow-awakening house. What was the house waking to —to another normal day or to accusations and scandal?

Mr. Ferguson did not approve of tea before prayers, but while he was having his bath she slipped down to the kitchen, got the cook to brew some, and drank it quickly.

At twenty-five past seven the servants began assembling in the hall, and at twenty-nine minutes past exactly Mr. Ferguson came in. He said good morning to his brother and sister and to Cordelia without particular significance of expression, and prayers were read. Then they went in to breakfast.

The meal as usual. Uncle Pridey said the rain had spoiled the roses;

Aunt Tish said she'd said all along it had been going to rain yesterday, her corns had been springeing that bad. Mr. Ferguson was a little more silent than usual. Cordelia forced her breakfast down, though each mouthful stuck like a lump in her throat.

While the servants were out of the room Mr. Ferguson said steadily: "Did you hear anything last night, Tom?"

Pridey grunted. "Rain in plenty. Mr. Gladstone was restless. Perhaps he's got corns like Tish."

"There was someone about."

"Someone about? What d'you mean: burglars?"

"Eh, don't say it was burglars, Frederick. I'd never rest easy in my bed, nay, I wouldn't that."

"I came down for a book shortly after midnight and found the french windows in the library not only unlocked but swinging open."

"At *that* time? What was Hallows doing?"

"That I have yet to inquire. I locked the windows and considered rousing the house, but that seemed a little alarmist; also I thought if there was an accomplice within the house . . . So I waited in my study until well after two. The top bolt of the french windows makes a distinct noise, and I knew I should hear it if anyone opened it again. No one did, but this morning I examined the flower-beds carefully, and two geraniums had been broken off in the bed under the dining-room window."

"The dining-room window! Was that open?"

"No, securely locked. Did you hear anything in the night, Cordelia?"

She said indistinctly: "I'm afraid I fell asleep rather early."

"I shall see Hallows straight after breakfast and see what he has to say," said Mr. Ferguson, breathing. "In any case I shall inform the police. In the meantime say nothing to the other servants. I intend to get to the bottom of this."

So we are safe. *Just* safe. Hallows will get a blowing up. And the police will be warned. Warn Stephen. He mustn't walk into a trap. But how? Can't go to Town because the Griffins and Dr. Birch and the Vicar are coming to tea. A message. Who would take it?

Upstairs in her bedroom she took a piece of notepaper and wrote:

All well but you must not come. Danger. C.

She sealed the envelope and addressed it to Stephen at his home. He must go back there some time during the day or evening.

About eleven she put on her outdoor things and walked down the Grove in the direction of Town. The day was warm and sultry but fine, and the heavy rain of the night had washed the drains and killed the dust. She walked on for half a mile until she came to an old man sitting with a wicker basket of artificial flowers. He had a cataract over one eye and was here most days of the week. She asked him if he knew where Moss Side was. He said he did. She then offered him a shilling if he would deliver the letter for her, promising to give him another shilling if the message reached its destination. He agreed eagerly and she returned to Grove Hall with an easier mind.

The tea-party in the afternoon went its humdrum way. In the middle of it Dr. Birch was called away, and this made things worse, for she liked his alert, modest, definitive way of talking. At supper Mr. Ferguson said Hallows had sworn he locked the window. The police had been told and would keep a special eye on the house.

She spent some time in the garden but was careful to put a handkerchief under the sash of her window just in case Stephen had not had her message. As dusk fell the gases were lit, and she read a book and watched Aunt Tish falling to sleep in her chair and wished she could do the same. At a quarter after ten Mr. Ferguson came out of his study, and that was a general sign for the household to move. By half-past ten, as usual, everyone was upstairs and the lights going out.

Alarm had slowly died in her. They had been tremendously lucky to escape, but chance and Stephen's enterprise had saved them. Now all the old perplexities remained but not, *not* the dreadful expectation of immediate exposure. She took the handkerchief out of the window-sash and began to undress. Because of this awful scare they had not been able to make any plans for meeting again. Just now even that didn't seem to matter beside the relief of being safe from discovery. If it ever *did* come to some break with her present life, then, please God, let it be open and above board, not secretive, not turned up ashamed to the light like a slug under a stone.

She folded her clothes and dropped on her knees beside the bed. She didn't seem to know the solution to anything any more. Last night she had prayed for deliverance from discovery, but tonight that didn't seem quite a respectable prayer. Even to return thanks for it——

She heard a footstep in her dressing-room.

On her feet in an instant, she turned and backed towards the curtains at the head of the bed and saw the door of the dressing-room slowly open.

It was Stephen.

He was hatless, wearing an old tweed jacket, grey trousers, soft rubber shoes. His eyes were narrowed with the light. They stared at each other.

"Stephen! Didn't you get my message!"

"Yes, I did," he said grimly. "What was wrong?"

"They thought it was burglars—told the police. They're on watch."

"Oh—the police. I wouldn't worry about the police. They didn't suspect you?"

"No. . . . How did you get in?"

"Through the window—like last night. Practice makes perfect."

She picked up her dressing-gown and struggled into it.

"When I heard your footstep I couldn't move, couldn't think——"

"You're shocked?"

"Not—exactly. But supposing someone saw you . . ."

"No one could. It's like a coal cellar outside."

"But I told you to stay away."

"I know. You can tell me." His eyes were heavy on hers, with something sombre and positive in their brown depths. "I know you can tell me; but it doesn't work, Delia. Brook will be back tomorrow. I had to see you tonight."

"It was madness to come."

He said: "Will anyone hear us talking?"

"Not—like this."

"Is your door locked?"

"No. . . ."

He went across and carefully turned the key in the lock. Hands behind her back, standing against the curtains of the bed in her white dressing-gown and white nightgown, she moved her head and watched him.

An unrelated act can sometimes change the note of an encounter. The turning of the key seemed to cut off from their minds all the substance of their first sentences. Last night—the police—the risk of discovery: they were locked out, outside the door; within was a sphere of its own, intimately held within four walls, close, personal, secret. He turned and stood with his back to the door and looked at her. And she looked back at him.

He came across. She seemed young and unprotected. But there was no self-doubt in his love just then. She put her hands on his shoulders with a half attempt to hold him off; she struggled in his grasp, turning this way and that, but with a feebleness that showed her own love.

"Don't be frightened, sweetheart, please," he said. "There's nothing to be scared of. We love each other, don't we? That's all that matters. You can't go on being lonely and unhappy all your life. What's the use of fighting against ourselves. . . ."

He went on talking, and she listened, not to what he said but to the tone of his voice, which flowed like a wave over her reluctance, softening and sapping the last reserves. She seemed to be sliding into a darkness without time or thought, and there came a moment when her life was lost and she allowed herself to go on madly without effort down the increasing slope.

CHAPTER SIXTEEN ❧ Brook was in exceptionally good spirits. A letter had been forwarded on to him from the Athenæum inviting him to read some of his poems at a *conversazione* to be held there next month. It was an honour he had hoped for for years, and it had fallen to him just at the right time, when his self-esteem was at its lowest ebb.

He was well, too, something so rare that his spirits went bounding up. He chatted away to Cordelia, his minor grievances forgotten. He didn't even seem to mind that she had been down to the dye works three times in his absence. Had she been in a mood to appreciate it, she would have realised that he lived perpetually with a sense of inferiority and for his very salvation he fought against admitting further encroachments.

They talked about holidays.

At length he said: "What's the matter, dear? Don't say *you're* not feeling well."

"No, I'm very well," she said. "It's this sultry heat."

"Did you miss me?"

"Of course."

"Did you have any visitors?"

She told him about the Friday tea-party.

"Friday?" he said. "D'you mean yesterday?"

"Oh . . . Was it only yesterday? Yes, I suppose so. It seems a long time ago."

"There *is* something the matter," he said. "Is it Father?"

"No. It's nobody. I told you. The weather's oppressive. I think I'll lie down for a while."

"Just as you say, dear."

Lie down for a while but not to sleep. Friday was yesterday. No, it wasn't, it was another life ago. You live a life in a few hours. At first, at the first onset of his love-making she had felt sick, half angry, humiliated, desperately frightened of discovery. He could not have chosen a worse time—with the previous night's escape still fresh, with the probability of police about, with some of the household certainly on the *qui vive*. She submitted to his caresses in a condition of mind which could hardly have been worse had she known Mr. Ferguson to be sitting in her dressing-room.

Somewhere, too, in the depths of her mind, hardly formulated as thought, was resentment that for this final acquiescence he had left her no freedom of choice. Yet he had conquered in the end. Her horizons of experience were enlarged beyond all imagining.

Brook did not press his questions any more, but several times he glanced at her and wondered. Like most ailing people, he was self-absorbed, but he was by no means insensitive to other people's feelings, and he felt there was some change in her adverse to him, though he was infinitely far from guessing the truth.

She saw no more of Stephen for a long time. She kept closely to Grove Hall and wrote to her mother saying that she was helping Mr. Ferguson and would not be able to see much of them for a month or so. Then she pressed Brook to take her away, and they spent part of July at Southport. She strove constantly to recapture her old feeling for Brook, but could not because she had never actually lost it. It was only that something stronger had come between. She could have fallen out of love with Stephen tomorrow and it would have made no difference. One can never go back on experience.

Brook, utterly lost as to causes, fumbled blindly with effects, which she could not altogether hide from him. His own love for her, perversely provoked, grew stronger, and there was an odd personal kindliness in their relationship with each other.

As for Stephen, she did not know what efforts he had made to see her; she only knew they had not been successful. But in fact Stephen had only made one or two attempts, and they were half-hearted. For most of the time they were in Southport he was in London.

On an afternoon in late July he walked down a pleasant street in Maida Vale and knocked at the door of a small house at the end of a row. A maid came to the door and he asked if Mrs. Crossley was in. She was a new maid and he had to give his name. She said she would inquire, and after rather a long wait she showed him into a white-painted sitting-room. There was no one there, but some needlework lying on a table looked as if it had just been put down.

He stared about him, gazed out of the window at a hansom setting down a passenger, picked up a book, and glanced at the title.

A young woman came in.

"Well, my dear, how are you?" he said. "You wouldn't know I was in London, I suppose? I thought I'd give you a surprise. You're looking very well."

She was in the middle twenties, with a slender yet slightly voluptuous figure. When she saw him her fine dark eyes had lit up, but at something in the tone of his voice she looked sulky again.

"Yes, it's a surprise," she said. "Have you had tea?"

"I've had some, but I'd like some more."

They chatted conventionally while the maid brought tea. He talked more than usual, she less; but gradually under his easy influence she thawed again.

138

"D'you like Manchester?" she said.

"Oh, it's all right. I get along all right."

"Trust you. I picture it sometimes," she said. "Drab streets, smoking mills, cobbles, and clogs. Is it like that?"

"Oh, no. And yes. It's got a social side. The people are interesting. Full of contradictions. They've been generous enough to me. We're doing well at the Variety."

She glanced at him.

"When are you going back?"

"Tomorrow or Wednesday."

"Is this just a friendly call?"

He smiled uneasily. "Could it be anything else?"

"Can you blame me for wondering?"

He got up, went to the window, stirring his tea. "I didn't think you felt anything any more."

"Oh." She shrugged. "I don't know that I do." But it was a lie and it made his task more difficult.

"I think you used to like having me about. I think that was it."

"Is that the way you remember it?"

"No. No, it isn't. We had fun for a couple of years. Lots of fun. Then—well, then it didn't work—things stopped going right for us. So what did we do? The only sensible thing surely."

She stared at him. "Of course. The only sensible thing . . . What is it you've come to say, Stephen?"

"We separated," he said. "All that side—all our married life is over, but there's no bitterness or hard feelings. It's all been for the best."

The best. Easy word. She said nothing. A fly was buzzing endlessly against the window.

"But we can't go on like this for ever," he said. "Tied and yet not tied. Like a horse on a rope. Don't you ever feel you want your complete freedom, so that you can finish the chapter entirely? We could still be friends. Much better friends. It must be irksome to you."

"Does that mean it's irksome to you?"

He said: "I've been thinking a lot about it for some time."

She put more milk into her cup but did not reach for the tea.

"Who is she, Stephen?"

He turned, met her gaze, his clear brown eyes a little embarrassed. After hesitation he said: "Nobody you know."

"Someone you've met in Manchester?"

"Yes."

"What makes you think it's—likely to last?"

"I just *know* it this time."

"Didn't you—'know it' when you married me?"

"I was a lot younger then. I'm—sorry, Virginia."

She poured her tea. "Yes, I'm sorry too."

"But in any case," he went on. "In any case it would be better for our break to be a complete one. It's all wrong to be as we are."

"Does she know about me?"

"Not yet."

"You think she'll marry a divorced man?"

"I think so."

"It's a terrible stigma—even on me. People would whisper, 'Oh, she's divorced,' and turn away and not trouble to ask whose fault it was."

He began to walk up and down the room. "It's no good pretending to you. You know I've not been an angel. But I've not felt like this ever before. It's only two important affairs there have been in my life: yours, and now this."

"Thank you," she said. "I'm glad I'm 'placed.'"

He bit his lip. "I hope you'll do this for me. It means a great deal. It means everything, in fact."

"I'm not at all sure. I'll have to think it over."

That wasn't enough. He began to explain his case. But after a moment she interrupted him defiantly.

"I'd like to meet the girl. What's her name?"

"That's not possible."

"Why? Are you ashamed of me?"

"No, don't you see, I want to keep her quite separate. I want this to be—to be nothing at all to do with her."

"When in fact it's everything to do with her."

"No, no, it is not." He was worried by her attitude. "Can't one begin——"

"Well, I think I'll wait some months before I decide," she said. "It can't do her any harm to wait."

"I've got to tell you," he said. "I don't like it but I've got to tell you that it won't make any difference. If you won't do this, then we'll go ahead just the same and let the legal fetters stand."

She watched him curiously.

"And will she be content with that?"

"If there's no other way, then I'm sure she will."

"You were always sure of your women, weren't you?"

"Always when it didn't much matter."

She made a wry face. "Thank you."

"I didn't mean that, Virginia. I didn't mean you, I meant the others."

"I used to believe I was different."

"So you were. I've told you so."

"And this one—she's different too? You'll stick to her—you think."

"I'll stick to her—I know."

"Is she very much in love with you?"

He raised an eyebrow in humorous deprecation.

"How can I answer that?"

"If she is—then I'm sorry for her. Poor girl—the disillusion that will come."

As she got up, he came behind her quietly, took her by the shoulders.

"Have you suffered so much because of me?"

She twisted her shoulders free and moved away from him. "Oh, leave me alone."

"You're not being fair, Virginia, are you? You're loading the dice against me. I was never as bad as that. It was six of one and half a dozen of the other between us. What's the good of pretending?"

"I tell you I'm sorry for her. And she'll be worse off than I am if she hasn't even respectability."

"You mean you won't free me?"

"What have I to gain?"

"You may want to marry someone else."

"I don't want to marry someone else."

He was staring at her, his handsome face frustrated and angry. One more effort.

"I wish I could explain it to you. I wish I could tell you all about it. Perhaps you'd understand better then. But I can't. I've shirked this visit to you. I should have come weeks ago. I want to do the fair thing by you both. I want you to do the fair thing too."

She looked up into his face. "Is she very pretty, Stephen?"

"Oh!" He made a gesture of despair. "What has that to do with it? I should have known better than to expect reason from a woman. I'll go now. I'll go and leave you."

She did not call the maid but followed him quietly to the door.

"I'll come in a week," he said. "Maybe it will be better that way. It will have given you time to think it over."

"No, please don't come again."

"Why not?"

She avoided his gaze. "I don't want you to come here again. But I'll promise to think it over. I'll write you. Same address?"

"Yes."

"Very well. Good-bye, Stephen."

He took her hand. "Good-bye, Virginia. And I'm—I hope you'll reconsider it."

He walked off down the street and heard her immediately shut the door and go in. He had an impulse to turn back and speak to her again in the old affectionate way, to try just once more to get her to see reason. But he realised that for today at any rate it would do no good at all.

CHAPTER SEVENTEEN ❧ The summer moved towards its close with a good deal of warmth and drought, which was very agreeable to the people living in the fine shady houses of the Grove. It was not so welcome to the thousands living and working near the banks of the Irwell and the Irk, which served as open conduits for most of the waste products of the populations concerned and stank to high heaven as they shrank, leaving pools of green slime and scums of grey filth at their edges.

Further heat in the minds of the knowledgeable was kindled by the Irish question, the Fenian outrages, the dissolution of Parliament, and whether Mr. Disraeli, who had made such a good job of the Abyssinian war, or Mr. Gladstone, who had expressed his intention of dealing with the Irish Church, should sit on the Treasury Bench.

The foundation stone for the new Town Hall, which was to outshine all other town halls ever built at any time anywhere, was laid, and women whispered that hats were to be smaller and that the crinoline was going out. There had been a scandal about a new dance, which had come straight from Paris, called the Can-Can, and which those who had seen it hinted was the height of indecency. The proprietor of the Lancashire Stingo tried to stage it, and all the idle gentlemen who hung about and chatted in groups at London Road Station, with no other purpose except to glimpse the ankles of the ladies coming down the steps, went in a body to the hall. But some spoil-sport on the city council got wind of the thing, and after one performance it was taken off.

Uncle Pridey sent his book to a firm of London publishers, who returned it after seven weeks, saying they thanked him for the courtesy of the offer but they were advised that the claims he put forward were not substantiated by the scientists of the day.

Two letters from Stephen. One was waiting for her when she got back from Southport, the other followed in a week.

With many false starts and wasted sheets she eventually sent off a letter which did not satisfy her all.

STEPHEN, DEAR STEPHEN,

Please don't write again; it isn't safe, for the letters in this house may well miscarry. So I beg of you, don't write again. Thank you so very much for what you say. Nursing my thoughts, I feel so weak—and yet so strong. Strong and rich in your love for me and in my own love. I remember and think of nothing but the hours we spent together, believe that.

Last night Mr. Slaney-Smith suggested we should hold a séance among ourselves just to see if anything happened; of course we did not, but it brought back my first meetings with you so vividly that I could settle to nothing all evening.

But it is better that we keep apart and do not see each other. Let us wait like this for a time; it's fairer to everyone. I have been away to Southport for two weeks and may go again, somehow it is easier when the distance is greater and there is nothing to remind one.

Essie's wedding is on the twenty-fourth of next month; I expect you will know that.

Your,
DELIA

Brook read his poems at the first autumn meeting of the Athenæum, and the *City News* commented on them as being romantic in tone and having a certain lyric quality suggestive of a minor Herrick. One was called: 'To Patience.' Others were: 'Your Silver Shoe,' 'Sing Only to Me,' and 'Helen.' Listening to them, and to the growing confidence with which, fortified by a large glass of whisky at the start, he read them, she was puzzled at the contradiction in him. She did not reason it right out but was vaguely distressed at this deep fund of romantic idealism in him, which their marriage, however hard she had tried, had failed to tap. He saved all his dreams for his pen. Stephen was the true romantic, not Brook. She hadn't stood a chance.

"Delia," said Esther next day, "we're all a bit perplexed about inviting Mr. Ferguson to the wedding. In a way he knew Hugh before I did, and it seems common courtesy. But we all feel he doesn't really like mixing with us Blakes—except you, of course, and everyone says you're quite a pet of his now. But you're Brook's wife and we're just troublesome in-laws. What d'you think we should do?"

"I'm not at all a pet of his," Cordelia said. "Why don't you ask him?"

"All right, I will. And what about Uncle Pridey? He's rather a lamb. D'you think we might?"

"Of course you might. But I can't pretend to guess what he'll say."

Uncle Pridey said: "This bacon is better than the last lot; nice and streaky with a good quality fat. I had an invitation this morning, young woman. Do they expect me to dress up, because I've nothing to dress up in."

"No, I'm sure it won't matter a bit, Uncle Pridey. They'll be delighted to see you just as you are."

"Suppose there'll be something to eat?"

"I'll tell Father there must be."

"Very well, then. Get me a card or something when you're out next time, will you? Expect they'd like it formal. Are there any more kidneys?"

Mr. Ferguson said: "I've had an invitation to Esther's wedding, Cordelia. I should like to accept. She's your sister, but you know yourself now how difficult it would be for me to spare a day."

He was watching her as he made the excuse, and she got a queer feeling out of the realisation that he cared a little what she thought.

"Of course," she said. "I'll certainly explain."

"In the meantime," he said, "will you give them this with my good wishes?"

When Esther was given the sealed envelope she found inside a cheque for a hundred guineas. She was so delighted that she went dancing and singing round the house, waving it under everyone's nose. Mr. Ferguson's stock rocketed.

Mr. Scott, Sr., was connected with the Cheshire Lines railway. They were people in a comfortable way of life, but they had no 'side,' Mr. Scott being a lanky grey-bearded man with a strong Glasgow accent, and Mrs. Scott, very much his junior, a plump Campbell from Oban. Hugh Scott had just been made a sub-editor of his paper.

Stephen was a little late at the church and she did not see him at all until afterwards. At the breakfast he was two places away, Teddy and a girl called Eunice being between. Mr. Blake had insisted on giving his eldest daughter an equally good send-off, so this, too, was being held at the Albion Hotel. Uncle Pridey took a particular fancy to the cold tongue and salad.

They had moved, she and Stephen, agreeably but distantly, like casual friends, overdoing it in their efforts to be natural. At the sight of him, after being near him for ten minutes, her good resolutions of the summer were already scattered. His mere physical presence . . . She struggled for judgment and failed at the very outset.

She thought: What is to become of us? If they ran away to London, as he had suggested once, perhaps they could get lost. But it was not *really* lost, could never be that. If only they could dissolve out of people's thoughts; that would be really starting afresh. Already she felt such a cheat. She had a fidelity towards and an affection for Brook. There was no getting away from it. What she was contemplating at this moment was something from which any decent woman would shrink in horror. She would become an outcast. Unclean, unclean! At present her family were proud of her. She would be letting them down—and *so* down. It was perhaps silly to let other people's opinions loom so important. They *must* not be the final arbiter. But because of them, if she ran away, she would never feel quite whole again.

A smaller party than Cordelia's, this; she was surprised that Mr. Slaney-Smith was here, less the prize boy than he had been at her wedding but still very much in prominence. She also saw Mrs. Slaney-Smith for the first time, a small, sallow, mottled little woman in lavender with an intense whispering undertone of a voice and a nervous habit of glancing over her shoulder. All her hurried movements seemed to be under the shadow of Mr. Slaney-Smith, dominant, criticising, eternally rational. She took a fancy to Cordelia.

The cake was cut and everyone was tremendously jolly. Mr. Scott, well primed, got up and made a speech which began with flattering references to his new daughter but somehow ended up in praise of Robert Bruce. Mr. Blake, warned off clocks by his entire family, hummed and ha-ed for a few minutes and then said that a happy marriage must be like a sundial which could be read in all weathers and found steadfastly showing its true bearings.

Then Hugh Scott got up to thank the fathers for their speeches and the guests for their presents. While he was doing this Cordelia noticed that Eunice Trent was looking very uncomfortable, and the girl suddenly gave one or two convulsive jumps. Then she leapt to her feet with a piercing scream.

"Oh! Oh! Something! Oh!" She gave a sideways leap across the room, past a startled waiter, shaking her crinoline skirt hysterically.

"What is it, what is it?" said Mrs. Blake. "Does she have fits?"

Two or three of the guests got up and moved towards the screaming girl. The waiter followed her solicitously. Then, in the sight of at least a dozen people, a mouse dropped to the floor and ran scuttering away under one of the sideboards.

At once there was panic. Women screamed and tried to scramble on chairs, two fainted, several waiters rushed towards the sideboard and dragged it away from the wall while Hugh Scott grabbed a knife and others took up fire-irons.

"It's gone!"

"No, there it is!"

"Don't drive it that way!"

"Open the doors!"

"I've got it! Look! Look! Hand me a stick."

They flushed the mouse from behind the sideboard, but it slid away and found refuge under a low table with a fern on it. They took away the fern and moved the table.

"Don't hurt it; catch it!" screamed little Anne, dancing round in an agony of apprehension. "Don't hurt the tweeny little thing!"

"Now then!"

"Careful! Those are my fingers!"

145

"There he is. Ach! Ach!"

At the last moment, when apparently caught, the mouse made a despairing dart for liberty and flew across the carpet, swerving round Mr. Slaney-Smith's shining boots, and escaped into the lobby of the hotel.

With infinite patience, quiet was restored. Some of the ladies looked sheepish as they were helped down from their chairs, and the two who had fainted were given brandy. Eunice burst into tears of shame at the dreadful thing which had happened to her. They tried to comfort her and patted her hand and told her there, there, but it was all over now, and gave her a drink of champagne. The manager of the hotel bustled in, gesturing and apologetic.

Mr. Blake and Mr. Scott were full of indignation. It was monstrous, they said, that any civilised hotel of this modern era should be so negligent as to allow vermin to be at large in the dining-room, and at a wedding party when there were many gently brought-up ladies to be alarmed and upset. This and much more they said, though Mr. Scott, who was now feeling very happy indeed, spoiled the effect by sticking a finger in the manager's button-hole and ending: "Ma dear-r fellow, why don't ye buy a cat?"

The manager was extravagantly sorry, but under his sorrow he was angry and suspicious; he saw the wedding guests back to their seats and then went off to cross-examine the porter, the boots, and the receptionist. In the meantime Hugh Scott, who privately thought the whole thing funny and was only afraid of making his private feelings public, prepared to go on with his speech.

But he found another man taking the floor and cracking his knuckles in concern as he tried to talk Hugh down. That uncle of Cordelia's with the tuft of beard and the lantern jaws. When Hugh saw that the old man was holding a small cigar box he gave up his speech and listened too.

"Of course," said Uncle Pridey. "Should have given you the present at the proper time, but what with one thing and another . . . And the lid must have come off in my pocket. Unnecessary fuss, in my view, over a mere mouse. Can't understand it, really I can't. Clean, healthy, inoffensive little things."

"What?" said Hugh. "What's that? Was that your mouse?"

"Was going to be yours," said Uncle Pridey. "Knew Esther liked them because she came and admired them one evening. Didn't know what to get you both for a wedding present and thought you might be interested. Tame they were, perfectly tame, able to do small tricks. But you scare the poor creatures making such a hullabaloo. They don't understand. Not used to so much noise."

146

"Oh, Pridey," said Brook angrily, "you *are* a fool. Haven't you sense enough to know other people don't feel the way you do——"

A word in the old man's sentence had caught Cordelia's attention.

"Were there more than one, Uncle Pridey? Are the others safe?"

He opened the box. "No, they're all gone."

"How many *were* there?"

"Only four," he said.

The pandemonium which broke out now made the earlier disturbance seem quiet and restrained. Those who had been foremost in assuring Eunice that it was all over now and that there was nothing at all to get hysterical about instantly saw the terrible experience she had gone through happening to them. Every other chair round the table was immediately occupied, elderly ladies leaping as fast as young, with screams and squeals—all except one of the faints who had not recovered and another who fainted to join her. The men, too, got a little confused, some shouting that the doors should be shut, the others to leave them open. One shouted for a bucket of water, and Mr. Scott, Sr., gambolling about with a glass of champagne in his hand, kept calling: "Why don't ye buy a cat? Why don't ye buy a cat?" Hugh Scott held the hand of his young bride and kept passing her up bits of wedding cake. Stephen sidled up to Cordelia, while Brook was expostulating with Uncle Pridey, and said: "This can't go on. I *must* see you. *When* can I see you?"

Then a second mouse was flushed from among the folds of the velvet curtains and ran a gauntlet of stamping feet and cracking pokers, to double across under the wedding table and to disappear between the manager's legs as he returned flushed-faced with the receptionist.

Shouting to make himself heard, Mr. Scott tried to explain the position, the manager nodding his head emphatically all the time as if to say, 'Just what I thought.'

Then Pridey put a hand in his pocket and said: "Oh, well, this little chap didn't get far," and took out a third mouse, wriggling between his finger and thumb.

He might have expected this to quiet things down, but instead it set some of the ladies off screaming again because they couldn't bear even the sight of a mouse, looking brown and mousy and sniffing and waving its forepaws.

Pridey opened the little cigar box and popped the mouse in and clicked the lid and Stephen said: "I *must* see you. I hear Brook is going away again next week. "

"It isn't decided yet."

"Oh, yes, it is," he said grimly. "He told me so today. Promise you'll see me then."

"I'll write," she said desperately.

The fourth mouse was not to be found. They hunted under the furniture and cross-questioned Pridey and raked about in odd corners. At last they began to conclude that this eccentric old man, whom someone had made the mistake of inviting to the wedding, had probably miscounted his own pets or lost one on the way to the church. The ladies were revived and reassured and the waiter went round with a new bottle of champagne.

"You promise?" said Stephen as Brook came across.

Brook was flushed and smiling, but angry underneath. "Did you ever know such an old fool? Sometimes I think he's not all there. I don't know what Father would have said."

"Pridey's got the courage of his convictions," said Stephen. "What so few of us have. When will you both be coming to spend an evening with me at the Variety? I'm sure Mrs. Ferguson would find it a refined and respectable show."

"Thank you," said Brook. "What do you say, Cordelia?"

"I should like it," she said. "May we let you know, Mr. Crossley?"

Everybody was settling rather gingerly back at the table. The tendency now was to treat the eruption as a joke. Even the manager began to smile again and brought the news that the first two mice had escaped into the street.

"Don't you like Stephen?" Brook asked in an undertone as they sat down. "You always seem a bit stiff with him."

"No . . . I think he's very nice."

And then the fourth mouse, which had been lurking under a table-napkin against the wedding cake, decided that it was time to bolt, and streaked down the length of the table, saw a friend in Anne, jumped on to her lap, and ran down her skirts to the floor, making a bid for liberty like its two friends.

CHAPTER EIGHTEEN "Good-bye, Brook, dear," she said, conscious of hypocrisy, conscious of guilt, of fear, of excitement.

One night, and on one night only, she tried in a panic to persuade him to take her, but he did not want to, and abruptly, her mood changing, taking a plunge, she agreed to stay behind.

Privately he had a selfish reason for wanting to go alone. He was taking a collection of his poems with him and wanted to arrange for them to be published at his own expense.

He was a little annoyed when Uncle Pridey came up to him just before he left and thrust *Habits and Heredity in Mice* into his hand.

"See what you can do, boy. Dozens of publishers up there. One of 'em ought to take it. It's worth doing for the prestige, even if they make no money out of it."

So Brook went off full of nervous excitement, unaware of what he was leaving behind and what he would bring back with him; and after supper that evening Mr. Ferguson said:

"I am going to Oldham late tomorrow. I shall come back here before I join Brook. I opposed your going with Brook because I wanted this to be your first big opportunity. . . . It will mean your visiting the works at least once a day, and Mrs. Meredith will have to manage. I'll leave everything in your hands—deliberately—to see how you go on."

She said: "I'll do my best, Mr. Ferguson."

"I know you will. And if anything goes wrong, don't worry. This is just a trial, and I shall be back at the week-end to see to everything. You can drive down with me in the morning and we'll go over the details together."

She drove down with him. They went over the details together. He left. She talked to John Simnel and some of the foremen. She stood in the counting-house of the great place, among the reek of the chemicals, slender and tall in her frock of fine brown wool with its brown velvet cape. She had been here so often these last months that they accepted her as a natural sight, but she wondered what they said among themselves: 'Another of old Ferguson's experiments' or 'She'll soon muck things up.'

The mysteries of dyeing, which had seemed so extraordinary to her on that first visit, were mysteries no longer. All through the summer she had been reading books. She knew something now of the properties of alizarin and purpurin, logwood and cochineal, and the new coal-tar colours. She did not understand, as Mr. Ferguson did, the chemical reasons why one dye was fast to some light and another not, but she was quick to grasp the practical problems. She understood also the commercial traffic of the counting-house and the offices.

She didn't of course quite believe anything yet. She couldn't give credence to these reins of responsibility which had been put in her hands. She half suspected that Mr. Ferguson was still hovering in the background, ready to pull the correct rein when she came to a corner. Any moment, she thought, he must change his mind and say, 'Well, after all, you're only a slip of a woman. And *your* place is in home. You couldn't expect to be taken seriously, could you?'

Only her reason told her that this was happening just as it appeared to be, that the man who in her heart she disliked and distrusted had given her this evidence of his liking and trust.

And she in return was unfaithful to any trust that had ever been put in her at all. At this moment, while outwardly business-like and calm, she was in dreadful conflict.

When she left the works she directed Tomkins to drive her to Albert Square. There she got down and told him to wait. She walked off casually and made her way down one of the side streets, asking her way of a beggar until she came to Spring Gardens. Very soon she found the Variety Theatre. In the dull October daylight the place looked shabby.

Signor Palermo, the World Renowned Impressionist. Bird Songs Imitated. Will play violin concerto without strings and FIVE musical instruments at one time.
Lottie Freeman. Lady Serio Comic fresh from triumphs at all the Leading Music Halls.
The Brothers Rouse. Double Juggling. Slack Wire Dancing and Chinese Postures.
Boston Minstrels.
Val Johnson, the Resident Buffoon.

Inside that building, with all its posters and its blue and gilt entrance lobby, Stephen was perhaps working at this moment. Should she walk in and ask for him? Wouldn't he be surprised? Up to now, all these months, all the advances had come from him. Perhaps he didn't think her capable of making a rash move on her own.

"Well, Mrs. Ferguson, waiting for the early doors?"

Dan Massington. Danger. Any moment of relaxed caution was dangerous.

"I was reading the posters. Do they really do all those things?"

"They do. But it's not quite the entertainment for Brook's wife. The Fergusons of Grove Hall. Tut, tut!"

In the daylight his complexion was bad. A dandy going to seed.

"How is Brook?" He fell into step beside her as she moved away.

"Very well, thank you."

"*Very* well? You must be doing him good, my dear."

She did not reply.

"I see he gave a reading of his poems the other week. I regretted I was not able to be there. What did they describe him as, a minor Shakespeare?"

"I'm not very interested in this conversation."

"I know you're not, but I think you're a damned pretty woman. Have I told you that?"

"Yes, you have, thank you."

"Too pretty for Brook! I wonder you stomach him, really I do. D'you ever feel in need of a change?"

"Of company? Yes! At this moment." She quickened her step slightly.

"If so," he said, "think of me. I'd give you a run for your money. Do you find me offensive?"

"Very."

"I thought so. Well let's change the subject. Come over and have a drink with me. There's a decent little place on the corner."

"No, thank you."

"You've fallen for them, haven't you," he said with a change in his voice, "hook, line, and sinker. You've accepted all their hypocrisies and subscribe to them yourself. When I met you that first time you were a pretty kid with a chance of leading a life of your own. Now you're a willing pensioner."

"Why do you hate them so much?"

"I don't. I despise 'em. I'd give a good deal to take 'em down a peg."

"Because your sister wasn't happy married to Brook?"

"Because they as good as finished her off between them."

She said: "For two years, every time we've met . . . Why don't you say what you want to say publicly—and have done with it?"

"Proof," he said, his lips closing over his teeth for a moment. "I've no proof or they wouldn't sit there so righteous and smug. But what happened to all the sleeping tablets that were missing? She was either driven to taking them herself or one of them gave her an overdose deliberately. There's no other explanation. Either way they're responsible for her death."

"If Dr. Birch had any reasonable complaint he'd have called in the police, you know that."

"Birch is a special friend of the Fergusons, isn't he? Went to school with Brook. He's where he is because of the old man."

"Do you think he'd risk his whole career just to oblige them?"

"Well"—Massington stared down at her—"he happens to owe them a lot of money. Did you know that?"

She drove home without seeing Stephen.

During the whole two years of her married life these unpleasant suspicions had been in the air, only once or twice given shape by Dan Massington but never quite disposed of.

She spent the whole evening reading Margaret's diary. There was very little in the later stages to support what Dan Massington had said. Yet the whole tone of the entries showed a progressive deterioration. They were the outpourings of an ill, a neurotic, and an unhappy woman. One day she was concerned only with the ultimate religious realities; the next she was worrying because she thought the maid had been at her chocolates and was going to hide them away where she could not find them. One day she had nothing to live for and had told Brook so; the next she was writing: 'I feel as if the world is slipping away from me. Sometimes I want to scream and clutch at the bed to *hold on* to life and the few things left that I care about.'

When Cordelia had finished it she took it back to the attic and buried it deep among the books, where it belonged. Later she stared round her own bedroom, trying to visualise the scene these walls had looked upon. The face of the miniature, in a bed something like this, dark sleek hair centrally parted, ailing patrician face, a bedside table littered with the stuff of illness, the oversweet warmth of a sick-room, old malices and contempts . . . She had been bitterly unhappy here. If Dan Massington's assertions were not true in one way, might they not be literally true in the other?

Twice before she got into bed she took up a pen to write to Stephen and twice she put it down. She needed him as confidant again. She needed his love still more. One reinforced the other and provided excuses to salve her conscience.

She woke next morning in a queer mood. For a time the mental turmoil was gone. In the night it had resolved itself. She picked up her pen a third time.

"Mrs. Ferguson thanks Mr. Crossley for his kind invitation to the Variety Theatre for tomorrow, Wednesday evening, and will be pleased to accept. She will meet him at the Town Hall at seven."

On Wednesday she was down at the dye works early, and stayed there all morning. At dinner she told Uncle Pridey and Aunt Tish that she was going to see her family that evening and that they need not wait up. Aunt Tish said it wasn't quite nice to be driving about the streets after dark even in one's own carriage.

Before dressing she fetched the diary down from the attic again and put it in her bag. She told herself she was going to consult Stephen about it. She walked a little way and then got a cab.

It was a fine night but windy. The cab took its time and she was early and in no hurry, peering out at the passing traffic and the wavering gaslamps. They drew up in King Street and she told the cabbie to wait. There was little traffic here. She watched a blind old man in a silk hat and a tattered opera cloak being led across the cobbles by a patient dog. In the distance somewhere was a barrel-organ.

She thought: This is madness: this is over the brink. I don't care.

She saw Stephen draw up in his own victoria opposite and get out and stand and stare about him. Then he came hesitantly across to her hansom.

"Delia! Is anything wrong?"

She gave him her hand. "Didn't you want me tonight?"

"Want you!" He paid her cabbie as she got out. "Where's old Mr. Ferguson?"

"Oh, just gone off for a day or two."

"My *dear* . . ." They crossed the road but he said: "Let's walk, shal'
we? It's no more than a few yards. We've time for a snack. . . ." He
took her arm. "I couldn't make head or tail of your note. I've been on
the edge of my chair all the day, not knowing what to expect."

"I thought it nice to be formal for a change," she said gravely.

"Absolutely monstrous! You've no heart at all."

"Oh, yes, I have," she said, "or I shouldn't be here."

He looked at her. "You're different. What is it? Lift your veil and
let me see your eyes."

"Are you surprised because I invited myself? Did it upset your arrangements? Had you to put some other lady off?"

He threw back his head and laughed. "Well now, I mustn't ask why,
for I love you like this!"

They reached the theatre. People were going in, and a crowd of
ragged children—bare-footed, loud-mouthed, and half starved—waited
round the entrance to see the people get out of their cabs and to take a
peep inside when the glass doors were pushed open.

The place looked very different with all the gases brilliantly flaring.
Above the door two enormous ornate lamps cast a warm orange glow
over the arriving patrons, to put you in the right mood, the convivial
mood, and as you pushed open the doors a glare of light came out, like a
paid hostess rushing to meet you. Cordelia was dazzled. Several men
of good appearance, heavy swells, tall and moustached and white-
gloved, turned to stare at her as Stephen led her in. She was glad of
her veil. Somewhere to the right a voice was saying, "Take your tickets,
ladies and gentlemen. Sixpence the body of the 'all, ninepence the
gallery, which is more select. No hadmission except by ticket obtainable
'ere. Sixpence the body of the 'all, ninepence the gallery, which is
more select."

Up the stairs; long crystal columns on the walls lit from inside; other
women here, some quite smartly dressed. At the top an attendant with
a lot of brass buttons touched his eyebrow to Stephen, glanced at
Cordelia with a flicker of interest as if to say, 'I like the looks of 'er';
then they passed a bar at which a few people were already drinking and
through a small door beside it into a private office.

There was another attendant in here, a boy not more than thirteen or
fourteen.

"Tell them we'll have supper right away, Maurice. And we're not to
be disturbed. Understand? I'm in to no one at all."

"Yes, sir."

They went into another room beyond. It was a small sitting-room with
a little table set for two. Stephen closed the door.

153

"This is wonderful. I can't believe it's happening. Tell me how it has come about. . . . We've time enough for a meal. I've told them to hold up the start until we're ready."

She looked around. "How very important you are, Stephen. To be able to hold up a performance just when you please. . . ."

"It's you that's important," he said. "May I?" He wanted to lift her veil.

She lifted it for him. They met each other's eyes.

"You see," she said, "there's no difference. I'm just the same."

His eyes travelled over her face with intense interest.

"You're never for a second the same. I don't begin to know you yet. Even this"—he touched her cheek—"even this changes its shape and colour so that I think I remember what you're like, and then . . . Lord, you're all different and new the next time, as if you've come straight from the mint and I've not set eyes on you before."

CHAPTER NINETEEN They had supper, laughing and chatting together. Her queer mood had lasted. She was reckless, high-spirited, the old doubts put away. The enormity of it all was lost in the excitement of it all.

Stephen was enchanted—and something of his enchantment showed in the gentleness of his own mood. Afterwards he led her along one of the passages and into a box which looked down closely upon the stage and had a thin trellis in front of it. It was furnished with gilt arm-chairs and crimson plush hangings.

"At one time no ladies were allowed on the floor of the house," he explained, "and these were built so that a few distinguished guests could watch the show without being seen."

She looked down. The first number had just begun. A man dressed up like a workman, with a clay pipe in his hand and a brimless silk hat, was singing a comic song. But for the moment she was more interested in the theatre. A long table was set parallel with the stage, and round it a group of men were smoking and drinking. Other tables ran down the auditorium, rather like a college dining-hall, and all these were full. Nine tenths of the audience was male. Overshadowing the back of the hall was the balcony, in which were more tables and chairs, and at the back of that was the saloon bar.

Her attention was half taken by the show, half by his presence so close to her; his was wholly on her, watching her, noticing her response to the different turns, full of the excitement of having her within the circle of his arm. Sometimes she would turn and smile at him, her face close to his; sometimes they whispered together, he in explanation, she in query or comment.

After each turn a refined, powerful, military-looking man with a waxed moustache would get up at the table nearest the stage and would lead the applause; and then when the last drop of appreciation had been wrung out of the audience by constant curtains he would take the enormous cigar out of his mouth and announce the next turn in a refined, powerful, military voice.

The ceiling of the theatre was blue with gold stars in unheard-of constellations. The arch of the proscenium was framed with white-enamelled scrolls and gold and silver flowers. The circle was lined with rosebud chintz. She was impressed; she knew exactly what Mr. Ferguson would say about it; nevertheless she was impressed.

Perhaps Stephen's presence coloured her feelings. She loved the Brothers Rouse, two sober little men with impassive faces and black moustaches and black tights, who tumbled about all over the stage and twisted themselves into impossible knots and boiled an egg in a pan on a stove on a slack wire, all without the slightest change of expression.

She didn't so much care for Miss Lottie Freeman, who came on dressed in flesh-coloured tights, a too-close-fitting bodice with spangles and cheap jewellery, and a curly-brimmed bowler hat. The costume was indecent and her soprano voice was high and harsh. But Miss Lottie was a favourite with the men, who hooted and whistled and cat-called for her again and again. Cordelia realised she was seeing life.

It was all rather warm and jolly and friendly, and nicer than she expected. She liked the little orchestra which accompanied as required. Just for the moment she liked its brassiness, its jiggy, easy tunes, and the way the players grinned and nodded and smoked. In the body of the hall knives and forks clattered occasionally, and here and there a diner lost interest in the show and tucked into his meal. But for the most part the audience was content with light refreshments and plenty of beer. The military man seemed to know everybody by a Christian name and chatted and joked with his cronies in the audience as well as with the people on the stage. As the evening went on a haze of blue smoke filmed the back of the hall.

Signor Palermo was ingenious but went on too long, and a few people got restive. Then someone gave a comic monologue and followed it with a pathetic one, all about a little dog that was frozen to death in the snow. When Miss Lottie Freeman came on a second time she was wearing a railwayman's coat and peaked cap, and Cordelia liked her better this time. She sang a song called, 'The Railway Guard,' and asked everyone to join in the chorus. It went:

> "I try to be merry but it is no use;
> My case is very hard.
> She left me as silly as a farmyard goose
> When she married that railway guard."

Absurd and catchy. Stephen and Cordelia joined in with the rest and laughed at each other when it was over. For the moment they had forgotten their separateness and become one of a crowd of homely revellers in out of the drab grey streets for an hour or two and making the most of the warmth and the light. Herb from over at the waterworks with the crippled wife; and Jack and Teddie, who had had a successful day on Change and were ending it suitably; Will the dhooti buyer from the shippers in Corporation Street; and Clarence the cotton broker who was dying of consumption; Arthur the teacher and Joe the medical student and Michael the Armenian Jew and Fred the bus driver, and the heavy swells leaning against the bar, stroking their moustaches and sipping their drinks.

The Boston Minstrels were the hit of the evening, four men made up as Negroes: curly wigs, shirt collars, shiny black faces, gaping mouths; something new. They had an accordion, a tambourine, a banjo, and bones.

They sang: 'I'd Choose to Be Daisy If I Could Be a Flower.' Fine voices with little artificial sobs; the queer, flat, quivering music had a strange appeal like the sighs of an old sad people long gone from their homes.

After that came 'Swanee River,' and everyone clapped and shouted for more. The refined, powerful, military man announcing it as a special encore, they sang. 'Massa's in de Cold, Cold Ground.' Cordelia's eyes were wet when it finished.

They saw the show right through, and at the end she came out of a happy dream to find it after ten o'clock. She said she must fly. He said:

"Do you need to go? What reason is there to be afraid? Only a couple of old people who won't even notice what time you come in. Stay a while and talk. Everyone will be going home. Aren't you hungry again? I can get you some sandwiches and there's plenty to drink."

But she wouldn't stay and, seeing her mind made up, he sent the page down to get his carriage. While they were waiting the barmaid came in. She was an overblown woman of about fifty with bleached hair, and Stephen said:

"Oh, Delia, this is Char, an old friend of the family. Char, this is a friend of mine."

"Evening, dear," said Char. "Pleased to meet you, I'm sure."

She smiled brightly, warmly, but her eyes were knowledgeable and assessing. Cordelia didn't quite like the look.

In the carriage she felt Margaret's diary in her bag. She had meant to show it to Stephen, to ask his advice. Now it seemed unimportant. Yet it was the spring which had released her reckless mood of this evening. That and what Dan had said.

He said: "It's been a wonderful evening. I wish we could have many more just like it. Just like it."

"I *have* enjoyed it. Thank you for everything."

"This fortnight," he said, "well, it's our heyday. Whatever may happen after, however we may plan, let's make the most of this."

"You suddenly sound very serious."

"Not suddenly. I deny it! Everything between us is serious—has been from the start. But nothing's sure and decided, is it? Then let's make certain of what is certain, tonight, tomorrow, the day after."

She stared at the shape of his head, silhouetted as he leaned forward a moment. Then some passing light brought light to his eyes as he turned to look at her. She felt the impulsive positive warmth of his presence like something new, freshly realised.

"Can you not come down again, as you did in July?" he said. "I'd wait for you; we'd drive to my house, no distance; a couple of miles. There's no one there; a few servants, and they'd be asleep. It's—too good to be missed. A chance in a thousand. Please say you'll come." He put his hand eagerly on her arm, trying to see her expression in the dark.

She said: "There's really only one way out; I dread it; but it's less underhand. In a year or two perhaps you will have moved. I can come and join you——"

"We can't wait for years, Cordelia. We love each other, isn't that all that matters? If we'd met a few years earlier the world would be giving us its blessing. Your marriage was a sad mistake. . . ." It was on the tip of his tongue to speak of his own, but he was not sure enough of her yet; such a confession might drive her away from him for this precious week, or perhaps for good.

"Yes," she said. "I know now. I don't owe the Fergusons all that loyalty, not with——" She hesitated to say, 'With the suspicion of Margaret's death hanging over them.' "But my own family . . . Oh, I don't know, forgive me, darling. I'm pulled both ways."

He pressed home his advantage, and at last she said: "That last time—being shut out—I should have no peace of mind."

"Then let me come to you. Your ivy is still as strong as ever."

"Oh, no!"

"Why not? It's the simplest possible climb."

She thought: In *that* room . . . Worst of all. Brook's room . . .
And with the memory of last time . . .

But it had also been Margaret's room. Wasn't Margaret really Brook's
wife? Mightn't she still be his wife if . . .

Thought gave out.

"All right," she said, plunging suddenly, recklessly down.

He said: "I hoped—when you came tonight. Something in your look.
But I hardly dared to think . . ."

Thereafter there is no going back. The chasm of yesterday becomes the
lover's leap of today and the accepted risk of tomorrow. Twenty-two
years of sheltered upbringing is the chrysalis that breaks, and the butter-
fly spreads its wings.

In authority at the dye works; in control of Grove Hall; in love. Here
is all the earth and all the kingdoms of the earth. But careful, says common
sense, that common sense taken from ancestors slow and steady, careful,
pride goeth; now show your mettle. Yes, Mr. Simnel, I know what
you're talking about when you speak of Norton's patent for tipping pile
goods with lacquer. Yes, Mrs. Meredith, Mr. Ferguson spoke to me
before he left; he wants the Welsh coal; oh, order two tons of it, we
have plenty of storage. I'm sorry, Madam Herbert, I don't seem to have
the concentration to play today, could we have the singing exercises
instead? Sometimes conscience raised its head, staring, unbelieving.
Sometimes the mind withdrew and held up a pointing finger. You.
You. Madness. Whom the gods would destroy . . . And then it all
slid away again into the blank unreason of knowing she would meet
him again, of needing to hear his voice.

Aunt Tish grumbled at her going out, but Uncle Pridey hardly seemed
to notice. He had bought some tree shrews and was making a special
cage for them.

Mr. Ferguson came back on Saturday evening, and Sunday was a day
back to normal. The early bath and walk and prayers, the presence
about the house, the servants just a little quieter, the breathing, the
elastic boots, the drive to church. Her father and mother and Teddy and
Emma and Sarah and Penelope; a pang at the sight of them. It's a
shame, Essie being at Newton Heath; that's two gone now, Delia, and
your father feels it a lot, though he doesn't say much. Dear Anne will
be fourteen next week; she's at home cooking the dinner; she seemed
to want to. Yes, and looking after Winifred and Virginia and Evelyn
Clarissa.

Father is greyer, she thought, and so thin; such a pathetic little neck,
but it could be so stiff if he felt like it. What *would* he say?

The drive home and the heavy midday dinner, Mr. Ferguson carving.

The specialist in Town had said half a pound of lean steak every day to get his weight down; he was doing that. An easy cure, he said, expecting everyone to smile. Afterwards a drowsy afternoon—no needlework allowed—then tea and more prayers. Rain came with the dark as they were leaving for church. They got back to a late supper with Aunt Tish wondering what Brook would be doing in that there London. Mr. Ferguson for one was tired and untalkative, and everyone was early to bed.

An oasis of respectability.

On Monday morning as they were driving down to Town together Mr. Ferguson ordered Tomkins to stop, and she saw the old half-blind man who had taken her message to Stephen coming eagerly towards them. A sudden moment of panic.

He came with his frayed coat, his wicker basket, the artificial flowers dangling; bowed nervously and grinned and said the weather was good and he hoped Mr. Ferguson was well. Thanking you, Betty's rheumatism was better this week; she only got worried when it cramped her hands. Mr. Ferguson gave him five shillings and he clutched the silver, his hand trembling in his anxiety not to drop it, not to let it tinkle on the road and roll away. Then he turned the blue eye that could just see and the paler blue one like a dead disc upon Cordelia and said would Mrs. Brook be so kind as to accept a flower, just a little one as a token of respect?

He knew her, then. The bogy of discovery suddenly leered at her. Suppose he said, 'I remember you from taking your letter to the gentleman.' "Thank you," she said, smiling.

"May it bring you luck, ma'am. The best of luck to all your family!"

They drove on.

"One does one's best for such people," said Mr. Ferguson. "Little enough as it is."

"Do you—know him?"

"I give him five shillings every Monday. It helps to keep them alive."

By what a narrow thread all her affairs hung. "He's always there," she said.

"Yes. They live in a cellar close by. It costs them four shillings a week. His wife works sixteen hours a day making artificial flowers for a factory. She earns about nine shillings a week."

"Nine shillings!"

"She's paid sixpence a gross for geraniums and twopence ha'penny a gross for buttercups. Not much, as you'll agree. Of course roses are more. But she only gets time to leave the cellar about twice a week."

Roses were more. She stared at the single red flower in her gloved fingers.

"If I'd known, I wouldn't have taken it from him."

"Oh, he wanted you to have it. Educated people don't believe in luck, but that was his idea."

"Have you been giving him the money long?"

"A few years."

When they reached the works Mr. Ferguson did not say much, but she could see he was pleased. There was satisfaction for her in that. Faithful to one trust if false to the other.

He left for London on the evening train.

Wednesday was fine and mild for the time of year. Only in the city was it smoky with a suggestion of fog.

For the first time at the works she found trouble and a decision to be taken. Simnel came to her the moment she got in and said the foreman of the steaming-room reported that the new colours they had begun printing yesterday were marking off. Calico when printed was steamed to fix the dyes, and marking off meant that dye from one piece of cloth left a stain on the next fold. The remedy was to wind a grey cloth between each fold of the dyed cloth, but Mr. Ferguson had told her he had abandoned this as requiring too much labour and cutting down the steaming capacity of the plant by half. She knew that great care was exercised when planning the dyeing to avoid this trouble.

To cover her hesitation, she asked to see the foreman concerned and also the head foreman of the printing machines. She could not quite be sure whether this was really something Simnel could not solve for himself or whether he was 'trying it on' and knew the answer all the time.

Just before they came back she remembered what she had been taught. She heard the steamer's report and looked at the cloth and then said:

"Has your steam been too moist? The cloth is still damp."

"Yes, ma'am. But you can do nowt else wi' madder and alizarin. Ye need wet steam an' low pressure an' a long standing to fix 'em safe."

"How long?"

"Oh, upperds of two hours."

She looked at the other foreman. "Mr. Ferguson will have planned this—these colours with you. Did he think there might be any trouble?"

"Nay. We did just same last month."

"But with wet steam you will be more likely to get marking off, won't you?"

Simnel spoke. "Best thing, Mrs. Ferguson, is to use the grey cloth. It's safest in long run."

She saw he was 'trying nothing on,' but she didn't like his solution. It was the natural easy one to take. But would Mr. Ferguson have taken it? She asked if they could deepen the engraving, which, she remembered reading, would allow of a drier steam for the same colours. Apparently they could not.

There was a moment's silence. They were waiting for her decision. She got up and went to the window, conscious that their eyes were on her. Each in his own department had far more practical knowledge than she could ever hope to have, but their knowledge did not extend beyond the confining limits of their own work, and if they had been left in authority they would not have known how to exercise it. Even Simnel. It was Mr. Ferguson's fault, as he had said. Moist steam, acids in the colours, oxalic acid . . .

She said: "Is the cloth going straight to the steaming or is there a delay?"

"Pretty near straight to it, ma'am."

"Well, it's a fine day. Can't you hold it up for two hours and let it air? Then perhaps you could cut the moisture by about a third and see if it helps. Is that possible, Mr. Trant?"

"Yes, ma'am. We can try it."

She glanced at Simnel, who was pursing his lips. "Of course, that doesn't solve anything, but it's worth trying. I can't help but think . . . Mr. Fry, is it the same dye that you used last month?"

"Aye, just same. Madder's a new lot, but it's just same composition."

She said: "Well, will you hold up the printing and make sure the madder is all right? It might have got acid in it or too much salts or something of that sort."

"It's all right," said Mr. Fry sulkily. "I saw to it meself. It's just same composition as last lot."

She said quietly: "Well, take Mr. Forrest along with you, and you can examine it together."

They went out. They were not very well satisfied, but they'd had their orders and although they grumbled they respected her more than they had done.

Thereafter followed a morning of anxiety. She knew how quietly they would come in if her ideas were wrong, how scrupulous they would be not to show any satisfaction they might be feeling. An hour passed before Mr. Forrest came in and the fact that Mr. Fry was not with him struck a hopeful note.

"Well?" she said.

"There's too much oil in the madder, ma'am. Far too much. I don't know how it happened; it may be carelessness or faulty mixing or poor ingredients."

Her heart leapt. "Would that account for——"

"Oh, yes, entirely."

"Have we much of it?"

"Yes, it's just newly mixed."

"Well, thank you. Will you tell Mr. Fry to get some fresh—and not to throw the old away yet? Mr. Ferguson will decide what to do with it."

"Very well, ma'am."

Inwardly bubbling with joy, she carefully went through some unnecessary accounts until Simnel turned up again just after noon. He carried a piece of cloth.

"I'm sorry, Mrs. Ferguson," he said, "the airing doesn't seem to have done much good. It's marked less, but it's still marking. It won't pass."

"No," she said, and told him the news Forrest had brought. He listened without change of expression.

"Well," he said, "that's good. But we must find who's at fault. What have you told them? Very well, but it'll mean rearranging our work for the week."

She looked at him, just as scrupulous not to show any of her triumph. "Yes, I expect so. Perhaps you'd help me to do that now."

In the afternoon she met Stephen some distance from the Grove, and they drove out to Burnage. The trees had lost their first yellow and were all copper and gold. The leaves lay thick in the lanes and made agreeable crunchy sounds under the wheels of the carriage. The hazy sun sent searchlights through the trees, and the cottages lay like old brown loaves long baked by the summer. They drove on to Northenden and had tea at an old inn by the river. The water had silk patches on it and dark broken shadows under the banks. They talked very little, being happy in each other's company and content with the memories of last week. This morning seemed to her a thousand miles away; it remained with her as something agreeable, a little pleasant triumph in the back of her mind, in a backwater of her life. This, her association with Stephen, was the main current. Several times she nearly told him about it, but a sense of shyness stopped her.

He thought: I haven't told her yet. I can't help it. But I must soon. Should I break all this peace now, say, 'Delia, I am married, it was all a mistake, but she won't let me go, not yet anyway'? What does it *matter* whether I'm married or not? There can't be marriage between us while Brook . . . It's only one more obstacle.

She said: "It doesn't smell like autumn today, but like spring. It's a sort of warm buttery smell there is in the air, and reminds me of picnics when I was about five."

"Would you like to have a boat?"

"No, thank you; unless you would. . . ."

He shook his head, and there was silence for a while.

Presently she began to hum, and then to sing in a low sweet tone:

>"I try to be merry but it is no use;
>My case is very hard.
>She left me as silly as a farmyard goose
>When she married that railway guard."

He said, watching her: "You're happy, aren't you? At least I've made you that."

She smiled, pursed her lips, smiled again. "Just at this moment I don't care for anything or anybody. I woke up last night in the middle of the night and thought, Is this happening to me, *me?* And I turned over and groaned in horror. But during the day . . . I think you must be a banshee—or whatever they call them in Ireland. You've cast a spell."

"It's nothing like as complicated as that. All I've done is help you to realise your natural self, to become sweet and passionate instead of stiff and constricted. And I've helped you to forget you're married to Brook. Isn't that about it?"

"Yes," she said. "Or at least . . ."

"I'm only sorry," he said, "that my spell doesn't carry you right through the night. When *I* wake up I'm filled with joy that I shall be meeting you again next day. Your conscience is still very uneasy, isn't it?"

"At times."

"I can't think why you worry about Brook. You never loved him. And he's happy enough in London. What the eye doesn't see, you know."

The words had slipped out easily. She glanced quickly at him. After a few moments she said:

"Why are you two people, Stephen?"

"Am I? I didn't know." He sipped at his cup. "Perhaps you're right. But aren't we all? You're about six people—and never the same two days together."

"And are they all equally likeable?"

"Likeable? They're loveable! Variety is the——" He stopped. "Well, go on; what were you going to say about me?"

"I don't know."

"Did you mean you didn't like me as much sometimes as others?"

She half smiled at him through her lashes. "It isn't a question of liking. . . . But sometimes I think I know you, understand you. Everything's fine. And then suddenly a stranger's there—says unexpected things." One felt suddenly separate again, alone.

He put his hand over hers. "Such as what?"

She looked down at his hand. "Beauty's in the eye of the beholder, don't they say? Perhaps the contradictions are in me."

"Perhaps the beauty is in you," he said. "Just at the moment you look like one of the seraphim come down from the Golden Gate to pick up your halo—and a very young seraphim, about seventeen. But glory be, I know that really your brain's working away inside your head like a squirrel in a cage. Tell me, what's the matter?"

"When can we go away together, Stephen?"

He looked at her with a flicker of surprise. "Do you feel that way about it?"

"Now that it's come to this. If we must sin, let's do it openly. Then at least there'll be no need to cheapen it any more."

He said: "D'you think I like sharing you with any man, even Brook, in any particular?"

Still they were not quite talking on the same plane. "Then . . ."

He turned her hand over, patted it, his face puckering briefly with the effort of decision.

"I can't drop my affairs in Manchester in a day. Somebody will have to take over. I shall have to have it out with Dad. I'll write him to come down this week-end. Yes. I'll do it tomorrow. It may take a fortnight. Will that do?"

"Of course." She was watching him, satisfied but unsatisfied, sure of his sincerity but seeking some inner grace that he hadn't yet got to give. "Are you quite certain?"

He turned and smiled now. "Yes, my very dear. Certain, certain, certain."

The warmth was creeping back into her. "And you'll not regret it?"

"No. Not ever. And you?"

"No, not ever," she said.

They drove back when the sun went down, and he left her where he had picked her up. They were not to meet that evening.

On Thursday as he went into his club to lunch he met Dan Massington. He would have nodded and moved on, but Massington said:

"Hullo, old chap, don't see you much at the club these days."

"No? Well, no. I've been busy. One thing and another."

Massington raised an eyebrow. "You're fond of fishing, I gather."

Stephen stared, a little impatient. "Not specially. I haven't done any for years."

"Not? I must be mistaken. I thought I saw you angling at Northenden yesterday."

Under Massington's cynical gaze Stephen felt a sudden flicker of anger following the shock. His thoughts raced.

"At Northenden? I don't know what you mean."

"Troubled waters, old chap. Believe me. Can't blame you for poaching, of course. Should do the same myself given half the chance."

"Possibly you'd make a better poacher than a peeping Tom."

He knew at once he had said the wrong thing. He should have met Massington on his own ground, laughed with him.

Massington said: "You're guileless for your type, Crossley. Holding hands is best done under cover of darkness. Otherwise the world notices these things."

"You'd be amused, no doubt."

"I was indeed. More amused than you'd ever guess. I'm related to the Fergusons, you know."

"Yes, I know."

"It was bound to happen sooner or later—a girl like that married to a spineless weakling. I shall laugh like hell when Brook finds out."

"Is there any reason why he should?"

"Oh, it would spoil the whole joke if he didn't."

"No doubt you'll go out of your way to tell him."

"Good Heavens, no. Not gentlemanly, old chap. Of course, one wouldn't be above dropping the merest hint."

"Naturally not. I wonder you haven't gone hurrying. If you haven't enough money, perhaps I could pay the cab fare."

Little spots showed in Massington's cheeks. He smiled. "Pay me later. It doesn't matter now."

As he moved on, Stephen felt the impulse to call him back, to plead or to threaten; but neither course seemed to have any prospect. He went into the dining-room, furious with himself for losing his temper.

There could now be no more of this turning away from the future. The crisis was coming too quickly and had to be faced. During the afternoon he sat rather morosely in his office and thrashed the whole problem out more thoroughly than he had ever done before. He was not a man who liked unpalatable decisions, but this was a turning point in his life and he recognised it as such.

He had not arranged to meet her that day. Mr. Slaney-Smith did not vary his routine because his friend was away. Monday was washing day, Thursday was Slaney day, and it was her business to be in to entertain him. But by five Stephen was in a ferment with his new resolutions, and he decided to pay her a formal call. He found her just putting her music away.

"Stephen!" she said in an undertone as soon as Hallows had closed the door.

"It's six weeks since I was officially here last, and I asked to see Brook."

"What is it? Has something gone wrong?"

"Shall we be disturbed?"

"Any minute."

"It's Massington." He told her briefly what had passed.

"Then—do you really think he will—say something?"

"I don't know. But we can't risk it. And I've been thinking all round. I can't ask Dad to come this week-end. In truth, if he cuts up rough he's quite capable of coming straight to this house and blurting the whole thing out to the Fergusons. And that's impossible with you still here. You must leave before I tell him."

"When?"

He glanced at the door. "I should like you to leave before they come back."

"Before *Saturday?*"

"Yes." He watched her face. "You could go Saturday morning. Travel up to London as they leave it. I can find you a hotel somewhere quiet, where you could be staying a couple of weeks till I join you. It's the only way."

A shock to feel it just round the corner; tonight, tomorrow, and then . . . But it was like an operation which had to be faced; if health and happiness lay on the other side . . .

She said: "If Dan Massington knows, then it's out of our hands."

"I could come with you to London, see you safely in, and then go to see Dad. Then back here till he finds someone else. Have you much to pack?"

"No . . . I shouldn't take much."

"You'll do it, then?"

"Yes . . ."

He took her hand. "It's a big move. All afternoon I've been thinking. I'll make it up to you, Delia."

She said slowly: "I don't want anything 'making up,' Stephen."

They rapidly discussed ways and means. At length he said: "Then that's settled. You'll come as arranged tomorrow?"

"It would be better not if——"

"Oh, yes, *please*. Come as you promised at six. It will be our last night together at the Variety. I hate the thought of spoiling tomorrow. Let's not spoil it."

She said, smiling: "All right. I'll come."

When he had gone she stood a moment by the piano, turning over the music with unsteady fingers. Only yesterday she had thought, All this can be postponed until later, the moment of flight, the direction of flight. They had ventured on a glacier and at first the movement had been barely perceptible. But slowly it had increased and at some point had passed the stage where it could be arrested. Now they were glissading down the slope and there was no escape from the precipice.

At supper she found Pridey had invited Robert Birch. Mr. Slaney-Smith, who had gone very thin and scraggy of late, tried to taunt Pridey into elaborating his views on spiritualism, but Cordelia and Birch quietly collaborated in preventing a clash. Thwarted of his chosen prey, Mr. Slaney-Smith tackled Birch on euthanasia, and having got a qualified agreement on this, he turned to Cordelia and began to tell her about his children, how well they had been brought up, and how one of them had got into trouble at school through refusing to stand when the Lord's Prayer was said.

What would all these people think? That they would condemn her for all their air of civilised broad-mindedness was certain. Even Mr. Slaney-Smith, despite his advanced views. It was bitter to feel that her father and mother would be shocked beyond measure. Nothing of Mr. Blake's disapproval of the Fergusons would help him in the smallest degree to condone her immorality. She would write to them when she got to London; in the leisure time before Stephen rejoined her, she would write at length and explain it all. But *can* I explain it? Can I put into words . . .

Hallows was bending over her. "If you please, ma'am, Mr. Massington has called."

Exposure now. An icy hand. Put off, even for two days. "What does he want?"

"He wished to see Mr. Ferguson. I explained to him that they were both away. Then he asked to see you, ma'am."

"Tell him—to call again on Saturday, Hallows. Tell him Mr. Ferguson will be back then."

"What's that?" said Pridey, looking up from his pie. "Who's called?" "Dan Massington."

Pridey grunted. "Useless sort of fellow. Mischief-maker. Wouldn't have anything to do with him, young woman."

"Tell him to call on Saturday, Hallows."

When the butler had gone she waited tensely to know the result, whether Dan would consent to be dismissed. Silence had fallen at the table. Although the hostess, she was still the newcomer among these men.

Slaney-Smith said: "Haven't seen the fellow for months. Wonder what he wants, what? Probably lost all his money at the races. You remember that time, Birch—no, it would be before your time, he turned up with a bailiff's man—brazen as you please. We found him in the drawing-room, legs crossed, impudent. Mr. Ferguson had friends . . ."

Robert Birch said: "I never knew him well. I hope Brook is enjoying himself in London, Mrs. Ferguson. He wrote me a note at the beginning of the week."

She met his gaze. "Yes, he's been buying lots of books. I'm looking forward to seeing them." I mean I was.

"That Mr. Crossley was here this afternoon," said Aunt Tish. "He didn't know Brook was away either. Brook should tell people."

Hallows re-entered the room, but went about his business without comment. She wanted to ask, to call him.

"Well, has he gone?" said Pridey, crinkling his eyebrows.

"Yes, sir. After a slight argument, sir."

. . . That night in her bedroom she took out Brook's last letter and glanced through it.

. . . It was raining on Saturday, and I think I've got a bit of a cold coming through getting my feet wet. . . . The National Gallery is magnificent, the pictures in it make our galleries look silly, but I went to a concert last night and the orchestra wasn't nearly as fine as ours. . . . I met a publisher today, and quite by accident he heard I was something of a poet myself, and he at once asked to see some of my work. Naturally I showed him a few things I happened to have with me. . . .

. . . Father has been busy all week, and it's not left me as much time as I'd wanted for seeing the sights. I long to bring you with me next time. . . .

Next time . . . Next time . . . She did not sleep very well that night.

Friday, the third of November, dawned with a low fog. As she drove down into the town it thickened and grew yellower and got into her throat, even though she had ordered the closed carriage. It seemed to lie on her spirits, which had been so high and carefree and reckless at the beginning of the week. When the carriage turned into Ancoats the mean streets pressed down and together, and the women's coarse voices echoed as in a confined space. Tomkins had to stop hurriedly once, the horses rearing in fright as a ragged child darted across under their hooves. The lights of the tiny shops were lit here and there, and at the works most of the lights were on. Simnel had bronchitis; the first fog of the winter always brought it; and his loose rustling cough punctuated the morning.

There was very little for her to do, but she stayed till twelve, knowing that this was the last time she would ever be here, that this was the end of her adventure in commerce. She didn't regret it, but there is always a nostalgic pull about the thing you are leaving.

After dinner she drove round to the shop to take leave of her family. Outwardly the casual visit, but inside saying, 'Good-bye, Father, good-bye Mother; good-bye, little Anne, with your mothering instincts, and Sarah who wants to be a singer, and fat, bald, gurgling Evelyn Clarissa, and I'm sorry Teddy isn't at home, and good-bye, shop, with your clamorous clocks and garden, with your old pear tree and drawing-room, rosewood piano and kitchen and all.'

Silly to be sentimental—in twelve months . . . "No, there's nothing the matter; I just happened to be passing. Am I? Well, I don't *feel* sad. But I ought to go soon. Yes. Brook's due home tomorrow afternoon.

Well, I expect I shall go with him next time; it was more convenient for him to go alone."

She'd arranged to meet Stephen at six, and have supper with him at the Variety and then see the show again. Friday was a good night at the hall and the fog had kept no one away. Outside the yellow vapour curled morosely round the glittering signs, but within was warmth and talk and light.

Supper was served by Char, who breathed stale port and a kindly benevolence over them. Cordelia was a little damped by her presence. Char and her overblown brightness, like a shiny figurehead, was something to be vaguely frightened of, not personally but because she stood for things.

Later Val Johnson came in. A big heavy man with a Mongolian turn of feature and a thick creamy laugh, he stared back in admiration and lively goodwill; and Stephen said this was his friend, Mrs. Blake, who was going to take over the management of his music halls.

"Oh, no, I'm not," said Cordelia, laughing.

"Come, come, is this a joke, eh?" said Val Johnson with a lift of his expressive eyebrows. "Lemme in on it, now, both of you. A joke 'tween friends, eh?"

"Perfectly serious, old man," said Stephen.

"Quite the contrary," said Cordelia.

"Because if there's any truth in it, miss, madam, or otherwise," said Johnson, "lemme warn you against it. There are fates worse than death but no fate worse than dealing with music-hall folk. Into an early grave you'll go and even the worms'll have the laugh of you. *Her-reh!* Lemme *warn* you before it's too late. I b'lieve there's a keeper wanted for the monkey house at Belle Vue: now there's a nice quiet job bi contrast. Or what about these gels who get pushed about in wheelbarrows on tight-ropes: that's a nice safe job bi contrast. But music halls—gimme strength and lemme warn you!"

"She's going to be my boss, so she'll be your boss," said Stephen. "It'll pay you to keep on the right side of her."

"Pay me," said Val Johnson. *"Pay me? Nobody and nothing ever pays me. Six, ten, sixteen."* He squeezed his face up into a great clenched fist of disgust. "Sixteen kids I've got—if no more's come since Thursday—and the missus takes in washing. *Washing!* She ain't particular. She'll wash anything for fourpence. I'm a cut line. *Her-reh!* Thrupence ha'p'ny I give her every Sat'day night. But *pay* me. It's sweated labour, this comic business. Talk of the song of the shirt. If they'd only pay me by the laughs I get—twopence a laugh, a penny a grin, a ha'penny a titter, I'd make me fortune and go and live in Salford."

"Very soon," Stephen said to Cordelia, "you'll have heard all his act and you won't need to go and listen at all."

"But no," said Johnson, trying to tighten his belt an inch but failing, "they keep me here and pay me just enough to keep body and soul apart. I hope you'll alter all that, miss or madam, and see that a labourer is worthy of his what's-it. Soften their hard hearts—you'll need about a 'undredweight of soda in the water but it'll be worth the try. Then when you've got 'em good an' soaked, try and squeeze a rise o' pay out of 'em, won't you, there's a good gel."

The comedian, arguing good-temperedly, was edged towards the door and pushed through it. Ten minutes later they went out themselves to see the start of the show.

It was all arranged now. Tomorrow she would leave the house as usual for the works and would drive there but get out at the gates and take a cab to the Variety. In the meantime Stephen would send up a van for her cases, which were to be left ready, and they would catch the noon train for London. 'So,' Stephen said, 'forget tomorrow, let's enjoy tonight.'

Val Johnson opened the show with a comic song, 'As I Was A-Walking beside the Sea-shore,' and then the Brothers Rouse did their turn, more sombrely and unemotionally than ever; and Miss Lottie Freeman sang ''Arry.' Everybody sang ''Arry.' Cordelia glanced down over the crowded floor and balcony; the hands beating time, the roar of men's voices, the smoky friendliness, everybody happy again. This was all condemned because it was slightly vulgar. But why should it be wrong for people with so little gaiety in their lives to come out in the evening and eat and drink and bang on the tables and sing at the tops of their voices? Eat, drink, and be merry, for tomorrow——

"You're not singing, my sweetheart," he said, putting his hand over hers.

"I was watching them." She smiled. "I like to watch them."

"Would you like to go out among them?"

"D'you mean——"

"On the balcony. It's more fun among people."

After all, why not? Tomorrow everyone would know.

"All right," she said.

So their future was decided.

CHAPTER TWENTY It was only a few paces down the narrow corridor and they were into the balcony. The Boston Minstrels had just come on, and one of them began the verse of a song called 'Put My Little Shoes Away.' The others joined in, singing in harmony. A sentimental song; but the audience liked them sentimental and roared at the end. She saw several men wipe their eyes, and one of the smart young men at the bar blew his nose before reaching for his mug of beer.

Stephen led the way forward, nodding and smiling to the men he knew. People were staring at her and she tried to feel unconcerned by their interest. She was glad she was still wearing her small hat and veil. Room was somehow made for them at one of the tables at the front of the balcony.

'Swanee River' again. She glanced around. Six men at the table besides themselves and one girl—a pretty girl, overdressed and painted a bit. The glare and warmth of the place was more pronounced at close quarters. It got into your blood like the fumes of wine, heady and a little oppressive. A little less pleasant. At the next table officers of the Volunteers were very conscious of their moustaches and their white kid gloves. Beyond, three men who might have been bookmakers' clerks whispered together over mugs, passing on the shady tip from the stable, then two women; then a group of middle-aged men, greying, thinning, sagging, but this all forgotten; in the corner Dan Massington sat looking at her.

"They're going to sing 'Massa's in de Cold, Cold Ground,'" Stephen whispered. "I told them it was a special request."

"Yes." She took up her glass.

"You did want that, didn't you?"

"Yes. Thank you, Stephen. You are kind."

"Ladies and gentlemen," announced Major Morris, taking the long cigar out of his mouth, where he had put it to clap. "Ladies and gentlemen, it is now my privilege to announce that as a special encore and at the special request of a distinguished member of the audience tonight the Boston Minstrels will sing their famous and renowned song, 'Massa's in de Cold, Cold Ground.'"

He was amused, triumphant. She didn't look again; the one glance had shown his little one-sided smile, lips just parted over prominent teeth. She listened in a dream. Well, what did it matter? Nothing more to lose, nothing more to fear. But she hoped Stephen did not see him.

"Your hands are cold! They've no right or business to be, in this warm place. You're not nervous?"

"Champagne must stop my circulation. I wonder why?"

"It's the betwixt and between stage. You'll soon be better. Let me fill your glass."

Val Johnson came on in a sort of holiday sailor rig, a straw hat with a black silk ribbon, spotted shirt with black flowing tie, velvet jacket with brass buttons over a white waistcoat and bell-bottom trousers. His big black moustache was heavily waxed, he wore an eyeglass on a ribbon, and an enormous cigar waggled in his mouth.

"The fellows look upon me—with a jealous eye.
The ladies all adore me—as I saunter by.
They titter and they blush
Then after me they rush;
The *heaviest* of heavy seaside swells am I!"

Stephen laughed. "I believe the old scoundrel is worth a ~~raise~~ rise. I'll see he gets it next month. Och, now, you're very quiet. Brighten up, me dear, it's Saturday tomorrow."

"Och, now," she said, "I was just thinking of that."

"Well, then, I'm sorry I reminded you."

"Not at all. I'm glad I forgot."

"Look here," he said, "are you more Irish than I am?"

"I think it's catching," she said, "like German measles."

"Or Scotch Haggis."

"Is that catching?"

"Well, you have to have a doctor."

"No," she said, "you're confusing it with lobscouse."

"Oh, I thought that was something to do with the drains."

Still laughing, he turned towards the stage, and as he did so the look in his eyes changed.

He said: "Well, well, our old friend Mr. D. Massington." He bowed and smiled. "Mr. D. Massington's here, Cordelia. In the corner. Bow good evening to him."

"I certainly shan't."

"But in our business," he teased, "we have to be polite to all our customers."

"I've already seen him."

"So that was why my Delia's hands were cold. I wonder how the devil he got in. What's the matter, my sweet? He can't hurt us now. Let him gibber in his corner like the wicked old monkey he is."

"It's a superstition. He's—tied up with all the things that have upset me in the past. Perhaps M. Gustave would be able to explain it."

"Shall I have him thrown out?"

"Heavens, no. Ignore him, as you say. In a bit perhaps we can slip back to our box."

"Oh, ho," said Stephen, "but perhaps he's not content to leave it so. He's got up and he's coming this way. Hold tight, my dear, this'll be fun."

Heart thickly beating, she stared at the stage. She never knew what was happening there. Someone was on it, and the orchestra was making the most of its brass.

"Oh, evening, Crossley," said Massington behind her. "Mind if I share your table?"

"What's wrong with your own?"

"Not convivial enough. I don't attract the ladies as you do. Won't you introduce me?"

"I'll do it with pleasure if your memory's so bad."

"Well, is it my young friend after all? While the cats are away the kitten will play? I'm afraid this kitten is in for trouble. Not that I blame her."

She glanced up at him. He was rather more than usually drunk.

"Not that I blame you," he repeated. "Remember when I saw you first I warned you life with Brook would be insupportable—that's unless you were as good as you looked, which I doubted. You'd obviously got to come to terms with yourself. My only complaint—my only complaint is that you couldn't choose a gentleman to teach you how."

Cordelia leaned her chin on her hand and watched the stage show. Do nothing, show nothing to make it harder for Stephen.

But Stephen was already in a losing battle.

He said: "For a gentleman you've a very peculiar way. You're always objectionable in places where it's hard to make a disturbance. I've a feeling that your tongue's the boldest part of you."

Massington smiled. "And for an upstart, my dear Crossley, you run entirely true to type."

"Ssh! Ssh!" people were saying round them as the show went on. But Stephen was too deeply involved to care.

"I've no doubt," he said, "that you'd wish to bring ill repute on our place by getting yourself thrown out. But maybe you'd like to *walk* out, and then we can settle this in the nearest alley."

"In the fog," said Massington, "with your thugs to see fair play?"

"Bring your own friends—if there's any will admit to that. And if you're afraid of getting hurt, no doubt we can find some boxing-gloves."

"I'm sure," said Massington, "you would be able to instruct me in all the latest fouls of the ring."

"I'm sure," said Stephen, "I should be able to instruct you in how to keep your mouth shut."

"But not permanently shut, eh, my dear?" Massington turned to Cordelia. "That must be worrying you. Or are you committed past caring? Has this glib-tongued little Cheap Jack really persuaded you that he means to be honest for once in his life? Tut, what women will believe! My father used to say, 'The prettier the woman, the bigger the fool: only the plain ones learn common sense.' I think there's something in that——"

Stephen was up and had taken his arm.

"Will you go out quietly, or will you be thrown out—and I give you warning, if you are we'll prosecute."

"Stephen . . ."

Massington looked down at the hand on his arm as if at something unclean. He had all the gestures of the aristocrat but none of the restraint.

"Take your damned hand away!"

"Ssh! Ssh!"

"Take it off, I tell you! I shall stay here as long as I like! I paid like everyone else——"

Stephen motioned to the two attendants who were pushing their way through the tables. "Fling him out and send for the police." He hesitated. "No, just throw him out and leave it at that. Please keep your seats, everyone!"

People at nearby tables had got up in alarm at the noise. Stephen released Massington and motioned to them to sit down.

One of the attendants grasped Massington's elbow.

"Now come along, sir. Out yer go."

Massington turned and stared at the little uniformed man, then abruptly snatched his arm away and gave him a violent thrust in the chest which sent him sprawling across the people at the table behind. Stephen's advice was no use now. People got up, some amused, some alarmed.

The other attendant caught Massington, but he twisted and fought in a violent temper. Stephen was on him; they went down in a heap; Cordelia backed among others. Massington rolled under the table, the attendant with him; the other attendant half pulled the table away, and Massington got up on all fours, lifted the end of the table on his back; glasses and mugs and plates sliding and rolling. The painted girl screamed, pressed against the rim of the balcony; the stage show hesitated, faltered, went on. The girl was free, Stephen having pulled her. But the table was going up; others shouted now, joined in; two attendants on Massington; but their impetus, though well meant, just tipped the table; it went over the edge of the balcony; Stephen grasped it, but the weight was too much; it pulled out of his hands, the white cloth fluttering—and *crash*: the crash and the shouts came up from below; it had fallen, perhaps killed or injured.

They had Massington securely, his face bleeding, his thin black hair; he'd collapsed, retching under their weight, his own fury, drink. Stephen was looking down; the show stopped, people were shouting, screaming, a new note from below. Others peered down, took up the cry. The white table-cloth had caught on a gas bracket on the balcony edge, was flaming, flaring, out of people's reach. 'Fire!' people were shouting. 'Fire!' The band had stopped; people were up, pushing, standing, already moving to get out.

Major Morris shouted at the orchestra to play on; two dancers stared stupidly from the stage; Stephen shouted and gestured towards the back. Someone turned out the gases which ranged the balcony and the walls.

A doubtful move, the lights only in the bar, on the stage; and the light of a burning table-cloth, the flame licking at the pink chintz round the balcony. The move to get out became a sudden great unthinking rush, like a rush of water, a rush of blood, a sudden boiling over, a breaking of chemical forces. Cordelia was pushed headlong towards the door. "Keep calm!" someone was shouting; it was Stephen, vain, futile reason, thin small voice in the clamour of panic. "No danger! Keep calm!" The half-light worse than the danger of fire. People standing on tables, over-turned; the band weakly wavering into "As I Was A-Walking." Val Johnson on the stage in shirt-sleeves.

"Cordelia! Cordelia! Where are you?" Torn both ways, Stephen had abandoned the hall and now sought her. "Stephen, here!" she said, a hand raised in the flood. A woman had fallen, was screaming; the half-light was worse than the fire: a little smoke and flame; but the great beast must get out. From the body of the hall you could hear it trampling too.

Massington was gone somewhere. Stephen plunged after her. They were moving towards the stairs, stumbling and climbing over chairs; the hoops in her skirt bent and were crushed. "Stop *pushing!*" someone shouted. "There's plenty of time." They were trampling over someone lying on the floor; no other way; you had to do the same or fall. A crashing and smashing of chairs behind; someone was fighting.

The bottleneck of the stairs; Stephen nearly caught her as they reached the first step. Down, one, two, three. "Stop pushing." "Look out there!" "Mind these women!" People were pressing down from the top, with one thought only, to get to safety away from the fire, out into the open air. And at the turn of the stairs they met a stronger flood coming up from the body of the hall.

Movement suddenly ceased and was replaced by pressure, pressure that became instantly unbearable. She stood there between three men, crushed, unable to move her arms. Whalebone snapped and her skirt tore. Pressure on her shoulders, her back, her breast; she couldn't breathe. "Please," she said. "Please." The pressure eased fractionally; she could just take tiny breaths of warm vitiated air, getting warmer. Dear God, if I die. O Christ receive my soul. Is that a poem? "Stephen."

"Here," he said. Blessed voice; but he couldn't move, couldn't touch her, over people's shoulders. "Get *back* there! Get back! Stop pushing! There's no danger if we keep quiet. Go back up the stairs! Stop pushing at the top. Go *back!*"

Talk to a blind beast bent only on freedom, cattle in stampede. "Gawd!" someone started shouting. "Gawd! I'm dying. Let me *out!*"

If you faint here you're done: you stay up because you can't fall, but when they move you'll slip slowly down till their boots go over you. Keep your reason.

"All right, miss?" The man next to her was peering at her. "It's a bit 'ot, ain't it? Keep your pecker up."

"I'm all right," she said, and then she saw *his* colour changing; somebody'd turned off the colour and it was running away, out of his face, which went green; his eyes turned up and his head lolled on his shoulder. But he still stood there.

This aye night, this aye night, every night an'all. Fire and sleet and candlelight, and Christ receive thy soul. That was it; old Scottish friend of her father's, one Christmas Eve he'd . . .

They went down a step. The *heat*, as if the fire was filling the air; and the smell, the terrible smell; the human animal reduced to its basest chemical content, crushed bodies in a terrible press. "Cordelia!" The wall lights were beginning to dance. Of all the ways to die. I shall scream with my last breath. God, God, God, God! Father forgive them for they know not . . . Groaning further down. "Cordelia, my sweetheart!" "*I'm going, Stephen,*" she said. Another step. One foot was off the ground and she could not find the ground. "Blast you! God and all the Saints! Blast you! Stop pushing! Give us air!" Something was trickling down the side of her nose, sweat from her forehead. Her limbs were soaking. Another step down, into the greater heat, the greater press. Another step, the groans were all round her; Stephen was fighting someone. They had reached the corner, the dread corner.

It was like a battlefield, like a terrible battlefield in which the vanquished, the dead, and the wounded could not lie down. But some were down. She could feel them underfoot. The man beside her was slipping, would take her with him; blood was thumping in her ears. Down he went, slowly at first, then with each step quicker until one moment his hair was level with her shoulder, the next with her waist, and then he was gone.

Eased pressure; Stephen could just touch her; she took a deep breath of warm foul air and then the gap closed. It saved her for a second or two longer. The lights were inside her head now. This aye night, this aye night, every night an' all. "*Cordelia!*"

And suddenly, like a great spout of water, she and others were flung

176

into the entrance lobby by the pressure; she was on her knees, a man under her; she was falling, but someone grasped her shoulders, dragged her on hands and knees towards the door. Among the glass from the broken door, towards the air; she heard Stephen groaning behind her. It was one of the attendants who had saved her. Half sick, half fainting, she was in open air, in the swirling, blessed, friendly cold fog. Stephen had reached her, his arm about her waist as she slumped against the wall.

There were people all round, half visible in the fog, sitting on the pavement, shouting, standing in the road. No fire engine yet. Was there any fire? People were coming out faster; the worst of the bottleneck might be broken, but many were injured if not worse. Ambulances needed.

"Are you all right; answer me: are you all right!"

"Oh, Stephen," she said. "I'm . . . I think so. And you?"

His face was black, his coat gone, his waistcoat and shirt torn. He kept saying: "I tried to stop it, I tried to stop it." He released her hand and put his head in his hands.

She was just able to stand against the wall, taking great breaths of the fog. "Is it on fire?" she said. "There's no sign."

He straightened up slowly, trying to stave off collapse, trying to shake himself free of the nightmare. "I thought you were gone. By all the Saints, I thought you were lost. Are you sure you're not hurt?"

"Bruised. Better in a minute. Oh, Stephen, thank God! It was horrible!"

His eyes went up to the building. As he recovered, professionalism grew in him again, the instinct of years.

"I must go in again and see. I'll get you a cab. You must go home."

"Don't go back. You'll do no good. I'm afraid for you."

A man came stumbling out. "They're lying there!" he shouted hysterically. "Dead! Dozens of them. All down the stairs! I can't face it! Has anyone seen my brother? He was just in front of me, but I can't go in—I daren't go in again and look."

"Ah, now, stop your shouting!" Stephen started forward and took him by the shoulders. "Hold all that hysterical talk or you'll start another panic!"

"Panic! My cripes, it's a disgrace——"

A cab came out of the fog, and now two policemen. The cab was commandeered to take three injured people to the infirmary and another one nearly bumped into it as it turned away.

Stephen said: "There's a cab rank round the corner. Quickly, I must get back."

He led her down the side street; they crossed in the fog.

"I don't know whether I'm on my heels or my head," he said bitterly. "And all our fine plans. If I can't come with you tomorrow—you'll leave just the same?"

"If you want me to. But don't go back, I'm afraid for you. Or let me stay too."

"And have you mixed up with all the police? Not likely. Praise to God, here's a cab. I want you to drive this lady to Grove Hall, please, as fast as you can."

"Quick as I can? Lucky if we get there at all. It's a proper thick 'un."

He glanced back, torn both ways, put his head in after her. Almost absent-mindedly: "You have the address? The time of the train?"

"You wrote it all down."

"Oh, my Delia, what an evening. When I'd hoped——"

"I feel it was all my fault——"

"Ah, nothing of the sort at all."

"You really want me still to go tomorrow?"

"Yes, yes, what else could we do? You were right about that fellow. Bad luck! My God, I could murder him!"

"Take care, take care."

"I'll write you tomorrow to London, let you know everything. Keep out of this mess. Now go home and don't worry. Good-bye, sweetheart. I must go."

With the pressure of his lips on hers she sank back into her seat, trembling, exhausted, and the cab moved off into the fog.

She leaned back then and for a time she must have fainted, because when she came round the cab had stopped and the cabbie was groping across the road towards where a lamp feebly gleamed. Presently he came back.

"Nay, I didn't know which end o' t' street we was." He coughed. "Reckon we're summat like right." He got up and the cab began to move again.

The smell and feel of the crowd was still in her lungs, in her mind. She wanted to be sick, her mouth was dry and bitter. Skirt torn, arms bruised, knee bleeding, hair down. Those terrible minutes would live with her for ever; she would never again be content in a crowd; there would be terror of the great beast. She feared for Stephen, but her exhaustion was such that she allowed herself to go on, to be driven farther and farther away, out of his reach and his danger.

Presently a change in the sound of the wheels showed they were off the sets, and she knew she must be nearly home.

Old instincts serving, she struggled to sit up, tried to put up her hair, to smooth her clothes. She didn't know what the servants would think, what her face looked like. If she could get in without being seen.

178

She stopped the cab at the gates and paid the cabbie. Then, limping unsteadily, painfully, she went in, up the drive. Lights in the house. What time? No idea. Hallows not put the bolt up yet.

Stand in the porch between the big pillars, cool your head on the cold stone. Grope for a handkerchief to wipe your face; is it dirty? Pat your hair. An accident. That was it, an accident in the fog.

She went in. The hall was lighted; nobody about. Gather your skirts; make for the stairs boldly. What did it matter? Tomorrow . . .

Uncle Pridey came into the hall.

"My 'cello: someone's been fiddling with it, let the strings down. D'you think it's that new maid, Flossie, Florrie, or something? Why, what's gone wrong with you, young woman? Where've you been?"

"There was an accident," she said, stumbling over the words. "My cab and another. The fog was so thick."

"Are you hurt? Don't tell me you're hurt?"

"No, no. I just want to lie down for a little."

"It's confoundedly annoying," he said, peering at her. "If we'd a child in the house . . . When the tension's let down it won't stay up, you know. Keeps going flat in the middle of a piece. You're the second one that's come in like that, just wanting to lie down for a little. I expect you know. Or do you?" He wrinkled his eyebrows. "Afraid your gallivanting's over for a bit, young woman. Have you been gallivanting? Don't know and I don't want to know. We're a dull lot. But it's over now. Brook's back."

She stared at him stupidly, looking into his eyes for the laughter that was not there.

He said: "Tut, look at your skirt. Looks like an umbrella that's been struck by lightning. You know, nobody'd any business to *touch* the thing. I'll keep the 'cello in my room in future."

"Did you say—Brook?"

"Up in bed. He's got a feverish cold or something. The usual thing: sniffle, sniffle, that's why he came home. He'll be glad to see you; you can hold his hand."

She went upstairs and into their bedroom.

CHAPTER TWENTY-ONE She went into their bedroom: Brook's and hers. Her box, half packed, was in the dressing-room; he must have seen it. This would mean facing . . . She could not face him just now, on the verge of collapse.

He was lying in bed; the same Brook, the long sensitive nose, the hair curling in front of the ears, the inlooking brown eyes; eyes unnaturally bright tonight; was it with a temperature or with the growing suspicion of the truth about her.

"Cordelia!" he said. "I thought you were never coming. Where've you been?"

"Why, Brook," she said, "I didn't know. I didn't expect you." She hesitated, then bent over him.

"Don't kiss me," he said. Oh, she thought, and then he added: "I've got a fearful cold. That's why Father sent me home."

She kissed his forehead; the kiss of Judas, head hot, feverish. Did he notice anything? "What's the matter, Brook? Is it your throat again?"

"No, not really." He explained exactly how he felt. A cold last week and a fresh chill on top of it; he'd been awake coughing all last night and this morning his father had told him to come home at once. He'd shivered and sweated all the way in the train.

"But we must send down to the Polygon at once," she said. "It's bad to neglect a temperature. He'll be able to give you something." The homely mothering things, the pampering things she had learned these last two years.

"I've taken some fever curer," he muttered, half unwilling to be persuaded that he was really ill, yet desperately absorbed in his own symptoms.

She said: "I'll just change my frock; then I'll slip down and send one of the maids." She met his gaze for a second, frankly, assessingly. "I was in an accident, Brook, the cab I was in—in the fog, you know—it collided with a wall."

"Ah? That was bad. It was thick at eight when I came home. It's made my cough worse." He wasn't interested in her accident, in her lies; she was ashamed of them as soon as uttered.

In the dressing-room her case stared at her accusingly; she had not even bothered to close the lid; anyone could see it was half full. She turned to the glass. Dreadful. Hair pinned up anyhow, face streaked with dried perspiration. But inwardly she was a little steadier; the shock of Brook's arrival had countered the effects of the ordeal. Hastily she sponged her face, changed her frock, pushed the case into a corner. She didn't know what effect his return would have, and for the moment she was too sick and exhausted to care. For the moment her body carried on in the old familiar routine, acting and moving without her mind's direction. She heard Brook coughing. It was a thick, rustling cough, heavy and ugly.

She returned to the bedroom, slipped out, and fled down the stairs. Aunt Tish in the hall, heavy with a tale of the servants' neglect; she greeted her kindly, soothingly, and slipped past. On her way back she again met her and this time the old lady would not be thwarted and she said, "Yes, Aunt Tish," and, "No, Aunt Tish," and, "I'm sorry; I'll speak to them," hearing nothing of the complaint. Oh, to be free from all this, to be in bed and forget the happenings of tonight.

Robert Birch was not long in coming. He couldn't afford to neglect his best patients; perhaps he didn't *dare* to neglect them, suggested Massington's old poison, working, stirring in the blood still. Tall, reticent, rather ugly in a not unattractive way, he strode up the stairs with her, greeted Brook, talked of the fog. Brook as usual was a bundle of nerves at the sight of his friend, curiously anxious to deceive him into thinking there was nothing wrong, as if the doctor were the final arbiter of his condition and not merely the assessor. Robert took out one of the new clinical thermometers and found that his patient's temperature was 102 degrees. Not agreeable, but not yet cause for alarm; Brook's temperature shot up like a child's at the least thing. He sounded his lungs and said: "Well, stay in bed for several days; a very nasty cough; nothing solid, Mrs. Ferguson, but plenty to drink, must try to get the temperature down; the windows open as soon as the fog is gone; I'll make you up a bottle if the boy can come back with me; I'll be round in the morning; good night, good night."

Cordelia had been watching him. Outside on the landing he said slowly:

"I'm very sorry, Mrs. Ferguson, I'm afraid I've bad news for you. There's pneumonia well developed on both lungs."

She stared at him unbelieving, almost asked him if he was sure. Cry wolf, cry wolf. But he had never done that.

"Does that mean . . ."

"It means he's seriously ill, to say the least. With his constitution . . . Where is Mr. Ferguson? His father, I mean."

"In London."

"I should wire him, then."

"As bad as that?"

He stared at the wall with his deep-set eyes. "I certainly hope not, but it's as well to be sure. D'you think you'll be able to manage tonight?"

"Oh, yes."

"We'll see about nurses in the morning. I'm afraid you may not get much sleep. Give him a sip of brandy every two hours. If I don't hear I'll be round at eight."

That's the end of flight for a little while, Stephen. A rat can desert, but not surely the most faithless wife. Brook never did me any harm, unless to marry a woman before she discovers . . . I'll write in the morning; Stephen's got to stay in Manchester himself now; it will mean postponing for a few days, a week, or until Dan Massington denounces. But he is probably one of the injured. I *can't* leave with Brook ill. Suppose this illness *solved* our problem. Traitor thoughts . . . 'I try to be merry but it is no use. My case is very hard . . .'

"All right, Brook, it's me, Brook, Cordelia. Drink this." He was a bit delirious; once he had called her Margaret, but at least not in a voice of love. Heavens, I'm tired; I shall be asleep in a minute: mustn't drop off. That dreadful panic: it's still in my ears, in my stomach. Poor Stephen, I pray he's safe; I hope that man wasn't right, shouting about people dead. Did I really *tread* on people? It felt like it. It was go on or go under. I shall *never* forget it. "No, Brook, not out of bed; it's not morning yet: look, the curtains are back and it's dark. . . ."

I wonder if Dan Massington will come. And is Val Johnson safe, and . . . 'I try to be merry but it is no use . . .' It will all be in the papers. A police inquiry? Shall I be called? "No, it's brandy, Brook. The doctor said you were to have it. . . . He's not here, he's in London; don't you remember?" I shall be wandering myself soon; if only I could sleep.

In the end she did sleep and Brook slept, too, in the early morning just before daylight came. And then he woke with a terrible cough, and when Robert Birch came he was hollow-eyed and exhausted.

All that morning she was busy. Birch insisted they should engage a day nurse, Cordelia undertaking to see the nights through. A special surgical woollen jacket had to be bought to secure the patient against chill, all the requirements of a prolonged siege laid in. Brook watched it all keenly, rather suspiciously, like one viewing preparations for his downfall; he was aware now that he was seriously, perhaps dangerously ill for the first time in his life; all the other false alarms were as nothing, all the sore throats, the bronchial colds, the attacks of colic, the bouts of indigestion. Yet he did not ask about his ailment, as if he was afraid of its being given a NAME.

Immediately after breakfast she ran downstairs and asked for *The Examiner,* but Uncle Pridey had taken both it and the *Guardian* up to his room. She had no time to slip out for one and so waited until dinner. At dinner, to which she came late, Uncle Pridey had forgotten to bring the papers down. She was dead tired and had no appetite, and Aunt Tish's advice about Brook seemed interminable.

She said at last, interrupting: "Was there anything interesting in the papers today, Uncle Pridey?"

"What? What papers? Oh, yes. Yes, there was indeed. Some ignoramus writing of Verdi's revolutionary harshness. Always intend replying to these silly people. Never get the time. By the way, did you interfere with my 'cello last night, Tish?"

"There was that there terrible accident," said Aunt Tish. "Eh, they were telling me about it in the kitchen. It's what comes of going to those places."

"What places?" said Cordelia.

"Theaytres, dear. There's been a terrible fire at one of the theaytres in Town, so they were saying in the kitchen. Dozens burned to death. Fire engines and ambulances and police . . ."

"People shouldn't write about what they don't understand," said Pridey. "They forget that all genius looks revolutionary to the dullards and the stick-in-the-muds."

"Did you see it, Uncle Pridey, about the theatre?"

"What? Oh, yes. At that place belonging to that friend of Brook's. The one we went to the concert with."

"Mr. Crossley?"

"That's it. Stuff and nonsense, Tish, there weren't any burned to death at all. Crushed in the panic. Cattle in a stampede. Can't reason with a crowd. I just glanced at the headlines. Twenty-three, it said."

"Twen—— You mean injured, Uncle Pridey?"

"No, dead. This toast is like biscuits, Patty. You cut it too thin and cook it too slow."

"Sorry, sir. I'll tell cook."

Cordelia stared at her plate.

"Twenty-three," said Uncle Pridey, chewing. "More than twice as many as were killed in the Peterloo massacre. But these people won't be sentimentalised over. You see? The coroner will say there ought to have been another exit door; jury will pass a rider; nobody'll do anything about it, and the music hall will be open and playing to capacity again within a week."

"Were there—many injured?"

"Don't know. Just scanned it. Believe it said young Crossley got knocked about a bit. Agreeable fellow, I thought. Agreeably impudent."

There was silence.

"I think I'll go for the papers," Cordelia said, getting up blindly. "Where are they?"

"On my dressing-table. Send Patty if you're in all that hurry."

But she wouldn't listen. She had to see what it said in print, alone.

Trembling, she sat on his bed and read it, her eyes skipping in panic down the page.

'Injured.' 'Among the injured were . . .' No sign of it there. Dear God . . . 'The theatre was bought by Mr. Patrick Crossley two years ago when extensive alterations . . .' No.

She couldn't hold the paper steady and had to spread it on the bed. 'Mr. Crossley, in an interview this morning, stated . . .' So he was that well. But which Mr. Crossley?

Here it was. 'Mr. Crossley, Jr., re-entering the theatre with the fire brigade, had the misfortune to be on the stage when part of it collapsed, and he was admitted to the Royal Infirmary with a fractured leg and bruises.'

Somebody was arriving downstairs. Mr. Ferguson; he was due about one. There didn't seem to be any release, any relief for her in what she had read, in knowing at least that Stephen was not permanently injured. She stared at the great headlines. You could hardly expect anything else: it was the worst disaster of its kind that had ever happened in the Town. Eye-witness accounts of the panic, editorial comment, lists of the dead and injured. She felt so terribly sick again at the thought of all those people, as if their death lay on her conscience. Tears began to run down her cheeks, but they were not tears of remorse. Weakness and unhappiness and sheer desperate fatigue. She could have collapsed on Uncle Pridey's bed with all the mice and the shrews staring at her with bright, quiet, inquisitive eyes.

'The cause of the panic is not yet known but is believed to have been caused by some drunken men.'

Must go down. Nothing has happened, Mr. Ferguson; the dutiful wife, the business-like daughter-in-law; your son is desperately ill; if I look tired and colourless it is after being up all night nursing him. 'She left me as silly as a farmyard goose when she married that railway guard!' That song; it went round and round in her head, round and round, endlessly repeating. She would die with it.

Sham and deceit. Well, the pretence must go on for the time being; there was no other way out. Unless Dan Massington called today as arranged. Then it would be all over. She would face it—almost with relief. Cordelia the straightforward, the honest. If things had gone right she would by this time be an hour gone on her journey to London.

She picked up the paper to fold it, and as she did so she glanced down the column of names of those who were dead. Unbelieving, she saw: 'D. Massington, Esq, The Dower House, Alderley Edge.'

CHAPTER TWENTY-TWO ❦ Mr. Ferguson had come back a little irritated at the recall. It showed in every mannerism, in every impatient breath he breathed. But having seen Brook and Robert Birch, his attitude changed, and there was just the faintest flicker of uneasiness at the back of his self-opinionated grey eyes.

Nevertheless he was determined to have as much say in the matter as possible. Birch was sent off in the Ferguson carriage to call on

Mr. Plimley of St. Ann's Square. Mr. Plimley, the lung specialist, came and saw, and his report was bad. Lobar pneumonia, well advanced, as Dr. Birch had said.

"I won't say that the position is by any means hopeless, Mr. Ferguson, but I should be wrong to encourage you by overoptimism. Your son's heart is very flabby and there will be a great strain put upon it in the next few days. By the way, don't on any account let him be given any more of that patent cough medicine stuff. It will ease the cough, which will be fatal, for if there is to be a salvation it must come through the cough, distressing though that is. Dr. Birch was quite right to prescribe an expectorant I think I can perhaps let you have something a little more efficient. For the rest—well, it depends very much on the patient. And it depends on the nursing." He smiled gravely at Cordelia. "It is a great help to a patient to know that one of his loved ones is near."

After the specialist had gone, Mr. Ferguson came back into the drawing-room and stood breathing before the fire. Cordelia had not risen from her chair.

"I partly blame myself for this," he said heavily. "Brook has had the chill on him for some days. He would have come home earlier if I had allowed him."

"I expect he was well looked after in London, wasn't he?"

"Not like home, as you must know." One hoped to comfort and earned a mild reproof.

She got up. "I must see if he wants anything."

"Nurse Charters is here, isn't she?"

"Well, she's new, and I thought——"

"What sleep did you have last night?"

"I don't remember." I *can't* be praised for my devotion already.

"Well, if you'll take my advice, go and get the blue-room bed made up and sleep in there. You'll need all your strength for tonight."

"Very well." But first I must write to Stephen. Just a note to the infirmary. 'Stephen, dear Stephen, I can't go yet. Brook is dangerously ill, and with Dan Massington being—now he cannot come. I am so very concerned about your injury, please write to me at once and tell me how you are. I will be round as soon as ever I can. . . .'

"Is everything satisfactory at the works?"

"It was yesterday morning." She went into details.

"Good. I'm glad you did that. It's a great pity that your first period of responsibility should end this way."

As she got to the door something made her say: "I see Dan Massington's dead."

He looked up keenly, his brows knit. "Massington? I didn't know he was ill."

"No . . . He—it's in the papers this morning." She haltingly explained.

"At the Variety? There was a notice in the London paper. That's Crossley's music hall, isn't it?"

"I didn't have time to read it all."

"Fortunate it was not a Saturday or Mr. Slaney-Smith would have been there. Well, I think that will finish the Crossleys in our city."

His complacency provoked her. "I'm *sorry* for their misfortune," she said hotly. "I'm sure they'd be sorry to know of ours."

But it was useless. "As for Massington," he went on, not listening, "it is not our place as Christians to condemn. Naturally I wished him no harm, but I won't pretend that his death will be any loss to us. He was very little comfort to his sister while she was alive, but when she died he made as much fuss as if we had forced her to take her own life."

And didn't you? she thought, going out and closing the door. No, common sense said, not Mr. Ferguson, the owner of Grove Hall, the councillor, the dyer and printer and mill owner, the sturdy Christian.

Sunday saw little change, but by the evening Brook's temperature was up to 104 degrees, and he was delirious on and off all through the night. She nursed him devotedly.

Towards the morning he came to himself but was plainly weaker. The heavy loose cough shook his thin body again and again. After only two days his frame was wasted and there seemed no bulk at all under the bedclothes. Now that he was rational there was no time or thought for ordinary conversation; his whole being was absorbed in the struggle for survival. His eyes followed her but he seldom spoke.

After a particularly bad bout of coughing he said: "Suppose you gave me—a dose of that—Walker's Cough Syrup."

"I couldn't do that. Robert said not."

"Well, his stuff—doesn't seem to soothe—at all."

"No, dear. They said it was necessary; it seems hard but they say the coughing helps to clear the congestion."

He said, rustling deep in his breathing: "I can feel it coming now. Give me one dose. No one will ever know."

No one will ever know. "I can't, Brook. I daren't."

"I don't believe—you want me—to get better."

"It's because you must get better that you mustn't go against what the doctor says."

She was relieved and exhausted when Nurse Charters came. She slept for two hours and then was up again for Mr. Plimley's visit.

Mr. Plimley did not expect Brook to live through the day, but he did not put it into so many words.

When he had gone, Mr. Ferguson said: "I think I shall not go down to the works today. I will—send word." He looked at Cordelia from under lowered brows. "Don't despair, my dear child. While there's life there's hope. We are doing all we can. The rest is in God's hands. I— lost two of my children. We had great hopes for them. Great hopes. They were fine fellows, vigorous, intelligent, had never ailed until then. It was a terrible blow. I trust that this final loss—will be spared me. I think I will summon the servants and say a brief prayer. When two or three are gathered together . . ."

By the afternoon's post came an ill-written letter from Stephen:

My Dearest,

Bless you for your note. I am *very* sorry to hear of Brook. I had pictured you in London by this time away from it all. Go soon, please. It was terrible when I got back to the theatre, like a shambles on the stairs. They wouldn't let me in at first, but later I got past them and found the fire brigade still pumping water into the theatre just as if they'd lost their witless heads. The fire was out; I swear it would have gone out on its own. Everything was deep in water and I could smell gas, so I went up on to the stage. But the great swill of water that had been draining down towards the stage had weakened the supports, and, as soon as I went blundering on in the dark, part of it gave way—and me with it. So I am here for a week or so, bad luck on it.

Do not admit to having been at the theatre on Friday, there is no reason why you should be in it. I told Dad this morning that we were going to leave M/c together. He didn't much like it. But I have talked him round and he'll give me a management in London, where, as I pointed out, the breath of scandal need hardly reach us.

He is of course all of a work about Friday; that's another reason why I think you should not be in it at all. I have told him a long story about how the trouble began. Dan Massington, at least, will not contradict me.

Oh, my sweet, I'm so longing to see you again.

Stephen

Brook lived through the day. He was terrible to watch, for he was never still except during one or two periods of drugged sleep. For the rest he was twisting and turning and pushing away the bedclothes and trying to get out and wanting to be lifted farther up the bed and complaining of the pillows, all the time conscious but not quite rational. One wondered constantly at the reserves of energy in a man who normally was so lacking in vitality. It was as if all the old hidden stores in him had been set alight and were burning up the accumulation of years in a day.

Towards evening his father took a turn at nursing him, but Brook did not seem to like him there. He kept sitting up and peering into the darker corners of the room and asking for Margaret. It was only when

Cordelia came in again that he sank back reassured, as if he knew then the difference between nightmare and reality.

At midnight they gave him another tablet and he slept a while. When he woke he stared at Cordelia with great earnestness, following her movements and allowing himself to be given a sip of brandy.

Then he gave a nervous titter and said: "When I marry again? *If* I marry again, you mean. I don't see the hurry." A pause. He stared at Cordelia, frowning patiently. "Who? The Blakes! What! Rather a change from the Massingtons of Alderley Edge, isn't it?"

He looked so natural and so rational that she found it more than usually hard to bear.

"Hush, dear, don't talk any more now. Just lie back and rest."

"But I must talk, Cordelia. What's Mr. Slaney-Smith to do with it? No, we don't want another sickly woman about the house. . . . Oh, I'm tired of lying in bed. Give me a drink, will you?"

He had just had one, but she gave him another. Anything to stop him talking. He turned over restlessly, terribly hot in his woollen jacket, wasted and weak. Then he began to cough. She had to hold him up and thought he was going to die. When it was over he said:

"Put—the cough syrup—on the table. If I need it—I'll take it."

"I've told you, Brook. It will stop the congestion from clearing. You mustn't take it."

To divert his mind she began to talk to him, empty stuff about the house and the garden. It helped to divert her own mind too. One had the most fantastic thoughts, coming unbidden: a flock of vultures scared away but quickly returning. Whether you admit it or not, Brook is the obstacle to happiness; if he goes, Stephen and I; gone his father's objections, the need for flight, the scandal, the disgrace. Brook never loved me; it was an arrangement of the old man's to gain his own ends. No doubt they looked into my family's health and history. Not like Margaret—no more sickly women—someone young and healthy, it didn't matter much who.

She'd been the victim of an arrangement which didn't take her own happiness into account. If she now sought that happiness in her own way the world would do its utmost to crush her. Her place was not here but by Stephen's side wherever he might go. One flickering life . . .

"Oh, God!" she said aloud, breaking off from what she was saying and getting up. She left him there and stirred the fire.

There was no real temptation in it. It was not that there could be any real impulse to act but that the thoughts would not let her alone. Supposing that a woman lay helpless here, a dark-haired, thin-faced, complaining woman, disliked in this house and disliking, supposing that

Brook stood by the bed and that the woman barred the way to his freedom. . . .

A slight sound drew her attention and she turned her head and saw Brook out of bed and tottering to the table where the cough medicine stood. How he had the strength . . . Like a wraith he moved, a fine cord of obstinacy leading him on.

She jumped to her feet, ran across the bedroom. Catch his arm at the table. "My dear . . ."

"Leave me—alone——" Voice a breath of wind, puff and I'm gone.

"Please, Brook . . ." He was collapsing on her arm even while he tried to fend her off. He put out a quivering hand for the bottle, and to humour him she put the bottle into his hand, turned to lead him back to the bed. It needed all her strength to support him back. When one was so low one was scarcely human. He collapsed on the bed, shivering, his purpose forgotten, allowed her to take the bottle away, to lift in his legs and cover them. He lay back among the pillows, the spark still there but only just there. He struggled to speak.

"They're—going to—publish—my poems," he got out in a whisper.

"I'm so glad, Brook. I'm sure everyone will like them."

"Bend down, I——" She bent over him. The words came. "I'm sorry—to be so much—trouble, dear. This fog—very bad."

"Yes. Very bad."

"I never made—a will, Delia. I somehow—didn't like to. But Father—will see you're all right."

"Yes, dear. But you must get better."

"It's too late. I'm so tired. You and Father get on—well together—don't you?"

"Yes," said Cordelia.

"Very glad. Different from Margaret. Margaret—wouldn't make any effort to—understand Father. He's—very kind man if—you make an effort to understand."

"Yes, dear, but don't talk now."

"Must talk now. I love you, Delia—want you to be happy. When I'm gone. I shan't see—another morning."

"It'll be light in two or three hours, Brook," she said.

"Don't cry, dear. I shall—be all right. I dreamt last night I was—having tea in the garden—with Mother. She looked so young, as if she was only—— She said, 'Well, Brook, you've come at last. I've been waiting.'"

He was silent for a time then, holding her hand. His last grasp of life. At times the grip tightened convulsively as if to reassure him that it still held.

At length he said: "Kiss me, Delia."

189

She bent over him and kissed him.

"You're—sweet girl," he said. "Too good for me. Perhaps some day you'll—marry again—have children, be really—happy. I don't mind."

"Shall I fetch your father?" she whispered.

"No. I'd rather—like this. Quietly—just with you. Hold my hand, Cordelia—I'm—— Oh, Heavenly Father, receive Thy servant—— It isn't bad. I'm going. . . ."

The grip on her hand relaxed and he fell into a quiet sleep. The greasy perspiration on his face slowly dried. His mouth fell open. She sat by his bed and watched. Sometimes the breathing could hardly be perceived.

When Mr. Plimley came in the morning he said that the patient's temperature was coming down by lysis and that there was now a slightly improved hope of recovery.

CHAPTER TWENTY-THREE For five days more it was touch and go. Having with curious tenacity overcome the greatest obstacle, Brook's strength was not enough to go any further. It flickered weakly and preserved itself at something just above extinction.

With the devotion of an unquiet conscience she nursed him as if her own life hung on it. She wrote to Stephen again, and he replied that he was in good health and spirits and was only waiting for his leg to mend. The full inquest had been adjourned until he could attend.

By the following Monday Brook was showing slight signs of recovery. His temperature had been sub-normal for three days and he was taking milk foods. She decided that today she must make an effort to see Stephen. All the time at the back of her mind was the niggling anxiety that he had been minimising his injuries to save her worry. Mr. Ferguson was at the works, and she took their own carriage to Piccadilly and dismissed it there and walked across to the infirmary. At the door she was told that Mr. Crossley had left yesterday.

Taken aback, the tense expectancy going out of her, she said:

"Did he leave any address?"

"Yes, ma'am. He's gone home. We have the address here. , . ."

"Oh, it doesn't matter, thank you. I know the house."

Out on the pavement again, she hesitated a moment or two. Would it be unwise to call? His father might be there. But his father knew all about her, might be less prejudiced against her if they met. And soon the news would be public property anyway.

She had difficulty in finding a cab and it was nearly four before she reached his house. She must be back before Mr. Ferguson.

The girl who opened the door looked at her blankly.

"Is Mr. Crossley in, please?"

"Yes'm. What name shall I say?"

She was taken in, and waited a few moments in the drawing-room, then went upstairs behind the maid. Her heart was thumping with the excitement of seeing him again.

Stephen in bed. He flushed to the temples at sight of her; she'd never seen him do that before. For a moment they were formal while the maid withdrew, Stephen even looked alarmed. Then in each other's arms.

"My dearest!"

"Delia! I never expected! Who told you I was——"

"Stephen, I went to the hospital." She explained. Something in his voice. She found herself explaining more than she need. He had all the good looks, the attraction Brook lacked. Not sick, only hurt, all the difference.

"I came home yesterday; but, Delia, it was a bit rash coming here. I've written to you."

"Does it matter?" she said, surprised. "Is your father here?"

"Why, no. But he may be. Perhaps we can talk quickly for a few minutes. How's Brook?"

"A little better. No, don't pull a face."

"I can't help it—why be a hypocrite? I'll swear your nursing would bring a man out of the grave."

"I've only done what anyone else . . . But it's been a terrible week."

He put his warm, long-fingered hand over hers.

"Horrible for you. Poor sweetheart——"

"But don't let's talk about it. I've been so worried because I was afraid you were badly hurt."

He laughed self-consciously. "I was fit enough from the second day if it wasn't for this leg. I'm pinned down like a fly on a paper, and it'll be weeks yet. That night—I shall never forget it."

"How did—Dan Massington——"

"They say he was found on the stairs. Cordelia, I'm expecting the Inspector of Police this afternoon: they're still trying to settle the blame. I don't want you involved. Can I let you know?"

"Yes, of course." She got to her feet. "Will you write me again?"

"I hate to see you go so soon. I think of you so often and now when you come to see me . . . When can you leave Brook?"

"Not yet. He's been so desperately ill. And he depends on me. If I left him in this state the shock might bring on a collapse."

"Don't you think I need nursing too?"

"Yes. Oh, yes." She smiled. "I should love that. In a few weeks perhaps."

"Do they suspect nothing?" His keen eyes scanned her face.

"Not yet. There's been no *time*. Brook's been too ill, and his father too worried. When is the inquest?"

"It'll start again on Friday. Don't stay with the Fergusons until they find out. Your room's kept at the hotel. Go soon, so that I can join you."

There was a moment's pause. The tempo of the conversation had increased, so that now they were talking as if against a time limit.

"Stephen, are you sure everything's all right?"

"Of course."

"You still—do you want to keep to our arrangement? Nothing has changed?"

"Good Heavens, do you suppose anything *would* change? Come here, my girl, I can't reach you; this leg is maddening. Cordelia, don't you believe me?"

She smiled at him. "Of course, Stephen." If he said so like that it was all right. "I'll go now. I'm sorry to have been an inconvenient visitor. I'll send you three days' notice next time."

He glanced away and said: "Tomorrow's Tuesday. Come Thursday, now. Can you come Thursday?"

She was about to reply when the bedroom door opened and a tall dark young woman came in. She was wearing a hat and a cape.

"Oh, sorry," she said, overcasually. "I didn't know you had a visitor. I've been to Town. Er—d'you mind if I come in, Stephen?"

After a second Stephen said sharply: "Well, it's all private. Come back in five minutes."

She was handsome, this dark young woman, her hair parted in the middle under her jaunty set-back hat, her dark eyes large and hostile. And the fair young woman was handsome too, with her hair in curls at the nape of her neck and her fine grey eyes narrowed with surprise between their long brown lashes.

It was too late to do anything; it had to come out.

"Are you Mrs. Ferguson?" asked Virginia.

"Yes," said Cordelia.

"I thought as much."

"I'm afraid I don't know who you are."

"Won't you introduce us, Stephen?"

Stephen stared bitterly in front of him. "I'm *married*, Cordelia—or was—and this is my wife. I've been trying to tell you for weeks. It's not important, it hasn't the least importance, for we've been separated for years and it's not at my invitation that she's here now. She came just to——"

"I heard of Stevie's injury," she said. "And after all I *am* his wife, so I thought I'd come and look after him. You're looking after your husband—for a change. Stephen hasn't raised any great objection. I think he likes to have a woman about the house—some woman. As I said when I came down——"

"Virginia! Would you *leave* us now? I want to talk to Cordelia." His face was angry, exasperated, anxious. "It happened this way. Every time I came to the point of telling you——"

"I've often wanted to meet you, Mrs. Ferguson," Virginia interrupted. "When we first discussed you some months ago I said, 'Well, why can't we all three meet like intelligent human beings?' And your husband, too, for that matter. What does he think about it all? Or doesn't he know yet?"

"If you don't leave us," said Stephen, "I shall ring——"

"No, please," said Cordelia. "I must go." I must go at once or I shall be sick.

"You must not indeed! Nothing of the sort. It was to avoid this that I wanted you to go, Delia, but now there's no hurry. I shall have to explain right from the beginning before you properly understand, and it's a long story. Virginia means nothing to me now——"

"Except that I happen to be his wife. . . ."

"I'll go now, Stephen," Cordelia said in a low voice. "Some other time, perhaps . . ."

"You *must* listen to me!" He struggled to get out of bed and fell back with a twitch of pain. Let me turn back to him, she thought, listen, listen, believe everything, anything. "It was wrong of me to have hidden it from you, but—Cordelia, are you taking any notice? I couldn't *prevent* her coming——"

"Why should you?" she said.

"Look," said Virginia, with a little brittle twist to her lips, "there's no need to go on my account. I'll leave you here in peace. If you feel like that about him, let him have a chance of explaining."

"I don't *want* an explanation," Cordelia said passionately. I must go, get out. She turned blindly to the door.

"*Cordelia!*"

"Oh, let her go. She'll come back; you ought to know that now; your women always do. . . ."

Out in the passage. He was shouting to her, half appealing, half commanding. For once he would be disappointed; *this* woman wouldn't come back. Get out before I fall. Down the stairs . . .

Stumbled on the last step. A servant. "Can I help you, madam?" "No, thank you." Through the front door. Steadily down to the gate, knowing the servant is watching. Door closed. *Now*. Grip the gate. Walk through. Out in the roadway. Oh, God, send me a cab. The day was heavy and an early dark was falling.

She walked along and saw a seat, a circular wooden seat built round a big tree. She sat on it, trying to steady her hand, her breathing, her heart.

Thereafter was a dreadful blackness of spirit like nothing she had known before. Through all the heart-searchings of Stephen's courtship, through the trials of Brook's desperate illness, there had been the uplifting knowledge that she loved someone and was loved. She was armoured within. But now the armour had broken and crumbled like shoddy tinfoil.

His letter was waiting for her when she got home, and later a longer letter came. It was his apologia. He explained his reasons for never telling her about his marriage, his consuming love for her at the beginning and his uncertainty about hers for him, his fears of her revulsion at the news, his putting off each time until another time, the lack of the right opportunity.

As for Virginia [he went on], her coming was Dad's idea. She means *nothing* to me now and has meant nothing for years. After I met you I went to her and asked her to divorce me, and I have been trying to persuade her to do so *ever* since. At first she said she would consider it in three months, then in six months. When I found her here waiting for me, I thought, If I turn her out there's nothing to gain, if I tolerate her for a few days I may be able to talk her into being reasonable. Anyway, whichever way it turns, it can't affect us for long. Oh, yes, she's in the way as Brook is in the way; but we love each other, and nothing can bedevil it if *we're true to that*. In a month's time we shall be away together and the world can go hang.

Write to me, please, to tell me you have forgiven me; I'll not rest easy till you do.

All my love to you, Delia,

STEPHEN

Oh, Stephen, she thought, everything you say is right and reasonable, except that in this one doesn't go by reason. I almost wish you didn't put your case so well.

She wanted to believe, to accept it all just as he said; half of her wanted not to be desperately hurt and affronted and humiliated. Any escape from this desolation of the heart.

Brook was making progress now; slowly, painfully, re-establishing his grip on life. A trying time. Cordelia felt ill herself with worry and anguish and overwork. The inquest was resumed and concluded. The tragedy had shocked the city, and the owners were going to have to do something about it. Crossley, Sr., aware of expensive repairs and his son's coming indiscretion, was negotiating to sell.

Still no breath of scandal. Cordelia was so low in spirit that she didn't care what happened to her, but chance and the death of Massington left her name untouched.

After a few days Stephen wrote to her again, but she did not reply. She realised that from his point of view her attitude might look indefensible. His marriage was no greater bar than hers. Even his secrecy he had explained and explained away. But to her nothing could quite excuse his lack of candour. It was something fundamental, a first principle. Their intimacy had been such that no important secret should have existed between them, could have existed on her side.

Well, there was pride as well, hurt pride. And Virginia's remark rankled like a sore. 'She'll come back, you ought to know that, your women always do.' She knew she was only putting off the issue. As soon as he was able to get about again he would be here in person to force a decision. Until then she must concentrate on getting Brook well. Only then would she feel able to make her choice freely.

Sometimes she felt cheated and deceived by everyone, and her deceit nothing compared to theirs. Often she felt like running away, not with Stephen but from the cynical impositions of life.

Robert said Brook must get away as soon as he was well enough. Another letter from Stephen. He said:

If you knew the purgatory I'd been through these lonely weeks, not knowing what you were doing or thinking, not having even a word from you. Haven't I explained that what I did I did out of love, out of the fear of losing you? It's so hard to say by letter what I can say to you in person in five minutes. Let me have just a line. I shall be able to walk a little in another week, and if you don't come this week I shall come to see you next, and all the Fergusons in creation won't keep me out.

The first day Brook went downstairs they had tea alone in the drawing-room and as usual she read to him after tea. He looked worse downstairs than he had up—more wasted, more frail.

He said: "You've been a good nurse, Delia. *You* pulled me through. I can never thank you enough for all you've done for me."

"Oh, rubbish," she said uncomfortably.

"It isn't rubbish. I shall never be able to repay you." He was silent a moment. "I only hope it will be worth it."

She put down her book. "In another month you'll be as well as ever."

"I was always ailing before; what shall I ever make now? I wish to Heaven I could at least sleep."

"You will when you can knock about more."

He said: "I couldn't fix Uncle Pridey's book up in London. Nobody will look at such nonsense. Anyway, you've got to have a scientific training in the first place."

"He was so set on making something of it."

"My poems will be out in February. I got a letter today."

"Well, that's wonderful. Isn't that something to look forward to?"

He stared into the fire, frowning. "It's queer," he said. "One of Margaret's chief troubles was insomnia. In those days I used to sleep like a log. Funny it's come to me."

"Yes, but she used to take something for it, didn't she?"

"Sleeping pills. She was always having them." He glanced at her. "I see you've heard all about it."

"I've never been told anything." She was unable quite to hide the bitterness in her voice.

"No, I remember now, Father said the fewer people who knew about it the better, and that it would only upset you."

"What would upset me?"

"Well, you don't want to bring a new wife into a home and fill her up with gloomy stories about the old. We may be lacking in some things, but give us credit for having the tact to see that."

"Wasn't it more than gloomy stories, Brook?"

"You mean the trouble at the end? Well, I don't know. Naturally we didn't want to advertise it."

"Is it true there was nearly an inquest?"

He glanced at her again, surprised at her tone.

"Yes, I thought that was what we were talking about. Robert had issued a new box of sleeping pills the night before she died. There were supposed to be twenty in the box and the next morning there were only four. I didn't know where they'd gone. I didn't even know she'd got a new box. I knew she sometimes took a second one in the middle of the night if she couldn't get off. Father was away for a couple of days in Oldham, otherwise he might have acted more quickly to stop the rumours. I expect you know how, if once a thing gets about, there's no stopping it whatever you do. Most people hear the truth, but there's always someone left to spread the old lie."

"What lie?"

"About her having committed suicide, of course."

"How do you know it was a lie?"

He said: "Why are you suddenly so upset about it?"

"I'm not upset. How could you stop an inquest?"

He bit his fingers for a moment.

"We stopped it by finding the pills. I found them the following day at the back of her writing desk. She'd put them away in an old box. I blame myself for it. I should have known. She got like that; she was—she grew suspicious of everyone and was always hiding things. There are some things we've not found yet and probably never shall find."

Cordelia did not speak.

"Like that diary you mentioned once," he said. "And one of the household accounts books, and—and some ear-rings I gave her. Oh, well, I'm glad that time's over anyway."

They'd found the pills. She thought all round it. Mr. Ferguson had not even been in the house.

"When you didn't tell me anything about it," she said with a sort of inner anger, "did it ever occur to you that *I* might hear—the old lie?"

"What?" He looked at her. "Why, did you hear something?"

"D'you think I never met Dan Massington?"

"Oh," he said with contempt. "Him. Well, he was just being malicious. Anyone could see that."

"Perhaps you knew him better than I did."

"Of course. But you don't mean to say you believed his stories, do you?"

"I didn't know what to believe."

"Well, why didn't you come and ask me?"

Why didn't she go and ask him? Because she didn't love him, she supposed. "I did try several times, but you always put me off."

"I'm sorry," he said. "I don't remember. I expect it was with Father trying to hush it up. I really don't recall you asking at all. I thought you naturally would if you wanted to know anything. Anyway, it's not really important. You know the truth now."

Not important. Somebody else had said something was not important: a trifling matter of being already married. Had no one any imagination, any conscience, any concern for what she might feel? "Dan Massington said Robert Birch owed your father a lot of money, so it was in his interest to hush it up."

Brook smiled thinly. "Robert isn't that sort of a person, Delia. You ought to know him by now. It's his fault it ever got out. When this practice came vacant Father helped him to buy it. He's paid about half back. But I don't think Dan had any room to talk about borrowed money. D'you know how much Father lent *him* altogether, over about five years? Nearly six hundred pounds."

"What for?"

"He was always in debt. It was Father's idea that a relative of his should be given a chance to start afresh. He paid all his debts twice. But I don't think he ever got any thanks for it."

That night she sat in front of the mirror in her bedroom brushing her hair. Brook, who had been in bed since eight, lay watching her. He liked this time of his invalidism best.

Suddenly she put down her brush and burst into tears. Greatly astonished, he stared at her. In all their married life she had hardly ever cried before, certainly never like this.

"Whatever's the matter? Aren't you well?"

She didn't answer but sat there with her hands in front of her face. He said again: "What is it? Aren't you well?"

She put her head on her hands and sobbed and sobbed. Impatience began to give way to alarm. He sat up further and pushed back the bedclothes.

"What's the matter, Cordelia. Can't you say *something?* Cordelia!"

She still would not answer, or could not. Laboriously, shakily, he got out of bed, moved towards her.

"What on earth's the matter?"

"Go away," she said in a muffled tone. "Leave me alone."

But although he could be petulant with the best he could at times also be patient. He put his arm round her shoulders.

"Tell me, dear."

She got up quickly, glanced at him out of half-hostile, glinting eyes, and moved quickly to the window, holding her side, trying to choke back her sobs. But they came like sickness, shaking and twisting her body. He stood looking after her, plucking at his lip, convinced now it was something he had done, but not knowing what.

He waited a time and then poured out a glass of brandy and water. She was a little better and gulped it down, then she returned to the dressing-table and put her face in her hands again, her fair hair falling forward. He put on his dressing-gown and drew up a chair and sat beside her and waited.

"Tell me what it is."

There was silence. Her face was streaked and she was inclined to shiver. His first alarm was passing with her tears.

"Look," he said. "I'm sorry something's upset you, but I don't feel well enough to sit here all night. If you still don't feel like telling me what's the matter, why don't you come to bed? I expect you've over-tired yourself."

She said: "I haven't overtired myself."

"Then what the devil is it?"

"Do you really want to know?"

"Of course I do!"

She slowly raised her head and pushed back her hair. She gave him a deep strained look.

"I'm going to have a baby."

She never forgot the expression on his face. After a moment she couldn't stand any more, but got up again, walked to the window, winding her handkerchief round her fingers. How was she to tell him the rest?

Quickly.

"Cordelia!" he said. "Are you *sure?* Are you absolutely positive?"

"Yes," she said. "Yes. Of course I'm sure." Only ten minutes before the whole realisation had come. "But there's something else I must tell you too. You've got to listen——"

He was standing beside her. "By God, this is the best news you could possibly give me!" He took her by the shoulders. "Oh, my dear, you don't know how delighted I am. It's the greatest possible joy for me. Why didn't you tell me before? How long have you known?"

To blurt it out madly like this: the last thing ever thought or intended. But the chill of horror, the abyss of nervous collapse, and Brook persisting, persisting.

"And you crying over it! Yes, I know. I expect it's the way of things at these times. I thought I'd offended you! It was before I went away, wasn't it? By God, Father will be pleased!"

She stared at his flushed face. He looked as if someone had left him a fortune. He looked thin and weak and flushed and revitalised.

She said: "It was while you were away——"

"I wonder if Father is in bed," he said. "He doesn't usually put his light out until eleven. I've a good mind to go and see him tonight. I could just slip across——"

"Brook, there are other things——"

"Another Ferguson, eh? He's always wanted a grandson. It's been—it's been—— Sorry, dear, if I go on like this. I know you must feel off colour and a bit below par, but I can't help feeling the way I do, can I? You wouldn't want me to feel any other way, would you?"

He turned away, then abruptly turned back as if he had forgotten something, and awkwardly kissed her. She watched him put his feet tremblingly into his slippers.

"Where are you going?" she asked hysterically.

"I'll see if there's a light under his door."

"But not tonight!"

"Yes, indeed, tonight," he said, smiling at her, and moved to the door. She said: "Brook! You *mustn't!*"

"But I'm going to. Sorry to offend your modesty, my dear, but we must at least tell him. I'll be back in two jiffys. Brrr! It smells cold on the landing. I think there is a light. Yes! My Lord, won't he be surprised!"

She said: "*Brook!*"

"Yes?"

Half out of the door, he turned at last. His weak, kindly face was suffused with an enthusiasm she had never seen there before. He waited for her to speak.

"Yes, dear, what is it?"

She sat in her chair at the dressing-table and struggled with words, and when they wouldn't come she watched him turn again and go out. Nausea had seized her, and behind that was a sudden new impulse to burst into hysterical laughter.

She fought it down and fought it down, and sat there silent but quivering, her head in her hands.

CHAPTER TWENTY-FOUR Sham and deceit. Those are the words. Lie and pretend. Will they all be taken in? Well, if the lie's to go on . . .

Did you ever intend to tell him? Yes, I tried, I began, he kept interrupting. Why didn't you blurt it out, then? People can get anything out if they really want to. Did you ever really intend . . .

She won't divorce him. Whatever Brook did, my child would be illegitimate. All its life, that stain. Marked on its birth certificate, branded for life. It's wrong, society's wrong, the parents if you like, but not the child. A social leper, that's how they treat it; I remember Sally Farmer, when they got to know, and it's worse if it's a boy.

But for the hysteria she would never have flung the thing at him. The maddest thing, before even a chance of reflection, before reason . . . Tell him the whole truth, she thought. Face him: if you will go on asking, if you want to know the worst. But at the last moment his delighted face had broken her intention. Several times since she had been on the brink again. Let them turn her out of the house. She wouldn't go to Stephen. She wouldn't go to her family. Right away somewhere. It was the thing one read of, woman with child staggering through the snow. (Only there was no snow, only rain, and no child as yet.)

Life had cheated her, and now it was cheating her even of the melodrama. Instead of scorn and contempt . . .

"My dear child," said Mr. Ferguson, "what Brook told me last night. I don't think you can realise how happy. For reasons, for various reasons

200

that I do not wish to explain, succession is to me the most important thing."

It was their half-hour of business; but the house was forgotten. He was staring at her with extraordinary benevolence in his steely eyes. She had never seen such a look. It was doting. It's easy to say, tell him the truth. Hard, incredibly hard to do it. Yet how long can I go on with it in face of such an attitude? Why can't they be normal, treat it normally? Just for a little while.

He got up. "My father started the dye works. Did I ever tell you how we came to the town?"

"No."

"My grandfather was a farmer from Carlisle. He heard of the prosperity to be found in this growing city and he decided to move here. I was a child at the time. It was a great upheaval, almost like emigrating to a foreign land. We came by boat and the journey took fourteen days. Then the vessel stuck on a sandbank and we had to take a small boat and row the last twenty miles down the coast to Liverpool in a strong wind and sea. We were all sea-sick, my mother tells me, even the rowers. From Liverpool we came here by a carter's wagon. We had very little money, but my grandfather took a shop and in time saved enough to buy some land on the edge of the canal, and there my father began dyeing velveteen. The present works wasn't built until just after I married." He turned and breathed at her through his lips. "The bare account. Only one who has been through it from the start. The toil and endeavour, the scheming and contriving, the borrowing and the building. Can you wonder that my greatest desire is to be assured—to be reasonably assured that all the effort shall not be wasted—to see another of the same name and blood . . ."

And what of Stephen? What would Stephen say?

"I feel I must get away, Mr. Ferguson," she said in panic. "I'm so tired with nursing Brook I'd like to go away somewhere quiet—for a month or perhaps longer." A month would be no use. Twelve months. Time to think. What am I doing? Is it even possible?

He said: "I confess it was silly of me, but I thought it was not to be. That was why I wanted to take you into the business. At least that way the name would go on for a time. Brook, I had always felt, would not live to be old. Perhaps that is wrong; after this last illness one thinks of the creaking gate."

Had he really much affection for Brook except as an instrument of his will?

"Your—other sons, Mr. Ferguson; were they young when you lost them?"

"What d'you say?" He puffed out his lips a little disapprovingly.

"Yes. They—— It was scarlet fever. One was seven and one was four. It was a great blow." She saw that his disapproval was at being reminded of the greatest loss of his life. In weakness he'd referred to it that night of Brook's illness. But not now.

"I'm sorry," she said.

"We had such hopes of Vaughan, the eldest. The Lord moves in a mysterious way. . . ." He shook his head. "Oh, well. It is old sorrow now. We must think of the future. The future is bright."

The future is bright. From now on she would be the Queen Bee, jealously guarded, cared for, nourished.

Kindness itself. But for how long? Supposing rumour, which she had not cared about until yesterday . . . Massington might not be the only one who could whisper, and sooner or later a whisper might drop into the wrong ears.

Kindness itself. Margaret's death was perfectly natural. Was there really no mystery, nothing important to hide, to hush up—their silence, their reticence nothing more than a natural wish not to talk of something unpleasant in front of a young and impressionable second wife?

That afternoon when Robert Birch called he stayed talking to her for a while in the drawing-room. She knew he liked to talk to her, and she thought his outward reserve prevented him from having many friends.

She said abruptly: "Brook was telling me yesterday—I'd never heard before—about Margaret's death. I'd heard rumours, rather unpleasant ones, but——"

He flushed. "There was some unpleasantness with her family, yes."

She said: "Could you please tell me exactly what happened?"

His penetrating brown eyes met hers in some surprise. She did not look away. He said after a moment: "Brook's first wife suffered from sleeplessness. I used to prescribe her a simple narcotic. I supplied her with a bottle of twenty pills the day before she died. At her death only four could be found. There was nothing unusual in the death, but I thought it necessary to draw Brook's attention to this—and the nurse's when she came. It was a very unpleasant duty on my part. Fortunately the pills were found; but not before there had been a certain amount of talk. The nurse was indiscreet, and Mr. Dan Massington chose to believe there was more in the incident than there really was."

She thought: The first time I saw Dan he was sober and didn't mention it. After that, every time, the brooding spiteful mind inflamed with drink . . .

She said in distress: "Could you answer me one thing, Robert—as a friend?"

"Anything I can. Believe me."

"Dan Massington also implied it was the fault of the Fergusons that Margaret was ill because she was so unhappy with them here."

He put one hand in his breeches pocket, frowned with uneasy distaste. "You're asking me something I can't possibly answer with any certainty. I can only give you my opinion—and that——"

"Please tell me what you think."

"The pernicious anæmia she suffered from was nothing whatever to do with them. But I'm simply not qualified to tell you that the state of her mind had no effect on her physical condition. In entirely happy surroundings she might have lived longer—another six months, a year."

"*Why* was she so unhappy, Robert? Was there anything between her and Mr. Ferguson except——"

"Except fundamental dislike? I don't think so. Only——" He stopped, and she knew instantly what he could not say, 'Only there were no grandchildren.' "It's very difficult for me to be frank, Mrs. Ferguson—Cordelia—may I call you that?—because I should feel disloyal. Mr. Ferguson is a man of—very strong will. To live with him I think you must be weak enough to give way—or strong enough to give way. Margaret was neither."

She got up then. "Thank you so much for telling me." She wondered which he thought she was.

They left on the Friday for North Wales. Brook was hardly well enough for a long journey, but he was ready now to indulge almost any whim. And her whim, if he only knew it, was a panic-stricken need for flight. Once the first move to retreat is taken, each step is faster than the last.

They went to Llandudno for a few days and then, at her suggestion, took rooms at a farm near Abergele; the nearest she could get to complete obscurity.

She wrote Stephen a dozen letters before leaving home but never posted any. Then, half an hour before they must leave for the station, she scribbled a hurried note and sent it off.

STEPHEN,

Brook is still very frail and needs me. I married him quite freely and no one persuaded me into it. Therefore it's my duty to keep my promise and to stick to him.

This is the end, Stephen. *Really* the end. *Please* don't call. We have had such happiness together, and I shall never forget it. But let's both realise that the other way would have meant unhappiness for us all—for all four of us and for many others besides.

Good-bye, Stephen,
CORDELIA

It had been an agony to write; and almost when she got to Wales she wrote again contradicting it all and telling him the whole truth and saying she would join him anywhere at his bidding.

The first two weeks were the blackest of all. She was distraught, on edge, turning her problem over endlessly, leaning first one way and then the other; waking in the night with a sudden start of fear, convinced she must fly before she was found out; sinking slowly back on the pillows in resignation, her mind in control again, working out the risks, the sacrifices.

Brook, curiously, was the greatest help. He was kind and considerate, and unexacting in his own needs. His own health improved, so that very soon he was able to go on walks with her over the fields to the sea.

Mr. Ferguson travelled down sometimes to keep an eye on them, but his absences were a relief to them both. Every time he came she would watch his face carefully to see if it showed any sign of his having heard rumours.

Christmas came and went so differently from last year and the year before. No house to think of, no suppers or evening parties to prepare for.

Emotionally she at last came to a state of semi-quiescence. At bottom she was no less unhappy, no surer than when she left Grove Hall, but all the stresses of the previous months had left her worn out, defeated.

Just after the New Year they went to Rhyl for the afternoon. They drove along the promenade, went on the new pier, walked as far as the end. They peered over into the sleek grey-green water swelling and shrinking under them and then retraced their steps and had tea in the pavilion. As they sat down Brook said:

"Good Lord! Isn't that Stephen Crossley?"

So it's come. . . .

"Hullo, Crossley. Astonishing meeting you like this. Didn't know you had any interest in Wales. Won't you join us at tea?"

"Thank you. Good day to you, Mrs. Ferguson. I thought I saw you walking but I couldn't believe it."

An exchange of courtesies, old but not intimate friends. The same charm, the same easy-flowing masculine gracefulness which she half loved and half feared. He sat opposite her at the table, virile and clean-cut and strong.

"No," he said. "I doubt if it ever will be reopened. We've sold it, you know."

"Oh?" said Brook. "No. I didn't know. I've been very much out of circulation for two months."

"Some people called Pemberton. I think they will be pulling it down and building a block of offices. They're not in the show business."

"I'm sorry. I rather enjoyed my two evenings there. I'd like to have brought Cordelia some time."

"Ah, I was looking forward to it," said Stephen gently.

"What are your plans, then? Shall you stay in Manchester?"

"No, I shall manage one of the London places for the time."

"Are you thinking of opening a hall in this district?"

Stephen smiled politely at the joke. "I am not. It's business connected with my divorce."

Brook looked startled and a little uncomfortable. He glanced at Cordelia, saw her looking at him.

"You're serious, are you?"

"Of course. Why wouldn't I be?"

"Well, I didn't even know you were married."

"Few people do. It's not in me to boast about it. We didn't get on from the start, Ferguson. You wouldn't realise all that means, you who are happily married and maybe have hardly had a cross word with Mrs. Ferguson all the time. My wife was madly jealous and possessive. She couldn't bear to see me talk to another woman. If I went out I had to tell her everywhere I'd been. It got in the way of my work. . . . Now, pardon me, am I boring you, Mrs. Ferguson?"

"Oh, no certainly not. . . ." Her eyes moved away; passionate feeling stirred somewhere in their clear depths, flickered and was hidden again.

"But what?"

"As a woman I think it's a pity your wife is not here to speak for herself."

"Don't you believe my story?"

"Of course. But perhaps it has two sides."

"Every story has two sides, Mrs. Ferguson. Only prejudiced people deny a fair hearing to both."

"That's what I meant," she said.

There was a brief silence. Stephen looked at her in exasperation.

"Well, I wasn't blameless," he said. "One meets a lot of attractive creatures. But it was all harmless and meant no more than that scud on the sea, as she ought to have known. I make myself out to be no saint, I assure you. . . . But a woman of character, a woman with love in her heart as well as petty pride, should be able to set aside the unessential things and see the truth in a man."

"Perhaps it's hard for her to know the truth if she never hears it from his lips."

"It's hard if she can think of nothing but her own self-esteem."

"Perhaps she would say that what you call self-esteem is really self-preservation."

Brook passed his cup. "I think you told me once that you were interested elsewhere," he said pacifically.

"Yes. As you put it."

"Didn't you say, though, that she was married also?"

"That's so. But I think that if people love one another truly enough, then nothing can stand in their way, no man-made laws are going to stop them from coming together as they ought."

There was silence.

She said: "I think we ought to go, Brook. You're not supposed to be out after dark."

They talked for a little while longer, and then parted amicably enough. As they were jogging home Brook said:

"It's queer, you two always rub each other up the wrong way. You never have liked him, have you?"

"Oh, it isn't that."

"He's not a bad fellow really. . . . Though I did think it a bit unnecessary for him to go into details of his divorce in front of you. After all, it's not a very savoury subject." He brooded. "It only shows."

"Shows what?"

"One doesn't know one's friends. One reads of the loose morals of people connected with the stage, but I'd thought of Crossley as different."

She said: "Well, if people have made a mistake and recognise it, isn't it better to try to put it right than to live in misery all their life?"

He glanced at her in surprise at her tone.

"By divorce? I don't know. It's very unpleasant. It entails all sorts of things you may not realise."

"Oh, yes, I realise."

"Yes, well, personally, I'd go through a lot before I went through that. And in any case I shouldn't discuss it over tea as if I was simply changing houses."

She didn't reply and he let the subject drop. Women were incomprehensible and their sudden changes of front didn't make sense.

She kept close to the house all that evening, and it wasn't until the following afternoon that she walked down alone into the village to post a letter. As she turned away from the tiny post office Stephen was coming to meet her from the direction of the local inn.

He raised his hat. "This is well met. D'you mind if I walk back with you as far as the stile?"

She said: "I meant what I said, Stephen. I *can't* come to you now."

He fell into step beside her.

"All because of Virginia? You couldn't bear to think I was married, was that it?"

"It doesn't matter now. It doesn't matter what my reasons are. But

206

while Brook was ill I made my choice. I realised that I cared for him more than I thought."

"I can't understand it and I don't believe it. What's come over you?"

"Nothing's come over me." She added with a sudden softness: "I'm sorry—*sorry*. Don't think it's easy for me."

They had reached the end of the village. The day was overcast and the bare country lane stretched out before them, dry and rutted and hard.

They argued for a while. She longed to tell him the truth, to justify what she was doing.

At length he said: "If you won't come away—if nothing will persuade you—would you be willing to go on meeting as before?"

She shook her head vehemently.

"What's to stop us? Massington is out of the way."

"I'll never do that again."

He said with a hint of anger: "I might be asking you to be a holy martyr."

"That's the last thing I feel."

"Dad warned me once," he said. "He warned me that you'd let me down."

"Well then," she said, hurt and sore and wildly angry. "I've let you down and that's an end of it. What else did he say? Did he tell you your behaviour had been perfect and that it was quite all right to tell any lies you pleased so long as you got your own way? Who else have you told? Surely there must be others you've taken into your confidence over so trivial a matter. I'm sure they must all think it very wrong of me to have refused you at all. And now——"

"Be quiet," he said, gripping her arm. "If you——"

She wrenched it free. Careless of the cowhand gaping over the gate, she hurried on with Stephen stalking beside her. They walked on, right down the lane, into the copse, up to the stile. The old dead leaves crunched under their feet. The farm lay over the next brow.

"He warned me this would happen," Stephen said with great bitterness. "He said you'd withdraw at the last, he did indeed."

She took a deep breath. Anger was greater than grief. Welcome anger; let it blaze; let this be a fine fire burning up all the past.

"It must be a great consolation to you to know he was right."

She put a foot on the stile, but he grasped her arm again and pulled her back. He had never lost anything before in his life and he couldn't believe he was going to lose her now.

"Oh, Cordelia, have you no sense, sweetheart? We agreed to run away together."

"Please let me go," she said.

He said fiercely: "I believe you hate me!"

She tried to pull her arm away but he held it so tight that it hurt. She put up her other hand to help and he grasped her wrist, pulled her into his arms. With a sweep he pushed her hat off and began to kiss her. She made no effort to fight now but turned her face away so that for the most part he kissed her cheek, which was cold with the air and smelled sweet.

He seemed to try to warm it with his own passion. "I believe you hate me," he said softly, hoping for some sign that meant a denial.

"I do now," she whispered.

He released her so suddenly that but for the stile she would have fallen. He had gone very white.

He said: "I know I've not done all the right things. I'm no angel and've never pretended to be. But I do know that day in, day out, I've thought of no one else but you—all these months, all last year. Everything else has gone overboard. It's been *your* happiness, *your* welfare. . . . Well, if this is the way you want it, then you can have it this way and I'm finished. Go back to Brook. I wish him luck. Stay with him. This is the end. . . ."

He turned and walked off through the copse, beside himself with anger, hating her with all the barbed hatred of inverted love.

Blindly, wiping her face on her gloves, not knowing what she was looking for but only that something was lost, she began to feel among the undergrowth by the stile for her hat and veil.

BOOK THREE

CHAPTER ONE ❦ It was five months later that she carved her name on the broad maple-wood mantelshelf where it ran down beside the fireplace in her bedroom.

A thunderstorm drove her in from the garden one afternoon, but its passing did not clear the air. Everything was heavy and damp and breathless.

The day before she had opened one of the books on Brook's table and read a poem which began: 'When I have thoughts that I shall cease to be . . .' She had had many such thoughts of late. Today they were stronger than ever before, strong to the point of morbidness. She thought, If I die next month, Brook will marry again; his father will make him; I shall be a shadow, a name. Like Margaret. What did she leave: a diary hidden away, an accounts book, some hair combings; clothes, I suppose, which they hastily sold or gave to the poor. But I mustn't think of Margaret ever any more.

She had had her wood-carving tools out this summer, unused almost since her marriage. Now she looked at them and looked about the room and thought, Well, why not? It was a queer impulse, foreign to her; under the ordinary feminine sways she was usually so level-headed. But in late weeks all that had changed; odd needs beset her; so now the need to perpetuate her name. She thought, I'll leave some mark in this room.

She began. She had hardly made the COR when she began to feel aghast at her own impulse. She had no need to fear the anger of the household—everyone was too indulgent to her these days—but only its astonishment, and perhaps even slight alarm. She didn't like the thought of making a fool of herself, but having now begun she felt that COR looked slightly more insane than the full name would. So with inner defiance she went on.

She had finished DELI when a knock came at the door. She got up laboriously but hastily, glanced at the clock; it could not be the maid.

"Come in."

The figure of Uncle Pridey insinuated itself round the door. He wrinkled his eyebrows at the sight of her.

"Ah, I'm glad you're up, young woman. That's to say, it makes no difference to me, but I see you're open to visitors. That's the notice they have everywhere at Blackpool, isn't it? I went there once. The Something Gardens, Open to Visitors; the Something Solarium, Open to Visitors. What? What's this? A little fretwork? Jolly good. But you've left out an A."

She had flushed to her ears. "I haven't finished it."

"Well, go on, finish it, then. Don't let me interrupt you. I'll sit here and watch. Here, this'll do; this stool." He folded himself up like a pen-knife. "Now. I'll keep quiet. Naturally one has to be quiet. No creative work ever done in a chatter."

She laughed rather weakly. "To tell you the truth, I don't really know why I started. It was just a silly impulse."

"Very good impulse. Decorate the house a bit. Mind if I have a sweet? Here, try one, those in paper are the best. Have always wanted to put my initials on the piano downstairs—one of these days I will. Go on. Important thing about being silly is never to get self-conscious about it. Fatal."

She said, putting the knife down: "Well, I have now. Did you want to see me about something?"

"Just to tell you a bit of news. You're the only one in the house who might be interested." He fidgeted about on his stool for a moment, looking like an elderly lantern-jawed leprechaun. "Here, if you won't finish it, let me. Hate to see a thing half done; cake or a joint or a job."

She moved a little aside and he pulled up his stool. In a queer way he had made her irrational act rational. She supposed that was how really eccentric people looked at things; to them the slightly abnormal was commonplace, one's range of behaviour was enlarged.

In silence she watched him dig out the A. It was not a very good A, being curlier than her letters and slightly askew. Like Uncle Pridey.

"Now for the date," he said.

"Oh, I don't think that's necessary!"

"Course it is. No carving's any good without a date. Just 1869, I should say. Month doesn't matter. Year of Grace, eh? Civilisation expanding like a bit of elastic. Question is, where'll it snap?"

He began on the 1.

"And your news?" she said.

"Going to get my book published."

She said: "Oh, I'm *delighted!* That's splendid!"

"Ah. Thought you'd be glad. It's not quite all it might be: got to pay half the cost. But that's better than Brook did with his poems. And little he's got out of it. Little I may get out of it too, but at least the thing will see the light. And some day people will recognise it. Maybe you'll live to see that. Envy you, you know, being still in the twenties; you'll see things. Have an idea the world's been climbing uphill all this century; about next year, 1870, it'll start running down. Exciting."

He finished the 1 and did the 8. His tongue stuck out tantalisingly while he joined up the ends.

"Really, though, I wish we lived in the year 1777."

"Why?"

"All nice straight cuts."

She laughed. He said: "Can't have all the diagrams; costs too much; pity because people buy books with diagrams; makes it easier for the simpletons to understand; this knife's not sharp."

"But is it very expensive? Surely you've enough money if you wanted."

"Bit of coarse corundum stone," he said.

"What?"

"Nothing better for sharpening a good tool. Where should I have money, young woman? Frederick makes an allowance, and deducts so much for my keep. By the time my magazine subscriptions are paid, my——"

"I'm sorry. I didn't want to seem to——"

"No. Perfectly all right. Quite entitled to ask. But where should I lay my hands on a hundred pounds—a hundred more than I've already put up?"

"Well, the works."

"Oh, the works." Pridey waved an impatient knife. "Money's there but always tied up. Frederick's always expanding, never content to sit back and make money; always putting it into a new machine, a new extension. If I ask him I know. He's always making money for us but we never see it."

She said nothing. It could not be her concern to read Uncle Pridey his first lesson in treason.

"There," said the old man, sitting back with his fingers on his imperial; "that's done. H'm. What d'you think of it? Not so even as yours. Will have to do. Now for some ink."

"Ink?"

"Well, don't you think so? Always used ink on the desks at school, make it look as if it had been done by the boy last week."

Her depression had gone. "All right. I'll get you some." She brought some from the dressing-room and watched him again. "I see you're an expert."

"Used to be. Certainly used to be. It's going to rain again."

She stared out at the lowering sky. The leaves were dead and still, only now and then one quivered under the impact of a drop. Something splashed on the window-sill and spread like a damp star.

She said:

"Would you let me put up the last hundred pounds?"

He turned his head and frowned at her. "What? What nonsense! Spend your money in a proper manner. You'll have something to use it on in a week or two: christening robes! lace frocks! veils and velvets! I know."

"Brook will pay for all those things. This is money I'd saved up for—something else, an emergency, out of *my* allowance, and now—I don't think I'm ever going to want it—at least as I thought I might." She had *not* been discovered; there had been no rumours, no flight; against the run of probabilities their infinite precaution had held. "And I'd like to see the diagrams in. I liked the diagrams."

"And the tables," said Pridey, cracking his fingers in anguish; "the tables of breeding. And the genealogical trees. And the graphs. They've all had to go. Agreed to that."

"Well, it isn't too late to change, is it? You could wire them, couldn't you?"

He peered at her. "A whim. Nothing more. You may have the money, but it's just a whim."

"No, it isn't. I want to use it that way."

"I don't like it. A bad business. Sure you're quite all right, young woman? It isn't this condition you're in? People get queer ideas sometimes. Expect that's why you went off gallivanting those first weeks."

"It was only one week, Uncle Pridey."

"And not only people go queer, you know. I remember one of my best mice. She began to eat her own tail. Far better keep your money, you know."

"When you look at me like that," she said, "you make me feel like a mouse."

"No," he said. "You're not a mouse. You're a mixture. I've watched you. Don't think I haven't. Cool head and warm heart. Sounds romantic, but I mean it. Always warring, first one on top, then the other. Dangerous."

She said: "Well, I'm quite serious and sane at the moment. My head's clear and I can get you the money tomorrow. Why don't you wire them?"

The rain was coming. It sounded in the garden like the pattering of feet.

"All right," he said energetically. "It's a damned disgrace, but I will."

CHAPTER TWO ✦ At 2 P.M. on Thursday, the sixteenth of August, 1869, with a trained midwife, a doctor, and a specialist in attendance, and in a mild state of anæsthesia reluctantly sanctioned by Mr. Ferguson, Cordelia gave birth to a son.

Mr. Ferguson ordered extra prayers in the hall.

Towards evening he was allowed in to see the mother and child. The curtains were drawn to keep out the hot sun, and a mellow pink light filled the room. It gave it a sanctified grandeur so that one spoke in whispers and walked with quiet feet. To Mr. Ferguson's annoyance Mrs. Blake, being a woman, had been let in some time ago, and she stood now gazing down with complacent pride at the bundle in the cot. Brook, worn out with a night and half a day's anxiety, sat by the bed holding Cordelia's hand, saying nothing and not knowing what to say; and Cordelia, having done her part, decorated the pillow like a quiescent flower, content for the time to let life slip by, too tired for any irony which the evening might bring.

Mr. Ferguson's bulk towered towards the bed canopy, and she smiled quietly up at him.

He said: "Well done. Well done. Of course I'd never any doubt, had you, Brook? You must be very happy, my dear."

"Yes—I am."

"Mr. Slaney-Smith called to inquire. He was just off to his lecture and made a detour."

"Oh—that was kind of him."

"So I thought. He was naturally gratified at our news. He sent his compliments."

Mr. Ferguson's eyes were straying, and presently he said: "I will see the baby now. Show me him, Brook; bestir yourself."

Brook got up and went with his father to the cot. They stared down at the crumpled pink features of Cordelia's child.

"Isn't he a little dear?" exclaimed Mrs. Blake. "Taking it all in already and sucking his thumb as if he was two months old! Look at his little finger-nails, like little sea-shells, aren't they? And look at the little creases round his neck, Mr. Ferguson. Grannie's joy! You know, I never get tired of seeing a new-born baby, many as I've had myself. They're God's messengers, that's what I call them, straight from Heaven——"

"Yes," said Mr. Ferguson heavily. He wished the woman would go away. He wanted his first glimpse of his grandchild to be a private glimpse, a dignified glimpse, not one punctuated by a woman's chatter. Besides, it offended his propriety to see that she was in a certain condition herself; for a woman well over forty with a grandchild now of her own it did not seem quite decent. It was time she stopped all that. Sometimes life seemed more than a little vulgar.

"He's got the Blake eyes," said Mrs. Blake, "and the Ferguson nose. Look, he's yawning. Cordelia used to yawn a lot, I remember. The doctor said she was anæmic, but we cured that with cod-liver oil. When she was four she was the roundest, chubbiest, brightest——"

"Mother, dear," said Cordelia, rightly perceiving that Mr. Ferguson was not interested in her childhood.

When the interloper had moved off, Mr. Ferguson said: "It will be in the papers tomorrow, Brook. I sent it down by special messenger."

"Good. Thanks, Father. What a queer tiny thing. So young! What shall we call him?"

"Ian Frederick Brook," said Mr. Ferguson without hesitation. "After his father, his grandfather, and his great-grandfather."

"I'll—suggest it."

"The fifth generation since we came to this city. Though only the second born here. I am glad he has come, Brook, while I am not too old to guide him as he should go."

"Yes," said Brook.

Mr. Ferguson bent over the cot and fumbled at the bundle with his big hands. Presently he had a firm grip and picked it up.

"Oh, sir—careful, sir," said Nurse Grimshaw, coming forward, and Cordelia raised a sudden anxious head.

"I have handled children before," said Mr. Ferguson. He peered closely at the baby's tiny face, at its clenched fist and faint fluff of dark hair. "He shall have the same education as you, Brook: the Grammar School and Owens College. I disapprove of the public schools because they take a boy away from parental influence. And at Oxford they would turn him into a papist. The influence of the *home* is the most important thing in a child's life, the example and teaching of his elders. I have spoken to Cordelia about it once, but we must have a more general understanding."

"Yes," said Brook. "Well, it's a bit early to think of that yet."

"It's *never* too early to begin a child's education, to see that he has the right environment and leadership."

"When shall I bring your father?" said Mrs. Blake. "And the children are sure to want to come. Essie will be especially interested, what with her happy event due so soon. And you know what little Anne is like. And your Aunt Doris said I was to say . . ."

Mr. Ferguson said: "The christening it would be agreeable to have on the twentieth, my birthday. Let me see, the Bishop is holding a confirmation on the twenty-first. . . ."

Cordelia thought sleepily, lazily: There was that time at Easter when that woman said hadn't she seen me somewhere before, and the time when I didn't want to call at the inn at Northenden, and when I had to discharge that maid, Vera, and I thought she had guessed something. Well, I've done it all for my son; he's legitimate; he's *safe*. That's all that matters. They don't know. None of them know the dreadful never-ceasing aching loneliness. For a while it got better, not gone but bearable: three, four, six months and something adapts itself. Then had come his letter.

She knew it nearly all by heart.

I am going abroad for a few months [he had written], to see how I like it. But I should be grieved to go and leave things as they are between us. . . . I lost my temper and said unforgivable things. I know how you must have felt and I hope you'll be trying to understand. Yes, I was wild and wanted to kill you.

. . . Sometimes I wonder if you ever really meant to run away. Well—we shall see. In a year's time I'll come to call on you again. Be thinking of me sometimes, sweetheart, and try to forgive someone who was all at fault only in loving you too much.

She had tried so hard to harden herself, to forget him, to think that she was well rid of his attentions. But it would not work. Some chemical, physical affinity existed between them and nothing could break it. Sometimes she felt herself to be torn between two opposing impulses. Stephen she loved but doubted; Brook she liked but did not love. This was an oversimplification but it came near the truth. Sometimes she felt not only that Stephen had let her down but that she had let *him* down. Her association with him had meant something to him, something *more* than that physical affinity, more than any other woman had to offer him. She had no peace of mind.

Tonight, in this pleasant backwater, she was detached for the first time from the old ache and wondered if the detachment would last.

But then she was detached from everything, impersonal, unconcerned. She stared about the room with placid eyes at the people discreetly moving and whispering in the dim sub-solar light. She had heard them talking of her son and his future. She did not mind. At present she was weak and relaxed and passively content. And tomorrow and next week would be the same.

But some time she would regain her strength, this lost, empty, lethargic contentment would go, and then these people, these amiable—or fairly amiable—grandparents, deciding whose nose he had and where he should be educated, would find they had another person to reckon with, one not naturally contentious but moved by powerful instinct to protect her own.

From where she lay she could just see the carving on the mantelpiece. She was glad her mother hadn't noticed it. Brook had thought it a practical joke: when he found that it was really carved he had been as embarrassed as she. His chief concern was what the servants would think. She hadn't dared to tell him she had lent Pridey a hundred pounds. That would really have convinced him she was going queer.

"Mother," she said, touching her mother's arm, "did you know Mr. Slaney-Smith before I married Brook?"

Mrs. Blake tucked in two wisps of hair, and three fell down. "Yes, dear, why d'you ask?"

"It's just occurred to me. He called to inquire just now. He's always seemed—rather a general friend."

Mrs. Blake glanced across at the two men to make sure they were not listening. "Oh, yes, dear," she said in an undertone. "I suppose it doesn't matter if I tell you now, you being a mother yourself. Ted and I knew each other before ever I met your father. We were quite sweethearts in our teens. On his twenty-first birthday—at his party actually—he proposed to me. Behind the curtains in the kitchen at the vicarage it was. You know, his father was then vicar of a church in Deansgate."

"No, I'd no idea. I didn't know his father was——"

"The one that had its spire taken down when you were a girl—I thought it desecration and no one knew why—there were the three boys, Charlie, who was drowned, Ted, and Frank, who does something in the Bridgewater Canal; Ted always had a bit of a fancy for me. But don't talk now, dear. I'm sure you must be tired. Just be quiet and think about nothing."

Instead she lay quite quiet and thought about last Tuesday, when Uncle Pridey and Mr. Slaney-Smith had had a fine set-to. Mr. Slaney-Smith was more quarrelsome than usual these days, and it had happened in the drawing-room before Mr. Ferguson came home. Mr. Slaney-Smith had begun it by saying: "Well, Tom, so I hear your scientific book is to be all the rage after all, what?"

Uncle Pridey had untwisted himself from his 'cello and looked down at the other man. "It's to be published if that's what you mean. Don't suppose it will get its deserts. Can't expect all the philistines to rejoice, you know."

Mr. Slaney-Smith had said: "Oh, it'll get its deserts. The public's got a keen sense of humour." He winked at Cordelia, who tried not to see.

"Donkey's can bray," Pridey had said. "But they're not the best judges of corn."

Mr. Slaney-Smith's eyes had bulged. "Well, no doubt they can tell the wheat from the chaff! What? Don't deceive yourself, my dear fellow.

The general mass of people are getting more scientific-minded every day. It's harder to hoodwink them than you think."

"So I used to believe until this fellow Huxley came along and did it so effectively."

Slaney-Smith had stiffened. "Naturally everyone can't expect to understand the most brilliant man of the century."

"Your Mr. Huxley would have made a good barrister—rather on the shady side, you know—able to make a bad case sound good; but as a man of science . . ." Pridey cracked his fingers in agitation. "As for Mr. Darwin . . ."

"Uncle Pridey," Cordelia had said. "I think——"

"As for Mr. Darwin, a distinguished botanist, no doubt, following a well-worn track——"

"If you were not so ignorant of the common principles of science, what? The idle prattle of a silly old man——"

"—a well-worn track," Uncle Pridey had said, cracking away, "trodden before by Wallace, Buffon, Lamarck, Erasmus, Darwin. In a few years' time another nine days' wonder will have come, while the real men, the men who count——"

"Such as yourself, no doubt."

"Not at all. I'm important only in a small way, but——"

"This modesty is alarming. But then all great men undervalue themselves. We must see what we can do to persuade you out of your retirement when the book gets its proper welcome. . . ."

Names and epithets had been flung across the room. Brook had arrived and together they had broken up the argument and steered Pridey, still talking excitedly, from the room. The old man had been thoroughly roused by Slaney-Smith's sarcasms.

Cordelia thought: Heavens. If Mother had . . . Mr. Slaney-Smith might have been my father; I might have been brought up like his children, creeping about the house when he's at home, *scientific*: how strange. Then she thought: Heavens, what if other people do what I've done: what if I *am* his child! She glanced at her mother and saw how absurd it was.

"What are you smiling at, dear?"

"Nothing, Mother. Only I'm glad you chose Papa instead."

Mrs. Blake giggled, a faint girlish lisp, relic of a lost time before ever Cordelia was born. "So am I, dear. But I never really cared for Ted much that way. He always struck me as a bit too—well, methodical, even in those days." She looped up a loop of hair. "Don't tell your father, dear. He's inclined to be a bit jealous, you know."

She had never looked on her father that way. It came to her as in a sudden moment of understanding—long overdue, she instantly felt—that her father and mother did not look on themselves as old, and that the problems of today are only the problems of yesterday repeated. She felt curiously comforted and in a closer kinship with her mother than ever before. She might almost whisper to her: 'Look, Mother, I have something to tell *you* . . .'

But she knew she would never get further than that. Their kinship would never extend into the realm of the impermissible. She had committed the unforgivable sin, and her mother would never begin to understand how she had come to do it. Whether or not she joined Stephen next year, or whether she remained faithful to Brook all the rest of her life, whatever happened, this part of her secret was a part she must never share.

CHAPTER THREE Autumn came and winter, and the Irwell was in flood. The Suez Canal was opened. *Habits and Heredity in Mice*, by Thomas Pride Ferguson, was published and created as much stir as Brook's poems, which was nil. Spring followed late and another summer. The Prussians cut the French armies to pieces and advanced across Alsace singing, *'Nun danket Alle Gott,'* at appropriate intervals. Uncle Pridey muttered, "Horrible, horrible, the downfall of civilisation!" but Mr. Ferguson said not at all, and what else could one expect when one knew of the licentiousness of Paris?

Essie had a daughter and Mrs. Blake a son. 'A brother for Teddy,' they put in the paper. Teddy was twenty-four. William Edward Forster introduced something called Board Schools, objects of grave suspicion, to be paid for out of the local rates; and a progressive railway company perfected a safety chain which hung outside the window and stopped the train if you pulled it hard enough, only you were not to do it just for fun.

Stephen stayed on in America.

And Ian, his son, laughed and cried and grew, and came to crawl on a rug and could pull himself up by a chair and had ten teeth and fine-growing curly brown hair and was pushed about in one of the new prams.

Postcards were invented; and four-fifths of all the steamships in the world were British. Agriculture was the most prosperous ever. And Von Moltke, who had begun the campaign so brilliantly, continued it by taking Sedan, Metz, Châteaudun, two or three armies, and Napoleon the Third as makeweight. Parisians, it was reported, were eating maize, ground bones, and leopards out of the zoo. The *Guardian*, which was always humanitarian, made quite a fuss about it.

One day, when out shopping in the town, Cordelia met Mrs. Slaney-Smith. Mrs. Slaney-Smith looked more anxious and more furtive than usual, and after a few polite preliminaries, she began to ask Cordelia about Mr. Slaney-Smith, how often he visited Grove Hall in a week. From that she suddenly overflowed into tears and confidences she could no longer suppress. Mr. Slaney-Smith was out almost every night. Mr. Slaney-Smith was not being honest with her. Mr. Slaney-Smith was going with another woman. It had been developing for two years. She had no proof but she was convinced of it. Moisture blinking on her thin pale lashes, she assembled her facts: the letters he regularly received in a woman's handwriting, the mounting debts, his coldness and pre-occupation.

Embarrassed and distressed, Cordelia tried to comfort and reassure her. But Mrs. Slaney-Smith was beyond that. During the rest of the day and well into the night Cordelia could not get the sound of Mrs. Slaney-Smith's voice out of her head, the shabby grey dress, the finger-tips, dusty white and wrinkled with constant washing, placed distressfully on her arm.

"A hard life, Mrs. Ferguson, all this time, these years. He has *moods*, you know, won't speak to us for hours, for days. I used to say to him, 'Let me help you,' but he keeps me out, outside himself, as it were. He wrestles, I believe, *inwardly*, you know."

"Forgive me, Mrs. Slaney-Smith, I don't want to pry, but—has this sort of thing happened before?"

"Well, sometimes now I wonder. I wonder if it's all tied up, connected. I know of one time, a *maid* we had when our eldest was tiny; I caught them in the hall, you could tell by their expressions. But that was seventeen years ago and not *serious*. I've wondered since, going to those music halls, exposed to temptation. Is your husband a God-fearing man?"

". . . Yes, I think so."

"It makes a difference, say what you will, it makes a difference; this un-Godliness, it leaves one without a *guide*. It's very, very sad, Mrs. Ferguson, and all my poor children. The Grammar School won't wait for their school bills!"

"I wish you'd let me tell Brook, Mrs. Slaney-Smith. I feel sure he would be willing to help you—that way—if I could explain. . . ."

Mrs. Slaney-Smith flicked a glance behind her. "I assure you, Mrs. Ferguson, it was the very *last* thing I ever thought of, ever dreamed of. I feel quite ashamed of this outburst, I really do. But you've always been so kind. Please, please, don't mention it again. . . ."

Nevertheless in the weeks that followed Mrs. Slaney-Smith was persuaded to accept a loan—on the understanding that Mr. Ferguson should on no account be told.

Cordelia found herself occasionally visiting the dye works again, once deputising when Brook was ill and Mr. Ferguson away, once or twice going down with them for special purposes, to see the effect of the new coal-tar greens, to help during a rush period.

To her surprise she found herself accepted by the foremen; she was no longer a stranger or an interloper. Sometimes they even seemed to welcome her. She was a woman, but they had had something in common ever since that November day.

This, too, was a period which saw the beginning of a tactical struggle between herself and Mr. Ferguson over Ian. (The pram represented a minor victory for her, since it was his view that his grandson should not be pushed about for everybody to peer at.) Sometimes one triumphed, sometimes the other. There had not yet emerged a crisis on which neither found it possible to give way. An open rift occurred only once, when Cordelia came back late from shopping one day and found that Mr. Ferguson had insisted on Ian's having his meal with the family and then, when the child upset a glass of water, had rapped him across the knuckles with the flat blade of a table-knife. On this tearful scene she came, and there were angry words in front of the servants.

"A baby of eighteen months!" she said, struggling with overmastering indignation.

"A child should never need to be disciplined after the age of two. I never had to touch any of mine after. By the time a child is two it should be necessary only for the parent to discipline himself."

"And do you think that way leads to affection between a child and its mother and father?"

"I have not had cause to complain."

"My father never touched any of us," she said, "but I never remember disobeying him."

"Indeed," said Mr. Ferguson, with the look he always reserved for her father.

"And I've the *greatest* possible respect for him," she said stormily.

"Respect for a parent," said Mr. Ferguson, "is not a matter of virtue, it is a duty. I should naturally take it for granted that you respected your father. Where the upbringing of your own son is concerned it is understandable that a mother's feelings should colour your judgment; and it is there that my advice and judgment must be of use to you. I have had a long experience of family life, yours is only just beginning."

How hard it was to measure words with him. Knuckle under or rebel: there was no middle way.

"In future, Nurse Grimshaw," she said, "Ian will have all his meals in the nursery."

"Yes, Mrs. Ferguson."

The tone of her voice left no doubt as to her choice. He looked at her, and for the first time for many months she met the full force of his glance.

"I will talk it over with Brook," he said.

CHAPTER FOUR Cordelia was at the piano when the men called. She was playing a few of the easier pieces among Brook's music, the windows wide open looking upon the sunlit shrubbery, a bee buzzing against one of the panes, and Uncle Pridey sitting on the hearthrug making faces at his great-nephew.

This was a new occupation for the old man, and one which sometimes even kept him away from his mice. He showed all sorts of unusual talents in the entertainment of a small boy just past his second birthday. At the moment he had twisted his clenched bony fist in such a way that it looked like an old woman's face, and had pushed two boot buttons in for eyes and draped a handkerchief round to look like a shawl. The tip of his thumb stuck out like a little red tongue, and Cordelia had stopped playing the piano to listen to her son's laughter.

On the scene came Betty, who had followed Vera, who had followed Patty, who had married a bus-driver.

"If you please, ma'am, two gentlemen to see Mr. Thomas Ferguson."

Uncle Pridey took the card with his free hand and screwed up his eyes at it. "Simon? Simon? Never heard of him. Must be a mistake. He can't want me. Show them in. No, don't you go, young woman, stay at your piano."

He was still squatting beside Ian when two men entered, both in the conventional frock-coats and silk hats. Men of substance. The older and taller blinked round the room, said tentatively to Cordelia:

"We are looking for Mr. Thomas Pride Ferguson. I think there must have been some mistake . . ."

"Here I am," said Pridey from the hearthrug. "Was named after a great-uncle who owned a farm and lost his sheep in a blizzard and shot himself, but that wasn't until afterwards."

"Mr. Thomas Pride Ferguson? Author of *Habits and Heredity in Mice, with Some Observations on the Anatomy of the Common Shrew?*"

"And Behaviour. Anatomy and Behaviour. It's no good talking about the bones unless you say what they do with 'em."

"My dear sir, may I introduce myself? My name is Simon. Professor Simon, Principal of the London School of Biological Research. This is Mr. Crabtree Pearson, who, as you know, contributes to the best scientific magazines."

The handkerchief was still draped round his right fist, so Pridey offered the other. It was warmly shaken.

"A-den!" said Ian. "Do it a-den!"

"Sit down if you like," said Uncle Pridey vaguely. "I've dropped one of the shoe buttons. This is my niece. Tish will complain if I don't give her them back."

"Let me take him, Uncle Pridey."

"No, no. Fair's fair. He was here first. I'll do it a-den. They can wait."

Professor Simon said: "May I congratulate you, madam, on your brilliant uncle. His book has created quite a sensation—quite a sensation."

"Sensation," said Pridey, when Ian's gurgling laughter had stopped. "It's been out eighteen months and no one's taken any notice of it."

"That, if I may say so, has been an oversight. All that will be altered now. Mr. Crabtree Pearson is devoting two complete articles to it——"

"One article," said Mr. Pearson, adjusting his pince-nez, "will be so extensive that it will appear in three monthly parts——"

"And it is hoped that we shall be able to persuade you to lecture at our next quarterly meeting. . . ."

"Lecture," said Uncle Pridey, the eyes falling out of the old woman's face. "Here, don't you eat that. Naughty, ah! Stick in your gullet."

"I'll take him, Uncle Pridey."

The old man got up, the bones in his knees creaking. "Dangerous," he said. "At least with most people. But I've a friend called Cornelius who as a young man used regularly to swallow a safety-pin for a wager. I remember he was very indignant when it was suggested he always used the same pin." Pridey looked sidelong at his visitors. "Is this a joke, eh?"

"Do we give you that impression? I firmly believe that your chapters on the anatomy of the common shrew will be accepted as a classic contribution to the biology of our time——"

"Ah, hum."

"I may say, your publisher is not a well-known man, and the book did not circulate as it should. It was quite by chance that a copy——"

"Common shrew, yes. And what about the heredity of mice?"

"An interesting and stimulating essay. Meriting anyone's perusal. But your chapters on the shrew, proving beyond doubt that it has a common phylogeny with man——"

"It's an invaluable contribution to the new theories of evolution," interrupted Mr. Pearson, taking off his pince-nez. "I have taken the liberty of sending a copy of your book to Mr. Huxley, with whom I may say I have more than a passing acquaintance——"

"Mr. Huxley," said Uncle Pridey, knotting and unknotting his eyebrows. "How very peculiar. No, don't go, young woman. Where did I put my sweets? Ah. Am I to understand that you're serious in this matter? Say it all again please. Have one of these. Didn't understand you the first time."

They said it all again, while Uncle Pridey plucked at his imperial and fumbled in his paper bag. Occasionally he glanced sidelong at Cordelia to see if she was deceived too.

"I'd like," said Mr. Crabtree Pearson, putting on his pince-nez, "if you'd allow me, sir, to take down a few biographical details so that I might mention them in the course of my articles. Also perhaps I might be allowed just a glimpse of your laboratory, so that I could describe it——"

"Laboratory," said Pridey. "Haven't got one."

"Well, perhaps you don't call it that, but wherever you do your work. How do you approach your dissecting?"

Pridey took out a huge clasp-knife. "I keep it sharp on a piece of common corundum stone. Handy thing, y'know; saw, corkscrew, gimlet, screwdriver. Only thing I don't use it for is carving names on the mantelpiece. My niece has the tools for that."

"And do you work in this house, sir?"

"My bedroom. Cosy enough. When one of my little friends dies I put him on the washstand and carve him up. You ever seen a stuffed rat? Tried my hand at a grey muzzled old fellow called Lord Palmerston. When I'd finished he looked perfect, lifelike; put him on the mantelpiece; began to smell. Had to throw him out. Don't know what I'd done wrong. D'you say you came from London?"

"Yes, this morning. We got your address from your publishers. We are staying overnight in your town and shall travel back tomorrow. Mr. Ferguson, I wonder if you happen to have a photograph of yourself which would be suitable for reproduction?"

"Only been to London once, when I was twenty-odd; had a few days there; wasn't impressed. All the people looked as if they owed money—afraid of being spoken to."

"A photograph, Uncle Pridey. Have you got one of yourself?"

"No, I haven't, young woman, or I should have said so. But why should they want a photo of me? It's not me that's important, it's the mice."

Cordelia ordered tea, and they all sat round, Professor Simon and Mr. Pearson in deferential politeness, Uncle Pridey in a sort of distracted dream, eating cakes very rapidly and casting crinkly side-glances at

Cordelia. Aunt Tish came in and was annoyed that she hadn't been told there were visitors so that she could have changed her blouse.

Cordelia pressed them to stay to supper and would take no excuse. She wanted Mr. Ferguson and Brook to meet them. And tonight, she realised, was Thursday.

The door of the drawing-room was open when Mr. Ferguson and Brook arrived, and the two visitors could be seen talking to someone out of view. Mr. Ferguson at once put his hat down for the approaching Hallows to pick up and walked into the drawing-room.

"This is my brother," said Pridey. "Professor Simon of the London something of Biology, Mr. Pearson Crabtree. They've——"

"*Professor* Simon," said Mr. Ferguson. "I seem to know the name." He shook hands. "Mr——"

"Crabtree Pearson," said Crabtree Pearson.

"Of course. Yes, yes. I know your name too. It was good of you to call. Did Madam Vaughan suggest it? You didn't write me, did you?"

"No, it was rather on the impulse of the moment——"

"Cordelia, I hope you have given these gentlemen our hospitality. I was delayed tonight: the calls of business. Have you been here long?"

"About two hours. Your daughter-in-law, is it—has kindly invited us to an evening meal, and in view of the fact——"

"Capital. Exactly what I should have wished. Are you staying in the city long?"

"No, only one night, we expect."

"I'm very flattered by your call. Oh, this is my son, Mr. Brook Ferguson. The poet, you know. I'm more than gratified that you should have decided to spend your one evening in the city with us. It's in fact a very fortunate circumstance that this is Thursday. My most intimate friend is a prominent biologist and he will be coming to supper tonight. I expect him any time."

"Are you a biologist too, Mr. Ferguson? A talent has been known to run——"

"Well, only in the way that every common man is a biologist these days." Mr. Ferguson flicked a speck of dust off his coat. "We follow the discoveries and deductions of scientists like yourselves with the greatest attention, since what you deduce sometimes calls in question our pre-conceived beliefs. By trade I am a calico-printer and velveteen dyer, as you will probably have heard. I also have an interest in the Waverley Cotton Mills."

"Oh?" said Professor Simon politely. He turned and bowed slightly to Uncle Pridey. "I suspect that you are overmodest as a family. It has given us great pleasure this afternoon to have the privilege——"

"That's Mr. Slaney-Smith now, I believe," said Mr. Ferguson. "Mr. Slaney-Smith is the biologist I was speaking of."

"I don't recall the name. Has he——"

"Quite a brilliant man though a confirmed atheist. Indeed, one would go further——"

"I'm afraid many of us are being driven into a corner these days," said Mr. Crabtree Pearson, adjusting his pince-nez. "Agnosticism is the natural retreat of the scientist. In my article of the twentieth of June last——"

Mr. Slaney-Smith was shown in. Neat, aggressive, square-shouldered and shiny, he was introduced, and his nasal voice mingled with and slightly dominated the others. The scientists, having been in the house two hours, seemed to conclude that the newcomers knew why they had come, and Mr. Slaney-Smith was so used to meeting strangers at Grove Hall that he took the situation for granted. Uncle Pridey mixed in the company and talked rather more than Mr. Ferguson thought necessary, but it was merely a passing irritation and hardly worth a rebuke.

After a few minutes they all moved out into the hall for prayers, and when these were said they went in to supper. Uncle Pridey sat between Cordelia and Aunt Tish as usual, and Mr. Ferguson had a guest on either side of him.

"My friend, Mr. Slaney-Smith . . ."

"Oh, yes, you're a biologist, sir. Are you attached to the university here, or are your researches private?"

"Private," said Mr. Slaney-Smith through his nose, "I lecture—hum—twice weekly to adult classes at the Carpenter's Hall. The title of my Tuesday evening course, which begins in a month's time, will be entitled 'Whence Man,' and the Thursday course will be called 'Natural Selection and Free Thought.' The latter series is a development of the main theme I have been pursuing for some years."

"Ah," said Professor Simon. "Does Mr. Ferguson assist you or do you consult with him on the practical side at all?"

"Mr. Ferguson? Well, I can hardly say——"

"I think," said Mr. Ferguson, not displeased, "that you do me too much honour. It may of course well be that the frequent stimulating discussions I have with——"

"No, no, I'm sorry, I meant the other Mr. Ferguson, of course; Mr. Thomas Pride Ferguson."

There was a moment's silence. They looked curiously at Uncle Pridey, who was busy with the fried sole.

Mr. Slaney-Smith said: "No, I'm afraid Mr. Tom Ferguson's researches are too deep for me to follow, what?" and went on talking. He was so sure of his own joke that it didn't occur to him that the visitors took him at his word. And Mr. Ferguson thought that Uncle Pridey had been boasting in his absence and that a rebuke would be necessary after all.

"Atheism," said Mr. Slaney-Smith, "is a necessary condition in civilised man. It's not until one clears one's mind of all the religious cant . . . A student said to me at the last session: 'Sir, do you disbelieve in the human soul?' and I replied, 'Sir, I am prepared to believe in the human soul when you show me one on the operating table.' I fancy he had not looked at it like that before."

"Talking of operating tables," said Pridey with his mouth full, "I remember a shrew I had once——"

"Your reasoning's a little arbitrary," Mr. Ferguson said benevolently, ignoring his brother. "If you rule out everything you can't see, then you must rule out half the attributes of civilised life: conscience, humour, memory . . ."

They wrangled amiably for some moments and then, seeing that their guests were not joining in, Mr. Ferguson steered round to their own subject. Here again the scientists were reserved and Mr. Slaney-Smith was left to do most of the talking. He was not at all abashed by his audience.

At length Mr. Ferguson said: "But perhaps you don't agree with either of us, Professor Simon?"

"You're both well versed in the theories of modern biology," Simon said. "A theoretical acquaintance, of course, is not everything. But I believe Mr. Thomas Ferguson was about to say something."

"To my way of looking at it," said Pridey, "it's simple enough. We're all agnostics, eh? Aren't we? Aren't we? That's humility for you. You can't believe anythin' till you confess you know nothing. But atheism's not just a step on; it's a mile away. Because atheism's intellectual pride, and pride and humility are not partners, they're opposites. That's it in a nutshell. All the rest, all this dibbling and dabbling, is just poppycock. Can't get away from it. Pass the bread, Tish."

"D'you mind," said Crabtree Pearson, adjusting his pince-nez, "would you very much mind if I put that down while it's fresh in my memory? I should be very grateful. I have a pad here."

Mr. Ferguson and Mr. Slaney-Smith stared at the scribbling man. Mr. Slaney-Smith took out a snowy silk handkerchief and dabbed his moustache.

"I should like you," Professor Simon said to Pridey, "I should like you to meet Mr. Huxley. If you came to London I think perhaps——"

"*The* Mr. Huxley?" Slaney-Smith said. "You know him?"

"Yes, we were at school together. If you came to London perhaps we could arrange a meeting, Mr. Ferguson."

"Ah," said Pridey. "Don't know. It might not do. Shall have to think it over."

"It's unlikely," said Mr. Ferguson in his Olympian manner, "that my brother will ever go to London; but I shall have occasion to be there this autumn. I should like to meet Mr. Huxley."

Professor Simon looked at his host without much favour. "I don't know if that would be possible."

"Naturally I've no wish to push myself. It was you who put the suggestion forward."

"I put the suggestion to your brother, sir. Forgive me if I am blunt, but Mr. Huxley is not easily accessible to the ordinary public."

There was a dreadful silence. It felt as if the dinner-party might suddenly blow up.

Mr. Ferguson said: "And by what curious reasoning do you suppose that my brother could be more welcome in such a select circle?"

"I should have thought it plain. Unless you have written a book of the same calibre."

Another silence. Cordelia kept her head down, nervous now that she had let it go so far.

"A book?" Slaney-Smith stared incredulously. "D'you mean *his* book?"

Mr. Ferguson said: "Do we owe this visit to my friend, Madam Vaughan?"

"We came to see your brother. I thought you understood that."

Brook, speaking almost for the first time, with a flushed face, said: "Well, I'll be hanged!"

"There has been a slight misunderstanding," Mr. Ferguson said with a lisp. "Why are you interested in my brother's book?"

"We believe it to be the most important contribution to biology published for some years. We believe it will soon be generally regarded as such."

Mr. Slaney-Smith's face looked as if someone had been drawing the inner threads too tight.

"If someone," said Mr. Ferguson, "had been good enough to tell me earlier, if someone had been able to spare the time to inform me . . . Naturally in one's own house one expects to be kept informed of events which have occurred before one comes home. I would not have thought that asking too much."

Everyone waited for everyone else to speak. Cordelia knew she had to say something.

"I'm sorry. I should have . . ."

Mr. Crabtree Pearson glanced at Mr. Ferguson's face. "Perhaps," he said pacifically, "the misunderstanding was partly our fault. Sometimes these little misconceptions arise. We must apologise. And—I *think* it might be possible for us to arrange the meeting Mr. Ferguson desires. Don't you think so, Professor Simon? Mr. Ferguson might be able to see Mr. Huxley provided he went with his brother."

This concession seemed to have the opposite of the intended effect.

"I should never think of putting you to the trouble," said their host, with icy politeness.

Uncle Pridey was chopping the meat off a juicy lamb cutlet. After a minute he put his knife and fork down.

"This Mr. Huxley now. Appreciate your offer. Great man, no doubt. Capital fellow and all that. But misguided. If I met him I should have to tell him so. D'you think he'd mind that? D'you think he'd mind? Could I tell him I've been saying rude things about him for years?"

CHAPTER FIVE So it began, and, snowball-like, it gathered weight with every roll. Blinking like a hoary old rat, Uncle Pridey emerged from the obscurity of sixty-nine years to find himself famous. The town itself, or that part of it which took account of scientific developments, became aware of him. After the publication of Mr. Crabtree Pearson's first article, which spoke of 'the investigations and brilliant deductions of this distinguished Mancunian, who, working in solitude and with the barest technical equipment, has added so much to our knowledge of the phylum of human ancestry,' fame came in a flood. He was invited out to dinner, to lecture, to give prizes, to write articles, to subscribe to charities, to become a patron of this and a vice-president of that, to join a modern laboratory, to write another book, to go to London, to go to Liverpool, to go to the Antarctic. It was all rather exciting for his friends and trying for his relatives.

Mr. Ferguson and Mr. Slaney-Smith were very worried about it. Naturally they welcomed and rejoiced in Pridey's sudden triumph, but Mr. Ferguson was afraid that the excitement and the continual strain of meeting new people would have a bad effect on his brother's health and always unstable nerves. Mr. Slaney-Smith said these cases of sudden notoriety were dangerous because one went up like a rocket and came down like the stick. When all one's prestige depended on a single book—three chapters of a book—it was terrifyingly easy to get exaggerated ideas of one's importance. The public was fickle. When the newness wore off people would drop him as quickly as they had taken him up.

While exploring his delight in Pridey's success, Mr. Ferguson found cause for criticism in almost everything else. For weeks nothing pleased him, and the first and most obvious thorn was his own mistake in assuming that the first visitors had come to see him. Everyone suffered for this, Cordelia most of all.

For weeks there was an underlying spite on his side which made her very angry and uncomfortable. He offered remarks about her running of the house, about her management of Ian, which in aggregate were insufferable, but which separately could be instantly defended as well-meaning advice. She knew exactly what his attitude would be if she flared up, his injured tolerant patience, his patronising rebuke at her childish show of temper. She knew him well now. She was determined not to fight him on his own ground, and in front of Brook.

Jealousy from Mr. Ferguson and Mr. Slaney-Smith she had expected and took a certain pleasure in. Brook's jealousy was less expected and quite startlingly strong. The publication of his own book had been a damp squib to which he had become grudgingly reconciled. But this sudden burst into fame of his old and disreputable uncle hit him very hard. Even she did not realise yet how hard he found it to bear. It was the last straw.

One day there was a social tea. Mr. Ferguson had raised all sorts of objections, but when he found it could not be avoided he changed his tactics and decided to make the best of it. Mr. Crabtree Pearson was back again, and distinguished citizens of the town were present: the chairman and three members of the Philosophical Society, some from the Athenæum and the Discussion Forum, a single representative of the Church of England Sunday Schools, and one, who had somehow sneaked in, from the Destitute Children's Dinner Society. There were also two leading Unitarians—with which religion Mr. Ferguson was flirting these days—a representative of the Press, some wives, and a sonority of clergymen. Mr. Slaney-Smith had pleaded pressure of business.

Pridey didn't think much of the affair and was willing enough to let his brother take the leading part. Sometimes it might have been Mr. Ferguson who had written the book. In the end Pridey was persuaded to get up and make a speech, which he did in his usual jerky fashion. His greatest difficulty was to keep to the point. His mischievous mind ran off exploring any little side alley that came along. He was like a puppy on a lead, anxious to sniff out every corner on the way.

The thin dividing line between eccentricity and brilliance was plain this afternoon. The old man chattering in the bosom of his family was a crank, the old man saying the same sort of things to an appreciative audience was an original thinker. Before he finished he had touched on Lord Palmerston and his failure to 'keep' on the mantelpiece, Shudehill Market and the bad smells there, the civil war in Paris, Wagner's musical genius, the poor quality of the oboe playing in last winter's concerts, the ugliness of women's fashions, and why Welsh mutton was the best for stewing.

It was while he was talking that Cordelia noticed one man in the audience glancing at her. He was about forty years of age and well dressed. While tea was being served he came towards her.

"You'll pardon me, Mrs. Ferguson, but I seem to remember having seen you somewhere before. My name is Price."

"I'm afraid I don't remember it," she said, smiling, for once off her guard, after all this time.

Brook had moved away to speak to one of his friends, and Robert Birch, who had come in late, was behind her, helping a lady to sugar.

Price said: "Forgive me, didn't I see you at the old Variety one night? You know, the old place where they had the fire."

That struck right home. It was like a sudden dagger-thrust in that respectable drawing-room.

Taking the tea the maid was offering her, she said: "You must be mistaken. I don't go to music halls."

He bowed. "I'm so sorry. Perhaps I should have realised that. It must be a resemblance. The colouring, you know, if you'll forgive my saying so—unusual."

She was recovering. Keep a cool head. She took the sugar Robert offered and thanked him. As he moved away, Price said:

"It was some lady with Mr. Stephen Crossley, the proprietor. What I mean to say is, I naturally wouldn't suggest you'd be likely to be there in the ordinary way. If you see what I mean." He broke off in some confusion.

"Of course. Yes, we did know Mr. Crossley, and Brook went once or twice without me. But it must have been some other lady, Mr. Price."

He stayed talking for some minutes, making general conversation but evidently a bit confused. The shock was only now coming out in her. She kept telling herself that she had no need to be alarmed, it was the suddenness, just when she had begun to feel secure.

People began to go, and she watched them leaving one by one, watched for Mr. Price, convinced against all reason that he would return to the attack before he left. Instead, when it came to his turn he touched her hand apologetically and went out without a word.

. . . When the last of his admirers had finally gone Pridey turned and leaned his back against the door and looked at Cordelia.

"It's all very well," he said in an undertone. "It's all very well, I tell you. They come here overflowing with goodwill; talk, talk, talk. They all love it. But you know what I said to you at the beginning. They're still praising my book for the wrong thing!"

230

She tried to think what he was saying. They were praising his book . . . "But surely there must be something . . ."

"About the shrews? Oh, yes, it's good enough stuff, added as an afterthought. Could have written that years ago. Doesn't seem to me to be anything clever in it; just stands to common sense." He grasped her arm and led her slowly back towards the drawing-room. "What's the matter. You got a cold?"

"No, no, I'm all right. Go on."

"Thought you were shivering. Believe you were. They're ignoring the important part. All that about the mice: that's from years of study. All the graphs and charts couldn't be made without years of study. Ever heard of a man called Mendel?"

"No."

"No. Pearson Crabtree hadn't either. Said to him, 'Look here, why all this fuss about me when there's this Austrian? *He'll* be famous when all your pet favourites are forgotten. Go and see him and invite him to London.' They only smiled. Look." Uncle Pridey released her arm and began to fish in his pockets. "A letter from the fellow; he's a monk or something. Wish I'd thought of that; joined an order; one way of getting privacy; trouble is one has to spend so much time praying. And this mortification of the flesh, sleeping in cold cells, wearing hair shirts, don't agree with it. Though I believe they keep a very good table. . . ." Pridey stared in front of him for a moment, lost in thoughts of good tables. Then he unfolded the letter. "D'you read French? Pity. Anyway, look at the signature. He wrote a book, made mine out of date two years before it was published. Only read it last month. Wrote to him. This is his reply. I'd like to frame it. That's what I mean. D'you see? All this fuss over the wrong thing. I didn't want to prove their pet evolution theory right." He chuckled mischievously and rubbed his head. "In fact I think it's wrong. Always have. Goes too far. Makes the wrong inferences. Natural selection my foot. But you can't reason with 'em. One of these days they'll see their error."

She was about to follow him up the stairs when she saw that the afternoon post had come while they were all too busy to attend to it. She knew that the top letter was addressed to her before she was near enough to read it. Coming immediately after the other shock, this one was doubled in power. But as she picked it up she saw the post mark was still New York.

CHAPTER SIX 🌿 Mr. Slaney-Smith disappeared on the twentieth of October. It was not known until the Thursday following, when a distraught figure appeared in the drawing-room just before evening prayers, pulling at its gloves and glancing nervously behind.

They couldn't understand what she said at first, and it was Cordelia who, more knowledgeable of the Slaney-Smith house-hold, first began to grope towards the truth.

"Do you mean he's left you?"

"I don't know, Mrs. Ferguson, I'm sure I don't *know,* but I fear, I suspect the worst. On Saturday he didn't come back until late, until the middle of the night. He'd been *drinking,* I knew, could tell from his breath. On Sunday he was in one of his *moods,* only worse. All day he never spoke, not even to Susie, who took his meals, who's lame, you know, and his favourite. We lit a fire, he insisted, though it was so warm, so close; he sat over it all day, we didn't dare go *near* him, I've never *known* him so bad, so difficult before. On Monday he went as usual and never came back, at least, not yet. I haven't known what to do, which way to *turn,* and all the children crying."

During this Mr. Ferguson paced up and down with his hands clasped under his coat-tails. It was plain that he knew nothing and was angry that his friend had not given him his confidence. Mrs. Slaney-Smith had been to the tea warehouse where he worked but not yet to the police. She had wanted, she said, to avoid the scandal, and she glanced hurriedly over her shoulder as she spoke.

But Mr. Ferguson had no doubt in his mind what must be done, and drove with her after supper to the nearest police station. In the few minutes the two women had alone together before she left Mrs. Slaney-Smith said:

"Oh, Mrs. Ferguson, I'm very much *afraid.* I don't know, can't *tell* if I'm doing the right thing. If Mr. Slaney-Smith should return, I shall never hear the last of it. If he'd only left me a little note, as you say. I'd rather have known the *worst,* really I would, than be left in this suspense."

"You really think he may have come to some harm?"

"Oh, dear, no! He wouldn't do himself a mischief. I mean run off, eloped with that woman. You don't *know* the anguish, the torments I've suffered."

"Have you ever seen her?"

"Oh, no. They were too *cunning* for that. I *tried* once to follow him, but really I had to give it up, my heart was palpitating. But my friend Mrs. Appleton saw him one day in Albert Square walking with a young woman and talking with her animatedly, Mrs. Appleton said. I don't *doubt* he's been meeting her a lot."

Mrs. Appleton had seen them talking animatedly and had borne the tale home. There but for the grace of God . . . The whole of this conversation had a horrible fascination for Cordelia.

"It's a *family* disgrace, Mrs. Ferguson. And he a man of forty-eight and married eighteen years. I've tried to be a good wife to him. I've lost some of my looks perhaps, but I've done what I could to keep myself attractive—I've tried." Mrs. Slaney-Smith turned up her wizened face to the light. "These wicked women, these home wreckers, they don't think of that at all. And Mr. Slaney-Smith so hot-blooded, that's the *trouble,* all his life, at times it's been difficult for me; at times——"

Cordelia interrupted gently: "Have you asked at any of the music halls where he usually goes?"

"No. I wouldn't *go*, Mrs. Ferguson. I feel sure it's there he's met this woman. I couldn't bring myself, couldn't *lower* myself to make inquiries."

The police were willing to lower themselves, but when, in spite of Mrs. Slaney-Smith's resolve, some of her suspicions percolated through to them, their inquiries became less urgent. A runaway husband was not so much their concern as a prospective accident or suicide. Mr. Ferguson was formidably indignant with her, treating her with politeness but calling her in private 'a low woman whose narrow mind sought the most indelicate causes.'

So the week-end passed, and Ian developed a bad teething cold, and Uncle Pridey went down to Town and bought him a clockwork mouse which ran all over the drawing-room carpet and made Aunt Tish jump and mutter. On Tuesday, about eleven in the morning, Betty came into the nursery to say there was a young boy at the door with a message for Mrs. Ferguson, but he wouldn't part with it to anyone else. In the hall Cordelia found a thin boy of about nine with a long anæmic face and lank yellow hair.

She tore open the envelope. Scrawled in shaky writing were the words: 'Please, Mrs. Ferguson, can you come at once? He's back. I can't begin to tell you. Can you bring someone with you?'

She stared a moment at the boy, hesitating whether to question him or not, but he looked so scared that she turned away. Brook and Mr. Ferguson were at the works, Uncle Pridey out buying sweets.

"When did your father come back?"

"I don't know, ma'am. He was back when we woke this morning."

Betty brought her outdoor clothes. At the same time Mrs. Meredith walked across the hall and opened the door for Dr. Birch. He smiled his welcome as he put down his hat; he had been called in to see Ian yesterday.

"Robert," she said, "have you your gig outside?"

"Yes. Can I do something for you?"

She rapidly explained, speaking in an undertone.

"I shall be only too delighted. But there's not room for us all." He had coloured a little.

"Of course. We can manage. It will save ten minutes."

The front door of the Slaney-Smiths was opened before they got down. Mrs. Slaney-Smith ushered them through the curtains into the front room. Her hair was unkempt and her face streaked with emotion and tears. She trembled her way into a chair.

"Oh, Mrs. Ferguson, I'm so glad you've *come*, and Doctor too, so good of you. I've had a terrible, terrible night, I thought it would never *end*, never finish at all. He's gone again. I've been wrong, *dreadfully* wrong over everything. I shall never forgive myself, and my poor children terrified out of their *lives*. D'you think we could try to stop him even now?"

Robert said: "It's not possible to restrict a man's movements, unless——"

"He said he was going to *end* everything this morning. That's why I sent. I don't know if he means it or not. But he said good-bye to the children, kissed each one, and embraced them; and then it came to Alec and he said, 'Where's Alec?' and when no one answered, no one had anything to say, he said, 'You've sent him for the *police*. It's no good, Florrie, they'll be too *late.*'"

"Do you know where he was going?" Birch said, convinced now, and moving quickly back to the door.

"He went down towards the Town. Oh, my poor Ted, what a dreadful thing to happen!"

Robert said to Cordelia: "Can you drive?"

"Yes, of course."

"Drive slowly down. I'll run by your side."

With Mrs. Slaney-Smith squeezed against her, Cordelia picked up the reins and they were off, leaving Alec with his anxious, peering brothers and sisters. One hand on the panel of the gig, Robert ran beside it. They clattered past a stationary bus, overtook two or three carriages moving at a walk. They kept a sharp look-out among the people on the pavements, but no one like Mr. Slaney-Smith was to be seen.

About a third of a mile down was a railway bridge, come to be known as the Fenian Arch from the recent murders there; on one side of it was a railway goods yard with express lines and sidings. As they came up to this Cordelia saw from her high position that there was a crowd of people at the gates of the shunting yard and more inside.

She plucked at Robert's arm. "Over there . . ."

She slowed the gig and presently reined the horse in to a walk.

"Can you *see* him?" asked Mrs. Slaney-Smith. "Is he among these? I can't see anyone."

"No. But I thought . . ."

"Oh . . . Oh . . . I hope not, he hasn't . . . Oh, it can't be Ted."

Robert was about to push through the crowd, but almost at the wheel of the gig a policeman said: "Don't stop 'ere, mister. There's been an accident. They're bringing 'im out now. Take your womenfolk away."

"What is it? What sort of an accident?"

"Well, accident or suicide. Man jumped under that line of trucks, they say. Killed on the instant. Don't block the roadway there."

Mr. Slaney-Smith had done himself a mischief after all.

CHAPTER SEVEN "I was quite wrong," she said, twisting her dusty wrinkled hands. "There was no woman, not that way. I'm quite ashamed to have thought so, to have suspected it, but what else could I think? *Really*. I was asleep last night and dreaming of my dear mother when I heard the front door bang. I knew at once. As he came up the stairs I quite feared, quite dreaded. But he hadn't been *drinking,* at least not recently, and I sat up watching him as he lit the lamp. I took my courage in both hands. 'Mr. Slaney-Smith,' I said, 'wherever have you *been?* A whole week,' I said, 'and never a word, never a line. It's not *fair* to me,' I said, 'or to the children. We've been anxious, worried out of our lives.' But he didn't say anything in reply. He just sat on his bed. So I spoke to him again. At last he turned and looked at me, just like seeing me, *noticing* me for the first time. And he said: 'I've been in London thinking what to do,' he said, 'and now I know what to do. It's the only way out, Florrie,' he said; 'the only way for a *logical* man. I was made a dupe of when I was a lad,' he said; 'the miracle stories, the candles, the pious parables. And what did it lead to? You know about Father. Well, I'm not going to be made a fool of a *third* time. I'm a civilised man, I tell you,' he said—very fiercely—it was like as if something was burning him *up;* 'and I'll go in a civilised way,' he said."

There was a faint breath of eau de Cologne as Mr. Ferguson took out his handkerchief. The afternoon sun beat through the lace curtains across the crowded room, falling on the cheap bric-à-brac, the scientific books, the Japanese ware.

"He wasn't unreasonable, Mr. Ferguson. He'd got it *all* worked out. I wish I could tell you, explain to you; I wish I could remember it all. Just as I thought, it had begun, been going on for more than *two* years. You had a—a séance at your house, didn't you, and a man called Gustave who went into a trance or something?"

"Yes, of course."

"Well, this Gustave gave a *message*, Mr. Slaney-Smith said, about someone who had died, and he described Mr. Slaney-Smith's brother Charles exactly, dripping wet and carrying a crucifix. Charles turned Roman Catholic, you know, and he was drowned in the Mediterranean when he was only twenty-three. He had a terrible quarrel with Mr. Slaney-Smith before he left and they almost came to *blows*. . . ."

"I remember it well," said Frank Slaney-Smith. "It was like a red rag to him when Charles went over to Rome. It was just after Father died and after there'd been all that trouble with the kitchen maid claiming . . . We were all a bit strung up at the time."

"Mr. Slaney-Smith thought this message had come from Charles. He couldn't get it out of his mind. He says he tried to *forget* it, and tried to tell himself that it was all telepathy. But he said he hadn't so much as *thought* of Charles for a month before that night. You know what a man, what a person he was for scientific *proof*. He said he tried to find Mr. Gustave at the time but he couldn't, and so one day he answered an *advertisement* in a paper and got in touch with another medium, and joined her circle, just to see, he said, just to inquire scientifically, he said, into it further. And that's where he's been spending so much of his time, his leisure, with these people, these *spiritualists*, and his money, for over two years."

"He should have told me. What results did he get?"

"He became convinced, Mr. Ferguson. It must have got hold of him very strongly. He kept it secret even from me, you know, who might have shared his confidence, his *trust*. And I—I suspected something quite different; I shall never excuse, never forgive myself. . . ."

"Did something—go wrong?"

"Yes, Mrs. Ferguson. Only last Saturday night, a week last Saturday, I should say, he went as usual to the Victoria Music Hall, and on the stage, he said, doing conjuring and disappearing tricks, was this *man*, this Frenchman, under another name."

Oh, Heaven! thought Cordelia.

"So Mr. Slaney-Smith went to see Mr. Gustave after the performance. . . ."

Mr. Ferguson said: "I shall write to Crossley tonight and——"

"No," said Mrs. Slaney-Smith. "It's no good writing to Mr. Crossley. It was Mr. Crossley's idea. . . ."

"What——"

"Why did your husband go to London?"

"He went to see Mr. Crossley, Doctor. I think perhaps he was hoping . . . I don't know what he was hoping . . ."

He was still hoping that it wasn't true, thought Cordelia. But Stephen is away, and even——

"Oh, yes, he found him, discovered him. He'd just come home from abroad, Mr. Slaney-Smith said. He *taxed* him with it all. Mr. Crossley agreed, admitted everything. He said he'd been challenged—that was the word—challenged to put on a spiritualist turn, and he'd done it."

The woman made a little grimace as she lowered her head. You could see the thin hair scraped away from the central parting.

"We'll have tea," she said. "My friend Mrs. Appleton has offered. I wonder *why* I'm so calm when this terrible thing has happened to me. I remember two years ago a woman coming to the door, rather a *common* type of woman, I recall. From the way she spoke, the questions she asked, I thought she had known Charles as a boy. I told her what I knew about him. I never told Mr. Slaney-Smith about it because sometimes he'd fly into a temper if you brought up Charles's name. . . ."

Robert said: "But when it's admitted that all this is true, does it prove that these other people——"

"That's what I said to him, and he said: 'Of course they're cheats. If the *first* step's a lie the rest is lies too. All life's a cheat,' he said. 'From the cradle you're fed on lies, with your milk,' he said—forgive me, that's what he *said*. 'Life's a sham, an impertinence, a vulgar insult.' I can't remember all the words he used, and some I wouldn't venture to repeat. 'Humanity's a festering *sore,*' he said, 'with all the microbes crawling over each other and feeding on each other and decaying together. There's only one way of making a protest, there's only one sane way out.' "

"I'm sure you did what you could."

"Indeed, I did. But he was too *strong* for me, Mr. Ferguson. You know what I mean, too *clever*. I couldn't *argue* with him. If you had been here, it might have been different. I could only speak to him of myself and of the children. I said was it *fair* to leave us, all ten of us, practically destitute, to fend for ourselves in the world today? What, I said, would become of Alec and Bernard and Susie and James? But he said: 'Perhaps they'll grow up *free*, as I never had the chance to. Those that are fit to survive will trample on the others, and those that aren't will be crushed out.'That's the law and it's the only law.' I said to him then: 'And what of your work? Who will carry on?' He laughed. He said: 'What's the good of denying God when there isn't any God to deny!' " Mrs. Slaney-Smith looked up, glancing from face to face with intent humility. "It was the only time when I thought his mind—when I couldn't quite follow him. . . ."

CHAPTER EIGHT 🌿 "Hallows, the fire was almost out in my study before prayers."

"I'm sorry, sir."

"And the new servants were late coming in for prayers this evening. I had to wait for them."

"I'm sorry, sir. I'll see it doesn't happen again."

"The household is getting lax. It needs a tightening hand."

Is this where our pretty story is ending? Perhaps it wasn't so pretty. Perhaps it was just a sordid little love story, shadowed all the time by anxieties and fears, doomed from the start by his superficiality and my timidity. Those three or four evenings together; and the dance when I knew I loved him and we went round and round lost in a lovers' dream; the afternoon sitting quietly by the river bank in the misty November sun . . .

"No, thanks," said Brook shortly. "I don't want anything more."

"You don't eat enough, my boy. That's one of your chief troubles. You're so finicky in all your meals."

"I eat as much as I can."

Brook was sulky tonight. He had had words with his father; not an unusual thing these days; for the goodwill which had existed at the time of Ian's birth had long since worn away.

Aunt Tish had been disturbed in her afternoon rest and was trying to fall asleep at the table. Pridey was the only cheerful one, seemed the only likeable one. By the afternoon post he had had an invitation—the first of its kind—to write the programme notes for a forthcoming concert. Among the pieces was Liszt's Symphonic Poem 'The Slaughter of the Huns,' and he was considering how offensive he could be without having his notes cut.

Nobody else knows, she thought; I can turn to no one for comfort or advice. No one to tell about this morning, or how I feel now. If I were a Catholic and could confess . . . How the priest would agree with my decision. But it isn't for that, it never has been for that . . .

Mr. Ferguson said: "Did Cordelia tell you that Stephen Crossley called today?"

Brook looked up, startled out of his moroseness. "No! . . . Did he come about Mr. Slaney-Smith?"

"That is a matter of doubt. Cordelia refused to see him."

What else could I do? she thought, with Ian at my skirts and you beside me. What else *could* I do?

"I wondered at his asking for Cordelia. No doubt he concluded that no one else would be at home, that he could expect a sympathetic hearing from her."

"He'd be disappointed then," said Brook. "Cordelia's never liked him. As a matter of fact, I'd have been rather interested to hear what he had to say."

"I too," said Mr. Ferguson, "though not with the weak goodwill you no doubt would have brought to the meeting. I should have told him what I thought of his kind." He blew through his lips. "Cordelia, however, chose to override me."

Brook glanced at her in quick surprise.

"He *asked* for me," she said, just keeping the break out of her voice. "I didn't wish to see him."

"I believe you have always received courtesy from me," said Mr. Ferguson. "I have some call to expect it in return. And in front of a servant you were a little high-handed." He rose. "Will you come to my study when you have finished your supper, Brook?"

I said: 'No, it is for me to decide. I am not at home, Betty. I am not at home.' And that was all. If only I could have sided with *him* against *them*. And walked out to meet him . . . A common opinion is a potent thing, and there were no two opinions about the Slaney-Smith affair. But she had done her best to ignore that. All this week she had told herself she must ignore that; she had her own personal inner knowledge and must judge by that alone. Anyway, it had nothing to do with the main issue. A joke turned sour. Forget it. But he had come when, with Mr. Ferguson there, there had been no possible half measures, no neutral ground. . . .

In his last letter he had said he was coming to see her as soon as ever he was home—and he had come as promised. And she had sent him away without even seeing him, without even giving him a chance to speak, sent him away perhaps for the last time.

Brook said: "When did he call?"

She stared at her plate. "About eleven. I was in the nursery with Ian. Your father had come in to see me about the new sewing-machine."

"Which sort are you getting?"

"The Wheeler and Wilson."

"I wonder what brought him here this morning. He must have heard. It was a poor joke he played, really. All the same, I shouldn't have minded learning how some of the tricks were done. Those candles. It was pretty clever. What made you not see him?"

"There was—nothing to say to him."

239

"Well, I should hardly have imagined it worth quarrelling with Father about."

"I thought of beginning something like this," said Uncle Pridey, putting down his pencil and picking up his fork. " 'In Mr. Liszt's latest essay in the Symphonic Poem, which I confess to finding neither poetic in inspiration nor symphonic in form, the keen concert-goer, if he attends, will distinctly hear in the ninth and succeeding bars the sound of Count Bismarck's feet pacing up and down the chancellery in the Wilhelmstrasse. This is followed by a long confused passage which may be taken to indicate the beginning of that slaughter of the Huns of which many of us these days would feel inordinately proud.' Think that would do, eh? Think they'd print that?"

"You're supposed to be writing programme notes," said Brook. "Not criticism. Besides, it's nothing to do with modern history."

"Everything's to do with modern history. That's the trouble with people, they seal things off in water-tight compartments, trying to judge a man without knowing what his father was. Just like mice. There's only one science, really, and that's the science of everything."

What if I told Uncle Pridey, what would he say? But could he, or anyone knowing Stephen so little, see why I still want to go to him and what is in my way?

After supper Brook was with his father for some time. When he came out he said with an angry expression:

"Father wants to see you, Delia. In his study."

Go in, ready for conflict. It had been threatening some days. This morning's little brush . . . But it was the wrong night to criticise. She didn't care what she said.

"You wanted me, Mr. Ferguson?"

"Yes. Sit down, please. I'll be ready in a moment."

The only sound then his steady breathing. Queer, his personal force. In whatever mood one came here one soon felt like the applicant after a new post, the schoolboy brought before the head. But he was puffy, grey. In the three days since the funeral he had not been near the dye works, only once left the house. It was a measure of his disarrangement. He had lost his best friend.

After a minute he put aside his papers.

"You will remember I mentioned this morning I had something to discuss with you."

"Yes."

"It's about Brook and yourself. I have for some time felt a little dissatisfied with our relationship. It has lacked something—some cohesive force. I have been pondering the reason."

"I'm sorry," she said. Perhaps Stephen had come to say he was sorry. Dear God, I wish I could die.

"Yes. Some cohesive force. Let me say too, Cordelia, that during these last three months I have been conscious of some coolness in our own relations. Let us not for the moment consider whose 'fault.' Nothing is ever so simple as that. The first step towards removing it is to recognise it." He stared past her, judicial, impersonally fair, blew a little through his lips.

"Yes," she said again, thinking: He will be on his way back to London now.

"For my part I have been overworking, busy in too many ways. For your part you have a very active brain and perhaps too little to employ it. You have been much with your son, of course. It seems to me that Brook's discontent, and perhaps yours, may come from a lack of identity with the things I stand for. You know perhaps that Mr. Slaney-Smith died in debt."

"Yes. Brook told me."

"He leaves a widow and nine children. It's very serious for them. I feel I must do something to help them. In considering them it has given me the opportunity to review all my affairs afresh."

She waited, while he tapped the papers with his finger. He went on to explain.

His proposition was to draw up a new partnership agreement, increasing the partners in Ferguson's Dye Works from three to six, two of the new partners to be herself and Brook, the third to be a fifteen-year trust fund administered for the benefit of the Slaney-Smiths, the money then to revert equally to the other partners.

"The active partners would virtually be yourself and Brook, and I would continue to exercise a directing influence. The result would be to free me considerably and would give you both, I hope, a new sense of security." He clasped and unclasped his hands. "I try to put this before you in detail so that you may consider it all round."

One came expecting carping criticism, a sharp quarrel perhaps, instead this. It was a gesture. She knew she ought to be surprised, gratified. Instead she thought: What would have happened if I had gone out to meet him? But I *couldn't*. There was no choice.

"Slaney-Smith's death brings home to one the futility of allowing small differences to loom large in one's life. I am getting no younger. I have long wanted to give more time to civic duties. So I should get my own satisfaction out of the change."

She began to say something but he went on unheeding.

"I want you to think very carefully of this. It's fortunate you have had some experience: you know what is entailed. I'll confess"—he stared at

her now with his steely, opinionated eyes—"though this is between ourselves, I should not feel justified in making this offer to Brook alone.
Though he's my own son, I know his limitations. Frankly this offer is
made to you."

She attended with difficulty. Flattery again. He wanted something.
No. People didn't back hypocrisy with a lifetime's work. *He* was not
to know the underlying causes of today. It was not the first time he had
followed up some rather cheap little squabble with a sudden change of
front which put her in a position of thinking herself ungracious or mean.

"I have no doubt," he said, "that there will be business associates of
mine in the city who will be anxious to advise me of my imprudence in
putting such responsibility in the hands of a woman. That, however,
need not concern us."

"Thank you," she said, trying to force warmth into her voice. "You're
more than kind. I expect Brook—will be delighted."

He said: "Living the daily life, one comes to see things without perspective. Tragedy withdraws one temporarily, gives one a brief escape,
the opportunity for a new judgment, a new beginning. Brook? Oh,
Brook is seldom delighted about anything these days. But go and talk it
over with him. You may help him to see it with greater enthusiasm."

"What doesn't he like about it?"

"For one thing he sees any invitation to you as a reflection on himself."

"Yes—I know. . . ."

"For another, this rather absurd notoriety my brother has achieved
. . . Brook has been very difficult lately, inclined to resent the smallest
thing."

"I think it would be better if I was not named as partner."

"I should not go on with the proposition unless you were."

"But I can't accept if he doesn't want me to."

He got up. "I've been thinking. When on another occasion a king
divided his kingdom, one of his daughters was called Cordelia. But he
was a blind old man without any perception of her real failing, which
was pride, or her real virtue, which was loyalty. Ours is a different case."

She looked at him quickly.

"Quite a different case," he said. "I flatter myself I'm not blind. And
you are not proud. . . . Though I sometimes think it's possible for
loyalty to be a failing. Don't you?"

"I don't know."

"*Your* loyalties are so strong. There is a certain danger in that."

"It doesn't seem at all true to me," she said, speaking from her heart,
almost in tears. "Or of me."

"Well, I hope you'll be able to accept this offer."

"Thank you for making it," she said.

242

Before she left he had turned to the window and was gazing out over the lighted shrubbery.

When his surgery was over that evening, Robert Birch had an unexpected visitor.

Half the house was still used by his predecessor's widow, and for his bachelor rooms he kept only a daily servant who left with the last patient.

For a few seconds he did not recognise the man standing there; then Stephen moved into the light.

"Oh—it's Crossley. I—didn't for the moment—— Will you come in?"

His voice had shown various changes of tone and Stephen noticed them.

"Thanks."

He followed the tall doctor upstairs and glanced round casually at the small book-stacked room with its two shaded lamps and the old spaniel crouching on the hearthrug.

"Am I disturbing you? Patients or anything?"

"No, not a bit. Sit down. Do you smoke?"

"Thanks, I'll have a cigar; it's a brand I always carry." Stephen sat in an armchair and smoothed his hair. Robert thought his visitor was a little ill at ease. He felt conscious of his own shabby clothes.

He said: "It's some years since you were in this neighbourhood, isn't it?"

"Nearly three. I've been in America most of the time. But I happened to be here for a couple of days and thought I'd be looking up some of my old friends."

Robert was a little surprised at the description as applied to himself, but he said: "I'm very glad you did. Have you seen the Fergusons?"

"No." Stephen lit his cigar at the taper offered him. "Thanks. I called round but they were out. I'll try to fit in a short visit tomorrow. How are they getting along?"

"All very well. You heard about the old brother's amazing success?"

"I did not." Stephen listened attentively to the story. "And I always thought him a bit weak in the head. Perhaps that's an asset in modern science." They talked for some minutes, then: "And that other old boy, Slaney-Smith? They tell me he's committed suicide?"

"Yes," Birch said. "He got entangled with spiritualism as a result of that sham séance you held at the Fergusons' house."

"I know. And from what I'm told everyone would like to put the noose round my neck as if I'd pushed him under the train."

The doctor smiled and fondled his spaniel's black velvet ear. "Well, hardly as bad as that."

Stephen said: "Oh, I'm sorry it's happened, very sorry indeed. But, on my faith and soul, it's nonsense to reason like a Hebrew prophet. If we all weighed the consequences of everything we did down to the third and fourth generation we'd all have to retire into monasteries and let the world run down, we should indeed. You're a reasonable man, Birch."

"I see your point."

"It's just fine and silly. I can't follow the reasoning of these people. I could never understand Ferguson and Slaney-Smith getting on together in the first place. I suppose the old man will be at the bottom of all this bad feeling?"

"Not entirely. And I don't know that one would call it exactly that."

"I wonder he doesn't think of the harm Slaney-Smith may have done in his life, lecturing against religion, talking blasphemy, spreading his own lop-sided doctrines. I wonder how many people he might have driven into atheism, even into suicide, if he happened to come upon any with the sort of shaky mind that only needs a push to send it toppling over."

"I suppose," Robert said, "you can't blame a man for proclaiming his faith or his lack of it—only if he does it with his tongue in his cheek."

"He came to see me, you know. He came when I was just back from the States. I didn't notice anything at first. When he told me he'd seen Clodius on the stage I knew the game was up, so I told him the truth. He didn't believe in anything supernatural; I thought he'd be amused. It just shows. And talking of having your tongue in your cheek, what of the lectures he's been going on and giving these last two years while dabbling in spiritualism? Is that a sign of sincerity?"

"It was a sign of the conflict," Robert said. "His suicide was a sign of his sincerity."

"Good Lord, man, and a sign that he'd got no humour in him at all! Must we all jump under trains when our pet theories go awry? It would be a poor world!"

"I'm not trying to defend him. I'm merely pointing out what may seem to be the difference."

"Oh, they were so pompous! That first evening. You weren't there that first evening, were you? So self-important with their beliefs and disbeliefs. Just begging to be taken down a peg."

"Was that why you did it?"

"What? Well, more or less."

There was a brief silence. Each was annoyed with the other. Then Stephen said, trying to change his tone but failing:

"How's Mrs. Ferguson?"

"Very well, I think."

"Is Brook all right now? Recovered from his pneumonia?"

"Yes, he's pretty well for him."

"What does she do with herself these days?"

"Mrs. Ferguson? I don't know. The usual things, I suppose."

"It's a drab sort of a house for a woman to be in, don't you think. And with a sickly husband."

"The Fergusons have been very good friends to me."

Stephen flicked his cigar impatiently. "I'm not asking you to be disloyal to them. But I came to have a weak spot for Mrs. Ferguson. You know how it is. You'd think she'd want a brighter life than she gets."

"Well, they're always off to concerts or entertaining at home. The old man's very hospitable. Then she has her baby to think about and——"

"Her baby?" Stephen looked up quickly. "By all the Saints, I'd no idea. I hadn't heard that." A bitter expression crossed his face. "I hadn't heard that." There was silence. Then with a sudden glint in his eyes he said: "How old will it be?"

Robert had been watching him. He bent to his spaniel again. "Ian? Oh—nearly two."

The dog got up, shook himself, then curled against his master's leg again.

Stephen said: "Oh, well—in that case, of course . . . Yes, I fancy she'll have plenty to occupy her time. I can hardly think of Cordelia with a child. I expect it will have made a difference to her?"

"I haven't noticed any difference."

". . . And I imagine Brook is very pleased with himself? Another little Brook to follow in the shadow of the old man."

"I don't think Mrs. Ferguson is the sort of person to let her son be brought up in a way she doesn't want."

Stephen looked at the doctor with a long glance. "You think she's got a mind of her own, eh?"

"I do."

"Maybe you're right."

They talked then of general things for some minutes. But the interest had gone out of the visitor's manner. He was casual, asked Birch things, and then lost interest in the answers. He finished his cigar and tossed it into the grate with an impatient, angry flick.

"Well, I won't waste your time any more. I don't want to keep you from your wife. . . ."

"I'm not married."

They eyed each other.

"Not? That's rather unusual, isn't it?"

"Why?"

"Well, I don't know. I thought you might have taken to it in self-defence."

"No."

Stephen got up.

"And you?" said Robert.

"Oh, I was—not now. My divorce came off a few months ago."

"Bad luck."

"Yes . . . It was queer the way it turned out. A funny world, Birch."

"Are you staying in Manchester long?"

"I'm going tomorrow or the next day."

"And then?"

"I shall be in London for a time. And then it may be back to the States. A good country. I haven't yet made up my mind."

As he was shown out, Stephen said:

"Are you a cynic?"

The doctor said: "I don't know. I don't think so. I try to take things as they come."

"That's been my outlook. But how d'you take things when they don't come?"

Robert hesitated. "I don't know. Perhaps you learn to do without. I'm a doctor, not a philosopher."

"I suppose you couldn't know anyhow. Nobody has the answer to that. I wonder if Slaney-Smith knows by now."

They stayed a moment in silence. A few dry leaves drifted downwards in the breeze.

"Anyway," said Stephen, pulling on his hogskin gloves, "I'm not going to take his way of finding out. Not just yet."

Robert Birch stood on the top step watching the other man until he was out of sight. Then he went in and upstairs and re-lit his pipe. After a minute or two he let it go out again.

He didn't know quite why he had lied about the age of Cordelia's child. He had done it on impulse, in the act of speaking, and while a monstrous cloudy suspicion had loomed in the back of his mind. The suspicion had been blown away almost before it was properly formed. But he realised that if he didn't take care, if he didn't prepare his mind to reject it as a disloyal absurdity, it might well come back and try to stay.

BOOK FOUR

CHAPTER ONE

"Have you got a bustle trimmed with blue?
Do you wear it? Yes, I do!
When I go to meet my John
Then I put my bustle on."

Three little girls in pinafores with coloured ribbons in their hair sang this as if their lives depended on it, their thin, breathy, solemn, over-articulate little voices not quite getting hold of the jigging polka rhythm of the thing. Sitting and standing round listening were the eleven other members of the Christmas party, stiff with frills and shiny with food. At a distance, feeling slightly self-conscious and out of place, like liners escorting tugs, were the grownups: Essie, Mrs. Blake, Aunt Tish, Mrs. Thorpe, Mrs. Trant, Mrs. Slaney-Smith—still in weeds after fifteen months—and Mrs. Shrike, the Vicar's wife, in a bustle trimmed with yellow and stuffed with the *Manchester Guardian*.

Cordelia flitted about keeping the party going. She looked very young today, much more like the elder sister of Virginia than the mother of Ian. Essie, although only two years her senior, had matured with marriage and motherhood. Cordelia, for all the stress and strain she had been through, had changed very little. She had authority and had used it for five years, managing a house half a dozen times the size of Essie's; for twelve months, too, as part-time working partner in Ferguson's Dye Works—to the astonishment of her family and the scandal of the city; but when she had no need of it her authority dropped from her and she seemed to her mother's benevolent glance to be just the same slip of a girl who had somehow got herself married into this important family years ago.

The only notable absentee today was Uncle Pridey. His long promised visit to London had come off in October, and a week after his return he had casually announced that he had taken rooms there for a few months and would be leaving shortly.

Mr. Ferguson had very much resented the idea of someone moving

247

out of the orbit of his influence. He argued that it was a waste of money, was inconsiderate towards the family, would make Pridey a cat's paw in the hands of ambitious Southerners. He predicted disappointment, heart-burning, probably a break-down in health; and to his increasing annoyance, Pridey cracked his fingers and went on packing.

Pridey left early one Friday morning in two cabs, one carrying his suitcases, his books and his papers, the other himself and his 'cello and eight cages of rats, mice, shrews, and things in pickle. He had dressed for the journey in a long tight frock-coat thirty-eight years old, a white waistcoat, and yellow check trousers. He had also bought a yellow bowler hat while in London, but this was a shade small and sat oddly on his thick grey hair.

"Well, good-bye, Uncle Pridey," Cordelia had said rather tenderly, kissing one bristly cheek. "You'll come back and see us some time, won't you? We'll all miss you, you know; especially Ian."

"These cages," he said doubtfully. "All home-made, put together as you might say in bits and pieces. Hadn't enough nails for the side of that one and you can see the string is gnawed. I shouldn't have let 'em play about on top. Now what's troubling me is, will they stand the journey?"

Dozens of sharp patient little eyes watched him as he spoke.

"I'll get you some string."

"It's an experiment, y'know," he said, pulling his hat absent-mindedly to a rakish angle. "Don't think I should like to live in London for ever. Can't understand the people. Too polite. But what you must do is come and see me. Bring Ian up. I hope my shrews won't be train-sick."

"Are you sure you'll be able to manage at the station or shall I come that far?"

"My landlady seems an amiable woman. Understands some of the basic principles of cooking, which is rare. A cockney voice, though. Like a fret-saw. Goes on and on. Good-bye, m'dear. I'll write you the moment I get there."

The moment he got there proved to be three weeks later, which was the earliest, he said, that he'd been able to get round to writing. As she went about the room encouraging the children to join in a game of 'Shy Widow' her thoughts moved towards this letter—perhaps inevitably, for Essie had been talking a lot about London this afternoon, about the theatres she went to with Hugh in his professional capacity and how well he was thought of on his paper.

Pridey hadn't bothered to put his address or 'Dear Cordelia,' or any of the usual things.

"You will have given up," he began, "expecting a letter from me, which is clearly the appropriate time to receive one. My days have been overoccupied since I came, and this is the earliest I could bring myself to the business of literary effort. It was a tiresome journey. I was fortunately able to have a carriage to myself—one or two people looked in at Crewe but went away again—but there were several incidents. Mr. Gladstone, whom I should not have suspected of wishing to put me to anxiety, was very naughty and slipped away while I was dozing. This prank nearly cost him dear. Some foolish ill-tempered old man in the carriage next but one—a general, he said he was, and just home from India, and no doubt his liver was puckered with tropical excesses; if he is the sort of man, I reflected, who officers our overseas army one cannot wonder at the Indian mutiny, and I found myself breaking a lifetime's habit and sympathising with the underdog—tried to stab him with a Sikh hunting knife. Fortunately the train stopped as I intervened, because the general's wife, a hard-faced woman whose appearance would have suggested a different calling if I had met her in Albert Square after ten at night, was lowering the window to pull the emergency chain. I was able to recover Mr. Gladstone, who was sitting quietly enough on the luggage shelf, and so explained. There was however no courtesy on their side and therefore little shown on mine.

"At the London station I took a cab to my lodgings, which are central enough, off a square called Soho Square. The cabbie was not unmannerly and made no objections to my little friends being inside with me out of the cold, and when I paid him I expressed my appreciation of this. Whereupon he said it was all the same to him, and the last passenger he had had before me was a woman for the fever wards. It is a curious reflection that in this great metropolis these public cabs should be regularly used to take people to the hospital. If you come, insist on a hansom. I was anxious for more than a week, having been long convinced that both rats and mice can catch the same diseases as human beings. However, they've all been well, except that Mr. Gladstone is suffering again from catarrh. Before I forget, I met that man Crossley the other night. The one who hoaxed us all, you remember, over his spiritualism and set Slaney-Smith off after his last red-herring. I was going somewhere, I forget where, and did not stay with him long but he said I was to send you his regards. An impudent fellow at heart, but he has a taking way with him. He wanted me to go to some music hall of which he is manager. I could not, so we parted. It is not a small world, though my landlady insists on saying so; it is a very large world but overcrowded with our kind and in the endless permutations which occur one can expect these encounters, I suppose.

"I have no doubt whatever that I shall find plenty to occupy my time here for the next six months. For three successive nights I have been in argument with some friends of Professor Simon's on Darwin's hypothesis of pangenesis. I have told everyone repeatedly that I know nothing whatever about this peculiar theory and that I criticise it merely in the light of reason and common sense, but they keep returning to the subject, as I told them last night, like dogs to their vomit."

There was a good deal more than this. When Pridey wrote he sent good value for his stamp. She thought when she read it, How strange if I had met Stephen by accident in the street, after all the avoidings, the heart-burnings; so he has not gone back to America . . .

And now Pridey has gone and I am more alone than ever.

"Mummie," Ian said, his hot sticky hand clutching at her. "Can we play Blind Man's Bus?" He always called it this despite corrections. It seemed to him to make more sense. "Can we? Can we?"

"Yes, darling, if you'd like."

"Will you play, Mummie? Will you be the blind man?"

"Yes, if you want me to."

He darted off, screaming excitedly at his playmates. "Stop it! All of you! We're going to play Blind Man's Bus, an' my mummie's going to be the blind man! Stop it! Stop playing!" He fairly shook one little girl. "We're going to play Blind Man's Bus!"

Later, when she had eventually caught someone, she untied the handkerchief and found that Brook and Robert Birch, who was supping with them, had arrived and were watching the game. She invited them to join in, and Robert at once did so; but Brook smilingly refused.

"I've been telling Delia," Essie was saying to Brook, "how happy Hugh and I are in London, and why don't you come up and stay with us? Of course we've nothing grand like this, but it's comfortable and it's easy and right in the centre of things. My dear, we have literary evenings, when Hugh's brainy friends come in and they talk about Coleridge or Mr. Dickens's last book. I just sit and listen, but it's quite a treat for me. Hugh's doing awfully well and he thinks there may be a chance of an editorship soon. D'you know Fleet Street, Brook? It's awfully romantic at night. I've been down twice when Hugh was on night shift. They start printing about seven in the evening. . . ."

Cordelia wished she would stop. Brook pretended it meant nothing to him; his attitude was that in his own circle and in his own town he had a culture and a literary talent equal to anything London could offer, but underneath she knew that everything Essie said heaped fresh fuel upon his discontent.

By now the game of Blind Man's Buff was getting rowdy, so she put a stop to it, and as she did so she heard the front door and knew it was time to close the party. Alderman Ferguson was back.

Privately Brook was more sure than ever that his father had played a confidence trick on him. He and Cordelia had become full partners in the dye works only to find themselves more under his dominion than before. True he was absent a good deal, but they were more directly responsible to him when he came back. At the time Brook had tried to warn Cordelia. But she hadn't seemed to see it that way. She said: "After all, what have we to lose?" and to that question he could supply no answer.

Yet he still could not quite bring himself to accept Cordelia's position. He took no pride in being unconventional and, besides, it was his wife not his father's. He was sensitive to other people's comments. He got no pleasure out of hearing them discussing purpurin and verantin, or why rubian when decomposed by chlorine left grape sugar. There was a charitable scheme afoot for buying some old property near the works and building houses on the land. Sometimes she would go into Mr. Ferguson's study in the evening and be there for an hour or more talking over plans. He resented that a great deal.

But Brook's slow awakening had not stopped at common day; all the good things in his life he now took for granted and he saw instead only the lack of real freedom. Pridey's going to London was a constant gall, and Cordelia often found herself in the position of being the pacifying influence in the depleted household.

No one, to look at him at supper tonight, round-shouldered and pale and ascetic and listening to Essie's airy London talk, or turning agreeably to one of Mr. Ferguson's new friends, a Swedenborgian, as he spoke about the *Heavenly Arcana*, would have thought he was resenting anything. No one, certainly not Brook himself, had any idea that the final explosion was so near.

CHAPTER TWO It began a fortnight later with a letter from Hugh Scott.

The two men had written occasionally since Hugh's move to London, but with their wives corresponding regularly the impulse to exchange news was lacking.

Hugh wrote:

MY DEAR BROOK,

You may be surprised at hearing from me so soon after Essie's return, but things have been moving quickly while she's been away; and anyway this is something quite outside the womenfolk.

I'll put it briefly right at the start. There's a project afoot to start a new weekly, to be called, we think, the *Westminster Bulletin*. It will be Liberal in politics, though not radical, and will generally try to take an independent line. Lord Hirondel is at the back of it and will be managing director of the company and will direct the policy of the paper. You know the wide experience he has had. Brompton Jones is to be editor. I have been offered a sub-editorship, and think I shall take the political side. Now the point is this: there are two sub-editorships still vacant, finance, and the literary side, which will be small but very important.

There's no difficulty in filling these appointments, and two or three names have already been mentioned, but a preference will be given to any man who can put money into the company, and I think, if you wished to take it and could put up, say, five thousand pounds, I could get you the literary sub-editorship. I don't mean that *anyone* could *buy* a sub-editorship: that would be fatal; but you have your published poems to show and your reputation to set against your lack of journalistic experience.

Believe me, it's a wonderful opportunity—that's if you really mean what you've sometimes said, that your heart isn't in your present job and that you want to devote all your time to literary work. Brompton Jones has had ten years on the *News* and before that he was with *The Times,* and he's not the man to give up a fine job to join a new paper unless he's pretty sure of his ground. I have put fifteen hundred into it, mostly borrowed from Father. I've always wanted to start with a paper on the ground floor and to share in its growth.

If you are really interested, let me know as quickly as possible and I'll send you more details. The actual appointment will have to be made in about a fortnight, so there isn't much time to waste. We hope to begin with the first number in the middle of March.

And now I must thank you for having Essie and Jane; they both enjoyed themselves a lot, but I'm glad to have them back. I don't think I should take kindly to being a bachelor again. Essie is as excited about this as I am and she says there's a nice house to let in the next avenue from our own, and she's already getting excited at the prospect of having Brook and Ian and her dear Cordelia as neighbours. I tell her not to count the chickens, for of course I don't know how you are placed with the old man.

Believe me,

Yours ever,

HUGH

Cordelia usually went down to the dye works with them at eight forty-five, and when they were not returning to dinner she would drive home by herself at noon, this being the end of her day. But today they came back with her. She could see that Brook was excited about something. He had a rare flush in his cheeks and hardly spoke through the meal.

Afterwards, during the ten minutes before the phaeton arrived back at the door, he showed her the letter.

Walk warily over this.

"It *is* nice of him to write to you. It's an exciting idea. What shall you do?" If she had loved him there would have been no need to pretend her enthusiasm.

"It's the sort of thing I've always—well, not exactly on a newspaper, I didn't think of journalism; but the more I look at it the more I like it. And of course I've had articles published and things. It would put me right in with the people I want to know. I'm not interested in dyes, never have been. This would be living!"

He glanced at her with a queer look which might have been his father's; expectant, faintly imperious.

"How long have you got to decide? A fortnight? Shall you——"

"Yes, I'll have to tell him tonight. Of course, I know the sort of thing he'll say——"

"Brook, d'you think it would be better to write for more particulars before you say anything? It's all rather vague, and you'd have to go and see Hugh and meet the others. I don't want to put you off, but d'you need to say anything to your father until you're more sure?"

He shrugged uneasily, irritably. "I don't know. It seems perfectly clear to me. Anyway, I'll write to Hugh this afternoon . . ."

His voice died away as Mr. Ferguson came padding down the stairs.

So four days passed before Mr. Ferguson heard anything of it at all. Cordelia wondered if she had done Brook a disservice by delaying his first impulse. Yet if Brook's need was strong enough . . .

Brook's need was strong enough. On Saturday evening when they were in the drawing-room he showed his father the first letter.

Mr. Ferguson's first irrelevant and irritating comment was: "January the twelfth. The letter has been a long time reaching you."

"No, I got it on Tuesday."

Mr. Ferguson raised his eyebrows and began to read. There was a minute's silence during which his breathing occupied the room. Then he folded the letter and tapped it against the knuckles of his other hand.

"Young Scott was always an enthusiast. I hope he'll not lose his money."

"I don't see why he should. They're all highly reputable people in it. And Hugh is canny enough, you know, on the quiet. Coutts are the bankers, and the capital is to be forty thousand pounds."

"I didn't see those facts mentioned here."

"No, I—I wrote and he's replied again." Brook passed over the second letter. Now for it.

More breathing in the silence. It was a cold night: the fire was glowing with the frost, warm light reflecting from the ornate tiles of the grate.

"I confess I'm a little puzzled here, Brook. He writes as if you have expressed some enthusiasm for the project on your own behalf."

253

"Yes . . . I did . . ."

Mr. Ferguson read the letter again. "With what object in view?"

"Well, I thought I'd like to—— I was interested in the idea and wrote for more particulars."

"It might have been more thoughtful all round if you had consulted me first."

Cordelia said: "I thought it a pity to have all the—I mean it was a pity to trouble you if there were details which might put Brook off in any case."

"It's no trouble to me to advise my children. That is a pleasure and a duty."

Brook picked up the first letter and folded it and refolded it.

"Well, there we are. I haven't been put off at all." His defiant voice trailed away. He frowned across the room at the fire, bit at a piece of loose skin on his finger.

"Tell me," Mr. Ferguson said, "was your idea to invest five thousand pounds in this as a profit-making venture without taking a personal part?"

"Oh, no. I'd like to be in it as Hugh suggests—in the way he suggests."

"And what do you propose should happen at the dye works?"

Brook did not answer for a moment. "I thought you could do without me," he said sullenly.

"You think that Cordelia and I can run it while you accept a permanent situation in London?"

"No . . . If I went—well, obviously, Cordelia would have to come too."

Mr. Ferguson put the second letter back in its envelope. Not a flicker on his face. "And the dye works?"

"Well, nobody's indispensable. You could get a manager in."

"You're not serious, Brook?"

"Yes, I'm serious," Brook said angrily. "Why shouldn't I be?"

Mr. Ferguson got up, paced across the room. Aunt Tish had put down her knitting. Cordelia had a sudden sense as of something rushing to destruction. She wanted to cry, draw back, draw back!

"Where do you propose to get your money from?"

". . . There's my partnership—to say nothing of Cordelia's. Together they must be worth a lot more than that."

"Let me first see this quite clearly. What you propose is to sell your holdings in a very prosperous though perhaps unromantic concern. This concern pays a high dividend, a long-established, a family business, where you are your own master and where—if you're ill or want a holiday —you are always assured that other people, many other people, employees, are continuing to work for you. Instead you wish to invest this

254

money in one of the most speculative . . . Launching a new weekly magazine against all the keen competition of those already established. You want to take an undistinguished position as a sub-editor; exacting work at all hours of the day, no longer your own master but at the beck and call of others. Is that it?"

". . . Yes."

"And further, you'd leave a very large and comfortable house with nearly a score of servants and take Cordelia and your son to live in some little London suburban avenue—one maid to do the rough work, and two trees and a concrete path for a garden?"

". . . Yes."

Mr. Ferguson said in the same quiet tone: "Are you mad?"

Brook went white. "I don't—well, I don't look at it that way, Father."

"How do you look at it then? Pray tell me."

Brook stammered, licked his lips. A tremendous moment, to throw over the old fetishes to which he'd been bowing since a tiny child. The ruler at two, the frown at four, the inflection at seven. All the iron doors, deep overgrown and long forgotten, shaking and breaking. It was not only his father; he was fighting what had become a part of himself, thoughts and opinions of another man.

"It isn't always money that means happiness, is it? It's what you do with your life. I've always wanted to write, to—to be a poet chiefly, but you can't live by poetry. Or not many people can. I can't help it. I've never been interested in chemicals, never shall be. I know I'm secure here. But security isn't everything. I want to launch out—on my own. You say I'm independent here, but I'm—not really. Even with the partnership we're still really dependent on you. It's only exchanging one master for another. . . ."

"So you look on me as that. You will find there can be a great deal of difference in masters, my boy."

"It's only natural, isn't it, to want to strike out on my own? I want to make a home for Cordelia. We've been married over five years now. It's better for young married couples to have their own place. Did you live with your father and mother when you were first married?"

"Yes."

"Well—anyway, that's how I feel, that's how we feel."

"So Cordelia is in this too?"

"I'm Brook's wife, Mr. Ferguson." She said it with a dreadful sense of futility, of guilt towards Brook, of throwing her support into a cause already lost.

Mr. Ferguson walked again up and down the room. So far they had not progressed an inch. This was just striking on the outer walls.

"I didn't know you were both so unhappy here."

"We're not. That's not it at all, is it, Brook? But if you can understand——"

"I want to make my own life," Brook said obstinately. "This is an opportunity I haven't looked for——"

"Oh, haven't you?" Mr. Ferguson said, suddenly standing quite still. "Then what of the contents of Scott's first letter? It's plain from that that you have been expressing your discontent to everyone. The contemptuous way he speaks of your 'present job' as if it were an office boy's. Changing one 'job' for another. It's the language of the petty clerk. And he speaks of me as the 'old man.' How you stand with the old man. People adapt their style to the known outlook of the people they're writing to. It's perfectly plain what he judges yours to be."

"I've tried to put this to you as—as reasonably as I can. I knew it would be a disappointment. I knew there would be trouble——"

"Then I wonder you bothered to consult me at all."

"I'm not dead to the decencies, though you pretend to think I am." They were slipping rapidly now down the slope; she couldn't stop them.

"I'm glad you realise that there is something slightly unmoral in accepting a partnership in a firm one year and attempting to slide out of it the next *with* the money made over to you as a gift."

"I never wanted the partnership! Cordelia persuaded me to take it. We were freer as we were before."

"But short of money. You wouldn't have had this offer from your good friend if you had been short of money. They don't want you, you know—an untried youth with a few flimsy poems published at his own expense, a——"

"Leave my poems out of this."

"Please don't interrupt me. I repeat that they don't want you. Why should they? The whole enterprise smacks to me of a sharp practice, a ruse to get your investment. In a few months—the first time you are in bed with one of your ailments—they'll tell you it's all a mistake, they are calling in an experienced man. But you'll not see your money again."

"That's my concern, isn't it!" Brook said furiously. "If I care to make a bad investment that's my look-out. At least I shall have got away from you for a bit. At least I shall be able to breathe freely. And if I fail, well, I'll not come whining back!"

"Please, Brook!" Cordelia was between them, afraid that one would strike the other. She had never seen such anger, such hatred in men's eyes before. It was as if the blood relationship had festered and turned to something more ugly than could exist between ordinary men.

She knew Aunt Tish was quietly crying, tears running down her cheeks soundlessly as if someone had turned an easy tap. Across her, these two men were saying dreadful, unforgivable things, things that would rankle and be remembered for years. Did they mean it, were these the true thoughts and feelings, hidden until now and now tumbling out? Or was a single trickle of poison infecting all the rest?

Once Brook tried to push her out of the way, but she clung to him, feeling his arm trembling against hers.

"Brook!" she whispered urgently. "No more now! Let it rest now. Give it time. Talk again tomorrow. Brook!"

At length, exhausted by his own passion, he quieted down and the old man stood there staring at them both, staring at them with angry eyes which were blank and unrevealing, summing them up, condemning. He had shut them both out from himself, from understanding. If Brook went on with it there would be an irreparable cleavage, she saw that. The long dominion might be coming to an end, but there would be no acceptance of it, never any giving way on the father's part.

CHAPTER THREE Brook was going on with it. Later that night or the following day she half expected to find his mood changed, as it so often had in the past. Once the grievances had been ventilated . . . But not now. The revolt went too far and too deep. And the offer was an opportunity which would not be repeated. It was now, *now* or never on all counts.

For three days the two men didn't speak to each other. They drove down with her each morning, they returned together at night. Brook, who was usually upset to the point of illness at any quarrel, seemed to thrive with nervous malignance on this one. On the following Thursday he left for London and on Saturday afternoon he returned, exhausted but satisfied. There was a light in his eye as of one who has seen a vision, though yet far off. He had met Lord Hirondel and Mr. Brompton Jones and two others. If Father thought they were after his money he should have been there during the interview. Hugh had had to talk to them every way to get them to accept an untried man. The money had turned the scale, but only just. They were in deadly earnest to turn out the best magazine of the day. Contracts had already been entered into to secure advertising revenue. Prominent members of the Liberal party were interested and would consider it a matter of policy that the magazine should succeed. It was quite a different thing from starting a weekly without adequate backing. They were planning everything to the smallest detail.

Mr. Ferguson had gone to Oldham on the Friday evening and he did not get back until nearly six. He passed Brook in the hall as if he were not there and did not come down again until prayers.

In frigid silence they gathered there in the hall, Mr. Ferguson by the small table which he used as a sort of rostrum, the Bible open before him. The servants formed a line down the wall. Ian was now considered old enough to attend these prayers before he went to bed and had been drilled into rigid silence. He stood with his hand in his mother's and with Brook on his other side.

With open watch Mr. Ferguson waited for the second hand to come round to six-thirty and then began.

"When the wicked man turneth away from his wickedness that he hath committed, and doeth that which is lawful and right, he shall save his soul alive. I acknowledge my transgressions, and my sin is ever before me. The sacrifices of God are a broken spirit: a broken and a contrite heart, O God, Thou wilt not despise. Let us pray."

The moon was nearly full, and the bare branches of the sycamore tree latticed the long window beside the front door. The gaslight in the hall was turned low, and shadows lay on people's faces, hollowing them like the faces of the moon. A good fire burned but it was very cold.

"From all evil and mischief; from sin, from the crafts and assaults of the devil; from thy wrath and from everlasting damnation . . ."

"Good Lord, deliver us."

"From all blindness of heart, from pride, vain glory, and hypocrisy; from envy, hatred, and malice, and from all uncharitableness . . ."

"Good Lord, deliver us."

Was he going through it all? Ian was moving his hand in hers. She glanced suddenly at Brook. She knew he hated standing; all his weakly body complained. But he was stiff and taut like a bow.

"Christ have mercy upon us."

"Christ have mercy upon us."

"Lord have mercy upon us."

"Lord have mercy upon us." It was over at last. Was she wicked to think of it that way? Oh, God, she tried to pray, help us at this time, protect us from bitterness and selfishness. . . . Ian was tapping his foot on the carpet; she squeezed his hand to stop him.

"Oh eternal God, our Heavenly Father," said Mr. Ferguson, "who alone makest men to be of one mind in a house and stillest the outrage of selfish and unruly words, we bless Thy holy Name and pray that it should please Thee to quiet the voice of ingratitude which has risen up amongst us, most humbly beseeching Thee to grant to all of us grace, that we may henceforth obediently walk in Thy holy commandments, and leading a quiet and peaceable life together, may continually offer

258

unto Thee our sacrifice of praise and thanksgiving, through Jesus Christ our Lord, Amen."

The went in to supper.

At the meal Aunt Tish complained about the cold weather and said she wished the snow would come down and have done with it, but only Cordelia made a show of answering.

As they rose from the table, Brook said: "Father, I'd like a word with you."

Mr. Ferguson stared at him with his blank Olympian eyes.

"What have you to say?"

"I'd prefer to tell you in private."

Without replying, the big man led the way into his study. Brook held the door open for Cordelia and then followed her in.

"Well?"

"Look, Father," said Brook on a palliative note. He had been persuaded by Cordelia to begin this way, the soft voice, the reasonable appeal. "I know you think badly of me over this. Perhaps you've the right—I don't know. But anyway, it's no use us not speaking to each other. We've got to discuss some things. Isn't it better that we should all sit down together and try to—to talk it over as quietly as we can?"

"I prefer to stand," said his father.

". . . Well, I've been to London. I've seen everyone concerned, and I'm sure this is the opportunity of a lifetime. You're not interested in the details. Anyway—the main thing is, I've accepted a sub-editorship on the new *Westminster Bulletin,* and I've promised to start work in a fortnight. That's a concession; they wanted me to begin right away, but I said I couldn't. I've also agreed to—to invest five thousand pounds in the paper." He gave a nervous shrug of his shoulders. "That's all."

She had been watching Mr. Ferguson, and she saw now that privately under his harshness he had believed Brook would not have the courage. She saw the change in his eyes. From envy, malice, hatred? . . .

Abruptly she lowered her eyes.

"You understand that I've forbidden you to take this, Brook. You know I look on it as an unfilial act—unkind, sly, treacherous. Fifteen months ago I made over to you and Cordelia one half of all my property in the dye works. Now you've flung that generosity in my face, dishonestly betrayed my trust. You realise that?"

"I don't see it that way, but I see you see it that way. I'm—very sorry, Father. But my mind's made up. There'll never be another chance like this."

"You're willing to desert the dye works, deprive it of the two people I have been training to fill my place? You don't care if it goes to ruin?"

"You've always implied I'm no good. You only made me a partner so that you could make Cordelia one and draw her in. You've faith in her but none in me and never have."

"What of the capital you propose to withdraw. You're willing to cripple the firm?"

"Oh—*that* can't cripple it. I know the amount of business. . . . I should think each of the partner's shares must be worth eight or nine thousand pounds. But if you're short of fluid capital you could take another partner. . . ."

"Outside the family?"

"Yes, if necessary. But you won't need to do that. You've money in other things. What about the Waverley Mills?"

Mr. Ferguson stood with his hands under his coat-tails.

"Nothing I can say then can alter you at all? No persuasion? Even if it breaks my heart? Tell me quite frankly."

All the old marks of indecision were etched on Brook's face; no rebellion; no independence could ever smooth them away. He got out:

"I can't help it. Perhaps what I'm doing isn't fair to you, but it won't ruin you and it won't break your heart." He ended: "If you'd give way decently we could still be friends."

Their eyes met, for the first time after a week's enmity.

"But I'm not prepared to give way," Mr. Ferguson lisped at him.

Brook took a deep breath. "Well, then there's no more to it, is there? I'm sorry, but I shall be—be leaving here in about a fortnight—with Cordelia. If you'll arrange—with the bank to put five thousand pounds in my name——"

"I'll arrange for nothing of the sort."

To her it had seemed all along that the old man had some weapon in reserve, but Brook had not sensed this.

"I'll forgo the rest of my share," he said. "I'm not all that grasping. But I've got to have the five thousand pretty soon."

Mr. Ferguson turned his back on them both. "Well, it will not come to you from my firm. Did you take the trouble to read the articles of partnership?"

"What articles?"

"Those we signed when the matter was arranged."

"What's that got to do with it? A partner's a partner, and he's master of his own share."

"With some qualifications, Brook. I'm sorry that you didn't read the deed thoroughly at the time. Clause nine stipulates that not more than five hundred pounds may be drawn out in any one year without the consent of the other five partners. That consent will obviously be lacking. I didn't wish to take this course but . . . While you've been away I have satisfied myself that the clause is legally watertight."

Brook stared at his father's back. He seemed to be staring at something more, at his own impotence through all the years. One saw creeping back into his mind the old frustrations. Wait, wait, consider it carefully. Could he have chosen to build all his revolt, his precious bid for independence . . .

He turned suddenly, whitely, to Cordelia. "Is it true, what he says? D'you know?"

She said distressfully: "I don't know, Brook. . . ."

"There's a copy of the deed in that drawer," Mr. Ferguson said, with a lift of his hand.

Brook turned to the desk as if he would tear it apart, wrenched open the drawer, and then in a sudden spasm of weakness turned away.

"You look."

He sat trembling on a chair while she turned over the papers, found the right one, opened it.

"Yes, it's true," she said, hardly above a whisper.

There was silence in the room.

"The clause was put in as a general safeguard," Mr. Ferguson said. "I didn't foresee anything like this. I didn't foresee being betrayed by my own son."

Brook didn't speak.

"Mr. Ferguson."

He turned, looked her over with constrained eyes. There seemed to be a coarseness in the texture of his face: one saw it with new intensity.

"Will you," she said, "try to think this over, for everyone's sake?" Give me words to say what I want to say. "There can't be anything for you in frustrating Brook. Prisoners aren't cheerful companions. And you're so generous. You're always giving to others, trying . . . For—many years he's worked for you, in the business you've built. He's not been happy because he's not fitted to it, not interested; he can't help that. You've been disappointed. Well, he's done his best. Why not give him a chance now in something else? You might be surprised. If he fails, as you think, then he'll come back here and work for you again, won't you, Brook? And with a good heart. That's fair. But he might succeed. You'd be proud of him then. He's set his mind on it. If this hadn't turned up he might have stayed a calico printer all his life, made the best of it. But it *has* turned up. Now, *whatever* you do, he'll never try to make the best of it again—unless you give him his chance first. You can't compel him to be a good son. You can ruin his life—but it won't make yours or mine happier. You've still got the chance to be—to be revered by him instead of reviled."

He had turned his head away. The grim profile, the authoritative nose. But he was listening to her. She went on.

261

"If you'll agree to let Brook go, I'll promise to work for you for the rest of this year—or until you're absolutely satisfied with some manager. By then, by the end of this year, there'll be a good chance of knowing whether Brook is going to be happy in London. If he isn't, then there'll be no need to leave at all."

"And Ian?"

She hesitated. As in a sudden flash she saw that this was a crucial issue; he had put his finger not on Brook's weakness but on hers.

"What about him?"

"Suppose you don't return. Is Ian to lose his just inheritance?"

"That's a long way ahead. Ian can come into the dye works if he wants to. But he must be free to choose."

"As Brook must be, eh?"

"As I never have been," said Brook.

"Fortunately for you, or you would be starving in a gutter."

"That's your opinion."

"Brook, please." She had just been grasping at something solid, some hope of conciliatory bargaining. "Mr. Ferguson, do try to help us in this. We're as much in distress as you. There's been nothing 'arranged' about it—that's clear or we should have taken note of the partnership deed. Perhaps we're more in distress than you. You've always been kind to us. Well, help us now, help Brook now. There's nothing shameful in what he wants to do."

Mr. Ferguson took a deep breath. If only one could get at him, she thought, touch some responding chord, his proved generosity, his sympathy; separate it from the corrosions of self-esteem.

He said: "Well, then, you think there's nothing shameful in desertion, you think Brook must be allowed to ride roughshod over everyone else to gain a fleeting satisfaction that he thinks he's missed. And what of my life, what of my plans, my life's work, must that all go on the refuse heap to please him? For fifty years I've worked for my family. Something concrete and valuable to hand on to my son and my son's son. Do you think I've never had temptation? Do you think Brook is the only one to make sacrifices? If I had consented to take a leading part in the city's life when I was first asked, when I was still a young man . . . Or if I had gone into politics I should have been able to occupy one of the Liberal seats. But there was no one who could take responsibility, so I gave up my ambitions for the good of my family and to build the future. Rightly or wrongly I did just that. Now do you expect me in my late years to throw it all away so that my son shall gratify a whim?"

She was silent. Perhaps they, too, needed generosity and sympathy. But it's no good, she thought with sudden clarity, expecting a son to appreciate his father's sacrifices. At least it's no good expecting sacrifices in return. Because the father's sacrifices are a free choice, the son's are bound.

Brook said: "I've promised these people. I've made all arrangements. I can't go back on my word now."

"You can write and say you've changed your mind."

"But I haven't," he said desperately. "I haven't, Father."

"Or better still," Mr. Ferguson said, "go to your friends and say you're willing to become a sub-editor but that you have no money to put up. That will test their real desire to have you."

Brook got up. "Good God! . . . I've lived with you all these years as——" He broke off because Cordelia caught his arm.

"Go on," said his father. "Say what you have to say. Let us have it all."

Brook said, panting: "You talk of treachery. What about yours? You pretend you're giving us a partnership in your firm, and really it's only a sham, a window-dressing to make you seem generous. You've used me as a puppet all my life to—to—— You played on my feelings whichever way you thought best. Don't pretend you've done everything for my sake; you've done it for your own. Why should I have to bear the consequences of your life! Why didn't you go into politics if you wanted to; it was your choice, not mine!"

"Brook . . ." He would take no notice of her now. The resentment had to come out whatever the cost.

"Did you ever want to get into Parliament? Well, chance is a fine thing. I don't believe you ever had the chance or you would have jumped at it and forgotten me *and* the dye works. Now you want to make a virtue of it. Well, it won't work."

Mr. Ferguson turned and looked at his son with a dreadful glowing look.

"Then what are you going to do?"

"You say the job was only offered to me for the money I could put up. Perhaps it was. Perhaps I will go and see them and see if they'll take me without. But I'm not staying here, I'll tell you that!"

"Very well. Get out when you please."

Brook was gasping with anger. He shook off her hand. Disappointment and frustration and hatred made his face old, flaccid.

"And don't delude yourself that it's only my friends who are interested in money. Why have you got all these civic appointments, why were you made an alderman before others who were just as good? Only because you could give to this charity and that——"

"Be quiet!" said Mr. Ferguson. "Leave—this room—before I thrash you."

"I'll go," said Brook, trembling, hardly able to stand. "I'll go."

He turned, seeming to forget Cordelia, stumbled past her, grasped for the door handle, went out. He left the door open. She slowly followed. The quarrel had been like physical blows, knocking the strength and resistance out of the fighters. She moved slowly, past the desk behind which the old man stood; she reached the door. As she went out into the hall she heard the outer door slam.

CHAPTER FOUR He didn't know where he was going. He had turned down towards Town because the other way one got out into the country at once.

He was half blind with anger and weakness. His heart was thumping, and he strode on driven by a strength not like his own. Had victory come out of the quarrel he would have been calm and quiet, exhausted perhaps, but sure. It was defeat which was the poison.

He slipped on the icy road, recovered. The air was bitter, but he was warm enough, sweating even under his coat. The moon had gone behind thick banked clouds which had a silvery shining rim to them as they crept over the luminous sky.

Defeat. It would mean—he saw all that it would mean. A long letter to Hugh, some unconvincing apology, a slow resettling to the old ways, excuses to the two or three men he had mentioned it to. A settling down to serfdom—but with a difference. No *pretence* of affection, even of civility now. Open war in the worst circumstances, in the business, in the home. Unthinkable. At least his father could not stop them leaving Grove Hall. A house somewhere as far away as possible. No social intercourse. By God, he'd make the bully pay . . . Schemes for revenge.

His foot slipped again, and he saw a public house on the other side of the street. Usually he would have been self-conscious about going in such a place, but now he crossed the road and boldly pushed open the door.

The saloon bar was crowded and he ordered a whisky. Schemes for revenge. The old man should never see Ian. He would find that slave labour . . . And there would be no reconciliations, not ever. Cordelia must be forced to do as he said. This would be war to the very end.

The whisky made him sweat still more; he ordered another and unbuttoned his coat. He knew that he was conspicuous in here sitting alone, his sensitive weakly face, of which he was so conscious, the rather long hair and the way it was brushed, they picked him out as a man with an artistic temperament, a gentleman. People glanced at him. He didn't care.

All his dreams and plans. Revenge was dead sea fruit. *No* other way?

Would the Westminster people take him with only five hundred pounds, a thousand with Cordelia's, if he promised to pay the same each year? Suppose he offered to work without salary. They could live in London on his share of the interest and profits, of which even his father could not now deprive him.

But it wouldn't work. They wanted the money at once. Was that clause really watertight? What happened if a partnership was dissolved? Supposing one partner died, surely the partnership would be wound up, the assets valued, a fresh partner if necessary found. Could one partner not *force* a dissolution? He would see a solicitor in the morning.

"Hullo," said a voice.

A woman was standing with a hand on his chair. She smiled at him coolly. A black dress with imitation diamonds, and her hair was dyed. He couldn't for a moment believe that she was really speaking to him.

"Who are you?"

"I'm all right, Mac," she said quickly. "And how are you?"

They stared at each other. Her hard brown eyes assessed his innocence.

"What do you want?" he said, reddening.

"Like to come 'ome with me and have a nice time?"

"No, thanks." He got up, glad of the noise in the bar.

"Well, buy a girl a drink."

Flushing up to his ears, he put a two-shilling piece on the table and threaded his way towards the door. Someone was laughing and he suspected it was at him.

Outside, the cold air greeted him like a newly sharpened knife. He felt full of self-contempt. He couldn't even answer a woman of her sort without stumbling, making her laugh. He turned again towards Town. No return yet. Perhaps no return at all tonight. His father might feel a little anxiety. Perhaps they'd think he had gone the way of Slaney-Smith. But that would not be fair to Cordelia. She at least had stood by him.

He saw another public house and stopped, glanced in at the steamy window. Couldn't go on walking all night. A deadly fatigue was coming over him, superseding the false energy. Feet were very cold; he didn't usually come walking in these shoes. He went in.

Quieter in here. He ordered another whisky and seemed to drink in with it a deadly despair. Did anything matter? He was done for, defeated. It was not only a material, it was a moral, defeat. The pretty dream had faded—had faded into the fight of common day. Who had written that? Shades of the prison house. Well, he was back in his prison again. The songster in his cage can sing . . . Sometimes in the past he had assuaged his disappointments with poetry. Not writing of his disappointments the way some people did—that was too close. But putting something on paper was a help. He'd always dreamt of fame, the sudden discovery, the glowing reviews, being received among the great ones.

Daydreams had often served him, but they wouldn't work now. He had another whisky and took out an old envelope and a pencil. Perhaps for once he would write directly of his disappointment. Nothing else would hold his thoughts.

> The iron-bosomed cloud obscures the light;
> Halts my tired footstep in the frosty dark.
> Bitter my thoughts and bitter his delight
> As the lone wolf's bark.

> Forth from his glittering doorway's empty leer
> Skulks into light his friendship and his trust,
> A fatherly affection insincere
> As the harlot's lust.

> Before ambition and the greed for power. . .

He wrote on, the thing coming in a spate unusual to him. He felt it was good. There were flaws, but the whole framework, the inspiration, was sound. His feelings, the hatred in him, was a constant spur. Ideas, satiric images came into his mind and were set down. He ran out of paper and slit the envelopes open, scribbling on the insides. He didn't care now who watched him. He ordered another drink but left it untouched.

At length, with perspiration cold on his forehead, he could do no more. He had written twelve verses. Three more he felt would round it off, but although he knew the general shape of them, they wouldn't come.

Well, it was a big thing done. It would normally have taken him weeks to squeeze out. He was chilly and it was time to go home.

Yes, home. He could face it now—perhaps not the disappointment but at least the thought of Grove Hall. He had written the worst out of himself. Once again his poetry had come to his help.

He got up and drank the whisky off at a draught, gathered up his precious paper, buttoned his coat.

He didn't know how long he had been there but it was late. As he came out he found there had been a fall of snow, and more flakes were drifting in the wind. The buses had stopped running and there was no cab about. He settled down to walk, the wind blowing icy round his limbs.

The whisky had drained his soul of old ambition and filled it with new. The *Bulletin* would almost certainly publish this poem even if it would not get him for sub-editor. It might make his name. A fitting revenge upon his father—the only one to which there was no reply. If one could only write with this concentration, with this feeling, more often. He had gone to the limits of vituperation yet in the best tradition of verse, like Pope, like Dryden.

He had never drunk so much before and about halfway home he began to feel ill. He sat on a wall, deadly faint, and held his head in his hands. Then he staggered on a few hundred yards before he was sick.

He knew the way so well that he could not deceive himself as to the distance yet to go, and when the gates of Grove Hall at last showed up they were like an oasis to a fainting traveller. He sat in the snow to recover. There was pride to consider. He must go in with his head high.

He was not displeased when he saw the front door of the house open and Cordelia, muffled in a fur coat, standing on the steps.

He caught a cold; that was to be expected.

He refused to retire to bed, feeling this would help his father to justify himself on another count. On Monday he didn't go to the works, but when Mr. Ferguson had left he strode boldly into the study and helped himself to the copy of the partnership deed. Then he took it off to a solicitor—not the family solicitor—in Town.

His worst suspicions were justified and he came home frustrate and sickly.

For another day he postponed writing to Hugh, toying with bold and desperate schemes. He worked, too, on his poem, polishing and pruning and until only one more verse was needed to finish it off. But that one would not come.

His appetite as usual had left him, but he went down to supper determined to face his father out. This time there was to be no climbing down. He sat there at the table staring inimically at his father from time to time and saying over to himself the verses of the poem, applying each one to the man before him, savouring its effect.

Cordelia spent the meal in horrible discomfort, wondering every moment from Brook's expression if there would be an outburst. The slightest thing, she could see, would be enough to set it off. She sensed now that it had been hopeless to attempt a compromise. This cleavage cut right down to the roots of their association. There was no bridge.

It could not go on much longer: the frigid silences of the last ten days were nothing to this. She determined to make Brook keep to his room for a couple of days. Some time then she must face Mr. Ferguson. At least *they* could talk, could make plans. She and Brook must leave as soon as possible, find another house.

267

Breaking in on this decision was a curious sound beside her and she saw Brook turn his plate round with an impatient gesture and push it away. She looked at him and saw that he was staring straight in front of him and licking his lips. The maid came across to take his plate but he did not seem to notice her hand. Cordelia hesitated to say anything, to break the heavy silence. If this was the beginning of another outburst . . . Mr. Ferguson was breathing heavily while he ate.

"What's matter, Brook?" said Aunt Tish, in a frightened voice. "What's matter, love?"

Brook put his hand on the table and with a sudden sweep pushed a heap of crockery across the cloth, upsetting salad dressing and a glass of wine. For a second Cordelia thought, This is going too far, but then she saw that he didn't know what he was doing. His hand had clutched the table-cloth and he was trying to get up.

"Brook!" She pushed back her chair and was beside him, but not in time to prevent him falling forward across the table in a faint.

Curious, the almost relief. Not another and fiercer quarrel; here is something to deal with, rub his hands, send the servants for brandy, talk about something normal in a normal voice. Callous? But it pricked the swelling bubble; give anything for that.

In a few minutes he began to come round; Mr. Ferguson stood back, plucking at his lip with an air half of concern, half of hostile detachment. Get him straight to bed; overdoing it; needed rest; and send down to the Polygon just to be on the safe side. Robert came quickly, examined his patient, told him he'd got a chill; bed for perhaps a week, then he'd be all right again. Out in the corridor he said:

"What's he been doing, sleeping out all night?"

"No. He went out on Saturday and caught a chill." She looked up. "It's not—anything serious?"

He said: "We mustn't get alarmed unduly. I'd suggest . . . D'you know if Nurse Charters is available? No, well, I could call in as I go home. If she's not I think I can get someone else."

"But—does he need that? He's been upset, and I shouldn't want him needlessly alarmed. I'm sure I'll be all right tonight."

"Better with a nurse. You look tired, if I may say so. I'd advise it for your sake."

She flushed. "I'm very well, thank you."

He looked at her with that long perceptive look of his. "I'd advise it nevertheless. You have to be considered."

At the bottom of the stairs the old man was standing.

He said with a faint unfriendly inflexion: "Well?"

Birch repeated what he had said.

"Oh? Is that necessary? The boy is always ailing something. I think this business of having nurses in at the slightest excuse is bad for him. It gives him an overweening sense of his own importance."

Robert said: "There's more than the slightest excuse tonight."

"Why, what's the matter?"

"He has a patch developing again on both lungs."

They both stared hard at him.

"You mean pneumonia again?"

"Yes."

A sinking feeling in the stomach. Mr. Ferguson looked as if he would like to deny it all, as if he still suspected Brook of doing this with a desire to anger him.

"It's very singular. I confess I'm surprised."

"No more surprised than I was, sir. The last time I saw him he was very well."

"No doubt. No doubt. Well, Mrs. Ferguson can manage, surely. You can stop it before it develops. It's not likely to be so serious as last time."

"All the symptoms are there, I'm afraid. We shall be able to tell better in another twelve hours. I confess I was—disappointed when I sounded him."

So it all had to happen again, the nursing, the delirium, the crisis, the long convalescence. Horrified and weary at the thought. She mustn't feel weary. It was her duty to see him through again.

The old man did not move from the foot of the stairs.

He said: "Is there grounds for a second opinion?"

"I don't think anything would be served by it at the moment. But naturally——"

"You know, Birch, why I always feel this way."

"Yes. Certainly. It can do no harm. I'll send a note to Mr. Plimley first thing in the morning."

He still did not move, and they had to step past him, leaving him frowning up towards the landing above.

At the door Robert Birch picked up his coat and said quietly:

"Brook told me last Tuesday that he was taking an appointment in London. Has there been a quarrel with his father?"

"Yes . . ."

She waited but the young man did not speak. He was buttoning his coat, his face uncommunicative.

She said in rising alarm: "Is he very ill?"

"I don't know. I don't think so. But he seems to have such nervous exhaustion. I'll be round early in the morning, about seven-thirty. If you want me before——"

She caught his arm. "I can very easily do without sleep for one night,

Robert. I think I can help him. It may help if he feels he can talk freely about it all. Then Nurse Charters can come by day as she did before."

He hesitated. "Very well. I know he'll be in the best possible hands."

But everything didn't happen the same. From the start nothing was the same.

Brook was as rational as his watcher and talked with her until she bade him go to sleep. This he obediently did, but his sleep was distressed. About three he woke and said in a hoarse anxious voice:

"Pass me a pencil. I—think I've—got the last verse of that—poem."

She turned up the gas.

"You mean . . ."

He was too tired to explain. He handed her the sheets of paper, while he very laboriously began to trace the words that had come into his mind. She read the poem and was appalled at the increasing venom of each verse.

She said: "When did you write this?"

He read in a faltering whisper:

> "Blood on the altar of his greed, I am,
> The sacrificial lamb.

"Listen——" He looked at Cordelia. "If I'm—not well enough, send this to Hugh—tomorrow. Put it in his paper. Tell him. If I'm not well enough to—write and explain—this will explain." The pencil dropped from his hand and he lay back faint on the pillows.

A feeling of panic seized her. She felt she urgently needed company, some company, to see her through the rest of the night. She pulled at the lever bell on the wall and hoped that its tinkling would waken one of the maids. Then she opened the door and ran over to Mr. Ferguson's room and burst in without knocking.

Scarcely ever been in here. Smell of cloth and moth balls and eau de Cologne. He was instantly awake. Perhaps not asleep.

"Brook," she said. "He looks worse. I'd like the doctor."

A great creaking of the bed. He was out and she saw a dim bulk struggling into a dressing-gown. In a moment he was beside her.

"Let me see."

They went across the landing and she went in. Brook's eyes were closed and his breathing was coming very fast. But some instinct told him that his father was there. As Mr. Ferguson came quietly in he opened his eyes and half raised his head.

"Get out!" he whispered with intense hatred. "Get out of my room!"

Frederick Ferguson looked about him as if seeking a chair; finding none, he backed towards the door and went out with his hand to his eyes.

"Brook!" she said. "Please! Keep calm. You'll upset yourself. Please! It isn't worth it! For my sake. Brook!"

He lay back on her arm and looked up vacantly into her eyes.

" 'The sacrificial lamb,' " he said. "Strange. All day I tried to get the line. Then it came—quite easily—as if—I only had to pick it up." He frowned, trying to concentrate. "Remind me tomorrow, dear. Must look it over once more—before you send it. Get it written out . . . Drop a note."

A maid came hurriedly into the room, and Cordelia sent her fleeing for the doctor.

But before Robert Birch could get there Brook was dead.

CHAPTER FIVE Now of all times I must not give way to hatred, to hysterical resentment. To grief, yes—and true grief, though queerly mixed. Perhaps it's the shock that makes me feel so much. I never *dreamt* this time. Nobody did. It's as if he slipped quietly away, through our fingers, out of a room while no one was looking; one moment he was speaking, then we looked up and he was gone, and there is no coming back through that door.

"Yes, Ian, dear, only for two or three days. Grandma will find you lots to play with, and I'll come and see you every day. No, Nanny will stay here tonight and join you tomorrow. No, dear, your train's too big to take. Well, just the engine, then." Brook was like this not long ago, lace collar, linen suit, white socks; and another woman, perhaps like me, watched him romp, never guessing.

Brook playing croquet on the lawn that first summer of marriage. Brook in bed with this complaint and that, tiresome, irritable, ailing, yet grateful for her care, appealing to the latent motherliness in her. Brook playing Chopin Nocturnes on a May evening. Brook so pitifully proud of the son that was not his. The reading of the poems at the Athenæum, nervous voice growing more secure as he went on, flushed cheeks and subdued triumph when it was over. The curious oases of mutual concord, at Southport and in Wales, amid all the worst stresses of her affair with Stephen.

She had loved him a little, perhaps more than she realised. It was not in her nature to despise affection, and many times her heart had responded to his. Now it seemed to her that it had not done so with sufficient warmth and sincerity.

Oh, of course, there was the other side; dishonest to herself to forget that now, his sulkiness, his occasional meannesses, all the rest. But did not most of them derive from his sense of inferiority, his frustration? Where was it all now—flushed cheeks, shaky voice, thin curly hair, introspective eyes, the sentience and the understanding . . .

"I'm more sorry than I can say, Cordelia. I blame myself for not having realised how far the disease had developed; but it happened that the inflammatory process hadn't reached more than a fraction of the lung in contact with the chest wall. In those circumstances it's almost impossible to tell. And it was so unlike Brook to hide his illness that it put me right out in my estimate. Forgive me, you can't want my excuses, but I felt it necessary to say this much to you. I—felt it necessary—to explain. . . ."

"I think he'd exhausted himself. You weren't to know."

"Do understand—and this isn't a conventional expression of sympathy —if there's anything I can do to help you, anything at all, please let me know."

"Thank you, Robert." But there was nothing he could do to help— much as he wished to. Only these last months had she come to realise how much he wished to.

Perhaps there was some hysteria in her on those first lonely nights, but it seemed to her that only half the crisis was resolved and that, Brook now being beyond his father's reach, Ian might any time come into immediate danger. Frederick Ferguson must not be allowed to touch his life. With horror she pictured the sturdy little boy (already mouse-quiet at prayers) growing slowly into another Brook: overawed and overborne in all things, thinking as his grandfather willed him to think until . . .

Her mind turned back to Margaret and dwelt on her more than it had done for years. It seemed to her now that her original suspicion had not been so far from the truth. Poison of a sort existed in the very relationship.

First Margaret; now Brook. Who next?

It was all she could do to stay in the house an hour longer; she wanted to push a few things into a box and snatch her son up in his sleep. Hardly noticed, the process of subjection and dominion might already be far advanced.

So far she had done nothing about Brook's poem. No doubt Mr. Ferguson deserved to read the considered epithets his son had heaped on him, yet she shrank from this last vindictiveness. The damage was done and nothing could restore the past. If she could have seen behind the suffering mask of the old man's face and assured herself once and for all that it was only a mask . . .

Dignified sorrow. "The great loss I have suffered." "So kind and dutiful a son." "It has pleased God to afflict me in my old age." Hypocrisy or the simple truth as he saw it? The important thing was not to decide but to get away from a decision. Someone else could sit in judgment, not she. She was too tired, too grieved to condemn.

It was possible to be quite sincere and yet still to crush and extinguish the life of those around you.

"Thank you, Mrs. Thorpe, it's so kind of you to come and see me. No, Mr. Ferguson's seeing nobody at present. Most of the day he sits in his study quite alone. . . . Thank you, thank you, yes, I'll give him your message."

And I am free to go, Mrs. Thorpe. Wake up, heart, and beat more quickly at the thought. But the loss of Brook is still too close.

I will plan. Today is Saturday and the funeral already twenty-four hours behind. Tomorrow Ian comes back from Mother's. On Monday Mr. Ferguson will go down to the works again. He must go, for he has not been near since . . .

"Oh, thank you, Father, for bringing him. I was coming over later. Are you sure he hasn't been any trouble? But, darling, what a *beautiful* clock! Did Grandpa make it for you? And does it *really* go? . . . Yes, it's been a dreadful week, but I think the worst's over. Everybody's been— so kind. No, Mr. Ferguson's been no trouble. But at times he's looked so ill that I've wondered. . . . Uncle Pridey's ill, you know, that's why he wasn't at the—why he wasn't here on Friday. We wired him but he wired back that he was in bed with sciatica. . . . Yes, I'll do my best to get a holiday—I'll get away as soon as ever I can. . . ." Tomorrow, in fact, but I can't tell you yet. I'll leave a note tomorrow—a note for you and a note for him.

Her father stayed all the afternoon, and by the time he left it was snowing again. She stood at the door watching him tread sturdily down the drive. The light from inside the house showed up the drifting flakes wandering aimlessly down, the thin damp crust of snow on the ground. Footsteps showed black where the snow had clung to his heels.

It was time for prayers and Sunday supper and the servants were gathering uncomfortably in the hall. Three times during the last week Mr. Ferguson had not come out of his study to say prayers and as there was no one to deputise she had had to dismiss the servants again. She did so tonight; and she and Aunt Tish went in to supper. She sent Hallows to remind Mr. Ferguson and he said he would have his meal in the study. Relief. Although the dining-room dwarfed her and the simple-minded old woman opposite, the silence between them was a harmless silence untainted with passion or fermenting grief.

When it was over, Aunt Tish said she was going to bed. She had never really stopped crying since Brook's death: even now there was a moisture in her eyes which oozed out whenever she spoke or was spoken to, and the dewdrop on the end of her nose was not a permanent resident but a fresh visitor constantly wiped away and renewed.

Cordelia went up to see if Ian was comfortably settled, talked for a while with Nanny Grimshaw, came down listlessly into the drawing-room, and picked up one of yesterday's papers which still lay folded and unopened on the top of Friday's on the table by the door.

The fire had gone down and she pulled it together until it broke into a blaze. One somehow needed the warmth and light of the fires for other reasons than the cold. Warm your hands while there is still feeling, draw comfort where you can, for outside is the churchyard and the dark.

Someone came into the room, and she saw it was Mr. Ferguson.

CHAPTER SIX 🌿 He said: "You blame me, don't you? Blame me for it all?"

They had been sitting for ten minutes in silence, she pretending to read, waiting the excuse to escape. He had been staring into the fire. They had hardly been alone together all this week.

"You need rest," she said. "Aunt Tish has gone to bed, so I haven't had the fire made up."

"You blame me entirely, don't you? Answer me."

"I don't know . . ."

"I had three sons," he said. "Only one survived to manhood. It wasn't fair. If they'd all lived, things would have been so much different. You don't understand. No—don't go."

"It won't help, talking of it now."

"What do you feel about death? What is it to you—is it an end, a beginning?" He turned his hands over slowly and stared at them. The firelight made the fingers a flickering yellow. "'And though after my skin worms destroy this body, yet in my flesh shall I see God' . . . 'He cometh up and shall be cut down, like a flower' . . . I had *three* sons, not one. *You* were brought up to believe in the family, your own family. You should be able to feel . . ."

"Does it matter what I feel now?"

"The value of our family, the value of succession. I've told you, we came from Cumberland, we were very poor, badly clothed, ill fed. That sort of thing makes for cohesion in a family, a sense that the rest of the world is unfriendly, against you. From a few sovereigns carried in a leather bag we came in three generations to what you see us. It's something to be proud of. It's not just an ambition personal to me: it's a credo, a faith. The good of the family is more important than the good of one generation. I've made great sacrifices—it was true, though Brook . . . I thought he understood. It came as a great blow. . . ."

She did not answer. Outside it was still snowing, coming down stealthy and secretive; now and then you could hear a betraying drip on the window-sill.

"You are a mother now. At least you must know how I felt when Vaughan and Joseph died. . . ." He eased himself in his chair, by the arms, stared at the fire. "It was scarlet fever—I've told you that; they all got it, all my boys and my wife. They were isolated in the west bedrooms. It was Dr. Bagshawe in those days. He prescribed port wine every hour—and biscuits soaked in beef tea. When Joseph got so very bad I sent for a specialist from Town. When he came he said, 'Mr. Ferguson, by whose orders . . .' I made a gesture and he said, 'You're killing these children.' I often wonder . . ." He sighed and was silent.

She watched him warily, half fascinated, half repelled. His memory went back so much further than hers, gave him some claim on her attention, her sense of fairness.

"They were clever boys, Vaughan particularly. With them nothing was impossible. Progress wouldn't have stood still when my generation passed. It could have gone to the limits. When only Brook was left it was clear that the best I could hope for was a generation's pause. If I can hold on, I thought. When I have a grandson and my grandson is old enough . . . If I was possessive, then circumstances made me possessive. That's why I felt such great joy at the birth of Ian."

Suppose I told him, she thought.

He said with sudden emphasis: "My brother Tom was a great disappointment. My father wanted him in the business, but he wasn't any use. For a time there was talk of making him a doctor, but even for that he wouldn't study. So when my father died, though he left shares to Tom and Letitia, he left me with a controlling interest. At the time it may have seemed unfair to the others—but he wanted to safeguard the future. He bound up the money so that it could not be carelessly frittered away or withdrawn. The same principles as those I have acted on. But he had me to fall back on. I had *no* alternative to Brook—except you. When he wished to take you away as well—and also my grandson— could I do anything but stand in his way?"

She said: "Brook had his dreams too."

A dusky red came up to his forehead. He hesitated, seemed about to stop, then said, half lisping, with an obstructive tongue: " 'Men are not in Hell because God is angry with them; they are in wrath and darkness because they have done to the light as that man does to the light of the sun who puts out his own eyes.' Did you ever read that? I have been in wrath and darkness for many years. . . . That is something you will not understand, Cordelia. No one knows it. My father wasn't in the same position at all. He was strong, *strong* . . ."

"I'd rather you didn't tell me," she said, moving to get up.

He put his hand out to restrain her, touched only the edge of her chair. He was fighting the iron reticences of a lifetime.

"You think I'm a religious man, don't you; a man who makes religion a part of his daily life? Isn't that so?"

"Well?"

"Well, it's not so. Only the outward form . . . Oh, I was brought up with a firm belief. I held to it all my early married life. But it was when my children died—I tried to see it differently, rightly, as the will of God. . . . But have you ever seen a child, two children, who last week were running about the house, lying there . . ."

"No," she said quickly. "Don't tell me." This had tapped some spring of fear and pity. She mustn't respond.

"I fought it," he said. "I tried to put the thoughts away. I began to work doubly hard. I *tried* to believe the old things. But all the time some erosion . . . Intellect fighting faith. To cover over the doubt I began to go deeper into the tenets of religion. Where one form of religious belief didn't satisfy I turned to another. Then I met Mr. Slaney-Smith. . . ."

He blew his nose. The eau de Cologne was faint, a little stale.

"Our friendship was not so strange as some people thought it. We were each seeking the truth from opposite positions. We used to argue—long into the night. There was so much common ground. . . . Neither of us would stoop to admit that. It was a tremendous shock to me when I knew he had come to believe in spiritualism. I should *never* have thought it possible. Perhaps it would be just as much a shock to him to know what I am saying to you. It's possible, I've thought since his death, that though neither of us would give way an inch, the arguments of each had an effect. . . . While he preached his unbelief he was secretly dabbling in this thing, coming to believe in it. And as for me, while I continued to speak of my beliefs, the faith I had rotted, and rotted away. . . ."

His lips were parting with each breath as if gently blowing dust. She saw that he must go on now, say all that he had in his mind.

"Perhaps it's true that I put out my own eyes. But what is the choice? Life after death to me seems—an impossibility. Perhaps you're lucky enough to believe it all without question. I still accept God. But as for some sort of existence after death—I have no faith at all. I see no hope of it. The biological elements destroy, destroy; building up something different in their place. To me, Cordelia, there's only *one* survival of personality, *one* continuance of personal qualities. That is through the family, through inheritance, through the begetting of one's children. *That's* immortality—the only sort we can hope for. Oneself goes down, the discarded husk, leaving the young plant to flourish in its stead. All through nature it's the same. One can hope for nothing else."

In the fireplace one of the big pieces of coal was roaring with a bright gassy flame.

"D'you see now why I care so intensely what happens to my son and to my grandson? I've been wrong—I know it. I should have let Brook go. But it was *not in me* to do it. If he came back now I don't think I could do it. I want you to try to understand."

She found she was trembling.

"Do you mean," she said, "that you'd rather have Brook dead than working in London?"

"No. Words are so ineffective. I loved my sons. . . . If the choice was before me now I should have to say to Brook, 'Go free, gladly go and be done.' But it would be the sacrifice of my life for his. . . ."

He got up then.

She said: "Brook couldn't possibly have given way again. It would have been the end of him—just as surely as now. All he wanted was the chance to *prove* himself. If you could only have compromised, have given way a little . . ."

"Once I was tempted to, to accept your suggestion of a year's trial. But the thought represented itself as weakness."

She was silent. Did she believe that he had ever really contemplated giving way? Wasn't it an afterthought, put out of its sequence by convenient memory?

"You blame me for Brook's death," he said. "I know you do. I've seen it in your face all along, though you've been considerate enough not to put it into words. Well—whatever it led to, whatever the truth—I know that mine has been the wrong. I know it now. I've paid for it, and I shall go on paying. . . . If there was a personal God—if there was a personal God and I had to account for what has happened I should ask not for forgiveness but for understanding."

The coal had exhausted itself as quickly as it blazed up, the flame had vanished into a thin grey curl of smoke.

"What I tried so hard to preserve," he said, "it's been destroyed—in the most final of all ways. There's only one thing left to me, and that's the hope that through you and your son—in time, not now but in time, we may build up something again. A new foundation of trust. I can say no more. In all sincerity I can only ask you—you must feel bitter, I know —to try to—to see that what I've been trying to do is not to destroy but to create. I had it all. I thought I had it all. But there was a flaw, and I —pressed too hard on the mould. Now there's only the useless pieces in my hands."

CHAPTER SEVEN 🌿 He did not go to the works the next day. It upset all her plans, but she knew she must leave just the same. During the night, when she had slept little, she kept repeating to herself, "It's all decided. It can alter nothing now. Soon the break will be made, this will be behind me and I can forget it all."

She knew her decision to go at once was the right one. There must be no more emotional scenes like last night, plucking at her sympathy, her understanding. She could not forget the things he had told her, could not get them out of her head. Frederick Ferguson and his pride of house and his loss of faith; Slaney-Smith and his inverted atheisms; and Brook and the dye works and continuity and spiritualism and possessiveness and love.

After breakfast she packed her own small box with a few personal belongings, one frock, a change of clothes for Ian, the jewellery that Brook had bought her. She didn't know where Mr. Ferguson was, but she took a chance and carried the box boldly down the stairs. A door opened as she reached the foot, but it was Hallows.

He hastened across. "Can I take that for you, madam?"

". . . Thank you. Will you just put it in the porch, please?"

"Do you want it delivered somewhere, madam?"

"No, leave it there. Where is Mr. Ferguson?"

"In his study, I think. I'll inquire."

"No. I don't want him disturbed."

Ian usually went out with Nanny from ten to eleven-thirty, but she had told the nurse that she wanted him back by eleven today. There had been a thick fall of snow in the night, but it had thawed as it fell and all the trees were adrip.

By ten-thirty she was ready, and she took out a piece of notepaper and began to write.

Dear Mr. Ferguson,

In spite of what you said last night, I feel that I can no longer live with you in this house. Please understand I am not trying to sit in judgment. Nothing we can do or say can alter what has happened. We have to start a new life, but my life I know can't begin again as you suggest. So I am leaving with Ian.

Good-bye,
Cordelia

She read it through. Unsatisfactory, partly because it only stated half-truths. She had given him neither of her main reasons. But it was better left unsaid.

She put the note in an envelope and left it on her dressing-table. When Ian and Nanny came back she was sitting ready in hat and coat and gloves.

"Oh, are you going out, Mrs. Ferguson? It's a horrid day with a thaw wind."

"Yes, don't bother to take Ian's coat off. I want to take him to Town with me. Just change his shoes, will you, these are rather wet. Betty, will you get a cab for me? One of the gardeners will go."

"Yes'm."

Now to wait. This was a trying time. She hadn't written to her father and mother. Do that as soon as ever she reached London. But until the irrevocable move was made she could settle to nothing.

Ian came bounding back.

"Mummy, what makes snow? Nanny wouldn't tell me. I don't b'lieve she knows. . . .

"Yes, but what makes it white, Mummy? . . .

"Mummy, where are we going? Is Grandpa coming? Whose was that box in the porch when we came in?"

Waiting now. Round and round in her head; thoughts of last night, thoughts of today. Suppose there was no cab about. It was a nasty morning and she might wait here and wait here. Panic kept rising. She could only wait until twenty past eleven. If there was no cab by then she would have their own carriage out. Foolish timidity not to have it in the first place. What did it matter that anyone should know?

"Mummy, I throwed a snowball and it hit a cat and the cat jumped like anythink and slipped on the ice. It was proper fun. And there were some boys, big boys, throwing snowballs over on the cricket field and Nanny said they were naughty because they were shouting rude words but that we were to pity them because they didn't know any better and hadn't got any shoes and stockings on."

Twenty past eleven. She got up sharply, so that Ian looked at her in puzzlement.

"We'll go now," she said.

"Where are we going, Mummy? Can we go to the toy-shop? There's a *lovely* cannon that fires *real* cannon balls."

She looked into his wide round childish eyes with deep and passionate affection. Let me always, she thought, be able to keep my love in check so that it never becomes inverted and a source of hate.

She led him to the door. "Quiet now, darling, please. We mustn't disturb Grandpa."

She moved with him out on to the landing.

Mr. Ferguson was slowly climbing the stairs. . . .

Quickly she pulled Ian back towards the bedroom. He went protesting, chattering irrepressibly, and she waited breathless behind the closed door, wondering if the old man had seen them. The slow creak-creak of his shoes went past.

"Mummy, shall we play hide-and-seek? Oh, let's! You put your hands over your eyes and I'll call when I'm ready——"

"Not now, darling. You must be quiet when I tell you. Let's—let's pretend that we're Indians and have got to get out of the house without Grandpa noticing——"

"Yes, and Grandpa's a bear, and we're 'fraid of him. Like I used to play with Uncle Pridey. And we're Indians with arrows . . ."

She opened the door again. Mr. Ferguson was in his room.

"Now," she said, and like conspirators they tiptoed across the landing and down the stairs. It would be ten minutes before the carriage was got ready. What to do in that time? The kitchens were the safest place.

Betty crossing the hall. "The cab's here, mum. Farrow's just got back. He said there wasn't one nowhere."

"Oh, thank you." Relief. Get right away. "Come along, Ian. We're going out together."

"He wouldn't come in, mum, Farrow said, because he was afraid of turning. He's at the gates."

"It doesn't matter." Better still. Betty was standing with the front door held open.

"Oh, shall I take that for you, mum? Let me."

"Thank you. It's very light."

"You'll be back to dinner, mum?"

The last lie. "I'm—not sure, Betty. Tell Mrs. Meredith not to wait."

So out, and down the snowy, slushy drive. So to the cab and the driver sitting hunched up in his cape and the horse stamping its feet, its steamy breath rising in the grey morning, and a glance back at the roof of the house black-patched in the thaw, and the heavy lace curtains and the interbranch of trees, and far away in the quiet distance the sound of an engine shunting.

She took a deep breath. "London Road Station."

She said to the cabbie: "This is the address. It's just off a place called Soho Square."

"Soho Square. Orright, lady. I know."

For the first time in her life she was in London. It was not quite dark yet and the press of the traffic outside the station was startling and exciting. Because Ian had slept a good deal on the journey she had had plenty of time for thought, and breaking in on the sombreness of her memories had come sudden waves of excitement and apprehension about the future.

She thought: Well, it is all thrown overboard now; I am beginning a new life; and the hansom lurched out into the stream of buses and cabs and carts and carriages and coster-barrows, and she thought, It is all past, I can forget what I ever knew about Persian berries and the coal-tar greens and ordering Pernambuco wood; and I must forget the old man who has dominated every day of my life since I married his son, the old man who is sitting at home now in that great house. . . . And the horse struck sparks off the dry frosty road as they turned a corner past a policeman, and the traffic thundered to a sudden knot, halted, and then was free again. And somewhere in the future is Stephen, whose faults that sombre household caused me to see out of perspective, so that I was blind to the richness and colour of life and was frightened into accepting its narrow code.

The early darkness was closing in as the hansom turned into a quiet square and clop-clopped across it to a narrow street at the farther side. An organ-grinder was churning out unrecognisable tunes by the curb, and some urchins were gathered round watching the antics of the monkey. At the far end of the street a man was selling muffins. Suddenly she recognised one of the confused bronchial tunes as 'The Railway Guard.'

Heavens, what that brought back to her! For a moment she could not push open the folding doors of the cab, though it had stopped outside one of the narrow houses.

> I try to be merry but it is no use,
> My case is very hard . . .

Bitter-sweet memories of the theatre and Stephen and the warm buttery smell of that afternoon at Northenden, and dreadful memories of the panic in the theatre with the smell of burning cloth and the press of angry urgent bodies; and later memories of the sick-room and the smell of cough medicines and steaming gruel and watching the glow of the night fire on the ceiling. The strength of her sensations frightened her. They seemed to belong to another person yet to have been intimately experienced by her. She was detached from them, but dreadfully affected by them. It was like remembering some mental illness of childhood. For the first time she realised how much she had suffered, and how much she had changed.

A woman opened the door. She had sharp but friendly eyes and a thin cockney voice. Yes, Mr. Ferguson lived here. Yes, he was in. Yes, he was better. First floor. She'd show the way.

281

They went up. She tapped on a door. Pridey opened it, bow in hand. He looked younger but bonier and he walked with a stick.

"Uncle Pridey!" screamed Ian, leaping at him.

"Good gracious," said Pridey, gathering him. "And I was just *thinking* of muffins."

They had had a meal, and it had been arranged they should spend the night there, as she had hoped might be possible. Ian was already in bed but his sleep on the train had left him wakeful now. The door of his bedroom was open, and every few minutes he thought up some new demand to lure one or other of them inside. Over supper Uncle Pridey had promised to take him to the Zoo tomorrow and to the Tower of London on Wednesday. They had discussed trains and mice and balloons and soldiers and ships and the icing on cakes and how to make paper hats.

If she had been in a fit condition of mind to appreciate it, she would have seen that London and his success had already changed Pridey. He talked less jerkily, less aggressively. He was just as eccentric, but now it was with a faintly rakish, jaunty air. He had bought a new suit and some good linen. He was blooming late.

When at last Ian was settled, she told Pridey in detail the whole story of Brook's death. She also told him all that had passed last night.

He was silent for some time, scratching his head. Then he shifted his position.

"Damned sciatica. Catches me just round the great trochanter of the thigh bone. Makes me very angry. When I had it bad I used to swear at Mrs. Cowdray every time she came in. Long-suffering woman. Wish she hadn't got that accent. I was having an argument about accents the other day. When I say I'm going to have a bath I snap it, I don't sing it. Whether I sing or not *in* my bath's another matter. Great sense of propriety, Mrs. Cowdray. Have to mind my P's and Q's. Wonder if that lad's asleep yet. I must feed my mice."

He got up painfully and limped off into the bedroom. He was gone some minutes and then came back with a bag.

"Have a sweet."

"Thank you."

"If my brother was a mouse," he said, "I'd inbreed from him. Specimen. Find out the relative incidence of the type. *Homo napoleonus.* Dog Latin. Top-dog Latin. He was always the same. He'd always charm or bully himself into top place. Even did it at school. Made the wrong marriage, you know. Ruination of him. Should have married a woman who would have stood up to him. Not, 'Yes, Frederick. No, Frederick.'

Oh, I'm sorry for him now. He can't take more than six feet of his factory with him."

"I'm sorry for him too," she said.

"I've said before—all this dibbling and dabbling is useless—all nonsense. Everybody's catching it—it's the fault of the age. They all want to be certain—sure and certain. Babyish. If they push over one dogma they must put up another in its place. Proof, proof! It's a form of egoism. What does religion hold for *me?* The I, I, demanding survival. Proof that *I* shall live, precious self." Pridey chewed hard and wrinkled his eyebrows at her. "We all want to live on, I suppose. Some way. I do. Seventy years is no time. So far as I can see it, seems to me, if God has lit a spark in us, even the smallest, why should He let it go out? Doesn't satisfy me, but it comforts me. There's purpose in most things. This constant fiddling of Frederick and Slaney-Smith, where does it lead you? The railway siding or the mental dust-heap. Those who know don't argue, and those who argue don't know. Did you love Brook?"

She glanced up quickly in surprise and met his eyes. She looked away. "I'm not sure."

"Brook was all right. When he married Margaret I thought: Two of a kind. But not the man for you. I said to Frederick the day I first saw you: 'You're marrying April to a wet September.' He didn't like it."

"Brook was always kind to me. Kind and generous and considerate. I was very fond of him."

"You got that poem you were telling me about?"

She took the crumpled papers from her bag and handed them to him. After he had read it he sat tapping the papers with his big bony hands.

"Shouldn't publish it."

"I'm glad you feel the same."

"May have merit, I don't know. But too vindictive. Try it out in twenty years. Brook won't be any older then."

They were silent together. A queer thought. Brook wouldn't be any older then.

Pridey passed the sweets. "Got a lot of money belonging to you. Ninety pounds odd. People won't stop buying the book. Half of 'em don't read it, I bet."

"I don't *want* any more money, Pridey. It's your book. My money was a loan, not an investment."

"I'm going back next month, you know. Back to Manchester. For a while anyway."

"To Grove Hall?"

"I've an idea for a monograph on the rat. Get more peace there, not so

283

much of this inviting out. And the climate's better. London's too dry. A bit of damp in the air suits me."

He brooded for a few moments.

"In a way I'm glad," she said. "I think they'll welcome you back now."

Her phrasing showed that she would not be there herself, but he made no comment. Probably he hadn't noticed. But you could never tell what Pridey had noticed. She felt curiously comforted, released by this talk. He seemed to make things clear for her, to unravel the knots she felt powerless to attempt herself. Almost for the first time since Brook's death her nerves were at rest.

He said: "That fellow Huxley. More in him than I thought. And Darwin. Still disagree with them both. Disagree profoundly. But they have their points. Credit where credit's due . . . The people here are odd. Only last night—my first time out since this sciatica . . . Was that the boy?"

"No. He's gone off at last."

"A curious fracas. Went to the theatre with a man called Wilberforce. Stuff and nonsense about an earl. Right in front of me there was a woman with a bare back—couldn't get away from it. In the second interval, while Wilberforce was polishing his eyeglass, I saw a flea. Naturally I put my finger on it."

"What happened?"

"She screamed. Very flat. Might have been some indecent assault. The man with her was offensive. I showed what I'd caught—explained it, a common *pulex irritans*. No difference. No sense of proportion. I tried to explain that the plague of London was largely carried by the common flea. I was acting in the interests of normal hygiene. For reasons not apparent they took this as a further insult. Think there would have been trouble but the curtain went up."

Cordelia said after a moment, struggling with her voice: "Wouldn't they have done the same in Manchester?"

He said reasonably: "Well, her back wouldn't have been so bare. Incidentally, do you know that this street is where they buried nearly six thousand of the plague victims? I told Mrs. Cowdray. It didn't upset her. A staunch woman."

Cordelia struggled with her voice again, and the laughter in it nearly broke into a sob.

"Oh, Pridey . . ." she said, breathing it out.

"Have a sweet."

"I—don't love Brook, Pridey. I never did. Not properly, not the way one expects to. You know that."

"It's not all the world."

"I've—loved someone else—for years. Did you—guess that too?"

"I never guess; I leave that to the scientists. Wilberforce isn't a scientist; you must meet him. He droops."

"Pridey, I've been in love with Stephen Crossley for five years. Now that Brook's gone I couldn't stay in that house with Mr. Ferguson any longer. I've come to London to find Stephen. I've come to you to help me to find him, because you're the only person who knows where he may be."

Uncle Pridey began to crack his fingers. "Wish I did, young woman; I'd find him for you. Why should I know? There's four million of us in London."

"But you met him and he invited you to some music hall. You said he was the manager there."

"What? Oh, months ago. But I never went. Not my cup of tea. What did he say the name was? Royal Varieties. But he's running two or three. May be miles away by now."

"I know. Yes, I know that. Anything may have happened. But it's a chance. And I felt I'd—after all this time—you see, Pridey, last time he came to Grove Hall I wouldn't see him, and the time before that I sent him away. This week—after Brook's death—I felt I couldn't *breathe*, and I felt I must go at once to Stephen, to see him, to explain every-thing, to try to make things up. All these years—I felt all these years have been lost. . . ."

Pridey said after a moment: "That week Brook was away—before he was first ill, were you meeting Crossley then?"

". . . Yes."

He shook his head. "The way you used to come in. Like a daffodil that the wind'd been ruffling. Royal Varieties is not far from here. Found it once when I was looking for Nelson. Like to go?"

She looked at him, startled. "When? Tonight?"

"Please yourself. It's not nine yet."

Confronted with the thing she wanted, she had the impulse to flee from it in panic. Enough for one day . . . Perhaps about Wednesday. But what excuse? She had to write to her mother and father—and there was . . .

"Like me to come with you?"

"Oh, if you would! But——"

"Free tonight or Thursday. Do what you please. I'm going to Wilber-force's tomorrow to see some rabbits. He's bred a black one with two white rings. Uninteresting things, rabbits: no versatility . . ."

Well, why not tonight? "There's Ian," she said almost hopefully.

"Mrs. Cowdray can look after him. She's used to my mice."

". . . You'd really come with me, Pridey?"

"If you want me. Don't want to be in the way."

285

"Oh, no, I'd like you to come. That's if you promise not to take any mice with you. . . ."

A faint satiric spark showed in Uncle Pridey's glance.

"I'll get my galoshes," he said.

CHAPTER EIGHT ⚘ They travelled by bus down the Charing Cross Road, facing each other in the blue plush lamp-lit interior, jogging and shaking with the other eight passengers and shuffling their feet in the straw. She felt sick, and tried to persuade herself it was the jolting and the lack of air.

After a while the conductor let down a sort of trapdoor and put in his head and said: "Charing Cross," and they got out. Pridey was limping badly.

"Get this side of me," he said, "or I'll be sure to poke you with my stick."

They turned along the Strand. There was a slight fog near the river and the street lamps shone fitfully. All the shops were lit and many open, the orange stalls and the tobacco shops, the wine shops and the public houses flaring. Buses, carts, and cabs were still plentiful on the streets and boys and girls quarrelled, selling matches and newspapers.

They walked along, jostled by the crowds. She was surprised at seeing so many people. Bare-footed urchins, foreigners in long ulster coats, men with their tins of evening beer, women's painted faces, young girls in pairs with dyed yellow hair, well-dressed theatre-goers, crowds at the doors of the public houses, potboys, old men whispering in the gutters. The smells and the noise and the fermenting thrusting life were oppressive; she was glad when they turned off down a narrow street.

They came to a gas-glaring entrance not unlike the old Variety.

"Well, this is it, young woman."

She said: "Let's go in in the ordinary way, please, just as if we'd come to see the performance. We can ask afterwards."

In five minutes now am I to see Stephen? . . .

The show was already on. Four girls in tights and frilly black frocks were singing a song about their first young man. Perhaps because there was no balcony the place seemed different, one had to plunge right into the heat and the light and the noise. Larger than the Variety. The bar ran down one side instead of across the back. Many more women present.

They were given a table at the side against one of the pillars. It suited them well enough.

Uncle Pridey said: "Music hall's a gross misnomer. No one can surely mistake that brassy noise. Extraordinary thing." He put his stick on the table and said to the waiter: "Well, if you haven't got lemonade you can get it. Sciatica. Bring this lady her sherry. Can't see him, Cordelia, can you?"

She was staring about. The interior of the place was well-worn and a little shabby, some of the tables were sloppy with drink, and the air was smoke-thickened. The chairman was a fat husky-voiced man with a mottled red complexion. There were still a few empty seats at his table.

"He didn't always go in at the Variety," she said. "But let's wait."

Pridey glanced at her with a wrinkling of his eyebrows.

The girls had gone off and were followed by the big act of the evening, a sort of ballet in which a lithe man in a tiger skin danced on a reddened stage among women in ballet frocks and was challenged and defeated at intervals by a fairy with a lighted wand.

The waiter came back with the food they had ordered and with Cordelia's sherry.

"I've brought you ginger beer, sir. I hope that'll suit."

"This steak," said Pridey, "is undercooked. Not cooked in the right way either. Tell me about Mr. Crossley, Stephen Crossley. Is he still manager here?"

"Yes, sir. But if you want to complain about the food——"

"Is he here, Mr. Crossley? Is he here tonight?"

"I think he's coming, sir. He didn't last night because he was at the Golden Fleece. If you want to see Mr. Warburton——"

"We do not want to see Mr. Warburton. Will Mr. Crossley come in here if he does come?"

"I expect so, sir; he usually does." The waiter ducked down and away.

Pridey took up his knife and fork. "Whole secret of cooking steak," he said gloomily, "is that it be treated like an erring husband and well beaten with a rolling-pin. If you spare the pin you spoil the rump."

The ballet came to an end with virtue triumphant. It was something new and popular. The chairman could hardly make himself heard above the talk and the clatter that broke out.

"Interesting," Pridey said with his mouth full, "the misdirected talents of these people. Those frescoes on the walls. Imitations of the sort of thing you'd dig up in Greece. Well, if you're going to have Greece, have Greece. Why surround them with those cheap crystal columns that would offend any reasonable man? Eating nothing, young woman. You'd a good enough appetite not long ago."

"That's why," she said, smiling, though it wasn't true.

"Ever since we came in," said Pridey, "a man at the corner table's been making eyes at you. Looks on me as an elderly lecher, no doubt."

"Don't take any notice, please."

"More than an hour curling his moustache. They're even longer in this city. Wilberforce has the longest moustache in England. Like a straw mattress." Pridey waved his knife. "Let me tell you, you'll find Mrs. Cowdray's mattresses deficient in give and take. No question, but we've been spoiled. Frederick's a difficult man to live with but he knows how to buy beds. . . ."

She put her hand on his arm. Someone had come in.

There was no mistaking him the instant she saw his head. For the moment he was moving among other people by the door, but he was coming this way. It was something about the set of his head, the way he held his shoulders, which unlocked all the old feelings and memories. She kept her own head lowered, forgetting her veil, afraid of being seen before she was ready, until she was calm.

When she raised her head he was half way across the floor. At his side was a tall dark young woman in green.

Pridey said: "Don't worry about me if you want to go off. I'll eat your steak."

They had gone across to two seats at the chairman's table. The chairman bowed his welcome. A waiter held out the chairs, and the young woman sat down. The chairman leaned over and said something about the comic dancers who were now on the stage. Drink was brought, and a waiter lighted Stephen's cigar. The woman's head was close to Stephen's as they consulted the menu. Very strikingly dressed in that vivid green, she'd a way of throwing back her head to shake away her hair. About twenty-eight or thirty.

Pridey said: "He's put on weight since I saw him last. Can't be with eating his own steaks. Perhaps we should have had the cutlets."

It is not necessary always to hear what people are saying in order to know the sort of thing they are saying. *She* was doing most of the talking, saying something about the dancers and the stage, gesturing a little with one hand. He listened attentively, more than attentively. Cordelia knew that look.

"Same girl," said Pridey.

"What? What d'you mean?"

"She was with him before. When I met him that time I told you about."

"Months ago? You never mentioned her."

"Never occurred to me. Didn't know you were interested. Anyway she's probably just a friend."

"Ladies and—gentlemen!" announced the chairman in a hoarse convivial voice. "Ladies and gentlemen! I now have the *honour* and *privilege* of announcing to you that by special request . . ."

The girl clinked her glass against his and drank. In the silence that

288

suddenly fell she laughed, an easy, husky, sophisticated laugh. She turned to say something to a waiter, and Cordelia could see her face again, the creamy whiteness of her skin, the prominent cheek-bones, black straight brows, full lips curved down. Not pretty but fascinating; could one ever take one's eyes from her opulent feline face? A man dressed in tattered black clothes and with a shade over one eye had come lurching on to the stage.

In the orchestra a piano began to tinkle, and the man sang in a great growling voice.

> "Oh, my name it is Sam Hall, Chimney Sweep,
> Chimney Sweep.
> Now my name it is Sam Hall, Chimney Sweep . . ."

Special request. *Her* special request? In Manchester they had sung 'Massa's in de Cold, Cold Ground.'

The singer hitched up the belt round his trousers and rubbed the bristles on his chin. His malevolent eyes wandered round the silent room.

> "Oh me master taught me flam,
> Taught me flam,
> Me master taught me flam,
> Though he knowed it all was bam,
> And now I must go Hang,
> Damn your eyes!"

Stephen wasn't looking at the stage; he was watching the young woman at his side.

The people in the hall were as if hypnotised. No waiter moved or knife clattered. There was an age-old sense of evil here which went far deeper than mere words.

> "Then the hangman will come too,
> Will come too,
> Then the hangman will come too,
> With all his bloody crew,
> And he'll tell me what to do,
> Blast his eyes!"

Cordelia thought: I must get away before he sees me.

A sudden storm of clapping broke the silence. With scarcely any change in his scowl the singer acknowledged his applause. They brought him back again and again. The chairman glanced inquiringly at Stephen, who glanced at the girl beside him. She tossed back her head and made a negative movement with her hand. The chairman motioned to bring down the curtain.

"Ladies and—gentlemen!" he began, announcing the next number.

"I think we'll go, Pridey," she said. "I'll come round in the morning. He's—too busy tonight."

"Extraordinary song. Kind of hypnosis," said Pridey. "Man would have made a good preacher. Don't jump to conclusions, young woman. Go up to Crossley, say how d'ye do, see what he says."

"No, no, I couldn't. I don't want to tonight. No, I'm not jumping to conclusions. Truly. I want to be fair. And it wouldn't be fair—tonight. Let's go home. I want to. I'll come round in the morning. I promise I will."

"Y'promise. And what if he's away somewhere else?" Pridey fished out his stick. "How would it be if I poked that man as I went out? He's still ogling. Make him laugh on the other side of his moustache."

"No, no. Pay the bill, will you, please, and then we can watch our chance to slip away."

A giant about nine feet tall had come on the stage and begun to sing a comic song. He was constantly interrupted by a dwarf, and soon they came to blows. The girl in green was ignoring the show and talking to Stephen again. The vehemence and the vitality in her seemed to dominate him.

There was a roar of laughter as the dwarf took out a pocket-knife and sawed the giant's head off. Cordelia got quietly to her feet and did not look back till she was near the door. Their leaving had not been noticed. Everyone was laughing and clapping because the giant's severed head lying on the stage was now going on with the song in comfort while his headless body held the dwarf down.

As they were leaving, Pridey tipped their waiter and said: "Who's that lady with Mr. Crossley. D'you know her, eh?"

"Who, that? Yes, Miss Freda Gerald. The actress, sir." The waiter looked at the silver in his hand. Finding it sufficient, he added: "From the Garrick, sir. At least, that's where she was last."

"She often come here?"

"With Mr. Crossley? Yes, sir. Quite often."

They went out. A slanting cloud of fog was drifting up from the river. It passed veil after veil before the glimmering lights of the narrow street. A sailor was arguing with a prostitute, and the smell of soup came up through a grating. Beggars whined in the gutter.

"Wonder what flam means," said Pridey. " 'My master taught me flam.' Rather think it's something to do with humbug. Lying, hypocrisy, and humbug. Flim-flam. That sort of thing. Shall we walk for a bus or take a cab?"

"A cab, please," said Cordelia.

CHAPTER NINE Now be scrupulously fair. What did you expect, that he should stay away from all women for years on end in the remote hope of still attracting you? Did you think he should have pined away or taken to drink?

Or, be honest, is it the woman herself? Her feline beauty had suddenly come from nowhere, formidably, to stretch across all the future. In the dark, grope for knowledge, for lights and signs, for insight but not imagination. Freda Gerald. It did not connect. A name disembodied. That woman with her poise, her hard sophistication, the beautiful flamboyant clothes, her upflung head. And Stephen. 'Oh, my sweetheart, could you expect me to be faithful all these years?' Toss and turn and turn and toss, praying for daylight yet dreading daylight. Be a coward and run away and earn an everlasting self-contempt—or else face it out as promised to Pridey.

She dreamt too: of seeing Stephen in the music hall with the girl in green, and someone whispered, "Oh, don't you know who that is? That's *Margaret!*" She dreamt of Uncle Pridey lecturing to Mr. Huxley, of Brook wildly acclaimed as a poet, of Slaney-Smith the believer and Mr. Ferguson the atheist. Sometimes she was so near waking that thoughts and dreams wove themselves into a logical pattern hardly to be distinguished from the paradoxes of real life.

When morning came at last she dressed with great care. Last night, carrying immeasurable weight among all the other considerations, was the fact that she was wearing part of the mourning she had put on for Brook. In that she must look drab and colourless beside the jungle green of the striking frock. Whatever the outcome, that was not the way it must be.

By chance the one frock she had brought was also green, though of a pale apple green with a check underskirt and a tight bodice and lace at the throat and wrists. She had brought one other hat, a little feather toque of grey with a green ribbon. Uncle Pridey plucked at his beard when he saw her.

They arranged over breakfast that Pridey should take Ian to the Zoo.

"We'll meet at lunch," she said slowly. "I'll be back by then. In any case—I'll meet you here at one."

The fog had cleared. London looked different in the morning light, the character of the light seemed slightly different from the northern city. The traffic was as thick as ever, people pushed along the pavements; at least a quarter of them looked foreign. Not that she was unused to foreigners. Strange smells, stranger accents, strange clothes; she was in a new land.

She walked a little way, chiefly to steady herself, to be sure of composure. Then she stopped a hansom. They *tlot-tlotted* off at a brisk pace, pushing among the buses and the thronging pedestrians.

There was no one about at the entrance of the Royal Varieties. Hours early. The street looked drab and untidy. A woman was hanging out washing on the balcony opposite. Probably the place was closed and Stephen in some office miles away. She paid off the hansom. Unlike the old Variety, this building was not on a corner and there seemed no stage entrance. Tentatively she walked up to one of the glass doors and pulled. The door opened easily.

Inside all was quiet and very dark. Smoke and stale beer and dust. Far in the distance was the sibilant sound of someone scrubbing. She groped her way towards it, found narrow stairs. The sound came from up there. It was pitch dark on the stairs and she was glad to get to the top.

"Excuse me," she said.

The scrubbing stopped.

" 'Ullo?"

"I beg your pardon. I could find no one downstairs."

"What d'you want?"

The charwoman was on her knees not far away.

"I'm looking for Mr. Stephen Crossley. Do you know if he's here?"

"Yer up the wrong stairway, mum. It's the other one b'ind the door as you come in. 'Ave you got an appointment?"

"Er—no. But I think he'll see me."

"I'll show you the way." Wiping her hands on her apron, the old woman got up and squeezed past in her cast-off bombasine dress. Gin and carbolic soap.

So he was here. Down the stairs and across the foyer. Up some more stairs. Lighter here. A glass door. Tap-tap.

"Yes?"

"Lidy 'ere to see Mr. Crossley."

A middle-aged clerk with shiny hair brushed sideways.

"Got an appointment, miss?"

"No. Will you just tell him Mrs. Ferguson."

"Very good—madam."

Now for it. Oh, God. The sound of voices. The clerk moved aside. Stephen.

"*Cordelia!*"

He stood there in the open doorway. For a second he did not move any further, his eyes like a stranger's, then warming, brightening.

"Cordelia, I *never* expected . . ."

292

With sudden calm, Heaven-sent, she smiled back at him.

"I thought I'd call in—for a few moments."

"I thought it was a ghost. I really did. Come in. Come in. What are you doing in London? After all these years!"

He came across and took her hands, smiled into her eyes. Seek, seek now for a hint of the equivocal in his welcome. He was plumper than she remembered. But all the old long-remembered charm, the clear full brown eyes twinkling with vitality and the joy of life.

"I'm here for a few days' holiday. I felt—I must call."

"Of course you must call. I should never have forgiven you. Come in. Come in here. At once."

He led the way into his office, shut the door, and stood with his back to it.

"By all the Saints, so you've come to see me at last! Well, and so you should. It's five or six years since we met and all my letters unanswered and the door closed upon me when I called. I was miserable for years, you know."

Past tense. She said: "I thought you would have gone back to America."

"I very nearly did. But then I changed my mind. It's the way of things." He walked across to a table. "Drink?"

"No, thank you."

"Oh, do; it'll keep out the cold."

It would keep out the cold. "All right."

There was a moment's silence. A soda siphon fizzed. Find something to say. He came back.

"Here's to you, my sweetheart." He'd remembered that she preferred sherry.

He said: "Oh, yes," and sighed.

"Yes what?"

"You're beautiful. More beautiful than I remember. I thought you'd changed."

"It's only five years," she said, with a little smile.

"Yes, but . . . Well, what of it? You haven't, and that's the main thing." They talked hesitantly for some minutes, hand-picking words, without warmth, cautious only to say so much. He asked her how she had found him. "Is Brook with you?"

". . . No."

He lit a cigar. "I can't say I'm sorry." The conventional phrase. But the conventional phrase led his own mind on. He looked at her through a cloud of tobacco smoke. Something kindled in his eyes. "*How* long are you here for?"

"I must leave tomorrow."

"Flying visit, isn't it?"

"Yes."

"Must go as soon as that?"

"Must go."

His voice grown a little softer, he said: "After that last visit to your house I was so upset. I was in a Hell of jealousy and anger. I thought, Let her go, I hate her. I'll go to America again. But it wasn't as easy as that. You can't love and hate to order. I couldn't forget you."

"But in the end you did?"

"Do I look as if I've forgotten you? I've never been able to get you out of my head. You know you're the only person who's ever really counted."

She said in haste, trying abruptly to divert him: "Uncle Pridey's quite a famous man now. They've made a great fuss of him here, and there's talk of his being given an honorary degree at one of the universities. I hope I'm not interrupting you in your work, Stephen, not intruding, I mean. I felt I wanted to come for the sake of old times." Her voice sounded false even to herself.

He smiled his old smile. "And why shouldn't it be for the sake of new times too?"

She turned away, but his hand moved to her elbow; he pulled her slowly round to face him.

"Did you really come all this way just to go off again tomorrow?"

"Do you mind?"

"Yes, I certainly do."

They looked into each other's eyes. Drown there, one could so easily drown there. He suddenly bent to kiss her.

Don't shirk this. She gave him her lips, warm and unreserved, as they had once been. He put his arms right round her in an embrace in which passion seemed in a few moments to grow and flower.

His face was altering, the sleekness going out of it. Slowly she put her hands to his shoulders, and, aware of the pressure, he released his hold, withdrew his mouth.

"On my life and soul," he said, "you're lovely. I've never known anyone more lovely."

Queer sensations now. The old battlefield. Cool head and warm heart. Triumph and defeat.

He said roughly: "Now you're here you must stay for a few days."

"I have to leave London tomorrow."

"You can't!"

"I must."

It wasn't playful, conventional, as it had been a few minutes ago. His eyes were weighing on her.

She said: "What have you been doing all this time? Did your divorce go through?"

"Of course. I told you that."

"And since then?"

"Oh . . . I've been working hard. And thinking of you."

"And your wife?"

"Virginia?" He frowned a little. "She's all right. She's still living at Maida Vale. Listen, Cordelia, you must realise now that she means nothing at all to me any more——"

"Oh, I do."

There was a flicker of surprise in his expression.

"Well, that's good then. That's one obstacle cleared out of the way. Have another drink?"

She refused, wanting all her reason, and he went over to pour himself another. She wondered what he was thinking, could not yet fathom what was in his heart.

There was a mirror by the table, and she suddenly realised that he was watching her through it. She lowered her gaze. He was in just the same position, wondering what she felt and why she had come. Despite the physical attraction coming to life again in his breast, never dead in hers, they were strangers fencing across the debris of five years.

"My dear," he said, "this calls for a celebration! I wish we could spend the day together. . . . But I've work on hand. I wonder if I could cut it . . ."

Work? "No, please don't. I've promised to be back at Pridey's lodgings for lunch. Really, Stephen, thank you."

But his old ebullience carrying him on, over his own hesitancies, the outside obstacles, he said: "Have you ever seen London before? Good. Couldn't be better. Look, will you wait here while I make some arrangements? Five or ten minutes. I think I can fix it all right."

She protested, though not vigorously. What she had come for today was too important to be shelved. She could send a note. Stephen went off, and she was left to stare out of the narrow window into the unheeding street.

He came back and said it was arranged. He'd ordered his carriage. It was a good day for the time of year. They'd go a drive until lunch. Then he'd show her one of the best restaurants. After that . . . Well, after that they'd just decide when the time came. He'd arranged to spend the whole day with her. Not this evening. He couldn't manage this evening. But until then. He wouldn't have her going back to Manchester feeling she hadn't been royally entertained. He pressed her to have another drink, and put on his check coat and monogrammed silk muffler, and then the boy came to say the carriage was here.

It was a victoria like the one he had had in Manchester. The sight of it brought a flood of bitter-sweet memories to her, and while he helped her in he reminded her of some of them.

They drove out along the embankment to Chelsea, and he went on talking, persuasively. Did he realise that the memory of those old times had pain for her as well as pleasure?

He insisted on keeping his hand on hers under her muff. His hands were as she always remembered them, warm and firm, long-fingered.

Once, conscious of how little she had to say in reply, he turned to her, watching her expression and unable to read it.

"You're quiet, my sweetheart. What're you thinking?"

"I'm listening to you," she said, smiling.

"Well, it *was* good, wasn't it? Every moment of it was glorious—even the scrapes and the near discoveries, even Dan Massington's interference. The tragedy was the fire and Brook's illness—and of course the misunderstanding about Virginia. We've both paid for that undeservedly. Isn't it time we made up for some of the happiness we've lost?"

She said: "Can you ever make up for happiness you've lost?"

"That's a dismal thing to say."

"I mean—if you have happiness later—can it be the same?"

He was silent, glanced at a passing carriage smarter than his own, came back reluctantly to the question she had put him.

"Maybe not if it's a long time. But this is only five years; you said so yourself. When I met you last in Wales, was it January, 'sixty-eight? No, 'sixty-nine. Not much more than four, then. It isn't as if you'd changed. You're exactly the same, except a bit more grown up, and more beautiful. *I* haven't changed, have I?"

". . . Very little."

"Well, then, in that case, I don't see that there need be any difference at all. When I'm sitting beside you like this I fancy myself back in Manchester and it seems like yesterday. Does it seem like that to you? Don't you remember it all?"

"Yes," she said. "I remember it all."

They made a wide detour from Chelsea and came back through Hyde Park and St. James's. They drove up Piccadilly, but when the coachman seemed about to draw up half way along Stephen tapped sharply and said: "No, not here. I told you Berridges."

They turned off and got out at a luxurious and discreet little restaurant with a carpet like new-mown hay to tread on and royal purple curtains and softly lit tables in alcoves. He was on terms with the head waiter, who seemed to know all his requirements without being told and brought oysters and champagne and delicacies cooked on a trolley before their eyes.

Under the friendly influence of the champagne Stephen began to talk about himself, about the theatre he had managed in New York and the repertory in Boston. He said it had been a wise move of his father's to suggest the job: he'd learned a lot, unlearned a lot. One day he was going back, but at present . . . He stopped, and to cover his hesitation he beckoned the waiter and spoke to him about the port.

She said: "And your schemes for changing the character of music halls: are you still going on with those?"

"Yes, Dad is. But I've lost interest in it since the Manchester days. Possibly we were attempting what couldn't be done. It's confused thinking to imagine you can improve them and keep them the same."

"I think perhaps you're right," she said.

"Do you?" he said, again in surprise.

A man went past in a loud suit and a bow tie. Seeing Stephen, he veered towards him, then, catching sight of Cordelia, he hunched one shoulder and coughed and walked away again.

"Excuse me," said Stephen, and got up and went to speak to him. The man had a booming voice, and she could catch occasional words, ". . . the manager says . . ." and ". . . you can't argue with her . . ." and ". . . but it was his nephew they owed the money to . . ." He wore a sapphire ring that winked as he gestured.

Stephen came back, cleared his throat, and glanced a moment after the retreating figure, then returned his attention to her. It was a sleek transition.

She said: "Have you many friends in London? You must know a lot of people."

"Yes, I do. But I miss the old days. And I've missed you." He sipped his wine and frowned at her. "Yes, I've many friends but there's only been one Delia. I *wish* you'd understand what these years have meant to me. I don't think you do at all. You care for Brook more than I realised. It's the truth now, isn't it?"

"More than I realised too," she said.

"Well, you've got him. But I've had nobody. Some men would be content with second best. But I couldn't. Even in America it was the same. I've been miserable and lonely and restless all along. Well, you've come to see me again. I can't believe it was just out of interest—or pity . . ."

"No," she said as he waited. "It wasn't that."

She looked up suddenly, and he smiled to hide his feelings. His eyes had said: I remember you.

"Why must you leave tomorrow?"

"Tell me about your friends," she said. "I'd like to hear about them."

297

"Is Pridey staying up here all the time?"

"For a while. Do you often come here, Stephen?"

"Then couldn't you make an excuse—fairly soon—to spend a holiday with Pridey? We'd have such rare fun. I'd show you all the things you most want to see, the restaurants, the theatres, the operas. London can be very gay if you know your way about. I'd show you."

He watched her face as she stared dreamily across the room. "You're an enigma today," he said chidingly. "Once it used to be easy to tell what you were thinking. I could read what you felt in your eyes."

She turned and smiled at him. "I've grown up, Stephen. We've both grown up."

He said slowly: "When you wouldn't see me that last time after Slaney-Smith's death, I didn't know what to do. In the end I called on Robert Birch."

She looked quickly at him. "Oh?"

"He told me about you having a baby. I didn't know until then. For a minute—for a wild minute—I wondered if it might have been mine. When I realised it couldn't have been I was miserable. I went off determined to forget you for ever."

Had he been looking then he would have seen a darker, softer glance in her eyes than had been there all day. In that moment she nearly blurted out the secret she had kept so long.

"Was that when you decided to hate me?"

"That was when I decided to hate you. It didn't work."

She lowered her head.

"Listen," he said, "don't get it into your mind that there's someone else. You know me better than that. I've told you I'm in love with you still, haven't I, now? I'll tell you it every day you'll consent to stay on. I can't say more than that."

"No," she said. "You can't say more than that, Stephen."

The waiter brought the port. A little was poured out, first into his glass, then into hers. He sniffed it.

"It's the 'sixty-eight, sir. The same as you had last time."

"Very well." He waited till the man had gone. He gazed at Cordelia. "Here's to us, my sweetheart."

They tipped glasses and drank. He refilled them, only lowering his eyes a second to do so.

He said: "Presently—when we've had coffee, we'll slip away. I'll show you my rooms. There'll be nobody there. The man who looks after me lives in the basement and never comes up unless rung for. The fire will be laid. We can have tea cosily together. You'll make it for me, won't you? Then I'll prove to you, not only that I still love you, but that we can recapture all the old fun, yes, and the passion. You'll forget the four years, your little boy, Uncle Pridey, Brook. I'll promise you that. . . . Darling, you're so sweet, so precious. Will you come?"

She said: "And afterwards? If I leave Brook?"

His eyes travelled over her face. The last caution going now, without a thought, his imagination aflame. "Better still. We'll—go to America then. I can arrange that. Give me a month, that's all."

"And—you're not interested in any other women, Stephen?"

"I've told you. Why d'you doubt me?"

"What about tonight? You said you were engaged tonight."

He said: "It was a business engagement. An important one. But if you want me to I'll cut it. Anything you say."

She slowly looked up and met his gaze. Her eyes searched into his. "Am I really as important to you as that?" she said.

CHAPTER TEN Pridey and Ian had been to the Zoo. They had seen the leopards, the monkeys and the alligators: they had fed the sea lions and ridden on the camel. When they got home Pridey read the note waiting for him and said:

"Your mama'll not be home just yet. Where shall we go this afternoon, my lad?"

"Back to the Zoo, Uncle, please," said Ian.

So they went off again and this time tried the snake house and the polar bear pit and the small mammal house and the parrot house, and Pridey got into trouble with a cockatoo and its keeper, but chiefly with the cockatoo, for trying to pull out what he thought was a loose tail feather for the boy.

When they arrived home a second time Cordelia was not yet back and there was no further message. Ian was tired out with so much walking and so much excitement, and after tea he allowed Pridey and Mrs. Cowdray in tart collaboration to put him to bed. Then the old man limped round to his friend Wilberforce to tell him he couldn't come and see his rabbits that evening. Once there, he found such interest in seeing the rabbits he had said he was not coming to see that it was nine o'clock before they parted and nine-thirty before he arrived back at his lodgings, having forgotten his supper. A cold meal was laid, and Mrs. Cowdray was in the basement knitting stockings for her sailor son. No, she hadn't fed his mice, what did he think? No, Mrs. Ferguson hadn't come back. She wondered at people forgetting their duty like that. No, the boy hadn't wakened; if he had *she'd* have gone up to him. Yes, he could make a pot of tea for himself if he felt inclined.

Pridey brewed his tea and was going to limp upstairs with it, but Mrs. Cowdray slapped down her knitting and said, "Here, let me," so Pridey brought up the rear with his stick.

First there were his little friends to be fed and talked to and told about the rabbits he'd seen; then the top of Ian's curly head had to be furtively viewed; at last he was free to pour out his tea and kick off his boots and warm his hands at the fire.

On this came Cordelia.

She stood there in the door for a moment as if hesitating, not sure of what she would find, while Pridey wrinkled his eyebrows at her and the hot tea steamed his face.

"Neet brings crows home," he said. "Just in time for supper. Mrs. Cowdray's worst meal."

She came forward and sat in the chair opposite him, quietly and meekly, and slowly pulled her gloves off, unpinned her hat.

"Oh, Pridey . . ." she said.

He sipped his tea. "We've been all day at the Zoo. Seen everything behind bars except men. Suppose one has to go to Wormwood Scrubs for that."

She looked at him and her eyes were suddenly blind with tears. She tried to stop them but it was no use, they had been held back too long. They overflowed her lashes and she put up her hands to her face.

He said: "Here, here, this won't do. Calm yourself. Have some boiled ham."

She did not give way as she had done that other time more than four years ago, but she sat there silently struggling. Pridey put down his cup.

"Won't do at all. Go out for the day to meet your lover and come back and flood the place. What's the matter?"

She took no notice. Pridey was alarmed because she was trembling. He got up and rubbed his head and made noises at her. Then he rubbed her head for a change. He went to the door to call Mrs. Cowdray but changed his mind and came back. He poured her out a cup of tea and offered it to her. Conscious that she must at all costs get away to her own room, Cordelia chose this moment to rise, and her shoulder jogged the tea-cup out of his hand.

Coming now, the accident was just enough to steady her, to weigh the balance towards self-control. Apologising amid the ruins, not aware of any relief, as there would have been after a complete break-down, she went on her knees and helped him to mop up the mess.

He said it was a cracked cup anyhow, and the saucer was safe; he'd saved the saucer, and he'd heard tea was good for carpets; he remembered a case in his bedroom at home when tea had been spilt on top of an ink-stain and the effect was quite artistic, like a single chrysanthemum.

"I'm very sorry," she said. "I just couldn't help it. I'm so desperately tired and unhappy. I've never felt like this before I think I want to die."

"Nonsense," he said. "Can't want to die at your age. Go and wash your face. Do you all the good in the world."

"I feel awful. I expect I look it. I feel like Aunt Tish."

"Had a spare cup somewhere. Yes, I remember. Been keeping lentils in it."

He went out, and with an effort she got up and went into her bedroom and tried to bathe her face. When she came back he had found the cup and was sitting at the table stirring his second cup of tea. She slipped into her seat with a last surreptitious wipe of her nose.

"Wilberforce has some fine rabbits," he said. "Fat, flabby, helpless things. One has had forty-two young in twelve months. Terrifying!"

She said: "It was awful, Pridey."

"Should think it is," he said. "In four years, if they all lived, one rabbit could have over a million descendants. You must meet Wilberforce."

There was a pause. Outside two drunken men were shouting, quarrelling.

"I found Stephen quite easily this morning, at the theatre. We—went out together."

"H'm," said Pridey. He looked at her and pushed a dish across. "Have some salad."

"I can't eat," she said with the remnant of a break still in her voice.

"Why not go to bed? Tell me in the morning."

She watched him for a moment as he began his meal.

"Don't you want to hear?"

He waved his knife uneasily. "Talk away. Talk away. But don't think in the morning: wish I hadn't told that old buffer so much."

She said: "No . . . I won't do that. What I'm sorry for is not telling you before, years ago. I've never had anybody I could tell anything. There was nobody who wouldn't have been shocked."

"Well, you won't shock me. I breed mice."

She half laughed but checked herself. Laughter was so close to that loss of control which was still very near. At the moment her mind was clear. It must stay clear.

"In a way, I felt mean—underhand, not telling him what I knew. But he'd *got* to mention her first, because it was something important; anyone could see that. I thought before I went out this morning, if he says, 'Cordelia, I'm in love with someone else,' or even, 'I'm engaged or married to someone else'—if he'll say that straight out . . ." She twisted her hands. "But it wasn't like that at all."

Pridey helped himself to the ham.

She said: "I don't know if I've been conceited or blind. When I first

301

met him there were things . . . But there was another side—or so I thought—warm, generous, impulsive—that I came to love. I thought, from the way things seemed, I thought I was important to him—apart from being in love—that in a way he needed me. Well—if he ever did, if that was ever true, it isn't true any longer. Whatever might have been five years ago, now—it's too late. . . ."

"Go on."

She stared at the table-cloth, the embroidered velvet table centre, the artificial flowers. "I knew—by the time we finished lunch I knew I could win him back. I suppose I should have been gratified—she must be very fascinating. But really I'd lost. There was this something else. It wasn't that she had supplied it but that he no longer felt the need of it. Or so it seemed to me. It was gone. *That* was the something I couldn't ever win back. . . ."

"If it was ever there."

"If it was ever there. I feel as if I don't know anything any more."

"What did he say about Brook?"

"I never told him. I found I couldn't. If once he knew that, then he'd know exactly why I'd come to London, why I'd come to see him. I thought at first that, as he didn't mention the other girl, I never could mention her either. But gradually it came nearer and nearer to the edge of my tongue. . . ."

Pridey stopped in his chewing. His face creased into an encouraging smile.

"He—wanted me to go back with him to his rooms. Just before we left the restaurant, when he'd promised everything I asked, I suddenly found I couldn't hold it back any longer. I suddenly said to him, 'What about Freda Gerald?' He was astonished, of course. And annoyed. When I told him how I knew about her, he said I'd not treated *him* fairly. Then he started to explain. From being sweet to each other it gradually all changed. Sometimes I think we don't talk the same language. He jumped to the wrong conclusions, started making excuses for the wrong things. Of *course* I was jealous when I saw the girl last night. But how *could* I blame him? I'd given him no promise ever to see him again. I couldn't expect him to stay away from all women all his life. What I wanted was his confidence and his trust today. I told him so. He got angry then and said how could I expect him to know all that, seeing that when I last saw him with a woman I'd walked out and had nothing more to do with him for five years? And I said if he'd been honest with me in the first place I shouldn't have deserted him—ever. . . ."

Her voice faded away. It was impossible really to tell a third person. In telling, even as it occurred, it seemed so petty. After all these years it had apparently ended in a lovers' quarrel over another woman. The girl's name had immediately obscured all the real issues. Perhaps it was his fault. Perhaps it was inevitable.

For the real issues went deep, deep. They were as fundamental as those which had divided Brook and his father.

"I left him soon after that."

"D'you still love him?"

"I—don't know. At present I think I'm cured. Aghast. Like a great awakening. And brave. It's in two or three days—or perhaps tonight—I shall begin to feel it. I shall wake up then in a different way. For five years everything I've done and thought . . . I shall wake up and find all that gone. . . ."

"Where've you been since this afternoon?"

"Walking. I lost my way. I didn't much care."

"Silly young thing. You'll be doing the same as Brook." Pridey put down his knife and fork and sighed deeply. His glance roved round the table. "You know, Mrs. Cowdray's very mean with her suppers. I do miss a substantial meal in the evenings."

She put her face in her hands. "Oh, Pridey, what shall I do?"

"Do? It's perfectly plain what you must do."

"Is it?" she said through her fingers after a moment. "What?"

"Oh-ho, it's no good me giving advice. You wouldn't take it. People never do. Just wasted air."

"But what *can* I do?"

He limped off into his bedroom and came back with the old paper bag. "Have a sweet."

Reluctantly she fumbled in the bag. "Thank you." It was a good move. Difficult for one's heart to break while one is sucking a toffee.

He said: "Mr. Gladstone's developing a taste for tea. Most peculiar. Drinks quite a saucerful some mornings. I wonder if you'll be here on Saturday. Wilberforce is coming round in the evening."

"I can't stay here indefinitely."

"How old are you?"

"Twenty-six."

"Just the right age."

"What for?"

"Now, look," he said. "Do you want my advice or don't you?"

"Of course, Pridey. I feel lost. Terribly lost—as if I shall never know my way again."

"Very good then. You're twenty-six. And you've come up to London to join your lover, that's it, isn't it?"

"That was it."

"And you came to me. Now I'm an ignorant old man. I judge things as an ignorant man should—by the light of common sense. But I didn't say to you, Cordelia, 'You're a fool, throwing yourself away on that man,' did I?"

She shook her head.

"I didn't say to you, 'Look what you're doing; you've just got out of one bad marriage, now you're going to jump into another.' Why didn't I say that? Because I knew you wouldn't take any notice. And besides—it's not for me to manage your life. People should mind their own business. That's what's been wrong with Frederick—trying to interfere. When I feel like that I say to myself, God doesn't interfere. Do I think myself cleverer than God? Have another sweet."

"No, thank you."

"But you want my advice, so now I'll give it. Go back to Grove Hall." She stared at him wanly.

"Oh, that's impossible."

"Nothing's impossible—yet. Take your son back. That's where you belong. It's not a bad place. You should never've left it."

"No," she said. "I can't do that. I won't do that."

Pridey limped over to the fire, chewing excitedly.

"You're twenty-six. But so much older than your years—in the head, I mean. You know the value of money. Don't you?"

"Oh, yes, I know all that. I realise I shall be throwing away——"

"Throwing away a hundred thousand pounds. All round it'll be that. A house and a works and Lord knows what besides. There's my money and Tish's money—though we can't touch it—and Frederick's money. It'll all come to you. You're an heiress, even the way money goes today."

She said: "I do know all that; but I'll not go back there to a life of being under Mr. Ferguson's thumb. Brook never had any free life——"

"Stuff and nonsense. *You'll* not be under Frederick's thumb. Brook, maybe, and Tish and I, and all the servants. But not you."

"Oh, yes, I am."

"Oh, no, you're not. Don't you know you're his pet? Especially since you gave him a grandson. You can handle him. You've got the same sort of minds. Though you use 'em differently. Didn't you realise that?"

"I don't know what you're talking about."

"Well, why d'you think he's given way all along the line about Ian's upbringing?"

"But he hasn't."

"Oh, yes, he has. All the important things. The things that have seemed important to you. Remember about the perambulator. And the cold baths. And not having meals with the family except on Sundays."

"But I've given way on heaps of things too."

"Why does he let you go to see your family as often as you please? Why was the new greenhouse put where *you* wanted it? And the holiday last year, remember that? And why did he make you a partner along with Brook? Because he can work with you. He knows you're as clever as he is and will stand up to him when you choose to. Ah!" Pridey sat down. "Damned sciatica reminding me again."

There was silence.

He said: "You say you thought sometimes you didn't talk the same language as young Crossley. Well, you talk the same language as Frederick. Seen it over and over again. Doesn't mean you're alike in character. But when you choose to stand up to him you always do it when he's put himself in the wrong and his own judgment makes him back down. We people get wild at the wrong times, put *ourselves* in the wrong. Under Frederick's thumb! What nonsense! He'd be under your thumb in another year or two if you were *that* sort of a woman!"

She lowered her hands from her face.

"No, Pridey. It's not really like that at all. And anyway—I don't always want to be fighting. It takes so much out of me. And I should have to over Ian. I left more because of him than for anything else. If I saw him growing up into another Brook, cowed, beaten, weak . . . That's the *real* reason why I can never go back."

"Nonsense again. All stuff and nonsense. But if it was a tussle for a year or two, wouldn't it be worth it? Money counts. How old d'you think Frederick is? I'll be seventy-two in a few weeks, worse luck. He's just seventy. He can't go on and on. Every year you'll be stronger, he'll be weaker. In five years' time you'll *own* Ferguson's. Ian'll only be nine then. He can't come to much harm."

She said: "You make me feel—like some scheming peasant woman— adding up when so-and-so will die."

He clutched his beard. "Ought to've known better. Gave up arguing with women long ago. Thought you were different. No stability. No damned logic. Go on. Go and drown yourself in the Thames. That's feminine. That's understandable."

"I'm sorry. I'm sorry," she said, getting to her feet. "I know you're advising for the the best, but . . ."

"Well," he said. "You don't want that sort of argument. Sordid, you think. Mercenary. What about the other. You're twenty-six. Just the right age. You've got looks. You'll go on having looks for another fifteen years. They'll get better for five or ten. I know your sort. Even though I am ignorant I didn't always keep mice. You've just lost your husband and jilted your lover. Your heart's broken. So you think. Well, I'm sorry if it is. But has it occurred to you that there are twenty-two million odd people in England and Wales, and that somewhere among them there may be other men you could fall in love with? And that if you're a bit more experienced and a bit more choosy next time you may find one who's neither a weakling nor a knave. People aren't born wise in this life, they buy experience, and if they're lucky they buy it in time. You're not an unlucky heart-broken woman; you're lucky, lucky because you've learnt so much—I hope—and still so young. Stop being sorry for yourself and use your head again!"

"I'm not sorry for myself," she said indignantly.

"Frederick's not comfortable to live with. I ought to know. But he's not all black. Brook wasn't all his fault, you know. *He* didn't make him ail. And I don't suppose this last quarrel was all his fault. Longer I live, more sure I am there's no black and white in this life, only different shades of grey. He's masterful, sentimental, complacent, bit of a Pecksniff. But in his own way he's enlightened, philanthropic, go-ahead, got his own courage and integrity. Anyway, it's no good arguing over spilt milk. Brook's gone and that's that. What you must consider is what's best for you. You asked my advice. Well, I tell you to go back to Grove Hall. Tell Frederick any story you like. Say Stephen's married again——"

"Oh, he doesn't know anything about Stephen."

"He won't be too particular about the excuse you make. He'll be too glad to see you. Go back to Grove Hall and try to forget the past. Brook and Stephen as well. And any grievances you've got against Frederick. I've had some, but I've lost most of 'em. When you look at him the right way, he's not powerful, he's pathetic. Think of the future. You enjoy tinkering about down at the works, don't deny it——"

"I don't deny it."

"And think of the future. Don't go rushing into the first marriage you see. If you've got sense you won't tie yourself to the works the way Frederick's done. Enjoy your life. Come up to London when you please, go abroad if you fancy. Educate your son properly. Can't do that for nothing. Three things. Make him broad-minded. Teach him the value of money. Keep him modest." Pridey stopped a moment, fumbled in his paper bag. "If there's any danger to Ian it's from you."

"From me!"

"Yes. Don't get too close to him. Keep your distance. Give him room to breathe. Expect you will. You've got enough sense for that. But just keep an eye on yourself all the same."

"You make me feel awful. Perhaps you're right—about him, I mean."

"It's not a question of being right. It's a question of common sense. Using your head. Well . . . Are you going to throw everything away?"

She did not answer.

"Are you going to be a goat and go on butting your head against a stone wall, saying, 'I won't learn, I won't learn, I won't learn'? Pah! Believe you are. Really believe you are!"

She went up to him, diffidently touched his arm.

"I'm sorry, Pridey. I'm sorry to seem obstinate. But I don't think I could face it. I don't think I could ever go back there again."

CHAPTER ELEVEN The morning train from London was ten minutes late. It steamed into London Road Station, and from a first-class carriage a fair young woman in mourning and a little boy got out. The young woman looked tired and ill.

A porter lifted out the single box, and she allowed Ian to drag her up to look at the steaming engine with its enormous driving wheel and shining brass-work. Then they walked off towards the exit.

It was fine outside but grey. The afternoon was coming to an early close. London Road looked busy as they came down the steps; but it was busy with a slower-moving traffic: dray horses with magnificent hairy hoofs pulling wagons and striking sparks off the road, women in clogs carrying wicker baskets, a horse drinking at a trough, two covered dust-carts with spades sticking out of the back, a boy asleep in the straw at the back of an open lorry, buses toiling up the hill.

It looked like home.

They climbed into a cab and she tipped the porter. "Eh, that's right," said one woman to another, hastening to catch a train. The cabbie clicked to his horse and they moved creakily off, down the hill, not hurrying, at a jog trot.

She thought: So I am coming back after all. It's not as Pridey said, not all of it. But part of it's true. In two days of despair she had gone over every word Stephen had spoken, every gesture. Freda Gerald was not important—except as a symptom. The final break would have come without it and come unobscured.

Only five days ago, on the journey up to London, she had thought it the narrow standards of Grove Hall which had blinded her to the richness and colour of life with Stephen. Now she realised the narrow standards of Grove Hall could only be blamed for giving her the excuse to think that.

And then, having deceived her, memory had begun at once to whisper and confirm. Isn't this the man who . . . Isn't this in keeping? . . .

Some times other and contrary thoughts restlessly claimed her, whispering what she had said to Pridey; it *might* have been; five years ago when they were both younger, if they had gone away together, as he was then, it might have been; but now too late, too late . . .

Or did she underestimate some new element in her judgment, new maturity, new standards of comparison and experience which, had she

307

possessed them five years ago, would have made the adventure impossible at the outset? She didn't know, would never know.

Tlot-tlot, tlot-tlot, over the sets and round the Green.

She thought: I'm not going back for my own sake. But all—all Pridey says about Ian is true. She was going back to accept a challenge. She would take up the reins where they had been dropped. The house and the works, and the new houses for the men who worked there; and her position and her family, and . . .

She didn't know if Frederick Ferguson would still be in the mood in which she left him. Inevitably, if he was to live, he would recover from defeat, climb out of this abyss; inevitably, being the man he was, he would claim the old allegiances, put on some of the old pretensions. There would be conflict in the future as there had been in the past.

Yet there would be times, too, and it would be dishonest to disguise it, when she would find herself working along with him in amity, as she had done in the past. This morning early when she had been lying awake she had thought that but for Frederick Ferguson, for all his impositions, she might have remained a milliner's assistant, have married a tradesman and gone to her grave with such abilities as she had unrecognised.

And the queer thought had come to her that a cynic, looking at this phase of her life with a proper detachment, might say that ultimately the most important thing in it had not been her relationship with Stephen or Brook, dearly as these had cost her in emotion and grief, but that other relationship with Frederick Ferguson, crystallising in the background, almost unnoticed, through the years.

The familiar streets, the familiar sights, the familiar smells. Trees now, and muddy lanes and the Grove.

She thought: If people really knew, what would they think? That I'm a calculating, designing woman—or a prude—or a wanton? Some perhaps one and some another. I've been faithful and unfaithful, cared nothing for possessions yet at the last am coming back to claim them. In fact nobody will ever know, nobody, not even Pridey, will know everything—all the facts—except me. And to me it doesn't seem that I have been any of these things. But then, although I know most of all, I can judge least of all, for I have been the centre of it. So I shall go on—as everyone goes on—to the end of my days, blown by every wind that comes. And the only steadying force will be my own reason, my own understanding. I'm alone. So I must hope and pray for reason and understanding. And judgment and patience and faith.

She looked down at her son who was dozing against her arm. His fair curls were escaping from his hat. Alone except for Ian, whom she must guide without leading strings, influence without oppressiveness, love without demanding anything in return. Pridey had called her an heiress. But it was he, Ian, really who was the heir. Ian Ferguson. She realised she was returning to perpetuate the crowning paradox of all.

The cab turned in at the gates of Grove Hall. Everything the same. Dusk was falling. There was a faint smell of wood smoke. Somewhere far in the distance children were shouting; it sounded like bird cries on the still air.

Before she could ring, as she got down, helping Ian who was stupid with sleep, Hallows opened the door.

As if nothing had happened, as if she had been out for a drive, he said: "Oh, good afternoon, madam," and took her box from the cabbie. While she paid the man Ian wandered sleepily into the house.

She went slowly in after him. Although she had been away so short a time the familiar smell of the place, with all its memories, came upon her like a feeling of physical sickness. The hall was empty. She put down her muff as Hallows closed the door and walked with her box towards the stairs.

She cleared her throat. "Is Mr. Ferguson—in his study?"

Hallows stopped. "No, madam. Mr. Ferguson is in his room. He's been unwell for some days."

"Unwell?"

"Yes, madam."

She stared at the butler. "Oh." She couldn't bring herself to pretend. "I didn't know. What's the matter?"

"I think it was the bereavement, madam."

For a moment she did not reply. Hallows stood there waiting.

"Where's Miss Ferguson?"

"She'll be in her room, madam. It isn't quite time for tea."

"Oh, no. I forgot."

Seeing that she was going to say no more, he went on up the stairs carrying the box. She watched him out of sight and then followed Ian into the drawing-room. It, too, was empty. A big fire. Brook's piano.

Conscious of relaxing nerves, of anti-climax, of a dreadful loneliness settling on her, she began slowly to unfasten her cloak. Ian had run across to get two of his favourite books out of a corner. Betty hadn't dusted the clock.

The familiar things, friendly with habit, inimitable, with their clinging strands, waiting to welcome her back. Somewhere surely would be the embroidery half done, the book half read. Oh, Stephen. So this is the end of our pretty story—at last. Tears blinded her eyes and she brushed them away. *Really* the end. Not even hope this time. Her heart ached as if it would burst. It was all very well to say come back, but somewhere in the very depth of her being she still loved him and it would never be the same. She needed Pridey now, desperately, to reinforce and renew with his arguments the logic for her return. Almost, if she had had the courage, she would have turned tail and fled again with Ian, anywhere, anywhere away from this big silent house with its indescribable surge of memories from the secret heights and depths of her life.

She looked about her in desperation, in panic. If for a while she could employ her hands, her mind, on any routine job to fill the first empty minutes of return. What could she do?

Hallows was coming down again. She must go up at once, with Ian, before her courage completely failed.

She turned. "Ian. I want you. We must go and see Grandpa."

Up the stairs. Slowing at the top. Go into my bedroom first. No. Courage. Now or never. She went to his door and tapped. He called, "Come in."

He was sitting by the fire, did not turn as she entered. He was in his big black dressing-gown, a huge bulk become amorphous but topped by that old grey distinguished head.

"Yes, what is it?"

She cleared her throat to speak, and as she did so became conscious that there was someone else in the room. Robert Birch was standing by the window. So she missed Mr. Ferguson's first glance. When she looked back he was slowly getting up, gripping the chair. They looked at each other. There were shadows now in the room, lengthy planes of dark, but she saw his jaw muscles move.

He said: "We didn't expect you." Almost without expression, feeling his way.

"No . . . I didn't write."

Scarcely seeing it, she was yet conscious of Robert's welcoming look, his pleasure—of something more than pleasure.

She said: "You've been ill."

"Oh . . . just a temporary thing." The old man glanced again at her suddenly, keenly. "Is that why you have come?"

"No . . . I didn't know."

He moved his head once, slowly, as if with satisfaction.

Robert said: "It was a nervous collapse. There's nothing seriously wrong, but he'll have to take things easy for a time."

"Grandpa," said Ian, slowly leaving his mother's skirt. "Uncle Pridey took me to the Zoo. And I've seen an engine with ten wheels!"

Mr. Ferguson looked down, still uncertain.

"Ten wheels," he said.

The little boy broke into a sleepy patter. She glanced now at Robert. There was uncertainty in his look too. He said in an undertone:

"I've been here a good deal. It was the least I could do. Have you—come back to stay?"

"I—don't know," she said miserably. "Perhaps for a little while."

He said: "Cordelia . . ."

"Yes?"

"May I be the first to—welcome you home . . ."

"Thank you, Robert."

She had flushed, conscious of a creeping warmth, a complex anger, a weakness near to tears. Then she glanced again at Mr. Ferguson and saw that he was not listening to Ian. The old steely glance, but less militant.

"What did you say?"

Well, she must say it. "You got my first note, the one I left?"

"Yes."

"I've decided," she said, "I mean, I think I was wrong. If I may, I want to come back—at least for a time."

For a moment he seemed to search into her, to seek to read all those conflicting motives, the feelings, the impulses which had swayed her and which she would never explain to him. He put his hand on Ian's head, moved his fingers over the hair.

Abruptly he put out his hand to her, with more than a shadow of one of the old regal gestures.

"Then may I, too, say—'Welcome home!' "